Praise for *The Tudor Rose*

"A vivid picture of a courageous woman and a truly royal queen."
—*Baltimore Sun*

"There is a particular fascination when a novelist can transmute names and vaguely remembered dates into a story of flesh and blood people."
—*NY Herald Tribune*

"Another Elizabeth! Her brothers murdered by the uncle who usurped the throne, she made his death the price of her marriage to Henry Tudor, which united England and bore Henry VIII."
—*Literary Guild of America Recommends*

"The latest of this author's portraits of England's royal ladies…as absorbing as its predecessors."
—*Booklist*

"Miss Barnes makes her story come alive…very skillfully has she drawn the picture of royal sorrow and self-sacrifice."
—*Christian Science Monitor*

"This is a magnificent portrait of a Great Queen."
—*Boston Herald*

The Tudor Rose

The Tudor Rose

The Story of the Queen Who United a Kingdom and Birthed a Dynasty

MARGARET CAMPBELL BARNES

SOURCEBOOKS LANDMARK™
AN IMPRINT OF SOURCEBOOKS, INC.®
NAPERVILLE, ILLINOIS

Copyright © 1953, 2009 by Margaret Campbell Barnes
Cover and internal design © 2009 by Sourcebooks, Inc.
Cover image: Portrait of Eleonora di Toledo by the studio of Agnolo Bronzino
© Bridgeman Art Library

Sourcebooks and the colophon are registered trademarks of Sourcebooks, Inc.

Published by Sourcebooks Landmark, an imprint of Sourcebooks, Inc.
P.O. Box 4410, Naperville, Illinois 60567-4410
(630) 961-3900
Fax: (630) 961-2168
www.sourcebooks.com

Originally published in 1953.

Library of Congress Cataloging-in-Publication Data

Barnes, Margaret Campbell
  The Tudor rose : the story of the queen who united a kingdom and birthed a
dynasty / by Margaret Campbell Barnes.
    p. cm.
  1. Elizabeth, Queen, consort of Henry VII, King of England, 1465-1503--
Fiction. 2. Queens--Great Britain--Fiction. 3. Great Britain--History--
Wars of the Roses, 1455-1485--Fiction. 4. Richard III, King of England,
1452-1485--Fiction. 5. Henry VII, King of England, 1457-1509--Fiction.
6. Great Britain--History--Richard III, 1483-1485--Fiction. 7. Great
Britain--History--Henry VII, 1485-1509--Fiction. I. Title.
  PR6003.A72T83 2009
  823'.912--dc22
                        2009025672

Printed and bound in the United States of America.
  VP 10 9 8 7 6 5 4 3 2 1

Also by Margaret Campbell Barnes
Brief Gaudy Hour
My Lady of Cleves
King's Fool

For Ethel and Kit

And All That Greenways Stood For

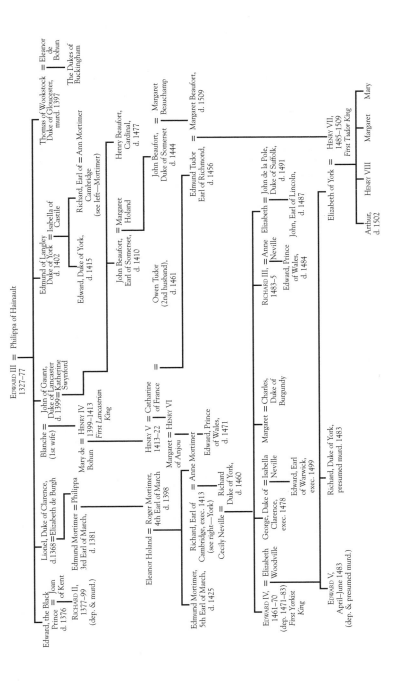

Author's Note

In Plantagenet and Tudor times so many parents called their children after royal personages that it gave rise to a confusing repetition of names. I have, therefore, altered the Christian names of a few of my minor characters. Also, in order to simplify the story, I have throughout the book referred to some characters by the titles they originally had, although higher ones may later have been conferred upon them.

My thanks are due to the librarian and staff of the County Seely Library, Newport, Isle of Wight, for their patience in producing all possible reference books on the period.

M.C.B.
Yarmouth, Isle of Wight

A LONG-DRAWN SIGH OF feminine ecstasy filled the room as the white velvet was lifted from its wrappings. Its folds hung heavily across a lady-of-the-bedchamber's outstretched arms so that every jewelled rose and fleur-de-lys stood out and sparkled in the morning sunlight. Other women, on their knees, reached eager hands to spread the embroidered train. Young Elizabeth of York, standing in her shift and kirtle, shivered with excitement as the dressmaker from France slipped the lovely material over her shoulders; for, princess or no princess, it is not every day that a girl tries on her wedding-dress.

"Oh, how beautiful!" breathed her English attendants.

"*Comme elle est ravissante!*" echoed the dressmaker and her underlings.

Because she was not sure whether such spontaneous compliments referred to the dress or to herself, Elizabeth, the King's daughter, called for a mirror.

"But, Bess, it makes you look so *different!*" complained her younger sister, Cicely, who had been allowed to watch.

Different indeed, confirmed the metal mirror. Where there had been a slip of a girl who still studied her lesson books, there now stood a stately stranger who might one day become Queen of France. The slender immaturity of her body made her look quite tall, the excited colour in her cheeks became her. Being a Plantagenet, Elizabeth had always been casually aware that she was beautiful—but never, surely, so beautiful as this! "Should there not be a veil?" she asked, overcome by sudden shyness.

"King Louis himself will be sending it," replied her aunt, the Duchess of Buckingham. "An heirloom of fabulous Cluny lace."

"And when I pass through Paris to Notre-Dame my hair will be unbound?"

"*Bien entendu,*" nodded the French dressmaker. "To signify that your Grace comes virgin to our Dauphin."

"Please—please—let us see *now* how it will look," begged Cicely from her stool by the window.

Elizabeth smiled at her, understanding as always. She realized that whilst all the others were interested in her as a bride-to-be, Cicely's first terror of parting had been born of seeing her standing there like a stately stranger, and that with hair unbound she would seem again the loving elder sister whom Cicely had always known. At a sign from their mistress two of the younger women loosed the Princess's headdress, letting her hair fall to her waist in a cascade of corn-coloured glory.

"With so much gold, child, you scarcely need a crown!" murmured Mattie, her old nurse, with tears of affection in her eyes.

"If Madame la Dauphine would but stand still!" shrilled the Frenchwoman, trying the effect of a makeshift veil with her mouth full of pins.

"And if Madame la Dauphine would but remember to talk French…" sighed the special governess her father had engaged for her.

"I must get used to this 'Madame la Dauphine' title," thought Elizabeth, and heard Cicely snigger from her stool. In private her brothers and sisters often teased her about all her new pomp and circumstance. Through the new window of leaded glass she could see the younger ones at play in the garden now, making a sweet childhood travesty of it: Edward dressed in a piece of trailing tapestry as the Dauphin, Ann with a nuptial daisy-chain on her head, Katherine as her bridesmaid, and Richard supposed to be reading the marriage service from one of their father's big books; while baby Bridget crowed delightedly at them from her nurse's arms. At sight of them out there on the sunlit grass a tender smile curved Elizabeth's lips, and suddenly she hated the white gown which symbolized the reason for her departure to France. "I am tired of all this trying on," she complained. "I pray you, ladies, put the dress away."

"But should we not wait for your English Queen to see eet?" expostulated its proud creator. "Her Maj-es-tie express a so ardent wish…"

"My sister the Queen promised to come," admitted Katherine of Buckingham.

"Were our mother coming she would have been here by now. She has been out from matins this half-hour or more, but hurried back to her apartments," vouchsafed Cicely, from her vantage-point by the window.

"Then something important must have detained her," the disappointed women decided.

So the wedding finery was reluctantly put away and Princess Elizabeth clad again in her everyday brown velvet with the square beaded neckbands. But before they could pin up her hair one of the King's pages, pushing his way through the protests of her women, came and bowed before her.

"Why, Almeric, how pale you look! Have you been making yourself sick again stealing the Queen's strawberries?" she teased.

"No, Madam."

"Madame la Dauphine," corrected the Duchess with asperity.

But either Almeric was mulish or he did not hear. "His Grace sent me to fetch you," he said, speaking directly and without ceremony to Elizabeth.

"Then wait while they bind my hair," she answered blithely. After so much standing about for dressmakers it should prove a pleasant diversion to see the King.

"No, Madam, by your leave," insisted the lad. "His Grace said 'immediately.'"

For a moment or two Elizabeth stood wondering. What could the King want with her so urgently? It could be some last-minute arrangements he had been making with the French Ambassador, of course, or even just some new book he wanted her to read. One of those wonderful new printed books, perhaps, fresh from Master Caxton's press. Or perhaps, with his usual impulsiveness, her father had bought her some amusing gift. Something from the tall-masted foreign ship which had just put in at St. Katherine's Dock—some strange spices from the very edge of the world, a little monkey or some other pleasant surprise. "You mystify me, Almeric!" she said with a laugh and a shrug; and, waving aside her women with their pins and their combs, she lifted the folds of her gown in either hand and followed him. Elizabeth almost ran through the long galleries of Westminster Palace, singing a gay little song as she went. It was always a joy to see her father. And nowadays, since this Shore woman had captivated him, she saw him so seldom.

Edward the Fourth of England was the fondest and most indulgent of parents. *Self*-indulgent, too, her mother said. And growing more indolent of late as his wife waxed more meddling. Their children often heard them quarrelling about it. But to Elizabeth, his firstborn, he had never raised his voice in anger.

Yet before Almeric had pushed upon the heavy oak door of the audience-chamber she could hear her father's powerful voice, and it was certainly raised in anger now. The easy-going King had been driven to one of his rare outbursts of Plantagenet rage, using that oath of his ancestors which always came to his lips when abnormally roused. "By God's breath, I will revenge this treacherous insult in every vein of his heart!" he was thundering, as she came into the room. There appeared to have been some sort of hurried Council-meeting, but it was over now and all the important men about him looked frightened as rabbits. Even Richard, Duke of Gloucester, the King's young brother, and Lord Hastings, his trusted Chancellor, stood silent; and the French Ambassador was cringing like a whipped cur.

"Even Guienne and Acquitaine, which my fathers fought for, I agreed to as her dowry," said Edward thickly. His strong hands were twisting a letter on which was impressed the seal of France, and presently he flung it to the floor and set his spurred heel upon it. His comely face was dangerously flushed and his tall body shook with anger.

"Will it mean war?" Elizabeth heard a man near the door whisper behind his hand.

"A year or two ago it might have," whispered back his neighbour. "But not now, perhaps. That harlot, Jane Shore, has softened him." No man in that great room had eyes save for the furious King. No one noticed his daughter standing in the doorway until Gloucester, whom little ever escaped, touched his brother on the arm. As the torrent of his rage subsided, Edward must have remembered that he had sent for her. Glancing in her direction and seeing her white frightened face, he tried to take a hold of himself. He strode across the room to her, his arms with their hanging crimson sleeves driving his courtiers before him as he went, so that every man of them melted away through the open doorway to discuss the dreadful purport of the French King's letter in some safer place.

Only Gloucester lingered, who—for all the battles he had fought—was not so many years older than herself. Although all the others had stared at her surreptitiously, Gloucester did not so much as glance at her, whether from tact or pity she did not know. "If you need me, Sir, I can raise an army for France," he offered, in that pleasant, unemotional voice of his.

But the King's oath had outrun his decisiveness. He only made a vague gesture of dismissal to his brother and drew her back with him to the centre of the room. For some moments it seemed that he could not speak. "That those false fiends should have done this to you!" he managed to say at last, when the door was shut and they were alone.

"Done—what?" she asked, trying not to see the offending letter trampled into the scented rushes at her feet.

"Broken their solemn betrothal contract."

Even then Elizabeth, so freshly come from all that femine preparation, could scarcely credit her understanding. Tall for her years, she stood close before him, looking up searchingly into his face. "You mean—the Dauphin does not want to marry me?" Her shamed words dropped slowly into the silence of the imposing room, reducing an event of world-wide importance to the personal feelings of a girl.

Shaken out of his anger at sight of her stricken face, the King would have taken her in his arms; but Elizabeth stood stubbornly still. This was an affront to her feminine nature. Something which would make her different in her own eyes as well as in the eyes of others, and which no man, however kind, could accept for her.

"He has asked for the Duke of Burgundy's daughter instead," her father told her, reducing his explanation to the same simplicity of terms.

Elizabeth felt as if someone had hit her a stinging blow across the face. She had been humiliated in public, so that the whole palace, the whole world, seemed full of mockery and belittling laughter. She saw herself again as she had looked in the mirror, a lovely bride in jewelled velvet. Madame la Dauphine, a future Queen of France. For a moment the figures on the wall-tapestries wavered uncertainly before her, but she was not a person given to fainting. Instead she just stood there, holding her chin a little higher. And in those searing moments she ceased to be the high-spirited child who ran singing through her father's palace, and became a woman. A woman aware of the ambitious cruelties of men.

"Bess, my dear!" implored her father, who could not bear to see such subdued bewilderment upon so young a face. And at sound of his voice, bereft of all but love, her mask of dignity slipped and she hurled herself into his arms. "C-couldn't they have sent their horrible messenger before p-people had seen me t-trying on my wedding-dress?" she sobbed out against his breast.

Edward sat down in his great state chair and drew her on to his knee. He stroked her unbound hair and tried to comfort her as if she had been small Katherine or baby Bridget, but with infinitely more understanding, since they two had always been very close. "It has nothing to do with you as a woman. You must always remember that," he told her. "This Burgundian chit might be as ugly as sin for all France cares. All Louis wants is to avoid war for the succession—the same horrors of civil war as we have suffered here. So, because my sister Margaret's husband keeps a Burgundian army which is a perpetual menace, the Dauphin must marry into their family." Explaining the matter to her, Edward almost came to see it from Louis the Eleventh's point of view, and his indignation waned. "You know how these marriages are, my poppet, with our daughters as the bait for political alliances."

"Yes," said Elizabeth, who had already been the proposed bait for several. But those other proposals had never been serious and she had been but a child. Whereas now the whole face of life was changed. She would have to readjust herself. "What a waste it seems, all the hours I spent learning to write French," she said, with a gallant effort at lightness.

But neither of her cultured parents would think so. "No learning is ever wasted," Edward told her gravely. "Particularly for people like ourselves who live in an era of expansion and invention, with William Caxton bringing the literature of the world within the reach of all. See here, child, how he had already improved his methods since I took you and your brothers to watch him at work. He is even illustrating his books with woodcuts." Reaching across a mass of state papers, the King picked up a box of small wooden pieces of type and scattered them on the table beside him. "That printing machine of his will turn out more books in a month than is done in years by the tedious script of monks."

"Will they ever be as beautiful?" asked Elizabeth.

"In time perhaps. And girl as you are, I warrant you a day will come when you will be glad that you can write a fair hand in more languages than one."

Elizabeth tried to fix her attention on what he was saying, knowing that he was trying to keep her thoughts from the shock which she had just sustained. He told her that she might come every day and read his books. "Not that I will have them taken away even by you," he stipulated.

"No, Sir," said Elizabeth meekly, knowing well enough that Richard, her younger brother, had one of them out in the garden.

Edward recommended *The Sayings of the Philosophers* for her piety, and Chaucer's *Canterbury Tales* for her diversion, but inevitably he had more serious matters to attend to. "I must go now and talk with your uncle and Hastings," he told her, getting to his feet.

And she must face again all those people who had so lately assisted in the preparations for her splendid marriage. Worse still, she must face them with red eyes, looking like any lovesick milkmaid jilted by her swain. "If it please your Grace," she asked in a small voice, "may I stay here a while?"

"Assuredly, my pretty," he agreed readily. "And I will send your mother to you."

Elizabeth stood twisting her hands together in the folds of her skirt. "Please, no…" she began, before she had time to think.

"No?" Her father, already gathering up some papers, awaited some kind of explanation.

Both of them, perhaps, had been tried beyond pretence. "She would begin—trying to put things right—to *manage*…" Elizabeth stammered, without reverence or caution. But before lowering her eyes she caught the answering gleam of amusement in his. "I mean, I would rather have someone who—who knows nothing of the matter. Someone who will not want to speak of it, or even be thinking 'The—Dauphin does not want to marry her.'"

With his free hand the King pushed her gently into his vacated chair. "But someone of your own, dear child?" he urged.

Elizabeth's only wish was to be alone; but even from this side of the Palace she could still hear the distant shouts of children at play, "Then I will have Richard," she said.

"A wise choice. I always find him a most engaging companion," commended the departing King. And from the doorway she could hear him calling an order to someone to fetch his Grace the Duke of York.

So presently Richard came to her, still struggling with the weight of the big leather book.

"Why, Dickon, it is *The History of Troy*!" she reproached.

"I know. I can read some of it. I took it from the King's collection," he said, with that look of complete candour which he had.

"But how *could* you?"

"We had to have a book for the wedding service." For all his sensitive air of delicacy there was a streak of obstinate daring in this ten-year-old which was not in the other royal children.

"Well, we shall not need it now," sighed Elizabeth. "So put it back with the others. Mercifully, our father did not miss it. I hope you let no dew from the roses get on it."

"I held it very carefully, Bess."

"I saw that you did."

"Where from? What are you doing?"

"I was in my room trying on—a dress."

"They are always making you do that. But now for once I have you to myself. I like books better than dresses, Bess."

"I believe that I do too, Dickon. Yes, I am sure that I do now." Having managed to heave his burden on to an appropriate shelf, the boy had more opportunity to observe things. "You are sitting in the King's chair!" he said, quite shocked.

"He invited me to. You know I would not sit here otherwise."

"Of course not," agreed Richard. "But perhaps Ned will sit in it one day."

"Not for years and years, I hope!" declared Elizabeth, still passionately grateful for her father's kindness.

"Is it specially comfortable?"

"No. Rather hard, in fact," she laughed, surprised that she could be so soon amused.

The boy was tired with his play and came and leaned against her, and it was strangely comforting to have him there. He began building wooden castles with Master Caxton's little pieces of type, and Elizabeth was able to think her own thoughts. After all, apart from hurt pride, why should she mind so much? She had never seen the Dauphin. And now, perhaps, she would be able to stay in England with Richard and the others. Her arm went round him, drawing him closer. She supposed him to be childishly absorbed in the construction of a tower; but with young Richard one could never be quite sure. Evidently his nimble brain had been pursuing some line of thought suggested by the troubled times of which his elders talked. "It is strange, is it not, Bess," he observed, hoisting a paper flag from his tower, "how many people want to sit in the King's seat even if it *is* uncomfortable?"

Chapter Two

MONTHS LATER ELIZABETH WAS wearing another new velvet dress; but this time it was black. As she stood at an open latticed window she could feel the sun hot upon the sombre stuff. There were gold tips to the little willows along the river bank, and lilacs scenting the Palace garden, and the invitation of an April morning made it seem all the more unbelievable that instead of planning some pleasant expedition she should be looking down upon the coffin of her dead father.

Because Edward the Fourth of England had been a soldier and a sportsman and had died quickly in the prime of his manhood the coffin was both long and heavy, and the bearers stumbled a little as they bore it out in to the sunshine from the dark Abbey doorway. Seen from above they looked oddly foreshortened creatures, so that Elizabeth wondered in a detached sort of way how they would lift so dead a weight on to the standing hearse, while that part of her mind which was freshly bludgeoned by grief recalled how briskly he had been wont to cross the courtyard in his lifetime. Following after, as if borne upon the sad sound of requiem chants, came the lords spiritual and temporal; and high upon the hearse went Edward Plantagenet's wooden effigy, wearing his sparkling crown and clad in his crimson cloak, so that it made a splendid splash of colour among the sombre crowd of Londoners who were come to gape at it. And to his eldest daughter it seemed that no living creature in the whole bareheaded throng would ever cut so fine a figure as he, who had dwarfed men by his height and dazzled women by his handsomeness.

As men mounted their horses and the procession began to move, a small piteous cry was wrung from her. Her father, who had always so cherished her, was leaving home for the last time. He had begun his last journey to be laid to rest at Windsor. More than anything that had happened during these past dreadful days, the slow, dull rhythm of mourners' feet in a stilled street made her feel bereft. So much more bereft than the daughter of any ordinary citizen; not by the measure of her grief but by the measure of her insecurity. It was as if the strong champion of her family's reclaimed inheritance were gone.

From the raised embrasure of the window where she stood Elizabeth turned for comfort to the living relatives who were left. They were all assembled there except the elder of her brothers, now so suddenly and frighteningly important, who was with his tutor at Ludlow. Elizabeth looked at them imploringly—at her mother, the Queen, sitting apart by the table, and at her younger sisters and Richard huddled in their unaccustomed mourning at the far end of the room. She had supposed that they, too, would want to come crowding to the window to watch the outset of the late King's funeral. That Cicely at least, who was rising fifteen, would want to look her last upon that effigy and wish a loving father farewell. But fear seemed to inform them; and it was natural enough, she thought indulgently, that in the strange circumstances of Death they should draw closer together and leave her, the eldest, to watch alone.

But a small gust of indignation rose in her as she watched her mother, marvelling that so newly made a widow should sit there dry-eyed, locked in some inward scheming with a half-written letter before her—trying, as ever, to improve on destiny. That *she* should not be too moved to do aught but mourn! But perhaps even that, too, was natural. For did not the whole realm know that Jane Shore, the glover's daughter, had more immediate cause to grieve? That most alluring of the late king's many mistresses who had dimmed the lustre of his name, causing him to smear with sloth and self-indulgence what should have been the well-earned years of leisured honour after his splendid wars. Jane Shore, reflected Elizabeth, must be a lost and frightened woman by now.

At seventeen Elizabeth Plantagenet knew all about her father's faithlessness; but knowing also his parental fondness, she found it hard to understand how humiliation can harden a supplanted woman's heart.

With tears in her eyes, she turned her back upon them all. Already the solemn procession was wending its way into King Street, and soon the velvet-draped coffin with the great silver gilt cross would be borne beyond the bend of the river, to be censed again by the lovely village cross at Charing. Was she the only one to care? But before it had passed from sight she heard the slither of a light step beside her and a cold hand was slipped into hers. "Where are they taking him?" whispered Richard.

"To Windsor," she told him, holding his hand reassuringly.

When he turned his head to look up at her the sunlight on his cheek made him look defencelessly young and fair. "Why not to the Tower, Bess?" he asked.

"Because people go there only to prison, sweet—or before they are going to be crowned," she told him, speaking softly too.

"Will our brother Edward go there when they crown him?"

"I expect so."

He thought the matter over in that quick way of his which often made her think he would be the cleverer of the two. "Ned is very young, don't you think, to be a King?"

"He is thirteen now, Richard, and of course he will have a regent to act for him."

"Who?"

"The Queen, perhaps. Or Uncle Richard of Gloucester."

"I wish it could be Uncle Rivers."

"But milord Rivers is only a Woodville uncle on our mother's side—not royal at all." And there, thought Elizabeth, lies a part of our insecurity—that our mother was not royal, but just someone the King married secretly when he was young.

But such matters weighed little with eleven-year-old Richard who knew only that he liked the gay and accomplished Lord Rivers and was nervous and tongue-tied with his Uncle Gloucester. He wriggled from his sister's hold and thrust his head through the open lattice, the better to look down. "How sad all the people look!" he said.

"And bewildered," added Elizabeth more to herself than to him.

"Because they have no King?"

"But they have, Dickon," she reminded him.

"Of course. Edward the Fifth? How odd it sounds!" he laughed involuntarily. "Is he that now, this very minute, Bess?"

"From the moment our father died."

It was a difficult thing to believe about someone with whom one had been arguing and learning Latin up to a few weeks ago. But for those silly chills he had had last winter, and his mother making all that pother about his seeing the King's physician, Richard supposed he would have been with Edward at Ludlow still. And now poor Ned would have to wear all that heavy ermine and sit through stuffy councils instead of hawking with him on the Welsh hills! Probably they would both have to live in London; but however horrible things were, at least Bess would be there. She wasn't going away to marry the Dauphin. "It is worse for us than for all those people, anyway," he sighed, kneeling back on his heels on the window-seat. "*We* have no father."

He leaned his fair head against the sun-warmed folds of her dress, and she bent over him tenderly so that a braid of her own hair mingled with his short, wind-blown locks. So exact were they in colouring, she noticed, that they might well have grown from one head. The new young King's hair was yellow like their mother's; whereas her own and Richard's were burnished with authentic Plantagenet gold. The thought pleased her, for, fond as she was of all her family, from tall-growing Cicely to baby Bridget, this slender, sensitive younger brother held her heart.

But it was Edward, the long-awaited elder son—Edward, the new thirteen-year-old king, who, with his good looks and sturdy health, promised to be as fine a man as his father—who was the widowed Queen's pride. Elizabeth knew instinctively that it must be he whom she was worrying about.

Through bad times and good she had always been her mother's companion, so she descended the stone steps from the window and crossed the great, richly tapestried room to stand beside her—pityingly, protectingly, her former flash of indignation forgotten. "He should know by now, Madam. The roads are in good condition and your messenger must have reached Ludlow."

Elizabeth the Queen stirred at last. "Yes, poor boy, he must know. And none of us there to help him bear the shock," she sighed. "He will not have dreamed of succeeding for years, Bess. And, as we both know, it is a sore thing in these days for a boy to inherit a crown before his sword arm is strong enough to protect it!"

Living through the bitter holocaust of civil war had taught these two Elizabeths the need of a strong man on their side. For years Yorkists and Lancastrians, sprung from two different sons of the great third Edward, had riven England for her crown. It was the old vexed question of descent through a woman from the elder son, or descent from the younger through a man. Their rival emblems, plucked during a furious quarrel in the Temple gardens, were a red rose for Lancaster and a white rose for York; and now the strong, thorned stem for their white branch was dead, leaving only a tender bud.

"Uncle Rivers is with him," said Elizabeth.

"And kind Sir Richard Vaughan. Don't you remember, Madam, how he used to carry us on state occasions when Ned and I were small, and how he always told us what to do?" joined in young Richard, who had followed her and was trying to add some comfort to his own.

Absently, fondly, the Queen stretched out a hand to smooth his ruffled hair. "My brother Rivers will stand by him, of course. And Dorset and milord Bishop of Salisbury," she ruminated, as if marshalling the Yorkist forces upon some imaginary battlefield. "And although milord Hastings never had much love for us 'upstart Woodvilles' as he calls us, your father made him swear that he would always protect our sons. That was some years ago, before your father came under the spell of this unspeakable woman. But he respected my acumen. In his will, which was read to me only last night, it is expressly stated that the arrangement of marriages for you girls is to be left to me."

"Though perhaps no European princes will be clamouring for us now!" thought Elizabeth, whose youthful confidence had been shaken.

Richard leaned across the table, eager and gallant in the morning sunlight. "The Cheshire men were all around Ludlow. I saw them armed and watchful as I came south to join you here," he was saying to reassure his troubled womenfolk. "Edward says they have always mistrusted the horrid Lancastrians."

"It is not the Lancastrians I mistrust," said the Queen surprisingly.

The boy's blue eyes opened wide. For him life was a simple affair where people were either on one side or the other, white or red, as in a game of chess. "Who then, Madam?" he asked.

But the Queen did not answer. Instead she asked him to light a candle that she might seal a freshly written letter which lay before her; and presently, wearying of grave matters, he slipped away to play catch-as-catch-can with plump, five-year-old Katherine.

"It will take much longer—a week or more perhaps—for the news to reach Uncle Richard of Gloucester in Scotland," said Elizabeth, when they were alone. "But of course he will come as quickly as he can."

The candle wick had run up foully and the Queen paused to snuff it before answering. She nipped it with wilful dexterity, as she dealt with most things she wished changed. "I would to God he would stay there!" she said, laying down the pewter snuffers with violence.

Elizabeth stared at her mother's sharp-featured face. The fair hair strained back beneath bands of white lawn gave her a spurious look of youth, and the high intellectual forehead was singularly unlined for one who had lived through so much strife and sorrow. It was difficult to believe that she had already been the widowed mother of two sons when first she met the King. "But Gloucester is my father's only living brother," exclaimed Elizabeth in bewilderment.

"Yes. By blood he was nearest," allowed the Queen.

"And dearest!" added Elizabeth, resenting the imputation simply because her father would have done so. "The most loyal to him of all."

"To *him*—yes."

"But, Madam, everyone knows Gloucester to be both courteous and capable." Both women were talking in undertones and although Elizabeth had no particular affection for her uncle she felt constrained to defend him with fairmindedness. "My father used to say that, although he does not look over-strong, he was the best soldier in England. Up and down the country, wherever there was trouble, when has he ever spared himself in our Yorkist cause? He must have worshipped the King."

The Queen opened her jewelled hands palm upwards as they lay on the table before her, seeming to intimate by the gesture how far she was opening her inmost mind. "But me he has always disliked," she said.

Her daughter's blue eyes opened wide. Uncle Gloucester's manner towards his sister-in-law had always been so suavely respectful. He had ever been tactful when people complained of the high appointments heaped upon her Woodville relatives and had never seemed to resent the jumped-up sons of her first marriage to Sir John Grey. Indeed, he had always seemed too busy soldiering or playing the useful younger brother to have time to mind such things. But then, of course, Uncle Gloucester was so reserved and inscrutable that it was difficult to know what he really felt. And so many people *did* dislike the Queen. Her marriage had been unpopular from the first when she had cast herself, the proverbial fair and penniless widow, on the King's mercy and stirred his hot young passion. By bartering her virtue for nothing less than secret marriage she had robbed England of some strong matrimonial alliance which might have helped to settle the constantly recurring Yorkist and Lancastrian counter-claims; and ever since, although she could not hold her indulgent husband's constancy, she had turned his less reputable passions to the advantage of her family by demanding power as recompense. Each time the popular King erred, men said, a hated Woodville rose. "If Uncle Gloucester dislikes her," thought her daughter, not undutifully, "it may well be because she has a mind as cooly calculating as his own."

"Mercifully, I had Dorset made Constable of the Tower," the Queen was saying, as if pursuing some similar train of thought. "So the defence of London lies in our hands."

Even before the funeral procession started she had sent for him, and almost at that moment he came, that modish half-brother of Elizabeth's, hurrying to kiss his royal mother's hand. "What news of young Edward?" he asked.

"I have written to your Uncle Rivers to bring him south immediately—with all those stalwart archers young Dickon has just been talking about," said their mother, holding out to him the letter she had been perusing. "If you will have a trusty messenger ride with this to Ludlow within the hour they should both be in London by May Day. Then you must send out a strong armed guard from the Tower to meet them, Tom."

Thomas Grey, Marquis of Dorset, thrust the letter rather reluctantly into his wallet. "Would it not be better to wait for the consent of the Council?" he warned.

But the woman who had had him made a marquis only laughed. "Never fear but what I shall get my way with them! Have you ever known me to fail?" she reassured him. "But this will give Rivers time to have all in readiness, and every hour counts."

"For my part I shall be glad to see Ned safely crowned," muttered Dorset, biting upon his nails as he was prone to do in moments of anxiety. "But I doubt if even Uncle Rivers—brilliant as he is—can raise the militia privately without an order under the royal seal."

To Elizabeth it seemed almost indecent that they should be thinking of such things before her father was halfway to his burial; but someone, she supposed, must think of them. Having been so set down by the Dauphin of France had sobered and shaken her so that she believed that she herself would never have the cunning so to spur forward fate, yet she admired and envied those who could. And towards evening when the candles had been brought and the younger children were gone to their beds she saw that her mother was right.

The Archbishop of York came in a great flurry of episcopal robes to hand over the Great Seal of England that it might be held in trust for young Edward. Dorset returned secretively from his errand. One after another men of consequence, returned wearily from Windsor, began to fill the room; and a hurried Council was called.

"We must prepare everything against the coronation of our Sovereign Lord King Edward the Fifth," began Lionel Woodville, Bishop of Salisbury, platitudinously.

"The first thing is to get his Grace quickly to London," urged Dorset. "I will send an escort as far as Highbury to meet him."

It seemed that all present were in agreement, except the rich Lord Stanley. It may have been because his own large band of retainers had not been offered the honour or because he had married the Lancastrian Duke of Richmond's widow, or merely because he considered too many Woodvilles had spoken. "Why so great a fever of haste?" he enquired, being a man of less impetuosity who liked to wait upon events and see which way they turned.

Everyone appeared to have forgotten Elizabeth standing in the shadows by the drawn window-curtains; and from where she watched, the men gathered round the candle-lit table looked like actors on a lighted stage, or like some Flemish painting in which the sitters' sombre garments throw into revealing relief the expressions on their faces. Just so the Queen's finely drawn features were illuminated as she sat at the head of the table, and the light emphasized the strength of Lord Hastings' profile as he stood at the foot. Elizabeth knew that her mother played in part a deceiver's role and that honest Hastings, come straight from a loved master's funeral, was too sore for subtlety; and with sensitivity rare in one so young she was aware of the antagonism between them. For years Hastings had practically ruled England. Scores of times Elizabeth had seen her father smile at him and say in that charming, careless way of his, "Do as seems best to you in the matter, my good Will, so long as you don't expect me to give up a whole day's hunting!" And she realized now how Hastings, who had never once betrayed that easy-going trust, must hate to see a managing woman sitting in Edward's seat and trying to ride him on a tighter rein.

"I suggest, milords, that word be sent to my brother Rivers to bring his young Grace immediately," she was saying as smoothly as though she had been presiding over the Council all her life, as guilelessly as though she had not already forestalled them. "Also that he calls out the Cheshire militia in full strength. If the roads are in good condition they should arrive by May Day. Pending the coronation, as is customary, his Grace will lodge in the royal apartments in the Tower. And if our good Lord Mayor will spare no pains to have his preparations under way I see no reason why we should not fix on May the fourth?"

"With milord Bishop of Salisbury, no doubt, to round off a family affair and do the crowning," muttered Stanley unpleasantly.

The royal widow's ears were as sharp as her still lovely features. "Why, no, my dear Lord Stanley. Who is more appropriate for that honour than our own Archbishop of York?" she reproved suavely. "But for the moment the main thing is to have someone to crown, and for that blessing I count the hours. For once within the capital my son will be safe."

She was carrying the meeting well until William Hastings roused himself from his cloud of surly gloom. "Safe from whom, Madam?" he demanded.

Elizabeth marked the start of surprise swiftly hidden by a bland smile on her mother's face. "From any who are his foes, milord," she was saying lightly. "He is so young…"

But Hastings was in no mood to be put off with vague evasions. His firm chin shot out aggressively. "And who does your Grace imagine *are* his foes?" he persisted, his deep voice thick with rising anger. "Valiant Gloucester, who has enough on his plate with holding down Scotland? Or our good friend Stanley here? Or myself, perhaps?"

Every man about the table grew tense with interest and the Queen's white hands were raised in pained surprise. "My dear Lord Hastings," she protested, "could the Yorkist heir be safer in any man's hands than yours, who served my husband so devotedly?"

The very fact that she could call a Plantagenet husband was a running sore to most of the proud nobility gathered about her. A sore which no longer need be kept decently covered. "Yet he must be brought to London by Lord Rivers, your brother—met by Dorset, your son—with a whole army of the best troops in England to lend lustre to the progress!" burst out Hastings.

"A fine fanfare for the power of the Woodvilles," scoffed Stanley, with a peculiarly unpleasant smile.

The sudden brutal words shook young Elizabeth. Although they were not aimed towards herself, they showed her where she stood. Never in her life had she heard anyone dare to speak even impudently to the Queen, and she could see her mother's face flush to red and knew just how hard an effort she must be making to rein in her fierce temper for young Edward's sake.

"I put it to the Council that the King be brought to London with all speed," she began again, ignoring Hastings.

"Madam, upon this we are all agreed," they chorused.

"Save for the archers," insisted Stanley.

"Are they not in my royal brother's pay," demanded Dorset insolently.

"And is not England a civilized country?" soothed the Archbishop of York, laying a churchman's appeasing hand upon the Queen's shoulder.

"I would have you consider, Madam, how little honour you do the late King in so belittling the love and loyalty his subjects bore him," pointed out Hastings, more gently.

Elizabeth Woodville, twice widowed, was hearing men's true untempered opinions for the first time. "During the time I have been Queen I have seen much disloyalty in unlooked-for places," she faltered.

"That is true, Madam," agreed Hastings, remembering how she and her young children had had to take sanctuary during the brief resurgent power of the Lancastrians after the battle of Edgecot. "But do you not suppose that seeing the new King escorted by a powerful army will set men's minds back to those very times? Can you not see that it is timorous folly to act as if there were any *question* of his being King?"

The Queen sat silent and rebuked. But this time it was not the Lancastrians she feared. Yet how to voice the instinctive mistrust she felt? Or how to make these well-meaning men see that had the suggestion of the archers come from any save a Woodville they probably would not have opposed it.

It was at that moment that the Lord Mayor of London suddenly saw fit to speak up, backing in Hastings a man who had done much for London's trade. "Let milord Rivers bring the King and I will answer for the welcome our citizens will give the sweet lad," he said bluntly. "But I do assure your Grace the sight of an army of hungry northerners and Welshmen bearing down on us will but drive my people to bar the city gates. They remember too well how their victuals have been eaten and their houses fired during their betters' arguments in the years of civil war."

"Then we are all agreed?" concluded the Archbishop of York; and the growled assent of twenty weary men went round the table, so that a mere woman's will could only batter itself against the barriers of their long pent-up jealousy.

"They are all so sensible. But, dear God, let them see that this time she is right!" prayed the slender Princess standing unseen in the shadows.

When she uncovered her eyes she saw that her mother had risen to her feet. Because she was no longer play-acting there was an appealing dignity about her. "Milords, if I have meddled in the past, or presumed to advance my family unfairly, I pray you forget it now," she begged. "I grant there is wisdom in what you say, but sometimes women have a kind of insight which outpaces wisdom. I…" For a moment complete candour trembled on her tongue, but the name of the man she mistrusted was too high above suspicion to be spoken, so she substituted other words. "I have here the Great Seal," she said, lifting the symbolic thing from the table before her, "and seeing that my son is but a minor, can make any order valid in his name. I entreat you once more, milords, to call out his loyal archers!"

For a moment or two it looked as if the Council, impressed by her earnestness, would be bewitched into believing in her fears. But Stanley broke the pregnant moment by flinging aside from them with a barely smothered oath, and Hastings strode forward to thrust a briefer order beneath the upraised seal. "You allow your womanish whimsies to ride you, Madam," he said roughly. "You cannot really believe that I—or any of us—would break our freshly made oath to him whom we loved and served, or leave anything undone which we deemed necessary for the protection of his son?"

The Queen could have refused to use the seal, knowing that in the absence of the Duke of Gloucester none other would have dared; but her brief essay to take command had burnt itself out. At the first shock of combined opposition her high-handed assumption of authority had dissolved into self-pity. In her blood was no stain of royalty to sustain her. "Then I must let myself be overruled by your counsel," she submitted. "And I pray God none of us assembled here may live to rue it!"

Chapter Three

R AIN BEAT UPON THE painted windows of the Abbot of Westminster's parlour, and every now and then a large drip from the smoke louvre high up in the middle of the roof would fall with a melancholy plop upon the May Day branches decorating the hearth. The tall candles guttered in the draught from a hole in the wall through which men had been bringing in furniture and chests of clothing from the adjoining Palace. And on the floor, low among the rushes, sat the Queen. She stared straight before her, scarcely noticing the strange disorder, and the pale hair which had once enmeshed an impetuous King hung like a yellow cloak about her.

Seeing her mother all abased and desolate like that seemed worse to Elizabeth than looking down upon the splendid coffin of her father—except for the fact that she loved him more.

"Do you remember, Bess, how we made our own May Day fun when we were in sanctuary before?" asked Cicely, picking wistfully at the withering green branches. To Elizabeth, sobered early to womanhood by the shame of a broken betrothal, the loss of such revelling meant little; and the others were too young to remember. But to fifteen-year-old Cicely small present disappointments assumed as big proportions as the portentous news that Uncle Gloucester had somehow intercepted Uncle Rivers and their younger half-brother Grey and imprisoned them in Pontefract Castle.

"We could not in any case have kept May Day with our father dead," young Richard reminded her, looking up from the book he was reading as he lay on his stomach by the Queen's side.

"All safe in sanctuary! Safe in sanctuary!" chanted small, pink-cheeked Katherine, dancing round and round the fireless hearth with outspread skirts. To her and to eight-year-old Ann, their change of fortune was all a new kind of game.

Only Elizabeth knew that it was not her daughters' safety, nor yet her own, that their mother was nearly crazed about. It was the thought of Edward in Uncle Gloucester's hands. Each time Richard would have sprung up to join in the younger ones' play the Queen's restraining hands reached out to fondle him. "As long as I keep them apart *each* is safe," she had said more than once, looking across the boy's smooth, burnished head to seek the comfort or corroboration in her eldest daughter's eyes.

This had been the Queen's instant answer to the ill news—her supreme strategy. Even with anxiety for her brother and her son Grey weighing upon her, she had roused the children of her second marriage from their beds and appealed to the Abbot for sanctuary, and he, poor man, not deeming it fit that they should share the asylum of felons claiming the Church's protection from justice, had given up to them his fine hall—never dreaming that in her desire for speed and secrecy the Queen would move in so precipitously as to wreck his masonry. Her move had taken everybody by surprise. To the saintly Abbot it must have seemed scarcely necessary, considering that the young King was already coming southwords in his royal uncle's care and had been proclaimed King in York by Gloucester's orders. But to the Queen's more suspicious mind, nurtured as it was on years of strategic struggle for the succession, the keeping of her younger son where no one could touch him seemed the most necessary move of all. As long as Richard was in safe keeping there could be no point in harming or dethroning Edward. "It takes a woman to outwit them," she had said triumphantly, as soon as they were installed.

Yet even Elizabeth felt that her mother was consumed by an unreasonable obsession about Gloucester. "After the beautiful letter of condolence he wrote you surely you cannot believe that he means harm to either of them?" she said consolingly.

"No harm!" flared the Queen. "When he throws my own relatives into prison!"

"Madam, may he not be only detaining them because it seems to him that they interfered—or at any rate acted too hastily?" ventured Elizabeth.

But the Queen was not to be placated. "Who is he to talk of haste when he swooped south like a vulture to intercept them at Northampton?" she said.

"I wonder how Uncle Gloucester could march a hundred miles farther than Uncle Rivers and yet catch up with him?" said Richard, closing his book.

"He could not have had the news so quickly either," added Elizabeth thoughtfully. "Unless, of course, the Earl of Northumberland or someone warned him."

"He can make his men do anything, your father used to say. Make them march without sleep—and go without himself, no doubt. He looks like it with that pinched face of his!" their mother railed shrewishly. "And as to interference, you talk like a fool, Bess. Had not the Council ordered my brother to bring the King? By the authority of the Court Chamberlain."

"It is true that milord Hastings *was* Chamberlain in my father's lifetime, but is he now?" began Elizabeth uncertainly.

"Had he let me order out those archers this would never have happened," said the Queen, with truth.

"Poor Uncle Rivers!" murmured Richard, sitting up and hugging his knees. "He used to show us the loveliest illuminated manuscripts and make all the old legends come alive."

"He is the most cultured man in the country; and of what can that misshapen clot of cold arrogance accuse him save of being my brother?" agreed the Queen despondently.

Elizabeth went and knelt beside her and began braiding back her hair. "I know how terrible it must be for you," she said, motioning to a hovering lady-of-the-bedchamber to bring a fresh headdress. "But, after all, perhaps the people *expect* Uncle Gloucester to bring him." Being a Plantagenet herself she could scarcely remind her mother that Anthony Woodville, Lord Rivers, was not.

Baby Bridget was asleep in her cradle and the two younger girls had wandered to a window, where they had drawn back a curtain and were whispering together excitedly. "What are you two looking at?" asked the Queen, instantly alert. "What is out there in the street?"

"Soldiers," reported Katherine stolidly.

"Soldiers with lighted torches," elaborated Ann.

That was too much for Richard. Feeling himself to be the only man of the party, he evaded his mother at last and ran to join them, clambering on to the window-seat. "Uncle Gloucester certainly *can* march!" he exclaimed, his nose flattened against a window-pane.

Elizabeth helped her mother to rise and went to look. "Are you sure they are his men, Dickon?" she asked, peering through the trickling raindrops.

"See the boar on their badges!" pointed out Richard conclusively. "And, look Bess, there is Uncle's old groom, Bundy, who taught me to ride my first pony. Over there, standing in the light of a torch."

So it was true. Gloucester had reached London.

"Come back, Richard!" called their mother.

The boy obeyed reluctantly, and Elizabeth could not help feeling that to be singled out for such express anxiety was bad for so imaginative a child.

"The yard is full of them. Do you suppose they are trying to surround us?" asked Cicely, beginning to be scared.

"They cannot harm us, foolish one. Not all the soldiers in the land can make us come out from here," Elizabeth reminded her.

"But they could prevent anyone else from getting *in*," pointed out Richard, the quick-witted.

"You mean they could starve us?" groaned Cicely, to whom no worse calamity was conceivable.

"Oh, for the love of our Lady, be sensible, all of you!" exclaimed Elizabeth, shooing the two smaller girls back to their dolls. "Why should Uncle Gloucester want to starve us? Probably he will ask leave to come and see us soon and bring you all some sweetmeats. Do try to remember that he is in as deep a grief as we are."

"He will go to his precious wife first," muttered Cicely, pouting at her sister's unaccustomed rebuke.

"And why not?" asked Richard. "I like Aunt Anne."

"It is one of the nicest things about him that he loves her so," reflected Elizabeth, feeling that so human a trait made him more like the rest of them and therefore all the less to be feared.

But the Duke did not beg leave to come and see them. Perhaps he was worn out with forced marches, or—as Richard suggested— had not had time to change his dusty armour. Or perhaps it was just that he avoided as much as most men the edge of an angry woman's tongue.

Instead they had a visit from their host, the Abbot. "The Protector is back, Madam," he announced, having been bidden to sup with the Queen.

"The Protector?" The title, if not the news, stunned her.

It being Friday, the Abbot helped himself to fish. "He styles himself so," he said, not liking to tell her that he had already by common consent had the title thrust upon him.

"And fills our peaceful courtyards with soldiery!" The poor Queen had scarcely eaten for days, and even now, in spite of her daughter's anxious urging, only picked distraitly at some fruit. "And what of Edward?" she asked immediately.

"The Duke has taken him to lodge the night in the town house of the Bishop of Ely."

Tears rose to her tired eyes. "Not with me, his mother," she said.

"Dear Madam," soothed the Bishop compassionately, "they say the young King was overtired from the long journey and needs immediate sleep."

"One is scarcely surprised after the shock of seeing his favourite uncle, who was appointed his tutor and who has always done every-thing for him, arrested like a common traitor. Surely, too, it was enough to kill him, coming across England at that pace. I would have you know, my dear Abbot, that for all his sturdy looks he is not so wiry as young Richard here." After brooding on her wrongs a while the Queen added with inconsistency, "To-day is the fourth of May. He was to have been crowned this day."

"The heralds have given it out in every ward of the City that his Grace will be crowned as soon as he is rested."

"And who told the heralds?" demanded the widow of their late master.

"Milord the Duke."

"The Protector?" She laughed shortly. "Heaven send he proves to be one!"

"But is he not the most obvious person?"

"We will see what milord Hastings has to say about that. At least there will have to be a Council-meeting. I shall tell them—"

"But, Madam—"

No one present dared to remind the Queen in so many words that, having withdrawn into the sanctuary of the Church, she could no longer expect to attend Council-meetings; but during their embarrassed silence she sat realizing the possible results of the one grave mistake she had made. Everything must depend upon Hastings now. Being loath to admit the disadvantages of the situation, she changed the subject. "How did London welcome my son?" she asked. And all young Edward's family hung upon the Abbot's words.

"With every possible show of deference and loyalty, Madam," he assured her. "They brought the late King's cloak of purple and ermine for him to wear."

"Was it not horribly heavy?" asked Richard, leaning eagerly over the back of his mother's chair.

"Indeed it was, my little Duke," agreed the Abbot, with a twinkling smile for the boy who had always been his favourite. "But his uncle had a thought for that and bade old Bundy arrange it so that most of the weight fell upon the flanks of his Grace's little white horse. Gloucester rode bare-headed beside him, Madam," he went on, "and the Lord Mayor tells me that every now and then, wherever the crowds were thickest, he would make a motion towards the lad with his cap as if to say 'Here is your King,' and then reined back his great charger a little so that the cheers seemed only for his nephew, and not at all for his own victorious campaign in Scotland."

"That was well done," conceded the Queen. "And how did Edward bear himself?"

"As became your husband's son, save that he looked grievously tired. The children threw white roses in his path and many of the women wept."

"Wept?"

"Because he was so young, I suppose."

"I would we could see him!" sighed the Queen, thereby giving her host the opening for which he had been waiting.

"If you wish it, there is nothing easier, Madam," he assured her. "Milord Duke sent to me the moment he arrived. He entreats your Grace to return to the Palace and to bring the children with you so that you may all be reunited."

"Oh, Madam, and it please you, may we not go?" begged Cicely, putting a coaxing arm about her.

"No," said the Queen, her thin clever mouth set straightly and her gaze on Richard as he tried, laughing, to teach his new wolf-hound pup to beg for scraps.

The learned Abbot glanced round his cluttered room and lowered his voice persuasively. "I have also had word with Lord Hastings, and he thinks that perhaps your Grace's coming here was ill-advised," he ventured. "He feels that the late King's brother is the man of the moment and that you insult him unnecessarily by so much display of distrust."

The Queen was clearly tempted. She enjoyed the exalted surroundings that were due to her, all the more so because she had not been born to them. "You mean the spiritual lords who have been so loyal to us feel it would be wise for me to return?"

"They think it would be more politic both for your Grace's sake and for their own," said the Abbot. "For you must know how hard their lordships are having to fight of late to retain sanctuary rights at all."

The Queen rinsed her ringed fingers in the bowl a young monk had the honour to hold for her. "Then let Gloucester free my brother first," was her ultimatum.

And so the days passed and the children became cramped and irritable. They missed their rides in the royal parklands and their pleasant springtime expeditions by barge. Even Richard's gay temper began to be affected by the mother's anxiety on his behalf. News filtered in that Edward had been taken from Ely Place to the royal apartments in the Tower, and Gloucester, instead of asserting himself by staying in either palace, was lodged at Baynard's Castle, the home of his dictatorial old mother.

They were days of anxiety and uncertainty which played havoc with everyone's temper; and they were not lightened for the Queen when the Archbishop of York came imploring her to return to him the Great Seal. The Protector had need of it so that the young King could issue sundry documents, he said, and it was as much as his own life was worth not to be able to produce it.

"The first document he will persuade that poor innocent child to sign will be a royal recognition of his protectorship!" prophesied the Queen bitterly.

"There are so many orders to be signed," the Archbishop excused himself evasively, "now that the Duke has fixed July the fifth for the coronation."

That preparations were going on on a lavish scale no one could doubt. The hammering of carpenters erecting stands for spectators echoed around Palace and Abbey from morning till night, and carts rumbled in from the country laden with all manner of food. The tailor who was sent for to supplement Richard's single hurriedly made suit of mourning declared that he dared not undertake to do it, because even with these long May evenings he and his workpeople were still sitting crosslegged by candlelight to finish the fine new clothes ordered for his brother, the King. And one morning, while wandering among the roses in the Abbot's peaceful little garden, Elizabeth caught sight of the Duke of Gloucester himself crossing a courtyard towards the Star Chamber, accompanied by a posse of important people. "They must be making final arrangements for the fifth," she reported to her family.

"I wish that I could see the procession! I wish that I could ride my horse again!" fretted Richard.

All morning the great doors of the Chamber remained fast shut, but, the day being warm, the windows stood open, and lay brothers working in the Abbot's garden could overhear voices raised in angry debate. And before noon it began to look as though, after all, Richard would have his wish. For after the meeting many of the clergy came to wait upon the Queen. This time it was the Archbishop of Canterbury who led them, and the Primate's face was grave. "The peers of the realm feel it to be only fitting that his Grace the Duke of York should be present at his brother's coronation," he told her without preamble, as soon as he had given them all his blessing.

"But surely you forbade it! Are we not under your protection here?" cried the Queen.

"No one can touch you, my daughter. Neither you nor our two elder Princesses, who are young women and of marriageable age," he assured her. "But in spite of milord Hastings' objection and of all our arguments it has been decided in council that the term sanctuary cannot apply to children who are too young to sin. With a great hair-splitting of legal deduction it appears to have been proved that since they are incapable of guilt they stand in no need of the Church's protection."

The Queen sprang to her feet white with fury. "It is a trick! A dastardly trick to get Richard into his uncle's hands. And only one brain could have conceived it," she declared.

"Perhaps only with the very proper purpose of having him ride in the procession, Madam," suggested John Morton, Bishop of Ely, trying to calm her.

"Once Gloucester has him he will not let him go," she countered. "Is not his purpose clear? Do they bother to ask for Ann or Katherine or my baby Bridget?"

"Gloucester is now free to take him by force," the Archbishop reminded her.

"He shall not—the child is sick," lied the cornered Queen.

"But we of the Church want no violence," he went on, ignoring her desperate mendacity. "And should your Grace give in with good heart to the Duke's wishes he is the more likely to deal leniently with Lord Rivers and Sir Richard Grey."

"You mean that I must be reduced to choosing between the safety of this or that dear one?"

"He has not said so," admitted the Primate. "Come, Madam, I think you are sadly prejudiced against him. In this matter he has common sense on his side. For apart from the fact that the people would want to see the Duke of York at the coronation, I pray you consider how heavy a burden and how great a loneliness our late Sovereign's death and your removal here have laid upon the King, who himself is little more than a child. Milord Protector, who visits him every day, says that he languishes for his brother as a playmate."

Elizabeth, who so seldom put herself forward and who had accounted her mother's extreme suspicion as foolishness, found herself rushing in in loyal support. "Can no one else be found for him to play with? What of the young Earl of Warwick," she suggested. "Would he not do as well, being our late Uncle Clarence's son?"

The Archbishop ceased to be solemn and shook his head smilingly, for, unlike her mother, Elizabeth had no unfortunate knack of annoying people. "Apart from the fact that he is up in Warwick Castle, I fear your brother would find him but poor company," he said. "For as you know, my dear Elizabeth, he is but simple in the wits, having been born in that bad storm at sea."

"More likely because his treacherous father was fuddled with malmsey when he was begetting him!" scoffed the Queen. "I would not have my poor son lonely, but surely, as my daughter says, some other lads of his own age can be found for him. He might even be more contented so," she added, searching feverishly in her mind for yet more excuses, "for it is a known fact that children quarrel most with their own kindred."

"Oh, Bess, when did Ned and I ever quarrel?" whispered Richard indignantly, drawing his sister away from their arguing elders.

Elizabeth smiled down at him, knowing his sweet disposition. And understanding how bad it was for him to hear himself being the bone of so much contention, she went with him to join the other children. "All the same," he added apprehensively, "I no longer want to go."

"But you will have a new doublet and hose and ride in the lovely procession, Dickon, and see the City all decorated," said Ann enviously.

"Probably Bundy will bring you a new cob and you will ride next behind Edward with Uncle Gloucester," said Elizabeth.

"And when you get back to the Tower you will be able to see all the lions and bears and tigers in the menagerie there," added Cicely, goodnaturedly gathering round with the others to cheer him. "Don't you remember telling us how Dorset took you and Edward to see them fed and even showed you how the keepers shot the bolts of their cages?"

"Why, yes, it was as interesting as the printing press, and there was an ingenious kind of master bolt that could be worked from outside in case they turned savage," recalled Richard, his alert young brain being easily diverted by such things.

"You said they were called the King's beasts, so they must be Ned's very own lions now," lisped Katherine, round-eyed with awe.

"Yes, poppet, but I don't suppose he is allowed to go and look at them. Our half-brother isn't Constable of the Tower any more," remembered Richard forlornly.

"Why not?" demanded Ann, who had entertained hopes of being taken to see the fearsome lions herself.

"Because one of the first things Uncle Gloucester did when he reached London was to relieve Dorset of his command and to put Sir Robert Brackenbury in his place," Elizabeth told her.

"Well, Sir Robert is very kind," said Cicely. "Perhaps *he* will show them to you, Dickon."

The idea seemed to cheer him for a while, but their mother was still arguing with the beautifully arrayed churchmen. "Brothers have been brothers' bane, so how can nephews be sure of their uncles?" they could hear her contending in that penetrating voice of hers. "And I have such deadly enemies."

Whatever they thought, it seemed they were too pitiful to remind her that she herself had made most of them. "Madam, though this forward generation may nibble at our privileges, Holy Church is not without considerable power," the Archbishop comforted her.

"I know well your good intent and believe you can keep them safe if you will," agreed the Queen at last, with a profound sigh. "But if you think that I fear overmuch, take care that you, milords, do not fear too little!" She called Richard to her and, placing a hand on either of his shoulders, gave him a little push towards them. "To your care I commit him—Richard, Duke of York, the late King's younger son—and of your hands before God and man I shall require him again."

Frightened by her anguish and by the churchmen's solemn faces, Richard felt the budding manhood he had clung to so desperately deserting him. He turned his back on them and caught at her dress. For weeks her foolishly outspoken fears had been playing upon his sensitive nerves, sapping his courage; and now some nameless terror was being conjured up before him. She held him tightly to her, his head against her heart. "God send you good keeping," she prayed, the tears raining down her face. Then, cupping his troubled face in both her beautiful jewelled hands, she bent to kiss him with prophetic passion. "Kiss me before we part, my sweet son, for God knows when we two shall kiss together again!"

And because she wept Richard wept too, and they clung together so that the gentle Abbot had perforce to part them. The Queen turned away, covering her eyes with a dramatic gesture and leaving the boy sobbing alone in the midst of them. It was one of those devastating scenes which the Woodville Queen seemed almost involuntarily to create.

After a moment or two the Archbishop of Canterbury cleared his throat. "Your uncle is waiting in the Painted Gallery to welcome your Grace with all kindness," he told Richard, and at the gently spoken words the boy straightened himself. Uncle Gloucester, like his father, was a soldier and would stand for no womanish tears. His sister watched them go down the long hall to the door together, the prelate with an arm about the young Duke's shoulder so that his splendidly embroidered vestments seemed to be covering him like a protective wing.

And suddenly all the Queen's foreboding sprang to life in Elizabeth's heart. She would have given anything to hold him back—done anything to keep him. Seeing how bravely he was trying to play the man, she wanted desperately to say something to comfort him, to tell him how dearly she loved him. But no adequate words came to her. It was as if, surfeited with the prodigality of her mother's emotion, all expression of her own were damned. "Don't forget the lions, Dickon!" she called out cheerfully as he passed her.

He did not answer her, and she could have bitten her tongue for producing such an inanity. The great oak door at the end of the room was thrown open. A shaft of sunlight from outside shone all about her small brother, glinting on his red-gold hair and making a charming silhouette of his slender figure in its sad black velvet. And in the doorway he stopped, disengaging himself courteously from the Archbishop's protective arm. And to her great joy he turned and smiled at her, answering the unconscious fervour of love in her eyes.

Then there was the sharp thud of pikes as the guard outside sprang to attention, and, although the warm spring sun still shone, he was gone.

Chapter Four

A S THE DAYS WARMED to high summer the hammering
ceased. London lay decked and waiting for a coronation.
The spectators' stands were all set up, the merchants' gabled
houses draped with richly coloured damask, the civic banners bravely
flying. And in the Abbot's quiet garden out at Westminster, among
the red and white roses, paced the two sad women who should have
been the most radiant figures in the coming pageantry.

"All this preparation is for himself—for Gloucester, the false
usurper!" raged the widowed Queen. "Did I not warn you?"

"You were right, Madam, and I a blind artless fool," admitted
Elizabeth.

"He never intended to have young Edward crowned. It was all lies,
lies!" The Queen's black skirts swished angrily against the low box
borders, stirring a bitter sweetness from their sun-drenched greenery.
"The moment those credulous clerics had wheedled Richard from me,
what did the fiend do but have my brother and my first husband's son
executed at Pontefract? My poor brother Rivers was so handsome, so
brilliant…Gloucester was always jealous of him."

"My father would never have believed this of Gloucester,"
mourned Elizabeth. "It is bewildering to recall how he trusted him."

"And now the unnatural creature dares to justify himself by
calling your trusting father's children bastards! You, Cicely,
Edward—all of you. Trying to strengthen his case by reminding
the world that the King and I were married secretly."

"It is only the legitimacy of Edward and Richard that really matters to him." Elizabeth of York sank down upon a stone bench and drew her mother down beside her so as to put an end to the distraught pacing. In the noonday heat the combined scent of box and full-blown roses almost made both women swoon; but neither of them could bear to be cooped up with prying attendants within four walls. They had to voice the thoughts which were tormenting them. "Who was this Butler woman whom they now pretend my father married first?" asked Elizabeth, who had never dared to speak of so intimate a thing before.

"One of the King's earlier loves," shrugged his widow, inured to his infidelities.

"Was she—long before you?"

"Only a few months. She was just Joan Talbot, the Earl of Shrewsbury's daughter, when I first knew her. She was very pretty and Edward very ardent, no doubt. If he could not get his way he may have *promised* to marry her."

"But at the time of your coronation surely the Council satisfied themselves that *you* were his wife?"

"They saw my marriage lines," stated the woman who had been enterprising enough to insist upon more than promises.

"And you had witnesses?"

"Only my mother and two waiting-women. But the testimony of my mother—Jaquetta, Duchess of Bedford—cannot be lightly set aside. That is why, for all their talk of secrecy, the only hope of my enemies is to prove that the late King married Joan Butler first."

"But surely after we have lived among them for so many years the people will never tolerate such lying injustice!" protested Elizabeth. "For whatever my father's faults, he was brave and open-handed and unbelievably popular."

"Whatever he was, it is only his sons who matter now," said the Queen wearily; and suddenly she covered her face with both hands and began to sob uncontrollably.

"My poor sweet, you have scarcely slept through all this terrible time!" comforted her daughter, kneeling on the grass to put strong young arms about her. "Let me ask the good Abbot's physician to prepare a soothing draught for you."

"What can that old dodderer do for me? It is Life which has already done so much!" wept the Queen. But Elizabeth produced a handkerchief with which to dry her mother's cheeks, and held still her pathetic, fluttering hands. "There is that clever Doctor Lewis who attends the Countess of Richmond," she suggested. "You remember how highly she speaks of him, and since he is a priest as well there will be no difficulty about his visiting you here."

"The Richmonds are Lancastrians," objected the exhausted Yorkist Queen.

"But now that the Countess has married Lord Stanley she is always received at Court."

"Yet her son is still an exiled traitor to our house."

"I am not asking you to see Henry of Lancaster, whom men might call our arch-enemy," smiled Elizabeth, "but this man Lewis who is reported to be so clever."

"Then perhaps to please you I will," conceded the Queen, bending to stroke her daughter's bright hair. "You are very good to me, Bess. You always did take other people's sorrows to your heart— even the younger children's small disasters. But I do assure you I am not sick. It is only that I am crazed with anxiety about the boys. God knows I should never have let them take Richard from me!"

It was the same useless lament with which Elizabeth Woodville had wearied herself and others for days. "Well, at least let us go in out of the sun so that you may rest," coaxed the younger and more practical Elizabeth. And when they came into the house they found the Queen's eldest son, Dorset, booted and spurred as for a journey and talking earnestly with Thomas Stafford, Buckingham's son, who had been brought up with them in the late King's house-hold since he was a page.

Seeing a visitor from the outside world, the Queen stopped in the doorway. "It is true, is it not, that Gloucester will have himself crowned?" she demanded dramatically.

"Yes, Madam," confirmed Stafford, bowing low. "At first he made some show of refusing it, but the Council have pressed it upon him." Being ill-pleased with the answer, she ignored him. "And the boys?" she asked, sweeping past him towards her eldest son.

"Stafford says it is thought that Richard will be allowed to attend the ceremony—to provide some show of avuncular regard, no doubt," hazarded Dorset, in order to comfort her.

"And not our Edward!"

"Even Gloucester would scarcely dare risk that, I fancy," smiled Dorset, settling the folds of a riding-cloak his servant had put about his shoulders. "Why, even those people who see in a proven man more security for the Yorkist line and more prospect of peace might be moved to cheer for him."

"Those same self-seeking people who so short a while ago wept for his appealing youth!" sighed the Queen, seating herself wearily in the midst of them.

"Richard always wants to see everything, but he will hate going without him," said Elizabeth.

In spite of the Queen's displeasure, handsome young Stafford fetched Elizabeth a stool and waited beside her. "He will scarcely have time to look about him, for if he goes he is to hold the new Queen's train," he told her.

"My son—a Plantagenet—to carry a Neville's train!" exclaimed King Edward's widow. And then, as if noticing for the first time that her eldest son was dressed for travelling, she cried aghast, "What! Are you leaving us and the protection of Holy Church?"

"I may be of more use to you raising help abroad, Madam, than skulking here," he explained. "Besides, Tom Stafford here says it is no longer safe..."

"'Tom Stafford says'!" she mocked contemptuously.

"Your pardon, Madam," began that sturdy young man in self-defence, "but such is the Protector's enmity towards all Woodvilles—"

"That you think it politic to forsake our household for his," snapped the most ambitious Woodville of them all, liking him none the better because of the indignant gesture of remonstrance which Elizabeth dared to make.

"Had Tom not been with Gloucester he could not have served us by coming here to warn me," pointed out Dorset, in his friend's defence. But the Queen's fingers still drummed sharply on the arms of her chair. "Then perhaps since he is so useful an emissary he can tell us whether any of the other turncoats there had the courage to protest when my children were proclaimed bastards?" she enquired bitterly. "And whether it is likely that, when all my kin are dead or fled, Hastings, who was our Chamberlain, will find it expedient to be of the Protector's household too?"

There was silence in the Abbot's disordered parlour while the two men exchanged glances. "Why, Mother, have you not heard?" asked Dorset at last, coming to her side.

"Heard what?" she asked, turning the rings on her fingers. "What fresh horror has been kept from me?"

Dorset seemed as if he could not bring himself to tell her, and finally it was Stafford who spoke, keeping his eyes lowered from sight of the shame that must be brought her by her shrewish tongue. "Milord Hastings will grace no man's household again," he said, telling the thing as briefly as possible. "Days ago, when the Duke of Gloucester first sounded the Council on the expediency of bringing into doubt the validity of your Grace's marriage, William Hastings refused point-blank to have anything to do with it. All his life he had served the late King, he said, and no one should have his allegiance save King Edward's true-born sons. He was absolutely immovable; and for the first time in my life I saw cool Gloucester lose his temper. He stretched out his arm with the old battle scar that shrunk it, and shook with rage. All his life he had fought for his country, and for years the Woodvilles had been the curse of it, he said; and even now, because of a pampered Woodville child sitting on the throne, they tied his arm so that he could do nothing to consolidate the Yorkish cause and so strengthen England."

"Go on!" ordered the Queen, when Stafford dared say no more; and with eyes still lowered the unfortunate young man took up his tale. "Jane Shore and women like her had dissipated his brother's life, the Duke said, and you—the so-called Queen—his substance. And now it had been proved that owing to a precontract with Lady

Butler 'the Woodville woman' never had been the late King's legal wife. Those, Madam, were his terrible words."

Without flinching the Queen lifted her ravaged face. "Did no one protest?" she asked.

"Some of the bishops and Lord Stanley, and were arrested for their pains," he told her tersely. "And before that stormy meeting was concluded poor Lord Hastings was dragged from the council-chamber and executed outside in Tower yard."

"You mean—then and there? Without either trial or shriving?" asked Elizabeth in horror.

"Some priest from the Tower chapel was hastily called, I believe," said her half-brother, finding his voice at last. "And it is a byword how instantly Gloucester's men obey him. They did not even wait to fetch a block, but laid poor Will across some timber lying ready for the coronation stands."

"God forgive me!" whispered the Queen. She rose from her chair and swayed against his shoulder, where she stood a while with covered face. Then, freeing herself from the precious comfort of his arm, she began to fasten the collar of his cloak. "You do right to go; and I beseech you go quickly!" her children and household heard her saying, as they drew away pitifully to leave her some privacy for so sad a leave-taking. "You must get ship for France. Not Brittany. Henry of Lancaster will be there. Try rather my sister-in-law, the Duchess of Burgundy. For the great love she bore her brother Edward she will surely do what she can for you—"

Moving to the seclusion of the Abbot's cloister, Elizabeth of York turned instinctively to Stafford. He had been the comrade of her youth, although of late her mother seldom suffered her to speak alone with him. "I am proud that my father had so fine a friend," she said, her voice soft with awe and grief. "Why, why would my mother never trust him?"

"She does not trust me either," said Thomas Stafford, worrying sulkily at a loose flagstone with the point of his shoe.

Elizabeth stopped by an archway and stood pulling at a trail of ivy while she looked across the sunlit grass outside. "Perhaps people who intrigue and plan find it difficult to believe that others are just ordinary and straight-spoken like ourselves—and poor Lord Hastings," she said. "But, oh, Tom, I wish she would not insult you so!"

Her sympathy wiped all the dark resentment from his face and he looked down at her adoringly. "I have only myself to thank," he grinned. "Having spoken with Dorset, I need not have waited. Indeed, if it should reach Gloucester's ears, it is not very healthy for me to be here at all."

"Then why did you not slip away?" she cried, all anxious contrition at once.

"Because Cicely said you were in the garden and I hoped to see you. To be able to comfort you a little perhaps."

Elizabeth smiled back at him, and the dark threatening shadows in which she had been living seemed to lighten, letting in the warmth of trusting friendship.

"Oh, Bess, you do see, do you not, that I am no turncoat, though I could never be a Hastings?" he implored boyishly, drawing her down gently to the long stone seat beneath the cloister arches. "We all followed Gloucester—thinking we were following young Edward the Fifth. It was this swift snake-like turn—these surprise tactics—which have landed us all in a completely false and unforeseen position. Even Gloucester himself, perhaps."

"You mean that at first he may have meant Edward to be King?"

"I don't imagine anything else occurred to him. Not during the shock of those first few days. He was white with grief for his brother. I was there, Bess, when he had young Edward proclaimed in York, and I would stake my soul that everything he did was sincere."

"He had my Uncle Rivers and my younger half-brother put to death," she reminded him.

"He was furious because they had tried to forestall him in fetching the new King to London. He looked upon it as a plot. And perhaps as he rode southward he began to think about his own little son, whom he had just seen and had to leave behind in Middleham Castle. Or it may well be that once he had reached London and was in Baynard's Castle the old Duchess of York persuaded him."

"My grandmother was always a managing woman, and he her favourite son," admitted Elizabeth.

"Or, perhaps, when it came to training your brother for his kingly part, Gloucester was disappointed."

"Disappointed?"

"Oh, I know Ned is comely. But the Protector cares supremely for the strength of York," explained Stafford hastily. "And Ned is not very—adventurous, is he?"

"He is not quick to teach, like Dickon, if that is what you mean," she agreed, mollified, and suddenly, in spite of all the tragic happenings, she gave a little spurt of delicious laughter. "How Dickon, in his place, would have loved playing the part! He would have made the most of every opportunity and risen to every dramatic occasion," she said. "Do you remember when we used to have plays at Twelfth Night how he always acted better than any of us?"

"Because he has more imagination, I suppose," agreed Stafford, with a reminiscent smile.

"Or because he inherits some histrionic sense from his mother."

"It was a handicap, perhaps, that young Edward naturally takes his importance so much for granted. As we escorted him down from York I used to watch him riding bored and weary through the cheering crowds. And not trying to hide his weariness, poor lad."

"Whereas Dickon would have found it all so exciting. Although he might have been dropping with fatigue, I suppose he would have smiled that devastating smile of his and charmed the hearts out of people. Perhaps it would have been harder then for Gloucester to steal all the fanfare for his own."

"I doubt if it would have made much difference," said Stafford, watching her tired face with concern.

"Nor I, really," sighed Elizabeth. "What else goes on in the outside world, Tom? After all the fun we had in my father's lifetime it is so deadly being shut up here."

Stafford searched his mind for news which might interest her. "You know, of course, that Gloucester has taken up residence in the Tower and sent for his wife to come down from Middleham?"

"We supposed that he would do that. Actually we heard through

Piers Curteys, who makes our dresses, that he had been ordered to make Aunt Anne a purple velvet dress in two days. Imagine, a coronation dress in two days! And I used to have to stand about for hours being fitted when—when it was a question of my going to France."

"It would seem that Gloucester marches his women as quickly as his men!" laughed Stafford.

Although they had the rare opportunity to talk intimately, they were not really alone in the cloister. A procession of monks passed them with downcast eyes and a slither of sandalled feet, and then Cicely, pursued by her sisters, escaped from the parlour blithely intent upon some childish game; but Elizabeth, pursuing a train of thought, seemed scarcely to be aware of any interruption. "You see my uncle daily, Tom. Do you really believe him to be such an ogre as all my Woodville relations think?" she asked, chin cupped in hand. "It is so puzzling, because only a few days ago we were all thinking of him as a fine soldier, a temperate sort of person, a dependable man of honour."

"They say a sudden glimpse of power can change a man."

"But even then, when he could have had anything he asked, he was never one to put himself forward for power. He loved my father as I do, and seemed content to serve him."

"Does it not occur to you, Bess," suggested Stafford, choosing his words carefully, "that in some odd, distorted sort of way he may be seeking to serve him—or his kingdom—now?"

"For Heaven's sake do not let my mother hear you speak like that!" warned Elizabeth, with an anxious glance over her shoulder. But she herself sat in silence with the thought, and when she spoke it was in a more hopeful tone. "Well, anyhow, I am glad that Anne Neville has come," she said. "Both the boys like her, and she will be kind to them."

Stafford put his hand on hers as it rested on the stone sill beside him. "I doubt if she will have much opportunity of seeing them," he said gently.

"Tom! What are you trying to tell me?" cried Elizabeth, her frightened gaze searching his face.

"It was awkward for your uncle, I suppose. Particularly with his own son coming. So he has had your brothers moved to the lodgings over the gatehouse."

He used the word lodgings euphemistically, momentarily forgetting how well she knew the labyrinthian lay-out of the Tower since her half-brother's governorship. "But those rooms are always used for—state prisoners," she said, looking down almost unseeingly at their joined hands. And then, as Stafford made no reply, she asked piteously, "Does it mean that they will really not be allowed to—go out?"

"There is a walk on the leads of the battlements," he reminded her. "From there they will at least be able to watch the ships go by."

"Who, then, will look after them?" she managed to ask.

"A man called Slaughter—Will Slaughter."

"God in Heaven, what a name!" ejaculated Elizabeth, crossing herself involuntarily.

"He was a trusted archer of Gloucester's troops. Black Slaughter, men call him."

"Why do they call him so?"

"Because he is dark and hirsute, I suppose."

"Let us pray it be for his hair and not his heart!" she murmured.

Seeing her blue eyes all awash with tears, Stafford put aside ceremony and lifted her little hands in his strong ones to cover them with kisses. "Do not worry so for them, dear Bess!" he entreated, his dark head bent close above her fair one.

For a blessed moment or two they stayed close in that sweet companionship. How good, she thought, to have a strong man hold one—a man who cared. So must girls feel, she supposed, who were answerable only to their husbands and not to the State. How easy, she thought, to care for some small country manor, living to please one man. How doubly sweet to bear and bring up children. Against the warmth of Tom Stafford's shoulder her generous mouth curved into a happy smile. For a moment she imagined herself playing with *his* children on some ordinary sunlit lawn. But even the escape of dreaming was short-lived. She was a Plantagenet and must obey her destiny, walking head high with tragedy if need be. "I will try not to worry, dear Tom," she promised, gently withdrawing her hands. "But perhaps you could come again and give me news of them—after the coronation?"

Much as he longed to come, Stafford hesitated. "I am no longer of the Queen's household—"

Elizabeth laid her fingers persuasively on his sleeve. "I know how she insults you, and the risks you run. But if it be possible come to me here. I will walk alone in the cloister before vespers. I have lost so much happiness that it would be hard to think I shall not see you again."

Daring and ardent was Stafford's kiss on the palm of her hand, but brief as ardent. A memory for a girl to live on. Not enough to hold her his, perhaps, but a stirring of the senses strong enough to teach her hunger for some other man's love.

It was days later before Elizabeth saw him again, and then it seemed impossible to recapture the enchantment of their former mood. All the fanfares and shouting of the coronation were over and only the deep-toned vesper bell vied with the renewed clamour of carpenters now taking down the stands.

"It seems incredible how orderly the streets look again after so much preparation," Stafford said, standing in the shadow of the cloister wall and having to shout unromantically against the cacophony.

"So much careful preparation," Elizabeth repeated dully, thinking of all the plotting which must have gone on within the lovely walls of Baynard Castle, and of how persuasive her domineering old grandmother could be.

"Anne Neville's purple dress looked gorgeous," he said at random, trying to break the constraint which lay between them.

"Did you see my brothers?"

"No."

"Then, after all, Richard did not hold her train?"

Stafford shook his head. "No, Bess. The Countess of Richmond held it."

"And she a Lancastrian's widow!"

"She is Lord Stanley's wife now. And Stanley has so many

retainers it pays to keep in with him. In his quieter and more calcu-lating way he almost becomes a kingmaker, like the new Queen's father, mighty Warwick, was."

"I know. I suppose that is why Gloucester freed him almost as soon as he had got rid of poor Will Hastings. At least there is one thing nobody has accused my uncle of yet, and that is of being a fool!" Stafford noticed that her voice had borrowed some of her mother's bitterness so that she seemed far removed from the girl whose tears he had comforted.

There was a lull in the half-hearted hammering, so that only the Abbey bell broke the afternoon peace. "It was unbelieveably good of you to come; but I must go now or they will miss me," she said; yet still stood a while, the book of prayers her father had given her clasped whitely against the sombre velvet of her skirt.

Tom Stafford waited for what he knew she would ask. He realised that, although he had risked much to come, her ultimate thought was not with him. "And you are sure my brother Richard was not there?" she insisted. "Not anywhere?"

"No," he answered grimly. "The only one of that name was King Richard the Third, with pale Anne Neville, his Queen."

Chapter Five

"D EAR TOM, WHAT HAVE you brought us?" chorused the younger Princesses, running to greet Stafford when at last he contrived to visit Westminster again. After weeks of dull seclusion they would have welcomed any visitor from the outside world, but he had always been such a favourite with them that they danced around him in delight.

"I give you three guesses," he teased, trying to keep their marauding hands from the basket of gifts which his servant had just deposited upon the Abbot's table.

"A new dress!" cried dainty Ann.

"Some new toys to play with," lisped Katherine, most of whose childish treasures had been left in the Palace.

"And you, my lady?" asked Stafford, smiling across their bobbing heads at their grown-up sister.

"A new dress would scarcely come amiss," laughed Elizabeth, ruefully holding out the worn folds of her one-and-only black velvet. "But just to see you again is the best surprise of all." Inevitably their visitor went red with pleasure, and, embarrassed by her own spontaneous candour, she turned hurriedly to her fifteen-year-old sister. "And what about you, Cicely? What do you hope Tom has brought us in that intriguing basket?"

"Food," said Cicely, with equal if less romantic candour.

Elizabeth made a shocked little gesture of reproof and Thomas Stafford was all concern at once. Having shared in the culturally rich life which their parents had hitherto provided for them, the idea that they might need the bare necessities of life had never occurred to him. It shocked him so much that he left his open basket to be rifled by Ann and Katherine and came to look more carefully at Elizabeth. She had always been attractively slender, but now it struck him that she had become altogether too fine drawn for a girl of eighteen. By the light of a long window by which she stood he could discern small hollows beneath the lovely moulding of her cheekbones so that it seemed for the first time that she bore some resemblance to the sharper beauty of her mother. "Does that mean that you are actually hungry?" he demanded, with rising indignation.

"No, no, of course not!" she denied cheerfully. "It is just that Cicely, as you know, is a horrible little gourmand. All the same," she admitted, compelled by his searching gaze, "it seems a long time since poor little Katherine had any sweetmeats, and I do wish the good lay brothers would sometimes devise some dainty morsels to tempt the Queen's appetite. Though I suppose it is ungrateful of me to say so when we must all be such a sore burden to them."

"But surely you can send your servants out to buy whatever her Grace fancies, or your friends can bring in a capon or some fruit?"

"It used to be so until a few days ago, Tom, but now it is not so easy. I am sure we are quite safe in sanctuary, for my uncle is not the man to violate the protection of Holy Church. But, as my astute brother foretold, he can set a guard outside to prevent anyone from getting either in or out."

"Set a guard?" exclaimed Stafford. "I had not heard of it."

"It has happened only within the last day or so."

"Come and see, Tom," invited Cicely, catching at his hand and drawing him closer to the window. "Look, there is John Nesfield, that horse-faced squire of his, barking orders at the men-at-arms. Bullying them for allowing you to pass, no doubt."

"How *did* you manage to pass?" asked Elizabeth, who had been too overjoyed at seeing him to think about it before.

"No one challenged me, and I am afraid I did not even notice Nesfield's men," confessed the warlike Duke of Buckingham's son, shamed by his absentmindedness.

"Then you must have been making up a sonnet to Bess's eyebrows!" giggled Cicely.

"The fact is that as soon as the Countess of Richmond had your message she asked me to bring her physician to see if he could be of service to the—to your lady mother. I suppose she must have persuaded her husband, Lord Stanley, to get the new King's permission, for certainly Doctor Lewis was conducted immediately to your mother's room."

"That was very kind of the Countess, and I pray you convey to her my deep gratitude. Although her sympathies must be Lancastrian, I sometimes think she is one of the best and ablest women in the realm."

"And certainly the greatest patron of learning. You should hear the students up at Oxford and Cambridge singing her praises!"

While Cicely joined her younger sisters and shared in the gifts he had brought to relieve their tedium, Stafford beckoned to his servant to bring the book of poems he had chosen for Elizabeth, and they sat for a while reading some of his favourite passages.

"I so much miss the books my father used to bring me," she said gratefully, poring over the exquisite illuminations. "This will help to pass the hours and be a kind of—escape."

"You do not need to stay here. King Richard would willingly have you all at Court, you know."

"In his power, you mean."

"I think he would be kind."

"Ah, well, my mother is so certain this is best for our security; though, for myself, I would barter security for freedom."

"Because half your heart is in a place you cannot get to."

"Yes. I would sooner be a servant in the Tower so that I could make my brothers' bed!" Elizabeth forgot the poems and began moving restlessly about the room. "Is there still no news of them, Tom?"

"My father, although loyal at heart to all of you, is often called there to Council-meetings, and he makes what enquiries he can," answered Stafford, quietly laying aside the book. "But no one in the royal household ever sees them."

"They do not play with Anne Neville's little son? Nor share his tutor?"

"Not that I ever heard of."

"Nor ever go out riding in the sunshine, of course. Oh, Tom, how they must long to speak to us, and how heavily the hours must hang!"

"At least I have something to tell you which may comfort you," he said, having kept his best tidings to soften the rest. "I invented some errand which took me by boat down-river, and as we rowed past the Tower I saw them looking out from the walk upon the battlements. I was not near enough for speech, of course, but one of them waved to me."

"Oh, that is wonderful! How kind of you!"

"It is no more than many others do. I do assure you that many a good citizen of London grows anxious for them and takes boat that way. And several swear they have seen them."

"Then it is certain they are alive!"

"Why, Bess, my dear, you must not let yourself think like that!" he remonstrated, taking her firmly by the shoulders so that she must stand still and heed him. "We, who have grown up in a country rent by civil war, know only too well the danger of a weak King from whom any man with ambition may try to snatch the throne. It is to prevent such wanton bloodshed that my father and Lord Stanley ultimately supported those who offered Gloucester the crown. But neither of them would have done so had he not sworn to them that no harm should befall the Princes. They say that when Stanley was released, after Hastings' execution, he made that a condition in return for his powerful allegiance. The times we live in have forced your uncle to violent deeds, but he is not an inhuman monster. Why must you torment yourself so?"

Elizabeth turned her head aside and stood plucking at the tassel of a cushion, as if debating within herself whether to tell him something. "I had a terrible dream," she said at last, with slow reluctance.

"When?" asked her cousin, releasing her.

"A few nights ago. Just before Gloucester set the guard, I think."

"What was it?" asked Stafford, gently taking the cushion from her and throwing it onto the stone window-seat.

She tried to smile at him, as if deprecating her stupidity. "Truly, I cannot remember. It was one of those nebulous nightmares, full of feelings rather than of facts. You know how sometimes one does not even see the people in one's dreams but is only aware that they are there?"

"Yes, of course."

"It was Ned. He was crying out to me. Calling me in some horrible fear, and I could not get to him to help him. That was really all. Except that my feet felt heavy as if I were shod like a warhorse so that I could not hurry. I tried and tried, and all the time his desperate, pitiful crying grew fainter and fainter until it was smothered in the blackness of the night…"

There was such urgent horror in Elizabeth's voice, and she—unlike the rest of the family—was a person so little given to imaginings, that even Stafford, who wished most to reassure her, could think of nothing to say.

"It may have been because I was worrying about my mother's health," she added, striving to speak more lightly. "Or because someone told us that ever since he understood that the coronation was not for him Edward has seemed to care for nothing. That he is not eating his food or bothering to dress properly. Poor handsome Ned, who used to think so much about his appearance! But, there, it may not be true. One hears such rumours!"

"I should try not to give heed to them," advised Stafford. "After all, as I told you, I saw them with my own eyes standing in the morning sunlight."

"But how long ago was that?"

"Only a week, perhaps."

"Ah! Before my dream."

"Please, Bess—"

"Oh, I am sorry. I know I am behaving as dramatically as my mother," she apologized, blaming herself for scant filial sympathy in the past. "But tell me this. Did the boys recognize you?"

"I imagine so since one of them waved."

"Which?"

"Dickon, I feel sure."

"It must have been a great comfort to them. Oh, how much I wish I could go on the river too. To see them. Just to see them!"

"You worry about the Dowager Queen's health and she is prostrate with grief, while you go about your daily affairs. Yet I think the love you bear your family is beyond hers. It is incredible," said Stafford, watching her pitifully. "You try to hearten and instruct your sisters here while half your heart is caged with your brothers in the Tower. And best of all I believe you love that young imp Richard. Or ought I not to have said that?" he added, as she did not reply immediately. "Do I, perhaps, presume?"

Elizabeth laid a reassuring hand upon his arm. "No, dear friend, you who have cared so much for my griefs and joys could never presume. And you are more discerning than I had supposed a man could be. Yes," she admitted, almost as though voicing some newly realized truth to herself, "I do not know why, but best of all I love Richard."

"Better than she will ever love me," thought Stafford. "And why must I try to make her, since in all men's minds she is still the King's daughter and it could only bring her useless pain?"

And so he stood in silence until her glance, happening to come to rest upon the lad who had carried the book, gave birth to an idea. "Tom, that yellow-haired page of yours," she began tentatively. "He is about Edward's height, would you not say? Do you suppose he would like to have some gay old suit of the real King's, if I can find one, and leave that plain serving-man's livery behind?"

It was some moments before Stafford picked up the trend of her thoughts. "I can only imagine that he would be delighted," he laughed. "But I would not let him."

"Not if I asked you?"

"Not if you bribed me with all the kisses that I hunger for," he told her, with intentional lightness. "I can guess what is in that fond and desperate mind of yours, but I care for your safety even more than for forbidden ecstasies. There will be no boat-rides past Gloucester's well-manned Tower for you, my lady."

"Then I must wait and pray for patience, I suppose," shrugged Elizabeth, turning away. There was an edge to her pleasant voice which betokened nervous strain. "Doctor Lewis is a long time with the Queen. I thought her Grace would have sent for me," she complained presently. "I trust he finds her no worse."

Even as she spoke a door was flung open at the far end of the parlour and the sound of Elizabeth Woodville's voice reached them, lilting to laughter. "On the contrary, she sounds much better," smiled Stafford. "It would seem that he has effected a cure, and—since I fear my royal aunt's tongue even more in health than in sickness—I will, by your leave, await him in the garden."

To Elizabeth's surprise, her mother, whom she had left propped up in bed, walked almost briskly into the parlour leaning on Doctor Lewis's arm. It was weeks since she had looked so well, with brilliance in her dark French eyes, a spot of colour high on either cheek and much of her old becoming vivacity. "Bess, my child, you were wise as usual," she called gaily, as Elizabeth rose from a formal curtsy. "I am glad you persuaded me to see the dear Countess's physician. See how much good he has done me already!"

Glancing at the grizzled, simian-looking little man, Elizabeth decided that he looked clever enough to cure the Devil. "What have you prescribed, Doctor?" she asked, in that kindly way she had of putting even the humblest people at ease. "Some potent elixir of youth, I should imagine!"

"At least something to live for," laughed the flattered patient. "Come and sit beside me, Bess. Margaret Beaufort, Countess of Richmond, has sent us a message, and as it is confidential we will send the others away." With a wave of one bejewelled hand Elizabeth Woodville cleared the parlour, but to her daughter's surprise the physician remained. "Doctor Lewis will be attending me frequently. He understands my symptoms," explained the deposed Dowager Queen, with apparent irrelevance.

"Is it about the Princes, Madam?" asked Elizabeth eagerly, the moment the three of them were alone.

"No, there is no more news about them, alas! I begin to doubt if I shall ever see them again."

"Then what particularly is there to make life more attractive?" murmured her daughter, seating herself reluctantly.

But even while the pessimistic Dowager Queen sighed over her misfortune her acquisitive mind seemed to have moved on to some fresh field of interest. "The Countess sends me word how gifted and personable a young man her son has grown," she said.

"Naturally, since he is her *only* son," smiled Elizabeth.

"But all reports confirm the trend of her devotion. Doctor Lewis here, who has just returned from Brittany, has been telling me in what high esteem Henry of Richmond is held."

The clever little doctor was quick to take up his cue. "He is handsome and prudent and a great lover of learning," he said, his shrewd eyes having observed Stafford's gift book lying beside the Princess's embroidery.

"And his mother says it is high time he took a wife," added the Dowager Queen.

"Probably he will marry the Duke of Brittany's daughter. I heard the French Ambassador talking about it the other day," remarked Elizabeth, with polite indifference.

But her mother leaned forward and placed a hand upon her knee. "The message was particularly for *you*," she said impressively.

Elizabeth came out of her own private thoughts with a start. Her blue eyes stared almost uncomprehendingly. During her short life she had become accustomed to being offered as matrimonial bait for some political reason or another; but the implications of her mother's words appeared to have neither rhyme nor reason. "A message for *me* about Henry Tudor of Lancaster?" she exclaimed; and the scornful abhorrence in her voice was as unmistakable as it was purely hereditary.

"Better a well-disposed Lancastrian than a treacherous Yorkist!" snapped the Dowager Queen.

"But my father would never have heard of such a thing," stammered Elizabeth, realizing that the suggestion was being made in earnest.

"Were your father alive to hear there would be no need of such a thing," pointed out his widow. "But times have changed and we must change with them."

"Have you forgotten, Madam, that Henry Tudor is attainted of treason and still in exile?"

"He might be persuaded to come home."

"Persuaded?"

"Doctor Lewis goes back and forth, seeing to accounts of the vast estates and bearing loving messages from mother to son. The Lancastrian heir is not so cut off from affairs here as you suppose."

The fantastic scheme began to unfold itself as a reality. None but a Woodville, thought its victim, could have conceived anything so daringly incongruous. "What chance would he have of even landing here against the will and ability of Richard of Gloucester?" asked Elizabeth contemptuously, unconscious of the involuntary compliment she paid her uncle.

Her mother's slim shoulders lifted themselves in that inimitable French shrug of hers. "None, at the moment," she admitted. "But married to King Edward's eldest daughter—"

When an ambitious woman's world crumbles about her she can still meddle in the advancement of her children, thought Elizabeth bitterly. "Nothing would induce me to marry him," she said, and, having always rendered sweet obedience to both her parents, was amazed at her own words.

The Dowager Queen flushed red with anger. She dismissed her new physician with a gracious but hurried gesture. "I think you forget, Elizabeth, that in his will your father expressly left me charge of my daughters' marriages. Even our enemies who dispute your legitimacy cannot dispute that," she said.

Elizabeth knew that that was true, and that scheming was indeed the breath of life to her. This latest idea seemed so far beyond the realms of possibility that one should be glad of it, perhaps, since it helped to take the poor Queen's mind off cruel realities. All the same, it angered Elizabeth intensely. "Do you love the white rose of York so little?" she demanded, standing defiantly before her mother as soon as they were alone.

The older woman rose, too, and faced her. "I hate Richard of Gloucester," she answered, tight-lipped.

"So you must plot with a Lancastrian? White rose or red, I suppose it can be all the same to you Woodvilles!" accused Elizabeth Plantagenet, for the first time insulting her mother's birth. They were no longer Queen and subject, mother and daughter, as they stood there, but two women racked beyond endurance or courtesy. Yet without the memory of Stafford's kisses still warm in her heart Elizabeth could not have said it. Apart from her horror of union with a rival dynasty, he had made the thought of any marriage of diplomacy abhorrent to her.

Before such rare defiance the Dowager Queen's vivacity wilted to self-pity. She leaned back in her chair and asked for her women, complaining to high Heaven that the one person upon whom she had supposed she could always count should so insult her in adversity. Automatically Elizabeth began ministering to her, all anger spent. After all, it seemed, it had been but an idle conversation, ending in the kind of scene which her mother always worked up to whenever life began to stagnate. And surely there was no need for anxiety, since, however much she might want her daughters to marry, there was nothing she could *do* about it while shut up in sanctuary. "Probably I shall never marry anybody," thought Elizabeth, almost too harassed to care.

"You do not consider me at all," her mother was wailing, as Elizabeth dutifully dabbed rose-water to her brow.

"It is the boys who need considering," said Elizabeth, in the flat, unemotional voice with which she unconsciously countered her mother's facile spurts of emotion. "In what way would your proposal benefit them? Judging by what my father has told me of Henry of Lancaster, it would not get Edward back his crown."

"No, but it might save their lives."

Elizabeth straightened herself with the damp kerchief still in her hand, as though physically meeting the impact of the thought.

"We could make it a condition," went on the Woodville woman, softly pressing home the argument which Lewis had suggested to her. "You could offer him your precious Plantagenet blood, couldn't you, in return for a promise that he would keep your brother honourably in his household?"

An odd assortment of thoughts and memories passed through Elizabeth's mind before she answered. A passionate longing for the warm security of her father's presence—an enchanting echo of young Richard's laughter—the firm tenderness of Tom Stafford's mouth. "I do not see that Henry of Richmond has the least hope of landing," she said at last, with detached common sense. "And as for promises, has not Uncle Gloucester sworn exactly the same thing? Why should I sell myself in the hope that a Lancastrian's word may prove more reliable than a Yorkist's?"

"Because your uncle has already broken *his* word. He has not kept them in his household but in prison," pointed out their mother incontrovertibly.

Elizabeth stood aside as the solicitous waiting-women came to escort the Dowager Queen to her room. "I begin not to believe much in any promise," she said sadly.

Chapter Six

YOUNG RICHARD PLANTAGENET was kneeling on the window-seat in one of the smaller rooms of the royal apartments in the Tower and pressing his nose against the leaded panes in an effort to see something more interesting than the stone wall of the tower across the garden. "Do you remember when Dorset showed us the menagerie down by the moat where they keep all those wild beasts?" he asked over his shoulder.

His elder brother Edward, sitting at a table in the middle of the room, grunted disinterested assent.

"That day I left Westminster Cicely said I might see them again," persisted Richard, craning his neck in the likeliest direction. "And Bess called after me 'Remember the lions!'"

"They said it to cheer you, I expect," said Edward, listlessly turning over the pages of his book.

"Do you suppose Uncle Gloucester would let us?"

"Is it likely, since he keeps us cooped up in these two rooms and will not even let us dine in hall any more?"

"We could perhaps ask Will Slaughter to take us," suggested Richard, sliding restlessly to the floor.

"*You* could ask him. Surely it is not to be expected that I should ask a servant to let me see my own lions?" replied Edward pompously. "Besides, he will do anything for you."

"I expect nobody dares to disobey an order from Gloucester now he is King," decided his younger nephew, after turning over the chances in his bored but fertile mind. "Well, let us play at something instead."

"You can play soldiers with your chessmen," said Edward more kindly. "It will help to pass the time until Slaughter, or that ruffian Forest, brings the next abominable meal."

Richard stuck out his underlip at his chessmen. He was tired of playing alone. Cicely and Ann, although they were girls, had always entered into his ideas and been fun to play with. When he had first left them his uncle had received him charmingly and everybody at the Tower had been kind. Aunt Anne Neville's distrait gentleness had soothed his homesickness, and there had been amusing minstrels at mealtimes and his cousin Edward's puppy to play with. But now Will Slaughter or his cross-eyed underling, Miles Forest, always bolted the door when they went out, and it was days since he and Edward had seen anyone else. Sighing, Richard drew from his wallet two or three pieces of Master Caxton's leaden type and set them upon the table. There were not enough of them to build a castle, but somehow the sight and feel of them comforted him. He had been playing with them when he last stood by his father's table, and now he kept them as a kind of talisman. Gloucester, or the Council, had taken away his family and his fun and even his dukedom. He was plain Sir Richard Plantagenet now, so they told him. They could not take away his knighthood, he supposed. That and the little pieces of lead were all he had left of the wonderful things his father had given him. But it was not in Richard's nature to repine. "If you won't play let us learn to dance," he suggested, sweeping the type back into his wallet and tugging irritatingly at his brother's book.

Edward was much bigger than he, but, to Richard's surprise, instead of cuffing his head he flung away from him and went and stood with his back to him by the empty hearth. "It would be better to learn to die!" he said, in a strangled sort of way.

"Why, Ned!" exclaimed Richard, all the teasing eagerness wiped from his face.

And suddenly, as if strained beyond endurance, Edward covered his face with both hands and burst into tears. "Now that that fiend has taken my c-crown I pray to God he will at least leave me my l-life!" he blurted out between sobs. Richard watched his heaving shoulders and was terribly sorry for him; but this was the wild dramatic way in which their mother sometimes talked, and during his sojourn in sanctuary his highly sensitive nerves had been too often rasped by it. "Who should want to kill a boy of thirteen?" he asked. "What have you ever done to hurt anyone?"

"It is enough that I was born my father's eldest son," said Edward, who had been made to read more history.

"Well, at least we are with our own relations here," said Richard, trying to soothe him. "Not hunted, as our father was, by our enemies the Lancastrians."

"An enemy in one's own camp is more dangerous than a dozen outside," said the lad who should have been King, slouching despondently back to his chair. "I do not like it that nobody comes near us—or knows where we are."

"Perhaps the new King is busy and has forgotten us," said Richard forlornly. And then, seeing that his brother would not be comforted, he fell to dancing by himself. Up and down the sombre room he went, every now and then passing the high arched window through which a shaft of moated sunlight fell upon his graceful, childlike figure. And because it was not very amusing to dance alone he had soon invented a partner. Each time he reached the end of the room he would bow to her, handing her gallantly in and out of the intricacies of the dance and making her admiring little speeches under his breath as he had seen his father do when leading the dance with witty Jane Shore. His vivid imagination had created a world beautiful with candlelight and elegantly dressed guests and lilting music, and so happily was he living in it that he failed to notice the quiet opening of the door.

Edward's fair head was still hidden desolately in his arms on the table, so it chanced that neither of them saw their uncle standing there watching them. "So you can still dance?" said the new King, after a moment or two.

At sound of his pleasant voice Edward's head shot up angrily. His chair was scraped back with a gesture of defiance even while he made a shamed and futile effort to hide his tears. Young Richard, arrested in some strange dance steps of his own invention, just stared in surprise; then, recollecting himself, bowed politely.

As Will Slaughter closed the door from the outside King Richard came forward into the room. "And who is your partner?" he asked, still ignoring his elder nephew.

It was seldom that young Richard was tongue-tied, but, as he had once told Bess, he was never certain how to take the uncle for whom he had been named.

"Some May Day sweetheart? Or your wife, perhaps?" rallied the King, entering into his imaginings so as to set him at his ease.

"My wife is dead," said Richard solemnly.

The King looked momentarily bewildered and then laughed. "Why, yes, of course I remember. When you were about six they betrothed you to the rich Duke of Norfolk's daughter. Another of your mother's clever moves!"

"It was an honour for the Mowbrays of Norfolk!" spluttered Edward furiously from the middle of the room.

The new King's eyes narrowed dangerously, but mercifully at that particular moment Richard found his tongue. "Her name was Anne too," he volunteered; and either the name or the sudden thawing of the boy's shyness must have averted the older Plantagenet's anger. "So we two not only bear the same names but are both married to an Anne," he said, his manner wholly delightful.

"And it *was* my wife I was dancing with," confided his younger nephew, trying to pull forward a carved chair which was considerably too heavy for him. "We met only once, at our betrothal. You were away in Scotland, I think, Sir. But I wish you could have seen her. She was sweet as a rosebud, was she not, Ned? And she had a wreath of white roses on her hair. But the ceremony in St. Stephen's Chapel was very long and she grew very sleepy towards the end. I think I could have loved her almost as much as I love Bess."

At his invitation the King seated himself in the high-backed chair, stretching his long supple fingers along the arms of it. "You all seem to love your sister Elizabeth very much," he said. "I have been away soldiering so much that I scarcely know her. And when I come back your mother insists upon shutting you all up in sanctuary. What is she really like?" He paid them the compliment of talking to them as if they were grown people, and looked particularly at Edward, trying to charm away his sulks and draw him into the conversation; and possibly expecting from him a more disinterested report.

"She is not clever like our mother," answered Edward, more civilly.

"So I should suppose," said the King, his thin lips twitching to a smile.

"But when things go wrong she always knows what to do," put in Richard. In his eager loyalty to Bess and his joy at having a visitor he went and leaned against the arm of his uncle's chair much as the little Prince of Wales might have done; and the King, knowing himself to be awkward with children, was secretly pleased. "You mean that she has ingenuity?" he asked.

Their two intelligent, sensitive faces were close together and young Richard looked back at him, trustingly. And it was the trustfulness, more than the older boy's antagonism, which hurt. "I am afraid I am not quite sure what ingenuity means, Sir," he confessed. "But when Ned let his pet monkey loose at a banquet it was Bess who covered it quickly with her skirt so that it shouldn't pick walnuts off the French Ambassador's plate."

"I can easily suppose that too," said the King, realizing that, after all, he had not managed to get all the danger that was to be reckoned with safely imprisoned in this one small room.

Edward hated him the more for his sarcasm, but was learning the advantages which might accrue from courtesy. "It was kind of you to come to see us, Sir," he said.

The King seemed to pull himself back from the long vista of his thoughts. "I came to see you, Edward, because I am going away. To make sure that Will Slaughter is looking after you as befits the son of Lady Elizabeth Grey."

The sternness of his voice seemed to escape Richard. "Where are you going, please, Sir?" he asked, with the liberty which his own father had allowed his extreme youth.

Mellowed by the thought of being in the saddle again, the King settled himself more comfortably in his chair. "Up through the Midlands to Oxford—a few days in Gloucester, of course—and then to our own town of York." In speaking to this eager little kinsman he found himself talking of it quite involuntarily as "our" town.

"You will like that much better than stuffy council-chambers!" grinned young Richard, with quick intuition. "And will Aunt Anne—the Queen, I mean—go with you?"

"She will go direct to York. A gesture to our northern subjects which every wise Sovereign should make after his crowning in the south."

"And Cousin Edward?"

"We are both hoping so. But he is rather young for so long a journey considering that he has been sick these last few days."

If the King's anxiety was patent, so was his nephew's envy. "I am a little older and not at all sick," he stated, not daring to ask outright. And then, as the King did not answer, he fetched a prodigious sigh and added, "I do so *ache* to be out in the sunshine. The Duke of Buckingham gave me a new pony and I have scarcely ridden him."

The King laughed, rumpled his red-gold hair and got up, conscious of a queer reluctance. "Clearly, my dear Dickon, your duty is to stay here and cheer your brother until we come back," he told him, glancing disapprovingly at his elder nephew's slovenly, untied points. "It would be a good thing perhaps if you could teach him—to dance."

Disappointed, Richard watched him go. "Could you perhaps, of your kindness, give our love to Bess?" he ventured, seizing his final chance. "I think she may be anxious about us."

"Why should she be anxious?" enquired the King, in that thin kind of voice which made people feel foolish and uncertain.

"I—do not know," faltered Richard, made conscious of a lapse of manners which he scarcely understood.

"I would willingly be your messenger," said the King. "But short of pushing past the crozier of every bishop in the country I cannot."

They could hear him for a while talking with Will Slaughter just outside the open door. Telling him which horse he intended to ride on the morrow, discussing the state of the roads, and even laughing ever some campaigning incident of the past.

"He is certainly more at home in camps than council-chambers!" muttered Edward the Fourth's elder son contemptuously, though well aware that it was the same forthright manner with the common people which had made his father so beloved.

But presently Richard, who was nearer the door, began to prance noiselessly in pantomimic exultation. "Move them into the room in the Garden Tower," he could hear the King saying. "They will be able to get out into the sunshine sometimes."

The door was closed almost immediately, but Richard did not mind. It would not be for long, he thought.

Only Will Slaughter heard the end of the crisply spoken order. Heard it, and wondered. His hand was still on the bolt and the man he had always served already a few paces along the passage. "And by the way, Slaughter," he said, halting in his tracks.

"Sir?" From bending over the bolt Slaughter straightened himself smartly to attention.

"That younger one has courage and gaiety," said the King, without turning his head. "Whatever happens while I am away I would not have him unnecessarily—hurt."

Chapter Seven

"BESS HAS A CROSS bear on her back," complained little Katherine, whose nurse often used the old household expression during her own childish tantrums. And Elizabeth realized with compunction that it was true. All day she had left the children to their own devices and then, trying to lose herself in the sweet imagery of her new book of verses, had been furious with the noise they made. Even the fine singing of the monks at vespers had failed to restore her usual serenity. Half her mind was still seething over the coupling of her name with Henry of Lancaster's, and the other half kept straying to her brothers in the Tower. She longed to go out and see for herself what was happening in the outside world, and the monotony of austere monastic walls was beginning to suffocate her. The summer evening was so warm and lovely that she ached to be on the river or riding beneath the great beeches at Windsor. "But it must be worse for the children," she thought compassionately; and after a cheerless supper she went to see what they were doing.

She need not have felt so much compunction.

Guided by shrieks of merriment, she found them gathered in a room shared by Cicely and Ann, and the whole place in the wildest confusion. They had opened two old oak chests which had been brought from the Palace and which had stood in some dark corner ever since. Garments of all kinds were strewn across bed and stools and window-seat, and all four of them were playing at the age-old game of "dressing up." Even baby Bridget, half asleep in her nurse's arms, had her fair curls rakishly crowned with a garland of roses which one of her ancestresses must have worn as Queen of Beauty at some bygone tournament.

"I hope, Madam, it does not matter their ladyships creasing up all those lovely velvets," apologized her old nurse Mattie anxiously. "But it is so difficult to find occupation for them these long evenings."

Elizabeth smiled reassuringly. "They are only old things, Mattie, and it is good to know that my sisters are young enough to be happy in spite of everything."

"Come and dress up too," begged Cicely, who was struggling into a pair of hose considerably too tight for her.

"Take them off before you split them," advised Ann, with sisterly candour.

"But here is the doublet to match," said Cicely, diving afresh into one of the coffers. "It's the one with the green ruffles which Dickon fancied himself in so last Christmas. Do you remember?"

"Put it back," said Elizabeth sharply, remembering only too well.

"Well, come and dress up in something yourself," urged Cicely goodnaturedly. "Here is a lovely flowered gown which would suit you to perfection."

How dear of them to be so eager for her to join in their play, thought Elizabeth, and to bear her no grudge for her day-long churlishness! "I would willingly try it on but that it appears to have been made for a giantess," she laughed, perching herself companionably on a corner of the nearest chest.

"Then wait while I find you something smaller," offered Ann obligingly, turning over a mounting pile of garments.

"Look! There's brother Ned's suit with the roses," pointed out small Katherine, as well as she could for the flowing veil in which she imagined herself to be a bride.

"Bess doesn't want to dress up as a boy, *petite imbecile!*' said Ann, throwing the favourite old suit aside. But Elizabeth picked it up and examined it attentively. It was made of plain black velvet with white roses of York stitched all over it. "Edward is so tall for his age I believe I could get into it," she said, beckoning to one of the women to unhook her dress.

The children were delighted. Willing hands helped to fasten the doublet and to tie the points of the long black hose. "Why, you look wonderful, Bess!" exclaimed Ann, whose dress sense already bade fair to be excellent. "Here, *chérie*, let me tuck some of your hair under this black-velvet cap. And put your feet into these square-toed shoes. They are distressingly clumsy, but I cannot find Ned's." Dainty Ann knelt back on her heels and stared in astonishment at the transformation she had wrought. "You know, Bess darling, you make a wonderful boy. No one would ever guess, would they, Cicely?"

"You look like another person—the way you did in that grand French wedding gown," said Cicely, gaping with astonishment. "Only now, I am glad to say, you don't look grand at all. Except for the silk roses, of course."

"Bring me the mirror," said Elizabeth, and, suddenly finding herself in urgent need of more mature confirmation, raised questioning eyes to kind old Mattie.

"Truly, Madam, you might be his young Grace the King," Mattie told her.

"Or one of the pages, with those shoes!" giggled a gawky young nursery girl who had come to carry Bridget to her cradle.

"If only Dickon were here he would make up some play for us to act now that we are all dressed up," sighed Ann, exquisite in somebody's flame-coloured pageant dress.

"I will try to invent one in his stead," said Elizabeth, looking down with particular satisfaction at the incongruous shoes.

They clapped their hands with delight, and when it was acted and the hour-glass had run down to bedtime the girls declared that never since their father's death had they enjoyed so good an evening's entertainment; and the waiting-women were no less pleased because a considerate Princess insisted upon her sisters helping to tidy the room. She even began folding things up herself; but while they were all busy she slipped away, and none of them noticed that she had taken her own impromptu costume with her.

Far into the night, almost to the last gutter of her candles, Elizabeth, the King's daughter, sat diligently unpicking white silk roses; and in the morning as soon as the kitchen fires were being raked she dressed herself carefully in the plain black velvet, trying to hide the gleaming length of her hair as Ann had done. She drew close the curtains of her bed so that the servants might think she slept late, then donned the square-toed shoes and, with pounding heart, crept softly down the backstairs, uncomfortably conscious of the unaccustomed draught about her slender, tightly hosed legs.

As a child she had often seen inside the Palace kitchens, and by comparison the Abbot's looked intimately small. She had counted upon there being more people about so that she might slip out unseen. But on the other hand there were no complicated passages to negotiate. Near the backstairs entry, in which she stood, some of the servants were sitting on a bench still finishing their breakfast ale, while beyond them a couple of scullions hung freshly filled pots on the chains above the great open fire. A lay brother appeared to be superintending the cooking, and in the middle of the stone-flagged room a tall monk sat at an old refectory table with an account book, chequerboard and several little piles of coins in front of him. He was bargaining for country produce as the carters brought in their wares, and the going and coming through the outer door at the far end of the room was considerable. Through the blunt Norman arch of it Elizabeth could see the open courtyard and groups of peasants unloading fresh vegetables. Some of them, their produce sold, were already throwing back their empty sacks and departing. It should be easy enough, she thought, to pick up a sack and walk past the unsuspecting guard beside them; and once outside the Abbey precincts she knew the way to the Palace water-stairs. Ferrymen were always hanging about at the moorings. She had only to call "Hey, there, a boat for below bridge!" and step casually aboard as she had seen young 'prentices do a hundred times when going about their master's business. And then, once out in the early-morning sunshine, she would be borne swiftly away from the stifling walls of sanctuary upon the sparkling tide. There would be the breath-taking thrill when the boat shot expertly through a narrow arch of the bridge, and beyond it, solid and white and strong, would be the Tower with the water swirling through the portcullis of the gate into the sullen moat, and the grim, battlemented towers above.

Perhaps in a few minutes from now she would see her brothers again. If she were fortunate, one of them might wave—though, to be sure, they would not recognize her in doublet and hose. And if they were not yet up she would tell the boatman to row back slowly at slack tide, hoping to see them on her return journey.

Elizabeth had never in her life stepped into a swaying boat without the help of obsequious hands, nor had she the least idea how much the hire of a public one might be; but she had been careful to put some gold pieces and a groat or two into the little wallet attached to Edward's leather belt. As she felt with moist, anxious fingers to make sure they were still there someone hurrying in from the backstairs passage jogged her roughly, elbowing her out of the way. "Have you no errands to do, blockhead, that you must cumber the doorways?" demanded a consequential young soldier whom she recognized as a corporal in John Nesfield's guard.

It was a new experience for a Princess of England, but Elizabeth had the sense to keep her mouth shut. She moved obediently into the kitchen and looked about her, accepting a mug of breakfast ale with the rest.

The corporal called loudly for a glass of the best Malvoisie. With reluctant but unruffled courtesy the tall Benedictine sent a servant for it and went on with his accountancy, setting to shame the young lout's self-importance. For, as everyone knew, no one in the new King's guard had any right to penetrate even as far as the kitchen.

"Thinks he owns the Abbey just because the Captain sends him to report to the Tower ev'ry mornin'!" grumbled the old man who grommed the Abbot's mule, sore because the soldier had upset his ale.

"What is there to report about in this celibate backwater?" enquired a discontented scullion.

"Everything the Woodville widow and her clutch of daughters do, I suppose," laughed a coarse-looking individual sitting on the bench close by Elizabeth's side.

"But what's the good of sending reports about *anything* to London when the new King's gone up north?" asked someone.

"He's left trusty people here to act for him, never fear!" vouchsafed the corporal, overhearing him. "Gloucester never did leave anything to chance. He's the best soldier we ever had."

As he set down his empty glass and swaggered out into the courtyard the lay brother turned from the fire with a skillet in his hand. "A pity Sir Mars does not bring reports *back* again about what's going on in the Tower," he said, voicing the uneasiness of all.

But uneasiness and curiosity were drowned in laughter as a shock-headed swineherd drove in an unwilling pig for sale, and the Benedictine monk, after poking its lean ribs, sent him out again. During the scuttling and the merriment Elizabeth edged her way farther along behind the fast emptying bench. It was no good standing still like a frightened hen, or being shocked by the way the servants really spoke. She noticed an honest-looking farmer selling Father Ambrose a fat goose while his two boys waited with a basket of more delicious plums than ever reached her mother's table. "I will go out with *them*," she decided, settling the unaccustomed belt more snugly about her slender hips and looking for somewhere to set down her mug.

But before she could reach the table to join them the sunlight was momentarily blocked from the open doorway and the swineherd came running back again. He ran so fast and so blindly that he cannoned into the lay brother, who was in the act of tasting the steaming contents of the skillet with a long-handled spoon. "The Devil take you!" yelled the poor man, as drops of boiling liquid slopped over his sandalled feet.

The lad did not even apologize. "Have you heard?" he panted.

"Heard what, you clumsy numbskull?" growled the enraged Benedictine, sinking back on to a stool to hold his scalded toes.

"What they are saying all along the strand."

"The strand is always buzzing with some silly tale or other."

"People with nothing to do but hang about for fares have time to invent them," scoffed a second lay brother, coming in hot from the hard labour of kneading the day's dough.

In spite of so discouraging a reception, the country lad stood his ground in the midst of them all. "'Tis about the two Princes," he said, still too excited and short of breath to elaborate.

Cooks and scullions turned from their tasks, and the breakfasting servants ceased chewing with bread still bulging their cheeks. Involuntarily every man stopped to listen, for what was happening to the late King's sons was the subject upon which the ears of all London hung.

"Well, what about the Princes?" asked the monk in charge, grudgingly, thereby lending the uncouth newsmonger the prestige of his notice.

"They've been murdered."

The stark words, roughened by a rural burr, seemed to drop into the expectant stillness as separately as hard stones. Their harsh impact created a horrified hush, followed by a babel of questions.

"Where?"

"Who says so?"

"How do you know?"

In the general hubbub no one noticed a fair-haired lad stagger against the table, or a mug half full of ale clatter to the stone floor.

"Seems some sailors had it from Will Slaughter's doxie. They be all round her on the water-stairs now."

"And who is this Will Slaughter?"

"He looks after them, she says."

"'She says'!" scoffed Brother Ambrose, closing his account-book with a bang. "It is always someone else who says. And is this—loose-living person with so sinister a name supposed to be the murderer?"

The tale-bearer, not having thought so far, could only scratch his tousled head.

"It seems scarcely likely, Brother Ambrose," pointed out the cook with the scalded toes, forgetting his pain. "Or he would have been the last to start the news."

"Then who is supposed to have done this dastardly thing?" demanded the Surrey farmer, his gaze upon his own two sons and the Abbot's money lying forgotten in his gnarled hand.

For a moment it seemed as if some powerful presence they all feared were holding men's tongues dumb. Some of them glanced apprehensively over their shoulders in the direction of the Palace buildings. "He who has most cause to benefit, surely," suggested someone at last.

"There's but one man who stands more firmly through the slaughter of King Edward's innocent sons," persisted the farmer, uninhibited by such townsmen's caution.

"King Richard is miles away making a circuit of the north," Father Ambrose reminded him sternly.

"But, absent or present, there be those left at the Tower who still do his bidding," mimicked a falconer from the Abbot's mews, remembering what the upstart young corporal had said.

"And mighty popular he makes himself, remitting fines and prison sentences and such," added his mate.

The slender lad in black who had stumbled seemed to have recovered himself. To the amazement of all, he suddenly flung himself upon the bearer of the hideous tale. "*How* were they murdered?" he demanded, clutching at the other's coarse jerkin as if he would shake the truth out of him.

The hefty young swineherd goggled in surprise. "In their beds, they do say," he stammered.

"'They say' again!" raged the clear, accusing voice. "But, in God's name, do you *know*?"

"How should I, fool?" countered the country boy, fending him off.

"Then speak no more out of your ignorance, rending people's hearts!" cried the one in black, fetching him a stinging welt across the face with his open palm.

The placid peasant's anger was roused at last. He swung back a red ham of a fist which would have persuaded an ox from one furrow to the next. In that moment the lads' two faces, coarse and cultured, came very close; and some vague recollection, stirring at the back of his slow mind, must have stayed the blow. His mouth gaped and his arm fell to his side. Not until his whirlwind of an aggressor had vanished through the backstairs door did his wits begin to function. "'Twas like our true King," he said, awe-struck. "I saw him when they brought him through London. Close I was to him as I am to you, reverend Sir. And all white and pale he looked, just like him."

"'Twas his very clothes," confirmed a Smithfield man, who had often watched royalty at the tournaments.

"And the way he spoke—with that clipped Norman accent."

"Must have been the poor King's ghost," muttered the credulous old falconer.

And, to be on the safe side, the two lay brothers crossed themselves.

"Ghosts don't talk such common sense. Follow the fellow and bring him back," ordered Father Ambrose, despairing of ever getting any work done in his kitchen that day. But they all hung back. No one wanted to be the first to climb the dark and winding backstairs for fear of what they might meet there. And by the time the hard-breathing pack of them had pushed each other to the top the gallery leading to the living-rooms was deserted, and colour would be added to any tale that might be told against the usurper because every man among them would believe until his dying day that he had seen the avenging ghost of unfortunate young Edward the Fifth.

Chapter Eight

UNAWARE OF WHAT HER reluctant pursuers thought, Elizabeth regained her room. She, too, was thankful to find the gallery deserted; and more thankful still for the privacy of her small, makeshift apartments. She shot the bolt and leaned breathless against the door. "It can't be true! It can't be true! Uncle Richard couldn't have done it!" she kept telling herself. "That fellow was only a village half-wit, and the people will believe anything." She began fumbling with shaking fingers at the unfamiliar lacings of her brother's suit. "Instead of giving up my project I ought to have slipped out while they were all gaping, and by now I might have seen them—Edward and Richard—moving about in the ordinary sunlight, living…" She had peeled off Edward's hose and now stared down at it, lying coiled and empty as a dead thing about her feet. "But of what use to go if they be dead?" She shuddered, shutting out the significant sight with both hands.

She sank down upon her bed wondering how she could find out for certain. Frightening rumours like this had reached them before, but never so vividly and crudely. Her thoughts flew to Tom Stafford, who would help her if he could. But how to get a message to him with that lynx-eyed Nesfield outside? Lord Stanley would tell her, perhaps. He was Gloucester's acquiescent subject now; but for years he had been her father's friend. And Margaret Beaufort, his wife, had shown herself kind. But perhaps the likeliest means of all to get reliable news would be through the Duchess of Buckingham. She must care profoundly, being the boys' maternal aunt. But that would almost certainly mean telling the Dowager Queen, since they were sisters. And, however badly in need of comfort herself, the habit of years made Elizabeth feel that at all costs her mother should not be distressed unless one were sure.

"I suppose the simplest thing would be to speak to the Abbot," she decided, unable to bear the suspense any longer. "I will dress now and waylay him as he comes from Mass." But she had barely pulled on her dress again before the unusual quiet was broken by women's agitated voices and by footsteps hurrying along the passage. She had scarcely supposed that people would be up yet, but someone was banging urgently upon her door. "Madam! Madam! You were not in your room and we have been searching for you everywhere!" they called, as if she had neglected something tremendously important.

Hastily Elizabeth rolled up Edward's suit and crammed it into a corner of her clothes chest. When she opened the door they all came pouring in. Their relief at finding her was so great that they forgot to pursue their enquiries as to where she had been. "It is the Queen!" they tried to tell her, all speaking at once. "She is prostrate… We can do nothing with her. This will kill her… Mercifully the doctor is with her…"

"It is the boys," said old Mattie simply, coming straight to her and holding her hands for comfort much as she used to do when Elizabeth was small.

"How did you hear?" asked Elizabeth, speaking to her alone.

"That Welsh doctor of the Countess's was sent with the news almost before her Grace was dressed. He and the Abbot broke it to her as best they could."

So this horrible thing was no tavern rumour. It was really true.

"I will come at once," said Elizabeth, fastening the last hook and pulling a cap with long pearled lapels over her disordered hair. She pushed past the hysterical women dry-eyed. Almost running along the gallery to the Abbot's parlour, she remembered inconsequently how she used to run singing through the Palace to see her father. She had been happy then—happy and secure. And now girlhood seemed so far behind.

Coming into the parlour already shocked by experience and emotionally drained, Elizabeth could survey the scene almost sardonically. The Abbot was there, and Doctor Lewis—the one tall, the other short; one offering spiritual comfort, the other herbal remedies. And in the centre of the scene her mother, who had now lost every male relative except Dorset. The hour that followed was Elizabeth Woodville's and unforgettable. Alternately she paced the room and threw herself down among the rushes on the floor. Her fingers tore distractedly at the fairness of her prematurely greying hair. And all the time she called aloud the names of her young murdered sons, until the whole building seemed to be filled with the torment of her grief. It seemed that Cicely and Ann had tried to comfort her and retreated, inept and frightened, before an anguish beyond their comprehension. Now they were crying quietly for the brothers in a corner. Their relief at Elizabeth's appearance was patent. For Bess, and only Bess, would understand and know what to do.

By forgetting her own grief which ran too deep for frenzy, and emptying herself out in a tide of pity, Elizabeth could help. Both pity and the need of it were utterly sincere. Surely, she thought, cradling her mother's thin shoulders in loving arms, no woman could have been called upon to bear so much. That she might have aggravated fate did not lessen her suffering. "It may not be true," murmured Elizabeth.

"It *is* true!" cried the Queen Dowager, spurning false-hope. "After my brother Anthony and your brother Grey what else could we expect? I knew it when I let Richard go. It is the very kind of devilry that that Gloucester fiend would do." And standing slim and straight before them she cursed him with the cruellest curse of all. "O God, if there be any justice, avenge my innocents!" she cried. "And make Richard of Gloucester's only son die too!"

There was something so awesomely prophetic about her that the children huddled, silenced, in their corner. The Abbot came to her reprovingly, holding out as if in expiation the jewelled cross that hung upon his breast. By sharing the burden of her anguish Elizabeth managed to quieten her at last, and Mattie coaxed her, in her exhaustion, to accept a few hours' merciful oblivion by means of the sleeping draught which Doctor Lewis had prepared.

"How did you hear this—terrible thing?" Elizabeth asked him, when at last the Queen Dowager lay quiet on her bed.

"The Countess had a message from milord Stanley and sent me here immediately, fearing some chance rumour or some rougher tongue might be the means of killing the Queen Dowager."

"If grief could have killed her Grace surely it would have done so long ago!" sighed Elizabeth, thinking that it is seldom the women who involve others in their lamentations whom sorrow kills, and herself longing for the ordinary relief of pent-up tears. "But it was very kind," she added, marvelling afresh that the woman who should by rights have been her worst enemy should have sent to help her over some of the worst patches of her life. "We have much to thank you for too, Doctor Lewis. To sleep and to forget is perhaps the greatest mercy of all." She stood for a moment or two looking almost enviously at her mother's quiet form, experiencing something of the relief that even death can bring to a household after days of a loved one's painful breathing. "But not for those who are very young!" her heart cried. "Not for Dickon, with all the shining adventure of life before him!"

Turning, she noticed the Abbot's pitiful gaze upon her; but the added reverence in his manner escaped her. "Can we be sure that it is true?" she asked, drawing the bed curtains close and shooing away most of the weeping women before walking slowly with him to the anteroom.

"I think so, Madam," he told her gently.

"But why this time, for certain?" Rebelliously, scarcely noticing what she did, she stopped before a *prie-dieu* and let her fingers drum upon the open book of devotions which her mother must have been reading when the news came. "There have been so many rumours. My brothers' bodies have been seen floating round in the Thames. They have been sent abroad. The young King was killed and Richard, Duke of York, kept in prison—"

"My dear child! That you should have heard such things!"
Shocked by the fierce hardness of her face, the Benedictine laid
a restraining hand upon her arm and Elizabeth relaxed. "Oh, what
does it matter what I heard!" she cried. "It is nothing compared
with what they must have suffered, my poor lonely loves." She
stood by the window, unable to speak, her lovely eyes suffused with
tears. But after a while, summoning all the courage of her breed,
she made a great effort to be practical. "You are able to go out about
London and meet people, Father. What convinces you this time
that it is true?" she asked.

After the trying hour he had been through the Abbot was
grateful for her composure. Her behaviour, he considered, merited
nothing less than the truth. "Margaret, Countess of Richmond, is
one of the wisest women I know. And also one of the kindest," he
began tentatively.

"The saintly woman with the paragon of a son!" thought
Elizabeth, who was growing tired of hearing this.

"Do you suppose she would have sent such tidings to you were
she not sure that they were true?"

"Not purposely, of course. But is she so infallible that she could
not be mistaken?"

"She would be more likely than most to hear the truth. You must
remember that Lord Stanley, her husband, is now Chamberlain of
King Richard's household."

"I remember that Lord Stanley was once my father's friend,"
said Elizabeth bitterly.

The Abbot moved to a side-table and stood absently fingering
the red-and-white pieces set out upon a chess-table. "There is also
something else which gives colour to the story," he said thoughtfully. "Sir Robert Brackenbury, as you know, succeeded your half-
brother as Governor of the Tower."

"And I have always felt that with Sir Robert they must be safe,"
said Elizabeth, coming to seat herself by the table and giving him
her complete attention.

The tall, black-robed churchman whose hospitality had been
so sorely tried looked down with real affection at the steady

intelligence of her lovely face. Small wonder, he thought, that the late King had loved her so. "Your intuition was probably right, Madam," he said. "And that is, I imagine, the reason why he was relieved of his command."

She was quick to grasp the implication. "Relieved of his command?" she gasped.

"For one night only."

"Was he ill?"

"No."

"How do you know this, Father?"

"That squire Gloucester always keeps about him—John Green, I think he is called—rode back from whatever town the Court had then reached on this northern circuit. Twice he came past Westminster. And I happen to know that each time he went straight to the Governor's lodgings in the Tower. The second time a close-eyed man called James Tyrrell rode with him, and when Green returned this Tyrrell person stayed behind."

There was silence in the Queen Dowager's bedroom and all that broke the quiet of the little anteroom was the low sound of their two absorbed voices and the singing of the birds outside. "What more?" prompted Elizabeth.

"Nothing much perhaps," shrugged the Abbot, "except that Sir Robert Brackenbury rode out of the Tower that evening with baggage for the night and a mere handful of servants. To spend the night with a relative on the other side of the river. I happened to meet him at the end of the bridge and he stopped to tell me so. It seems that he told several other people too, as he came along Thames Street. Which was strange in a busy man who seldom tells anybody his business. And he positively loitered over the bridge, almost as if he wanted to be seen by as many people as possible."

"You mean—so that they should know he wasn't in the Tower that night?"

"Yes. Brackenbury is no fool—although he did forget," added the Abbot with a reminiscent smile, "that he had told me not so long ago that he hadn't a relative nearer than Calais!"

Deep in concentration, Elizabeth began pushing the pawns into impossible gambits up and down the squares of the chessboard. "And this man Tyrrell?" she asked.

The Abbot folded his hands noncommittally inside the wide sleeves of his habit. "As to that, I know nothing," he admitted. "Only those within the Tower could tell you, Madam."

"But that night," deduced Elizabeth slowly, "*someone* must have held the keys."

"It was the eighth day of August," said the Abbot, as if some day it might prove wise to have committed the particular date to memory.

"The eighth of August," murmured Elizabeth. "With wild roses sweet in the hedgerows and dawn glimmering early over the cornfields. Merciful God, what a night to be young—and die!" Suddenly she pushed aside the disordered chessboard and stood up. Inaction was intolerable. "And Sir Robert is back?" she asked, almost lightly.

"Oh yes. He and I are both supping with the Lord Mayor this evening."

"Then I suppose you could not possibly—"

"No, Madam, for all his humanity, Sir Robert is a soldier who serves with loyalty the hand that pays him." Elizabeth thanked her host none the less warmly for sparing her his time. "I so miss my father that I have need of someone—like yourself—to talk to sometimes," she explained, and would have knelt for his blessing had not her shaking knees betrayed her.

"I shall always be at your Grace's service," he promised; and because there was more than ordinary insistence in the courteous words she looked up questioningly. His eyes were very grave although his lips smiled.

"Your Grace—?" repeated Elizabeth, fumbling for enlightenment. And suddenly, in the midst of her wild confusion of grief, the momentous realization came to her, whipping the blood into her pale cheeks. "If it be true that my brothers are dead," raced her thoughts, "then I am Queen of England."

There was a usurper on the throne and a Lancastrian pretender across the Channel, and there had been much venomous and hypocritical talk about illegitimacy; but neither Gloucester nor the powerful, turncoat barons could alter the true bloodline of royal descent. For years the family of Edward the Fourth had lived and moved, familiar and accepted, about the land, and Elizabeth knew—and in their hearts the people must know—that if his sons died childless, then she, his eldest daughter, must be Queen in her own right.

During some formless space of time, during which even bereavement ceased to be, Elizabeth Plantagenet stood withdrawn into her own consciousness, absorbing the sense of change in her own status. And as she did so a strange inner warmth sustained her, mingling with her awe and terror, and seeming to invest her with some second, and as yet unfamiliar, personality.

It was only a few minutes before Doctor Lewis came into the anteroom from her mother's bedside. "Madam, I must now entreat *you* to call your women and take some rest," he said with professional authority of manner.

But Elizabeth did not even hear him. In the light of royal obligation, she was thinking that whatever happened to her now there could be no more daydreaming about lovable young men who were commoners. And trying to realize that only an hour ago she had been nerving herself for an undignified *gamin* adventure. Well, there would be no need to nerve herself for it now. She wore Edward's difficult inheritance instead of his cast-off clothes, and she would never see either him or Richard any more. If only she could have shielded them with her own body! "Oh, Dickon, little Dickon!" cried her heart. "Did they hurt you hideously?"

"Madam, you have been through a great deal with vast fortitude." The doctor had given up speaking to her professionally and was now appealing to her with the ordinary compassion of a layman. "If there be anything at all that I can do for you—"

Brought back at last by his insistence to awareness of material things, Elizabeth caught sight of her reflection in the Queen Dowager's mirror. The last few tragic hours seemed to have snapped her youth. There were smudges of fatigue beneath her eyes, and their sad stare was set as a Medusa's. Yet she felt that both men were aware of her new-born regality as she answered, and she was glad that the Abbot of Westminster should be there to witness her words. He had been her confessor of late and had probably smiled tolerantly over all her foolish, immature sins. Now he would see something of her adult, naked soul. "There is nothing, I thank you, Doctor Lewis," she said, with a gesture of dismissal. "Except that I would have you tell the Countess of Richmond that I will marry her son if he will come back to England and kill my uncle Richard of Gloucester."

Chapter Nine

HENRY STAFFORD, DUKE OF Buckingham, first heard the horrible news when the royal party had reached Oxford. He was the greatest and most favoured baron on that northern progress and would not have credited the news for a moment had not his own son brought it. Even while surveying Thomas's concerned face and mud-bespattered clothing he could not bring himself to believe it.

"I honestly considered that a strong man like Gloucester would be best for England," he kept saying, pacing up and down within the privacy of a room which had been lent him in one of the colleges. "'Heaven help the country that is ruled by a child or a weak woman' is a wise old adage. How can this country survive, I asked myself, if she is to be rent much longer by these quarrels for the succession. Nor we ourselves, for that matter. Half the nobility have been wiped out during the wars. I did not want that to happen to you, Thomas, or to our family."

"And so you made that speech in his first Council which moved men to offer him the crown," said Thomas, who had never quite been able to forgive it.

"Yes, and would do it again for the peace of this realm, were I sure Gloucester would keep his word!" declared Buckingham. "For did he not swear to Stanley and to me that no harm should befall those hapless children?"

Thomas unclasped his riding-cloak and threw it wearily across a table. "And now the news is all over London that they are foully murdered," he said flatly, thinking of what must be Elizabeth's torment of mind.

As the splendid Buckingham lowered himself carefully into a chair the thought passed through his mind that either he must be getting old or that it took an exceptionally strong man to survive such troubled times. "Does the Woodville woman know?" he asked.

"Yes. They say it nearly killed her. And they say that the grief-stricken Princesses—"

"So much of it is 'they say,'" complained the Duke, whose journey in the new King's company had been so serene and enjoyable until this hot-head bore down upon him with his incredible rumours.

"It is true that I myself saw the Princes standing watching the ships a few weeks ago," admitted Thomas. "But no one has seen them since."

"And if anything had happened to two defenceless boys in that grim rabbit-warren of a place who could possibly know?" cogitated his father.

"Only the man who did it…"

"And if there has been no murder?"

"The King would know—just the same."

The handsome greying Duke swung round upon him. "Have a care, Thomas!" he warned sharply. "Your implication is treason."

Thomas shrugged and wandered to a dresser to help himself from a dish of fruit. He had been in the saddle since dawn and was ravenous. "Murdered or not, Sir, the King had gone to great trouble to have them both in his care," he pointed out, biting deeply into an apple. "We know that no one else would dare to lay a finger on them—and that no one else would have cause."

"In either case, what can I do?" asked his father, after a silence during which the crunching of the apple had been the only sound.

"You could perhaps ask the King straight out how they fare," suggested his son, more diffidently.

It sounded so easy; but the very fact that it was not magnified suspicion. "There are things one does not ask the King," admitted the man to whose help he owed most. And then, as if to turn his kindly mind from such sinister thoughts, Buckingham smiled quiz-zically at his son. "I suppose it is for the sake of Bess's beautiful eyes that you have ridden here like a fiend to badger me?" he bantered.

"What hope have I in that quarter? Particularly if this be true, since she is King Edward's eldest daughter?" Thomas tossed aside the apple core and strode to his father's side, impelled by love rather than by ambition. "Though there was a time when my hopes rose because you seemed to think our claim through the Beauforts at least as good as Gloucester's," he reminded him with tentative eagerness.

But Buckingham had made up his mind about that long ago.

"It was in order to save this very kind of bloodshed that I forgot that moonshine. Besides," he added, out of his fundamental integrity, "even on the Lancastrian side of the lineage the Countess of Richmond and her son come before us."

Thomas looked down upon him with affection. He knew that his father had loved King Edward and had acted for the best; and how sincerely concerned he was about the two boys. "I suppose it is partly because of Bess that I came," Thomas admitted, following his father's lead in. "But, believe me, Sir, in their shocked bewilderment all London looks to you. You are the most royal of all the barons. And, after all, are not poor Ned and Dickon your wife's nephews?"

"Yes, poor lads. But with King Richard one does not want to stress the fact that one is so closely related to the Woodvilles."

"Yet to you, I suppose, it must make this thing seem all the more horrible?"

The Duke heaved himself up and fell to pacing the room again. "So horrible that it becomes fantastic," he admitted. "I like the King. On this journey I am always about with him. In many ways—since we are speaking frankly—I find him finer than King Edward. He is just as manly and openhanded, and yet without his brother's lamentable lasciviousness. As everyone knows, his family life is impeccable."

"There is John of Gloucester, his bastard, who governs Calais. And some girl-child he would have married to the Earl of Huntingdon had she not died."

"Bah! Mere youthful pastimes when he was bored between battles, mending that arm of his," scoffed Buckingham, kicking aside a stool in his path. "I tell you he has *always* wanted Anne Neville, ever since the Kingmaker brought him up with his own daughters in Warwick Castle. Only consider what trouble he went to to get her!"

"Or the half of dead Warwick's wealth!" muttered Thomas, determined to hear no good of him.

His father did not hear him, but went on arguing out the issue half to himself. "He is capable and courteous. Not able to charm men and women into doing his will, perhaps, like Edward—but cool and cultured and friendly. How am I to believe, while chasing a wild boar with him or laughing with him at table, that he deliberately had murdered the sons of the man whom he so loyally loved and served?"

Because it seemed so impossible to believe, Buckingham felt that he must go straight to the King—to watch him at work, or catch him talking to others, all unaware. In order to look at him with eyes newly opened to this terrible doubt. For surely, if he had just ordered two innocent children to be put to death the hideous guilt of it must be written on his face?

But Richard Plantagenet looked much the same as usual. He was sitting at a table signing some papers with his secretary and one or two of his officers about him, and every now and then he would look up to question something or to give a brief order. And each time he lifted his face it was illumined by the torches stuck in iron sconces on the wall. They showed up everything that was there to be noted. The gentle, almost sad expression, belying ruthless activity and courage. The lines from eye to mouth, so weary for a man of thirty, which must have been etched by physical suffering of which neither friend nor foe had ever heard him complain. Every line of him, decided Buckingham, was a baffling contradiction. The taut body, quite as richly clad yet so much slighter than King Edward's. The slight hunch of the right shoulder, suggesting a clerk rather than a soldier. The long, thin hand holding the pen, which might well have been a monk's, and yet was more strong and supple on a hilt than any swordsman's in England.

How *could* one assess him, or be sure?

As if feeling such intentness of gaze upon him, King Richard looked up and smiled—and the case building itself up against him in his friend's mind was knocked endwise. "Why, Henry, you look as if something my cooks concocted has disagreed with you!" he said, handing the last parchment to the Captain of the Guard and rising with brisk relief.

"I wanted to see you—" began Buckingham, clumsily.

The King came and clipped him on the shoulder. "My dear fellow, have I not been visible all day?" he retorted good-humouredly, sending a small page scuttling for some wine.

Laughing sheepishly, the older man passed a hand across his forehead and was surprised to find it moist with sweat. "Stupid of me... Too much of your potent Burgundy at dinner, perhaps," he apologized. "But I just wanted to reassure myself, Richard. You see, if a friend you had always had—was not really there..."

The King quirked a mystified eyebrow at him as if he were mad. "It *must* have been the Burgundy," he said. "But I hope you are sober enough to take in the gist of something I want you to do for me."

"Work should be good for the whimsies," smiled Buckingham, getting a grip on himself.

"I have always found it so," said Richard, without smiling at all. "And mercifully just now this realm provides me with all the work I want."

"What would you have me do, Sir?" asked Buckingham.

Standing glass in hand, the King came to the point with his usual economy of words. "It is about John Morton, Bishop of Ely, who with the unfortunate Hastings opposed my succession. I want you to make yourself responsible for him. He is an enterprising sort of person, so his—host—must be someone I can trust."

"And so?" prompted Buckingham, shamed by so swift a lesson to his own distrust.

"I am releasing him from the Tower, and, with your permission, sending him under armed escort to your castle at Brecknock. That seems far enough away, in the wilds of Wales. I have just signed the necessary orders." Sipping appreciatively at the good red wine, he nodded towards the table where his writing things were still set out. "But I would like you, if you will, to send with them a letter to your Constable, telling him to have a comfortable room prepared and some books set out for the Bishop's use, and so forth."

"So you are releasing him from the Tower?" said Buckingham, surprised at such clemency.

"Why not? He is a man of unusual ability, one of our coming churchmen, I suspect, and if by some little show of friendliness we can win him over to our side, so much the better. In these times all our best brains ought to be used in the service of the country, not shut up to turn sour. And if you remember, my dear Henry, Stanley opposed me at that Council-meeting, too, and had to be hit on the head with a pike before he came round and saw reason."

"Would you say he has one of the best brains?" enquired Buckingham, who, having upheld Gloucester from the first, resented the pardon and easy favour shown his rival.

"Perhaps not," said Richard tersely. "But he has the most men."

"And you want me, I take it, to use my persuasive powers with Morton as a gentle substitute for a pikestaff?"

"That was my idea," smiled the King. "You will have all the long winter months shut up there with him, and you and Katherine should find his pithy conversation a godsend." Buckingham, who was ageing, had been looking forward to a few weeks' peace after such an avalanche of disturbing events, and his royal kinsman grinned at the ill-concealed glumness of his looks. "Or perhaps one does not want for pithy conversations when one happens to be married to a Woodville?" he laughed. "I fancy that is how my brother must have felt when he solaced himself with so many nitwit beauties!"

"Jane Shore is no nitwit," Buckingham reminded him defensively.

"No," agreed Richard. "Otherwise she would scarcely have lost so little time in getting first Hastings and then that odious Dorset to protect her."

"Is Dorset back in England?"

"Yes. Waiting to stir up trouble, no doubt. Had your Woodville wife not told you?"

And so, with Richard's pleasant friendliness fresh in his ears, Buckingham's horror would be lulled. But, again and again, as the days passed, he would find himself watching the King's face, seeing it as crafty and secretive; and then suddenly the Plantagenet would smile, and an impression of soldierly straightforwardness would remain. To Buckingham, the Sovereign he had backed with all his considerable standing became an enigma. Uncertainty chafed his days, suspicion kept him awake at night. He lost appetite at meals and accuracy at sport. He would recall pleasant scenes in which his friend, the fourth Edward, was playing with his children, and suddenly rage would surge uncontrollably in him. Remembering the good looks of young Ned and the charm of small Dickon, he would marvel how any normal person could have the heart to undo the Creator's work and still such animation. There were men, he knew, who seemed to have two personalities. It was as if in some strange way their minds were split in twain and good and evil stood apart, not humanly mixed, in them. Dangerous men, touched by the same supernatural forces which inspired witchcraft, in whose presence one felt beyond one's depth and shuddered. Could this youngest and most able of the great Duke of York's sons possibly be one of them? And if so, wondered Buckingham, was Anne the Queen aware of it? She did not seem to be. But could that be, perhaps, because she was not particularly clever or because she had been accustomed to Gloucester's ways since childhood? The whole idea grew frightening. By the time the royal progress had reached Richard's own city of Gloucester all triumph and enjoyment seemed to have gone from it for Buckingham, in spite of the tumultuous welcome. "I think, by your Grace's leave, I will go home to Brecknock for a while," he said, taking advantage of one of the King's rare moments of leisure.

"We have been working you too hard. Stanley was saying only last night that you were looking queasy. Is that the reason?" asked Richard, all concern at once.

"That—and some urgent affairs on my estate," lied Buckingham. Why in God's name, he wondered, could he not bring himself to take his son's advice and startle the truth out of Gloucester by asking straight out, "What have you done with our nephews?" If any man in England had the right to ask, it was he; but the question which had simmered so long in his mind stuck in his throat. And Richard was being so considerate, giving him permission to go—a little coldly, perhaps, supposing him to be peeved because Stanley had been appointed Lord Steward for the coming celebrations in York. "Anne will be joining us at Warwick Castle, which is always home to us, and I had hoped that you would be there to see our boy," he was saying, with the fondness of any proud father. "But perhaps, after all, it is just as well that you should be at Brecknock to keep an eye on Morton. He has the same kind of mind as the Woodville woman, except that when he meddles he has the strength of purpose to carry his schemes through. As well, too, that he is in Wales and she in Westminster," he had added, turning briskly to take cloak and gloves from his body squire, John Green, so as to satisfy the delirious shouting of his own people by riding through the streets again. "Else, being met together and finding some unity of purpose, those two might so ignite each other with their wild ideas as to blow up the whole country!"

Chapter Ten

AND SO THE MAGNIFICENT Duke of Buckingham set out, his mind already a breeding-place for revolt and lacking only impetus. And on his way to Wales he encountered his kinswoman, Margaret Beaufort. By chance—or so he supposed. And what was more pleasant or natural than that they should sup together? Margaret was as likeable as she was well read, as truly devout as she was wordly wise. Having had three husbands must have helped to make her such good company, he supposed, and even the fact that his rival Thomas Stanley happened to be the current one could put no blight upon a pleasant evening. Certainly it did occur to Buckingham to wonder why she should be travelling on the Bridgnorth road when her husband was bound for York; but women these days had so much liberty, and Margaret was a Plantagenet countess in her own right. The inn was excellent and it was days since Buckingham had enjoyed his supper so much. But inevitably afterwards, when their attendants had withdrawn, the minds of each of them reverted to their young relatives who had disappeared so mysteriously in the Tower.

"I am just come from the King," he said. "He never speaks of them, yet I find it almost too horrible to believe."

"And I am come from London where everybody believes it," said Margaret.

"One sees now why Gloucester was so set upon getting young Richard from sanctuary. Murdering one without the other would have been useless!" mused Buckingham, shuddering at the idea of such deliberate intent. "Did you send and let Stanley know?"

"Yes."

"Yet he does nothing!"

In spite of the urgency in her heart Margaret Beaufort's beautiful ageing face looked serene as ever in the candlelight. "The more reason why we should," she said, avoiding all discussion of her husband's affairs.

"We?" repeated Buckingham, feeling that he was being rushed into something bigger than he had intended. "Of course, if one wanted either to avenge the boys or to profit by their deaths," he added with reluctant generosity, "the Lancastrian succession centres in yourself."

"I am John of Gaunt's nearest living descendant," said Margaret, with a touch of her youthful haughtiness. "But I am getting to be an old woman and I ask nothing more in this world for myself. Only for my son."

And for him, it appeared, she was asking the very utmost—the crown of England.

Of course she had always adored him. In spite of three marriages, Henry of Richmond was her only son—by that Welshman, Edmund Tudor, long since dead in battle. Probably that marriage had been the romance of her brilliant life. The Tudors were people to be reckoned with, else how had Edmund managed to be sired by Henry the Fifth's French widow, who—though a daughter of the proud Valois—had loved her handsome Master of Horse, Owen Tudor, so desperately that she had married him. And probably it was the satisfying success of Margaret's own Tudor marriage that accounted for the way she managed still to be spoken of as Countess of Richmond and spent so much time travelling around by herself to relatives and convents and places of learning that could not possibly interest Lord Stanley. And why was she turning to a mere kinsman like himself for co-operation? "Even Stanley's wife doesn't trust him," thought Buckingham.

Though faced by the goodness of Margaret Beaufort's face, the simple truth did not occur to him. When she began to outline the design for her idolized son, he never supposed her to be merely too scrupulous to draw into such dangerous plans a husband who, although no Edmund Tudor, had never shown her anything but kindness.

"If both those unfortunate boys are dead," she was saying, "there is still Elizabeth."

"Elizabeth? Of course she should be Queen. But I supposed you wanted the crown for Henry Tudor."

Margaret looked pained at his slowness. "My dear Henry, do you suppose the people of England would ever accept him? We may be descended from John of Gaunt, but only through his older children's governess, when she was his mistress."

"He married her afterwards and Richard the Second passed a special law to make our ancestors legitimate."

"Which Richard the Third would very soon unmake! He seems to be proving himself a very able ruler, and, murderer or not, most of his subjects like him. That was a very popular move of his, removing the payment of benevolences, for instance. Particularly with the Londoners. To the people of Yorkshire and Gloucestershire, of course, he is almost God. So that even if we could raise enough supporters here and Henry could get ships from France and all Wales rose for him, the English people would still have none of him. Without Elizabeth. So he must marry Elizabeth."

"How," asked Buckingham, "when her fool of a mother keeps her in sanctuary?"

"I think her mother is no fool there, for if Elizabeth were not in sanctuary you can lay your last groat Gloucester would get her into his hands. Like he had her brothers. And then there would be *no* way out." Margaret leaned forward across the deserted table to lay a persuasive finger on the Duke's fashionably puffed sleeve. "Listen, cousin," she said softly. "I have in my household a very devoted doctor. A doctor both of divinity and medicine, who served the Tudors and the great Glendowers. He has initiative and discretion—and, like most Welsh people, a creative kind of courage."

"Creative courage?" Buckingham sat back more patiently in his chair, thinking how beautiful was the Countess's voice compared with the nagging shrillness of his wife's.

"He dreams. His dreams are set to music," explained Maragaret, drawing upon something she must have learned years ago in Pembroke Castle when she was youthfully in love. "And when the music of his dreams swells so insistently that it possesses him he has the courage to turn them into practical reality, though it may take a lifetime."

Buckingham began to perceive that he was destined to be the mainspring of those dreams and that they had already begun to materialize. "Then I take it that this invaluable pawn of yours has already made his first move—to Westminster?"

"Several moves."

"And that the women there know?"

"He attends the Queen Dowager, poor woman. In his medical capacity."

"Very well thought out! And I can well imagine that in her desperate situation the Woodville Queen welcomes any such scheme. But surely Elizabeth herself would resist to the last gasp uniting herself with a Lancastrian?"

"Do not forget what her feelings must be about her beloved brothers," said Margaret. "She has told Doctor Lewis that she will marry my son—on one very natural condition."

"And that is?"

"That when he comes he will avenge them."

"He will need to! For the Plantagenet is not likely to relinquish one foot of English soil save over his own dead body," said Buckingham, remembering the look of Richard's sword hand. For himself, he would have wished the thing done without that condition. It was natural enough, he supposed, and quite inevitable; though it sounded cruel on the lips of Margaret Beaufort. But even good women, when they wanted something for a loved one or saw it as ultimately right, could be more ruthless than men, he had found. Perhaps because they cared more passionately.

"I will think upon all that you have said," was all that he would promise. "For the next few months I shall be staying quietly at Brecknock, where the King has put the Bishop of Ely in my care."

Not by so much as the flicker of an eyelid did Margaret betray how prodigally Richard had played into her hands. "A churchman with an extraordinary fine intellect who should go far," was her polite comment. Nor did she think it necessary to explain just how far the prelate would go was dependent upon the success of this Lancastrian plan, since it had originated in his own fertile brain; or that even since his arrival at Brecknock the ubiquitous Lewis had been in touch with him.

Instead, being too wise to goad a half-persuaded man, the Countess was able to settle down to more amusing topics and to part company with her kinsman quite merrily, being certain that the fortunes of her son would be argued in the most favourable of circumstances by a tongue far more subtle than her own.

And so the long wet winter evenings in Wales were enlivened for the Staffords by their guest, although not at all with the kind of persuasive conversation that the King had hoped. For it was John Morton, who had refused to support his accession, who did most of the persuading. "All these gifts from various towns which he makes such show of refusing—for how long does your Grace imagine Richard of Gloucester will be able to live without them? With the Exchequer as it is he will almost certainly have to revive the hated levying of benevolences," he urged. "And then his popularity with the common man will wane. The people will begin to remember the brilliant Lord Rivers, who did so much for their arts and crafts—and William Hastings, an honest administrator if ever we had one. And now comes this hideous story about the disappearance of the young King and his brother. The news of it is running like wild-fire about the country, your Constable tells me. Gloucester's partisans up in York may still shout for him, but decent people who live within sight of the Tower and who are accustomed to seeing those two delightful boys about will not stomach it."

"We have no definite proof," Buckingham would demur.

"Then why does he not produce them?" his wife, Katherine Woodville, would be sure to shrill. Because she was their aunt it seemed impossible to keep her out of such debates.

And the Bishop would turn back the rich sleeves of his vestments, helping himself with delicate fingers to his host's best wine.

"The south would rise to a man for Elizabeth. They love her. Apart from being a very lovable person, she is for them a part of her father, who reigned over them affably for twenty years. And by all accounts this young man, Henry Richmond, is quite as gifted as Gloucester," he urged repeatedly. "Do you not see how such a union must bring an end at last to these interminable Yorkist and Lancastrian struggles which have been wasting the life-blood of the country? How it would give men a sense of permanent security in which this new invention of the printed word could bring enlightenment to all, in which our sailors would be free to compete with Spain and Portugal in exploring the uncharted places of the world, and how our craftsmen would have time to make things of lasting beauty instead of grim instruments of destruction? Can your Grace remain unmoved by the belief that so definite a clinching of this succession argument could promote goodwill and prosperity, creating a kind of golden age?"

"Simply by grafting the red rose upon the white," thrilled Katherine ecstatically.

Her pretty floral imagery left her husband cold, but Morton's more poetic mind was quick to cap it. "And so produce one indisputable, thornless, golden rose," he added.

"A Tudor rose!" agreed Buckingham contemptuously, hating to be coerced in his own castle.

"A son of Elizabeth's by Henry Tudor should be very gifted," her aunt reminded him. And for the sake of that son, as yet unborn, Buckingham found himself able to face the thought of inviting a stranger from abroad to fight a Plantagenet for the crown. "But suppose this paragon offends the people with his foreign ways, wants all the power or sells us to the French in return for Louis of Valois's help?" he asked, raising a few final objections.

"He must be made to take a solemn oath to marry Elizabeth immediately he lands," Morton told him.

"And at least he is no murderer!" said Katherine.

"Even if Richard *is* a murderer he would never sell a single sod of England!" muttered Buckingham. But the Bishop's silver tongue had beguiled him, and he was soon reaching for a map and pushing the memory of Richard's smile behind him. "Mercifully Dorset is back and can join forces with the Devon Courtenays to raise the west," he calculated, his voice gathering the old tones of command. "The Bishop of Salisbury, being a Woodville, can, of course, be counted on for Wiltshire. Then there is a useful man called Bray who was in the Countess of Richmond's service in the days when she was married to my uncle."

"Sir Reginald Bray is still with her and *au fait* with our plans," the Bishop told him.

"Then we must send him to sound the men of Kent."

"And it is imperative that we let the Queen Dowager and the Princess know the good news that your Grace is with us," said Morton, finishing off the wine.

"Doctor Lewis will gladly be our go-between again," declared Katherine. "You see, Henry, how easy it is to pierce the gloom of sanctuary!"

"I see how sensible it was of the King to set a guard about it, though many people called it uncivilized," retorted Buckingham.

And so Elizabeth Woodville was visited again by her favourite physician, and her health improved amazingly. With the threads of a conspiracy once more between her restless fingers she seemed to come to radiant life again. "When Doctor Lewis comes we are always sent to play in some other room," complained her younger daughters, weary of their confinement. But the privileged elder sister whom they envied listened with mixed feelings to the news their visitor brought. She was grateful for the carefully laid plans and her heart beat at thought of the important part she was to play. But her lovely face was no more animated than a piece of wood. "It is unbelievably good of the Countess of Richmond, my kinsman of Buckingham and the Bishop," she said, seeing herself as a pawn upon the great chessboard of England, being pushed frighteningly forward by the eager hands of two ageing women. She herself had given her word to go forward, swayed by a passion of pity for her brothers which cried aloud for vengeance. The same motive, perhaps, which in smaller degree had moved her Uncle Buckingham. But already revenge was growing cold—cold as their poor murdered bodies. Vengeance could not bring them back. All she really wanted was to get out of this suffocating place where one heard things muffled at second-hand—to have liberty to see people and ask questions—to search the Tower—to find out for herself what had really happened.

In her desire for freedom Elizabeth even consented to a wild plan whereby she was to be smuggled out of Westminster and join her relatives at Brecknock; but King Richard was better served than she imagined and that night Nesfield doubled the guard. Looking down upon the motionless, watchful figures in the courtyard Elizabeth of York, in her inmost heart, was thankful. No woman could have wanted to marry Henry of Lancaster less.

Yet Morton of Ely must have been right in his estimate of Henry's gifts, for once the names of places and supporters for the rebellion were sent abroad that young man moved so quickly and efficiently that the King of England had a bare week's warning. Of the shock that it must have been to him to hear that his friend had rebelled against him and that Henry of Lancaster might be landing at any moment, Richard never spoke. And of that bare week he wasted not a moment.

The courier system he had organized in his brother's time with relays of horses every twenty miles along the roads proved invaluable, enabling him to issue far-flung orders and to keep himself informed of the movements of his enemies. As usual he called upon his trusty Yorkshire-men, and brought every available man from London. He changed into well-worn armour, marched as only his men could march and took his enemies completely by surprise by setting up his standard at Nottingham, in the very centre of England.

"Where we can all converge and surround him!" laughed Dorset.

But Dorset was one of those men with a charmed life who always laugh too easily.

It was Buckingham who began to do the converging. With perfect timing, during the October week when Henry Tudor had promised to land, he marched a formidable army from Wales, with every promise of success. But Richard, anticipating the movement, sent two trusty knights to cut every bridge across the river Severn, and the Almighty abetted him by sending torrential rains. Such floods swamped the Welsh borders that neither man nor horse could live in them, and the peasants whose homes were swept away saw them as a punishment for treachery. "Buckingham's great water" they called that devastation; and even among his stauncher supporters the superstitious laid down their arms.

The Lancastrian came promptly with a fleet lent him by Louis the Eleventh of France; but the same fierce storm drove him back to Brittany, in spite of his manful efforts to land in little, landlocked Lulworth Cove. The rest of the rebels were defeated, and soldiers wearing Richard's cognizance of the white boar seemed to be rounding them up everywhere. Dorset and Morton were the type of men who usually escape, and Richard granted pardon to their soldiery. They had but obeyed orders, he said. For Henry Stafford, Duke of Buckingham, there was no such mercy. He was executed in the market-place of Salisbury. Sold for the sake of the reward by an old servant named Ralph Banister, with whom he had sought shelter.

"Why would you not see him before he died?" asked Anne, the Queen, seeing the bleak look on Richard's face in the midst of so much triumph. "Was it because your heart would have betrayed you into pardoning him?"

"That was not what he wanted. No man who wears the Stafford knot would have come cringing for his life," Richard told her.

"Then why did he beg so hard to speak to you?"

"Probably because he meant to kill me," said Richard lightly. "It seems he had strangled one of his guards to get a dagger."

"Oh, but, my dear! After you had been so kind to him?"

"In all probability he had been very kind to that Banister creature," shrugged Richard, trying to elude her questioning.

"But Henry Stafford must have had some reason for wanting to kill you," persisted Anne, with the obstinacy of a woman who is not very perceptive. "Particularly as all the blame was on his side."

Her husband took her by the shoulders and looked with exasperated tenderness upon the childlike face he had loved so long. He had cared too much for Buckingham to be unfair to his memory. "In this chancy world, my dear Anne, the blame is seldom all on one side," he said. "Henry did have a very good reason."

Which was as near as Richard Plantagenet ever came to showing anyone his tormented soul.

Chapter Eleven

I T SEEMED STRANGE TO Elizabeth to be back in Westminster Palace
again. To live in her own home as a guest—to put out her
hand for a familiar piece of furniture or a book and remember
that it belonged to someone else. She had been given the small
room where Mattie used to sleep, and her younger sisters climbed
a winding staircase every night to share a dormitory with some of
the Queen's younger ladies. It seemed strangest of all, perhaps, to
be called just "the lady Elizabeth."

"But the Duke of Buckingham has no bed at all save his
coffin—and he took the risk for our sakes!" she would tell herself,
whenever her pride rebelled. Besides, the King had been generous,
people said. After the rebellion he had been so determined to
keep his nieces safely in his own hands that he had tempted "the
Woodville woman" with advantageous terms. He would risk no
more dangerous marriages being planned to deprive him of his
throne. He himself would choose the girls' husbands, he said; and
they would be gentlemen by birth, but no higher in station than
was suitable for the late King's bastards. But he promised to provide
them with dowries and to treat them honourably. Before treating
with him the Queen Dowager had still had spirit enough to make
him swear to it publicly. And then, sinking into despondency after
the failure of her plot, she had at last agreed to come out of sanctuary—for her daughters' sake, she let it be known, so that they
might have some new dresses and enough to eat.

The children were overjoyed. The Abbot of Westminster, spreading his possessions about his own parlour again, must have been as much relieved as they were, Elizabeth supposed. But her mother, poor lady, had only exchanged self-imposed isolation for durance of a less dignified kind. The King kept his bare word. She had rooms in the Palace, but in some distant wing where the children seldom saw her; and with the hated Nesfield still on guard.

To the Plantagenet Countess of Richmond the King had been kinder. She, too, had been found guilty of treason; but so careful had she been not to incriminate her husband that he retained office as Steward of the King's Household. Indeed, bland Stanley benefited by her misdemeanours by being given charge both of herself and of her fortune, providing only that he kept her in one of his manors well away from London.

For Elizabeth, sharing their punishment would have seemed less humiliating than conspiracy contemptuously ignored. Having to live under her uncle's roof and eat his food was abhorrent to her. Had it not been for the new Queen's kindness her homecoming would have been even worse than being mewed up in sanctuary. But now at least she had a friend to talk to, a good horse to ride, with plenty of music and dancing, dresses and books, all of which she and her sisters enjoyed.

"Why are you so unbelievably good to me?" she asked her royal hostess with shy constraint, when they were alone in the garden gallery.

"Perhaps because I, too, have known what it is to be humiliated and unhappy," smiled Anne Neville, arranging some spring flowers which Ann and little Katherine had been gathering for her. "Besides, since my only sister died it is pleasant to have someone like yourself for company. And has it never occurred to you that you are a person whom it is easy to love, Bess?" Anne tilted her honey-coloured head admiringly as she tweaked first one blossom and then another to better advantage. "Richard likes you too, I believe," she added. "And Richard does not like everybody."

When Anne said guileless things like that, seemingly unaware of any tragic situation, Elizabeth was dumbfounded. How could Richard like her when she had tried to best him, and when her mere presence must be an embarrassment and a reproach? "Perhaps it is because I look like my father," was all she could find to say.

"Your father was his whole world—the man's part of it, as apart from me, I mean," said Anne, beckoning to one of her women to set the bowl of flowers where she could see them. "That is where I am so fortunate, Bess. The sort of marriages we have to make usually have so little to do with love. I imagine most royal husbands hate, or merely tolerate, their wives. But mine loves me!" She said the naïve words exultantly and began singing softly in a sweet, husky little voice. Clearly, Richard made her very happy.

Elizabeth stood and stared at her. It was all so irreconcilable. This ideal family life, Richard's dutiful affection for that grim mother of his in Baynard's Castle—and the things men said of him!

By tacit consent the two young women, who had both been through so much, never spoke of poor Buckingham's rebellion, although it might have provided one of them with a husband she did not desire and deprived the other of one she loved. And in return for the Queen's generosity in this matter Elizabeth tried not to plague her with questions about her brothers. Instead they talked of relatives they had in common and of matters of mutual feminine interest. But the questions burned all the time in Elizabeth's mind. "It is kind of the King to let you keep young Warwick in your household," she said, looking out upon the hopefully budding trees and skirting the subject ever nearest to her heart.

"Poor Warwick is so simple and harmless, and nephew to both of us," Anne reminded her.

"So were Ned and Dickon his nephews, but where are they?" burst forth Elizabeth, in spite of all her resolutions. Even if Ned had to be disposed, she thought, how wonderful to be able to see them both sitting at the King's table, instead of the witless Warwick boy who could not answer the simplest questions.

Anne sighed and laid down her scissors. Life had taught her patience. "My dear Bess, I have already told you that I do not *know*! I am sure they are being well cared for in the Tower, but even to me Richard never mentions them. And once when I questioned him for your sake he shut himself up in that terrible reserve of his and it spoiled everything between us for days. He is not usually ill-tempered," she offered an apology. "But he has been sleeping badly of late. It is having so many unaccustomed affairs of state."

"Or his conscience!" thought Elizabeth. But being a kindly treated guest she could not say so and hastened to change the subject. "Tell me about the time when you were hiding in London," she begged politely.

"I was hired as a kitchenmaid in a merchant's big house," began the Queen obligingly; and although everyone knew it to be true it always sounded fantastic as some old troubadour's tale.

"How you must have hated it!" sympathized Elizabeth, looking at Anne Neville's dainty little hands.

"I was horribly homesick for Warwick Castle. And the rough ways of the menservants frightened me. But most of all," explained Anne, in her inconsequent way, "I hated seeing nothing more beautiful than meat!"

It was difficult to imagine that this could have happened to a girl whose father had been so powerful that throughout the wars of the red and white roses his support could make or unmake Kings. But perhaps it had not been so bad for one who was not overburdened with imagination and who took such delight in simple things. Even now, as she came and sat by the fire, Anne folded back her skirts so as to enjoy the warm glow on her kirtle in just the homely way that Elizabeth had often seen her own women of the bedchamber do when preparing for a good gossip. "Did you sleep on the kitchen floor with the other servants?" she asked, thankful in the midst of her misfortune that at least she had never had to do that.

"Only at first," said the new Queen of England. "Afterwards I slept in a little truckle bed outside my mistress's door and was allowed to arrange her hair and clothes. She was quite kind and I suppose she saw that I was—different. But that, of course, was what I was most afraid of."

"Because of my Uncle Clarence finding you?"

"Yes. Having married my sister, he wanted to make sure of all my father's money, which had been left to us equally. So he kept me in his house—under his protection, he called it—so that no one should marry me. I was not even allowed to go out in case I might manage to appeal to King Edward or to Richard.

"Although he was their brother, Clarence was never so attractive as either of them.

"And when he was drunk I was terrified of him. And so was my sister. She warned me one night that he had said in his cups that he meant to get rid of me so that all the inheritance would be hers. So I ran away and hid myself in London."

"And no one recognized you?"

"Only Jane Shore. Her father being a City merchant, she used to visit sometimes at the house where I worked. But she never gave me away. It was she who pleaded for me to King Edward. But perhaps I ought not to say that to you?"

"In spite of her scandalous love affairs everyone knows Jane Shore is kind. It is only my mother who hates her."

"And then Richard came storming down from Scotland or somewhere," concluded Anne, with the warm trill of laughter which so belied her cold colouring.

"I remember about that because he appealed to my father," said Elizabeth—remembering with amazement, too, how hotly she had once sided with him. "And my father said Uncle Richard was to have you and that the money should be equally divided. Cicely and I were so glad, because we, too, disliked Uncle Clarence. But, of course, after the Scottish campaign Richard was everybody's hero, and ridiculously young to be our uncle."

"And almost directly afterwards, you remember, Clarence sided with my father against yours and was put in the Tower. He was a double-dyed traitor if ever there was one, yet when he disappeared some spiteful people put it about that Richard had murdered him because of the way he had tried to keep my money. I suppose it is because Richard is so successful that some people will believe almost any tale against him."

Elizabeth flushed with embarrassment, although it was quite likely that the thrust was not meant for her. "But you do not believe any of the tales against him, do you?" she asked, watching her kinswoman closely.

"Of course not," said Anne, settling her skirts more decorously at the sound of footsteps in the garden. "If one has known a person intimately for years one is more sure of the way he would act in any given circumstances than of the truth of what strangers say."

"So that even if you never saw my beloved brothers again you wouldn't believe—"

The Queen clapped a hand to the carved arm of her chair in exasperation. "Oh, Bess, why must you hark back to that?" she exclaimed. "I suppose that, loving Richard as I do, if God sent His archangel Gabriel to tell me he had harmed them I would not believe it."

The curtains at the end of the gallery were parted and, to Elizabeth's horror, Richard himself stood there. His riding gloves were still in his hand, and he had evidently come in unattended across the garden. "What wouldn't you believe, my sweet?" he asked, catching the end of their conversation.

"That you were bad," answered Anne, in that childlike way of hers.

"And has our charming guest been trying to persuade you that I am?" he asked suavely.

"No. We were discussing how well or ill one can know a person," said Anne, whose own hazards had taught her to be quick in loyalty.

"Because if she has we must try to be more expeditious about finding her a husband," went on Richard, just as if his wife had not spoken.

Anne turned to catch at his arm. "Oh, please, Richard, do not send her away from me just yet!" she entreated. "I find it rather—lonely—being a Queen. And you are always so busy yourself."

"You could have our boy with you more," he suggested, having been persuaded by her anxiety and her physicians to an unwilling parting.

"In the summer, of course. But these London fogs from this newfangled coal try his chest as much as they do mine," said Anne. "I am sure he is better in the country at Warwick."

"He certainly tires easily," admitted the ever-active King, anxiously.

"Perhaps it was all that ceremonial excitement up in York. You know, Bess, we walked all through the streets in our heavy ermine robes and with our crowns on to please the people, and although he is only ten that dear boy walked all the way, holding my hand. You should have heard the crowds cheer him…" Although she had turned purposely to include her discomfited guest, poor Anne stopped short at sight of the angry desolation of Elizabeth's face. "I always seem to be saying something tactless," she apologized.

Richard, coming behind her, lifted his wife's chin reassuringly. Although he was seldom demonstrative in public, there was something infinitely tender in the touch of his long, expressive fingers against the whiteness of her throat. Anne looked up and smiled happily, forgetting her *bêtise*; and Elizabeth, suddenly consumed by inexplicable envy, tried to slip away unnoticed.

But even while he was looking down into a woman's adoring eyes part of Richard was aware as a cat. "I would like you to come to my workroom after dinner, Elizabeth," he said, without moving. "My secretary has been preparing some documents which concern you."

If it was strange to be back in the Palace it seemed to Elizabeth the strangest and hardest thing of all to be standing once again in her father's room. And the new King kept her standing. In order to show her that he did not consider her the rightful owner of it, she supposed; or just to teach her meekness as the recipient of his hospitality. Of course he might really have been too busy to notice her, but in any case the way he went on writing made her furious, since meekness—as her father confessor frequently told her—was not one of her outstanding virtues.

Yet waiting gave her the precious opportunity to refresh her memory of familiar surroundings and to recall the happy security she had been wont to experience in them. She was grateful that nothing in the room had been changed. There were the same richly embroidered figures on the arras and the same hunting trophies, and the reflection of firelight from the great hearth still leapt warmly across the back of leather-bound books. It was all just as it had been the last time she saw it, that day when her father had comforted her about her broken French marriage and her young brother had stood beside her by the table afterwards, building castles with pieces of Master Caxton's type. To-day only the man in the great carved chair was different. But because he was different, so was Elizabeth's whole world.

While his brown head was bent so diligently over the documents spread before him on that same table she brought herself to study him closely, unobserved. He did not seem to fill the chair as her father had done, being slighter and quicker of movement, but he was just as gorgeously clad. Richard was meticulous about such things. And she had to admit that although his sensitive face was sometimes lined with weariness it was never slackened by indulgence or sloth. Even now, where his elder brother would have handed over such tedious clerical affairs to Will Hastings, Richard—no matter how long he might have been in the saddle— attended to them himself. In consequence there were no easy jests among the alert-looking men who waited behind his chair, nor grins or tittering among the pages. The Court was kept with more splendour than it had been since the days of extravagant, beauty-loving Richard of Bordeaux, so the foreign ambassadors said; but an almost military precision informed it.

"The deeds we drew up concerning allowances agreed upon for Lady Grey's daughters," Richard ordered crisply; and Kendal, his secretary, laid them instantly before him. At a snap of the King's nervous fingers, a page dropped to one knee, ready to hold the parchments from rolling back upon themselves. "Hand me a fresh quill, John," Richard bade his body squire. "And set a chair for the lady Elizabeth."

As John Green drew the chair forward for her Elizabeth took special note of him. "That bland-looking young man knows what happened to my brothers. He took his master's message to Sir Robert Brackenbury in the Tower," she thought. "If only I could find means to make him speak!"

"Recardus Rex," wrote the usurper King. Fascinated yet repelled, Elizabeth watched the signature flow in an exquisite, ornate hand which might have belonged to an artist—watched him hand to his secretary the grant which would decide the ease or penury of her future life, and then settle himself back in his chair. "Read the contents aloud, Kendal," he said, "so that the eldest of these ladies may hear."

The deed conferred upon each of her sister's estates to the annual value of two hundred marks to be paid out of the privy purse, and for herself five hundred. Ample for any ordinary gentlewoman, Elizabeth supposed, although she knew little of such domestic computations. There followed clauses promising husbands and dowries; but the long legal phrases swept over her uncomprehended, and almost unheard. It was a relief to know oneself provided for, of course, when one had known what it was to be hungry and ill-clad—but what did all these material details matter? It was not money but the sureness of someone's love she wanted. The protecting kind of love her father had given her, the adoring love of Tom Stafford or the demanding affection of young brothers. Even while she murmured formal words of thanks the tears welled slowly to her eyes, so that she was scarcely conscious of the dismissal of the King's attendants or aware of the moment when they were first alone.

The fact that he had left his work-table and was standing while she still sat recalled her wandering thoughts. "I purposely did not ask you here before," he was saying gently, so that she knew his watchful eyes must have seen her tears.

"This room—has memories," she apologized defensively, rising hastily as etiquette demanded.

"For me, too, it has memories," he said. And in that moment of common bereavement there was something which invited her affection in his beautifully modulated voice.

Elizabeth lifted her eyes and looked directly into his; and in spite of everything that lay between them the natural urge to go to him for comfort almost mastered her. He was young—a bare ten years older than herself—and a part of that familiar felicitous life which had been swept so suddenly away. He was so closely of her blood, and in the old days whenever something had gone wrong, either at home or abroad, it had always been the King's younger brother who had been sent to put it right. "I know that you, too, loved him," she faltered. "That is why it is all—so amazing!" Richard laughed shortly. "I can assure you that all the amazement is not on one side!" he said, taking up his stance before the fire. "Do you not suppose that it amazed me when, hastening to carry out my dear brother's commands as swiftly as ever I did when he was living, I found myself insultingly forestalled—with Rivers and Grey stealing a march on me to grab possession of his son? And when I had proclaimed him King in York and brought him royally to London, to find your mother making me out traitor by hustling you all into the Abbey for safety? As though I meant to eat you!"

"You mean that if we had trusted you and rallied round you to carry out my father's wishes things might have gone differently?" Elizabeth found herself saying with almost adolescent gaucherie.

"I am glad you have the sense to see it. And I hope you can comprehend how in a completely different set of circumstances I was forced to act differently. Even your father could not have foreseen that his wife's people would turn and bite me, trying to divide this poor ravaged country again."

"Whatever my Woodville relatives did, I deplored their distrust, Uncle Richard. At first I tried to persuade my mother—"

He was standing with his back to her, idly tracing the outline of a white rose painted on the great chimney-breast. "You were always the most intelligent of the bunch, Bess," he said negligently. "That is why I trouble to speak to you of these things."

A flash of discerning anger made her recognize the first flaw of deceit in his sincerity. "Say rather it is because you know that I matter and you want me to believe in you," she accused.

"It is too late to consider whether you matter or not!" he said, flinging round on her with a fine swinging of fur-lined crimson sleeves. "There was a time when I would have been content to hold the power as Protector. But not now. They were all here in the Palace at my brother's deathbed—as I would to God I had been! Hastings, Stanley, Morton, Dorset—all of them—while I was fighting for him up in Scotland. They, too, swore to carry out his wishes. And yet that day I held a Council-meeting, when everything was prepared for his son's coronation, I discovered that even those of them whom I had left unpunished were plotting against me. Even your mother—so frightened of me that she had to take refuge in sanctuary—had a finger in a plot upon my life. So I sent for your younger brother. It was to me—not to Anthony Rivers or any other accursed Woodville—that Edward left the care of his sons."

Elizabeth faced up to him like a young fury. "Yes, they were left in your keeping. No sane man denies it. But what have you done with them?" And when he did not answer she forgot all fear and threw herself upon him, beating at his breast with maddened fists. "What have you done with my happy, laughter-loving brothers?" she repeated, her voice rising like any crazed market-woman's deprived of her young.

But he was King, and it was treason to strike him. He might have called his men and had her sent to the Tower too. Instead he held her wrists and shook her from him with quiet strength. "I did what was best for England," he said, with something of the snarl of one of his own heraldic leopards in his voice.

For a few moments the fierce antagonism of their glances held. His face had whitened as hers had been flushed by leaping blood. Then realization of her helplessness came to her. Although her limbs shook, Elizabeth managed to sweep him a deep obeisance. It was her signal of surrender, but it also gave her time to master her emotion—time to add up the score of their encounter. Certainly he had betrayed the fact that she was a person of more importance than he would have deemed her had her brothers been alive. Whether he hated her or respected her the more for her outburst she could not be sure. All she knew was that there was that in his face which would intimidate her from ever asking him about them again. It was not until afterwards, in the seclusion of her small room, that it occurred to her that she was probably the only person who had ever dared to ask him at all.

If Richard were shaken he did not show it. With that light tread of his he walked back to the table and began turning over some papers. "I admire your courage," he said lightly. "Like that spirited younger brother of yours, you appear to have inherited more Plantagenet blood than Woodville."

Elizabeth took an eager step or two towards him. "Then you—like him?" she stammered, realizing that he was speaking as if the boy were still alive.

But the King took no notice of her interruption. "Since you are so solicitous for your family, you may be interested to know that I have offered your sister Cicely to Lord Welles, and that my good friend the Duke of Norfolk is agreeable for one of his younger sons to marry Ann. The others," he added, laying down the parchment, "are as yet too young."

Poor Cicely and Ann, who would naturally have made brilliant foreign marriages! So she was soon to be parted from them. But an even more intimate question arose. Curiosity consumed her. "And for myself?" she asked, in a small voice.

"I have not as yet arranged anything."

"Then for the present—I may remain free?"

In spite of the fact that it meant continuing to live as his guest, the relief in Elizabeth's voice was so patent that he looked across at her quizzically and smiled. "So your plotting was only half-hearted, although it cost Buckingham his life? You did not really relish the prospect of lying with a Lancastrian?"

His words struck so near the truth, and her remorse for Buckingham was so great, that she made no answer.

"How old are you, Elizabeth?" the King was asking.

"Nearly nineteen, Sir."

"Then it *is* high time you were married," he agreed, grinning at some devilish new idea. "All the more so as you always seem to fail to get the husbands of your expectation. Why, I remember in this very room offering to avenge you in France. Your poor father was so choleric about the way the Dauphin jilted you that it may well have hastened his death. And now Henry of Lancaster has failed you!"

"Oh, how I hate you!" murmured Elizabeth. And although she pressed both hands to her lips his sharp ears must have heard her.

"That is unfortunate, since our destinies have agreed that you must live in my house," he laughed. "But do not despair, Elizabeth Plantagenet. There is always Master Stillington."

"Master Stillington?" The name conveyed nothing to her.

"The son of our good Bishop Stillington."

"The Bishop of Bath who preached sermons proclaiming us bastards to please you!"

"But with no prejudicial feeling, I do assure you—since, being a churchman, this son of his must be a bastard too. All the same, he is a very able young man, and so useful to me that he merits some reward."

Elizabeth regarded her uncle with horror. "You mean that loathsome, greasy-haired clerk who leers at me from the lower tables in hall?"

"So you have noticed that he is already not without—desire?" jibed Richard.

"I do not notice the antics of menials," said Elizabeth, at her haughtiest.

Richard went to the door and opened it for her courteously. "But nevertheless I should bear the possibility in mind, Bess," he advised cheerfully. "Particularly when your singularly persistent mind is tempted to ask *other people* inconvenient questions."

Chapter Twelve

ELIZABETH HOPED NEVER TO see her father's room again, for all its sense of security was gone. If Richard had not punished her with public penance as he had the wantonness of Jane Shore, he had humiliated her for her persistency with the threat of this horrible marriage. "There is only Lord Stanley left to whom I can turn for help," she thought in panic, wishing that his kindly Countess were with him.

Being Steward of the King's Household, Stanley was always about the Court, and he had been her father's friend. Surely he would not stand by and see her married to some ugly byblow of a bishop. But although he was affable to everybody and always jovial to her sisters, she felt sure that he tried to avoid her. He did not want her to appeal or to be drawn in to taking sides even in so personal a matter. He was rich, generous and all the more popular, perhaps, because of his genius for avoiding controversy. Elizabeth had once heard the Duke of Buckingham say that Stanley's power lay less in the fact that he had twenty thousand armed retainers than in the fact that nobody could be sure upon which side they would fight.

Once, after finding the King's cross-eyed scrivener hanging about the passage to her room, she had insisted upon waylaying the Lord Steward. "Uncle Stanley," she had asked straight out, using the old affectionate title by which they had all called him as children, "do you suppose the King really intends to marry me to that awful Stillington creature?"

"I should think it highly improbable, Lady Bess," Stanley had told her imperturbably. "Gloucester may shed Plantagenet blood, but, with the fierce family pride he has, he is unlikely to demean it to that extent. And listen, child," he had added, seeing how alarmed she really was, "my squire, Humphrey Brereton, has always been crazy about you. I will set him as watchdog upon this menial and you will be no more troubled with his prying."

"But surely, milord, that will make two of them to fear," objected Mattie, who had gone along with her mistress.

"My dear lady, Humphrey Brereton knows his place," he had assured her, hurrying away upon some pressing or pretended business. He had spoken blandly enough, but the way he used Richard's old title and obviously attached no importance to the declaration of her illegitimacy set Elizabeth thinking.

"The King must trust a man very much to put him in charge of the very food he eats," she remarked that evening, watching the efficient way in which Stanley looked over the tables set for one of those lavish banquets by means of which Richard sought to ingratiate himself with the rich aldermen of London.

"Since Henry of Buckingham betrayed him I should think it unlikely that Richard really trusts anybody," the Queen had answered in that detached way of hers.

"But suppose Stanley were to poison him," speculated Elizabeth, wondering whether, beneath his bonhomie, the suave, thick-set Lord Steward were ever tempted to do so.

"My dear Bess, the things you imagine!" laughed Anne, who never imagined anything at all. "I am thankful Richard and I are going north to-morrow, if that is the way you croak. Only I do so wish he would not insist upon stopping to grant charters and things in every town we pass through, when all we both want is to push on to Warwick to see our boy!"

The unaccustomed querulousness in Anne's voice made Elizabeth regard her with anxiety. "Are you sure you feel well enough to travel so far?" she asked. "You have been looking so white all day."

"I am always white. Do they not call me the pale Queen?"

sighed Anne. "Besides, Richard disturbs me, sleeping so ill at night. He calls out, waking from some dream; and sometimes when he cannot sleep and the hours of darkness crawl he pulls on his furred bedgown and goes wandering about the Palace."

From the gallery where they stood Elizabeth could see him talking to Stanley in the hall below. "What ghosts, I wonder, go wandering with him?" she thought.

But she was recalled to reality by the touch of Anne's feverish fingers on her arm. "I wish you were coming with us, Bess," she was saying. "Usually it is great fun travelling with Richard. He makes such a pageant of it and insists upon my having so many new dresses. But this time, somehow, I feel as if there is something out there on the roads of which I am afraid."

"All tarradiddle, my dear!" scoffed Elizabeth, to calm her fears. "It is just that you have not been too well lately, and I am sure the fresh country air will do you good. Look, the King is ready now to lead you in to dinner."

Secretly Elizabeth had been longing to be left alone with her sisters—all the more so as the following day would be the anniversary of her father's death. But when the royal party rode out from Westminster next morning they made such a brave cavalcade that she found herself almost wishing that she, too, were going. As she pushed open a lattice to look down upon them the April air was sweet with spring. There were outriders, the King's standard-bearer, and men-at-arms, with Lord Stanley's imposing figure well in evidence. Lord Lovell, Sir Richard Catesby, Sir Richard Ratcliffe and most of the officials of the household were in attendance. Anne, dainty as a little ivory figurine, turned in the saddle of her white jennet to wave good-bye—looking far less fragile with that glow of excitement in her cheeks at the thought of seeing her son. And beside her, with his proud standard flowing in the breeze, rode Richard on his famous charger White Surrey, resplendent with gold-and-crimson trappings.

It was only as the gallant company turned northward out of the Palace courtyard that Elizabeth noticed something amiss. There was no handsome John Green riding a pace or two behind his master. "If *he* is left behind it can only be that he is sick," she thought; and, turning hurriedly from the window, bade old Mattie go and make enquiries.

"Please God it be so!" she prayed, laying her plans much as her mother might have done. "The young man has neither wife nor mother, so I can reasonably nurse him until he is convalescent. I will read to him and sit with him. I will even let him make love to me if only I can drag from him what message Gloucester sent to Brackenbury about the boys!" Her heart raced with excitement at the prospect of hearing something definite at last—and with fear of what, in the end, it might prove to be. Even the threat of sharing Will Stillington's bed would not hold her back from such a Heaven-sent opportunity.

But—even supposing Green's devotion to his master were not proof against any woman's wile—her heart's excitement was for nothing. "He is nowhere to be found in the Place," Mattie told her.

Elizabeth sent for an old groom of her father's who had taught her to ride. "Master Green's horse be gone—and his servant's. But the pair of 'em went yesterday, Madam—and southward," he said, gazing at her worshipfully.

And in the end the information she sought came to her quite casually. "Oh, John Green?" said the hated Stillington, who wrote out most of the King's orders. "Did you not know, Madam, that he is gone overseas?"

"You mean to France?" Elizabeth brought herself to ask, wondering if the trusted body squire had been sent to spy on Henry of Lancaster.

"Why, no, Madam, not so far as that," the King's clerk informed her unctuously. "Only across the Solent. If there is anything I can do—"

"Then he may be back soon?" snapped Elizabeth.

"Not for a long while, I should think, Madam," grinned Stillington. "As a reward for his devoted service the King has made him Receiver of the Wight."

"A dull appointment, on an island, for the best-looking bachelor at Court," pouted Cicely, who—like half the Queen's ladies—considered herself in love with him.

"But one where no one is likely to ask him questions!" murmured sagacious old Mattie, setting out her mistress's embroidery frame.

On the ninth day of April, that sad anniversary of the bereavement which had so altered their lives, Elizabeth and her sister were allowed to visit their mother. The King had been quite humane about it when Anne Neville, before departing, had begged the favour for them. "Providing John Nesfield is present," had been his only stipulation, thereby guarding himself against any further trouble from the Woodville woman's plotting. The poor deposed Queen Dowager was pathetically glad to see them and the loving prattle of her younger children helped to cheer her. The older girls were able to assure her of Anne Neville's kindness and more than once she sighed, envying them their freedom to live publicly at Court. Elizabeth, in Nesfield's presence, could not speak of the disadvantages which went with it when one's birthright had been taken away. All she could tell her mother was that the allowances the King had promised to make them when they left sanctuary had been legally confirmed. Of his proposals for marriages for Cicely and Ann the Queen Dowager was already bitterly aware, and Elizabeth had not the heart to add to her bitterness by speaking of the marriage threat he had made in private to herself.

The hours passed almost happily, but the Queen Dowager clung especially to her eldest daughter at parting. "When Uncle Richard returns I will ask if we may visit you again," Elizabeth promised, although she hated above everything to ask him for favours.

But a bare week later, when the King's courier rode in mud-splashed and breathlessly from Nottingham, she went again—alone and without permission. She went white-faced and shocked along the corridors to her mother's far-off apartments, and when Nesfield would have kept her out the preoccupied regality of her bearing silenced even him. "Let me pass, Sirrah. I must tell her Grace that my cousin, the King's heir, is dead," she said, passing through the open doorway without so much as glancing at him.

Her mother rose at sight of her, and by the look of triumph on her face Elizabeth knew that she had heard. "It is the curse you laid upon him. That dreadful curse!" she said, almost accusingly.

"When did the boy die?" asked the elder Elizabeth steadily.

"That day we spent with you—the anniversary of the very day upon which my father died."

"Then God has been good to me," the Queen Dowager said with slowly savoured satisfaction. "Three of my sons that fiend slew."

Elizabeth sat down unceremoniously beside her because she could no longer stand. "They had reached Nottingham when they heard. They were holding Court in the castle there. They did not even know the boy was sick. The messenger says they are beside themselves with grief."

The Woodville woman stared straight before her into the pit of her own sufferings. "Then they will know now what it is like," she said scarcely above a whisper.

Elizabeth, too, stared before her in the heavy silence of her mother's meagre room. So this was the fearful thing which poor Anne had felt was out there waiting to meet them on the road. Elizabeth recalled how bravely they had set forth, with their banners and their gorgeous clothes and their happy anticipation; and tried to picture their return—with the empty bleakness of their faces and of their lives. No matter what wrongs she herself had suffered, she could not but be sorry for anyone who had been as kind to her as Anne had been. Yet, strangely enough, in that hour it was Richard whom she was most sorry for. Richard, the man whom she hated. Whatever he had done had been done because he had this son and so could preserve the strength of the dynasty he had sinned for. And now, it seemed, the sinning was left denuded of its better motive, with nothing but the tattered shreds of remorse to clothe its shame.

The Queen's homecoming was sad beyond words. She had gone forth a gay and placid young woman, and came back a sick and heartbroken one. Her warm trills of laughter no longer spilled over the formality of Court life to inspire people's love, and the citizens of London, already deeply suspicious of her husband, saw the date of the Prince of Wales's death as an indication of God's judgement, and so withheld even their pity.

Elizabeth, the tender-hearted, seldom left her; and the King did all he could to comfort her. "You must grow strong again, my sweet, and bear me other sons," Elizabeth overheard him say, leaning over his wife's bed. But she also caught sight of his twisted face as he said it. For it was difficult to believe that Anne would ever get strong again, and the only child she had ever given him had been born eleven years ago.

Even if the lines about his mouth were deeper and his crisp orders sounded more impatient, he went about his affairs as usual. He was accustomed to suffering in silence and asked for no one's pity. And it was characteristic of his Court that the following Christmastide should be kept as splendidly as ever.

"Will the King let our mother be with us for Christmas Day?" little Katherine had asked wistfully, leaning against Elizabeth's knee.

"The Countess of Richmond is to be allowed to—Lord Stanley told me so," said her sister Ann.

"And so is his eldest son, Lord Strange," said Cicely, who believed in seizing all the fun she could before being hustled into a loveless marriage, and was looking for someone to replace John Green.

When the time came it was good to see her and young Ann being flattered by all the personable young courtiers and enjoying the dancing as they used to do; and to hear Katherine and Bridget shrieking with delight over their toys and sweetmeats and carrying out the spirit of the season by sharing them with simple Warwick, who was so much bigger than themselves. Even the Queen roused herself to take part in the festivities and sat in the midst of them to watch the Nativity plays and acrobats and mimes. "Although the mimes are but poor this year without our Dickon!" declared Cicely stoutly.

Since her return to the Palace Elizabeth had never known the King to be so gracious to her. He teased her about the new blooming of her beauty occasioned by freedom and fresh air, saying that his home evidently suited her. And when the Queen ordered a crimson gown pearled with holly leaves for Twelfth Night he insisted upon Elizabeth having one made exactly like it. "That crimson stuff will suit Bess now that she has wild roses in her cheeks," he had said, coming into his wife's room while the dressmakers had the exquisite stuff spread out. "Though I am desolate at the thought that they may be Lancastrian roses!" It was not like Richard to be tactless and both women knew that the comparison was unkind to Anne. Elizabeth saw the raised brows of the 'tiring-women. In any other circumstances the lovely creation she was being offered would have delighted her, but she was uncomfortably aware that to wear a dress exactly like the Queen's would cause talk about the Court; and, more important still, that Anne herself must be displeased. "How can Richard be thinking about clothes when we have no child to enjoy Twelfth Night?" she had cried indignantly after he was gone.

"Because he can feel two completely different kinds of things at once," said Elizabeth, realizing even as she spoke how odd it was for her to be explaining a man to his own wife. It used to be the other way round, but her mind had dwelt so much and so searchingly on the man of late. Seeing that all the preparations and festivities and dressmakers had tired the poor Queen out, she gently persuaded her to lie down upon her day-bed. "Madam, I did not seek this," she said soberly, when they were alone.

"I know that you did not," agreed the Queen at once. "Have I not already told you that when I know people well I trust their motives better than what other people say?" Impulsively she caught at her friend's hand, looking up at her with special urgency. "I know that I am often peevish these days," she added. "But, whatever may happen and whatever people may say, I want you always to remember that, dear Bess."

Chapter Thirteen

THE SEASONS HAD GONE round again since that splendid cavalcade had had all its gaiety quenched at Nottingham— his "castle of care," as Richard now called it. Elizabeth stood at the Queen's window at Westminster looking down upon the greening garden. "The spring flowers will soon be in bloom again," she said to cheer her.

But poor Anne was not to be comforted. "I shall not live to see the spring," she said listlessly from her bed. "Do not the physicians all agree that I have the same wasting sickness which took my sister and my little son? And now Richard tells me it is because of the contagion that he must shun my bed. But I do not believe him. There must be some other reason."

It was the first time that Anne had disbelieved anything that Richard had said. "Please God she does not think, in her distraction, that I am the reason!" thought Elizabeth.

"Why is he arranging marriages for your sisters and not for you?" asked Anne suspiciously, after tossing and sighing a while.

"Probably because he thinks mine is more important," suggested Elizabeth, carrying a cloth and a dish of rose-water to the bedside.

"Because you are the real Queen of England?" jibed Anne.

Elizabeth said nothing, but gently wiped her friend's hot forehead.

"Perhaps after I am gone he will marry you himself," went on Anne, determined to provoke an argument.

"He is my uncle," said Elizabeth coldly, setting down the basin. "You could get a dispensation from the Pope. The Spanish Duchess of Infantasgo and some of the Austrian royalties did." "Possibly. If we both wanted to. But it takes two to make a marriage," said Elizabeth. "And if there is one thing you can be sure of, my dear, it is Richard's love."

The words melted Anne momentarily to tears. "Oh, Bess, forgive me!" she cried weakly. "It is just that everything seemed to go wrong when we lost our son." But she spoiled her lovable contrition by adding with a hardness which seemed all the more terrible considering her natural childlike naïveté, "You got what you wanted *then*, didn't you?"

"Oh, Anne, don't talk so wildly!" implored Elizabeth, struggling with her anger.

"Well, if you didn't, your mother did. And whatever happened to your precious brothers they have been well avenged!" muttered the dying woman, hunching herself back among her pillows.

Long after Anne had fallen into an uneasy sleep Elizabeth sat by the window with her stirred and troubled thoughts. Had the poor Queen's words been so wild after all, she wondered? Or had she herself during these last few weeks been merely imagining things? That Richard's attitude towards her had changed must be patent to all. Her status at Court was very different now and many enjoyments came her way. To have been glad of it was only human; although with everything that she accepted from him went the self-abasing thought that she was being disloyal to her brothers. But now, reviewing her own feelings in the light of remorseless candour, she asked herself whether there had been something more? Some excitement because he singled her out—some strange attraction? Something unnatural, shameful, vile? Could it possibly be that Anne was right?

So often of an evening now that Anne was sick in bed, when supper was over and the musicians were filling the hall with sweet music from their gallery, she would find Richard at her side. Richard at his most charming. A grown edition of her younger brother— highly strung, mercurial, amusing, quick in mutual exchange of thought—speaking the same easy, expressive language of her breed. The sort of companion whom she so much missed.

As the threads of poor Anne's life grew more tenuous and she called constantly for them both, inevitably they were thrown more and more together. And when Anne died, as she had said she would, before the spring flowers were well in bloom, they shared a common sorrow. When the Archbishop finally folded the pale hands of the mighty Kingmaker's daughter across her small, cold breasts, for the first time in her life Elizabeth heard the hard-bitten Plantagenet sob—and yet by now she was almost sure that Anne's suspicions had not been groundless.

There were all the outward forms and ceremonies to go through, the solemn obsequies in the Abbey to be borne; and even while taking part in them Elizabeth was aware that some of the spectators remembered her replica of the dead Queen's dress at Christmastime and whispered, looking upon the withdrawn harshness of the King's face, that his tears had been the final hypocrisy. The mysterious disappearance of her brothers had dimmed his popularity, making people so suspicious of him that they were prepared to pin upon him any crime. There were even some of them, she was told, who whispered that he had hastened the passing of a barren Queen for the sake of young and healthier beauty. Elizabeth wished with all her heart that she could go away. But there was nowhere else for her to go. She was in Richard's hands. And, as the weeks passed, likely to become so quite literally.

"I suppose you avoid my touch because you still believe I butchered those brothers of yours?" he jibed, hating the way she tried to withdraw herself from his hold when the Court began to dance again.

"Produce them then!" she challenged, being now so much more familiar with him.

"But that is not the real reason, my sweet Bess," he said, ignoring her challenge and speaking too low for the other dancers to hear. "It is because you are afraid of what my touch does to you."

The tell-tale blood had sprung instantly to her cheeks and he had laughed, his eyes mocking her as he handed her in and out of the intricacies of the dance. His green eyes were flecked with brown and singularly beautiful, she noticed; and although he had not her father's grace, yet, being a man who took pains to be proficient in all he did, he was by far the best dancer in the room.

To all outward appearances their evenings were spent quite formally. No one overheard the frightening jibes and compliments he made and there was no one to whom she could speak about them save old Mattie. And as often as not there was nothing to speak about, because she and Richard would forget their antagonism and fall into natural discussion.

"You are no longer frightened of me," he stated one morning, as they rode leisurely through Windsor Park with Lord Stanley and Cicely and a string of courtiers dallying somewhere behind them.

"Oh, yes, I am—but only at times," laughed Elizabeth. "You change like a chameleon, Sir. You are so many different sorts of person."

"Convenient, perhaps; but rather exhausting," said Richard, interested.

"Convenient?"

"It always gives one the initial advantage not to look exactly what one is. If you had seen me for the first time sitting in a tavern—dressed in decent homespun, say—what would you have guessed me to be?"

Elizabeth turned to consider him in the clear June sunlight. "You might well be a scholar or a priest," she told him, unaware how devastating she looked when wrinkling her nose in thought. "Or even, when you are tired and with those long lashes of yours," she added wickedly, knowing how much it would enrage him, "a woman in disguise. One of those interesting-looking women who are nearly, but never quite, beautiful."

"God in Heaven, how horrible!" exclaimed Richard, almost letting his horse stumble into a rabbit warren. "But never by any chance a King?"

"Not in worsted," decided Elizabeth, remembering how her father would have looked like one in anything. "Not unless you spoke," she was quick to add in fairness, remembering Richard's voice.

"Nor yet a soldier?" There was nothing pompous about him, but her candour was hard to take. "Surely you would guess I was a soldier?"

"Only when I looked down at your hands." She looked, now, at his hands on the reins, trying to picture a side of him she had never seen. When he had been "the young Duke of Gloucester" men had clamoured to follow him into battle, and he was not much older now. "What is it like to go into battle?" she asked, knowing it for the foolish, womanish question it was.

Richard tried his best to answer her, however inadequately. "For different men it is different things, I suppose," he said. "Some go into it without fear or imagination, like well-trained chargers. For me it is plain hell beforehand, and once my sword is in my hand the wildest exultation this side of Heaven. Afterwards—well, it has been a proving to one's self of one's manhood and a bringing of the right to enjoy one's worldly status and one's woman. It would be just the same for one of my archers, I imagine."

"There is so much of your lives we women do not know," sighed Elizabeth.

Richard grinned down at her from his tall horse. "That is mutual," he said. "Do you not suppose that we often wonder about childbirth and the tigerish love you bear your children and what you really say about us when you are alone together? It is to these hours which a man and woman cannot share that their shared hours owe excitement. If there were no mystery one might just as well kiss one's page." He had turned in his saddle to beckon the others on. "That young sister of yours is practising her wiles even on burly Stanley!" he complained lightly. "Look, she is keeping the whole party waiting while she gathers pink chestnut blossoms to twine in his unfortunate sorrel's mane!"

But all their encounters were not so light. All summer Elizabeth walked with proud discomfort beneath the speculative glances of his courtiers. And then the thing which Anne had foretold happened. One August evening when the sweet scent of stocks was drifting in through the open casements Richard asked her to marry him.

"But you are my uncle!" she cried out, shrinking from him in horror.

"And the Pope is infallible!" he mocked, grinning at her across the chairback against which he leaned. "It would not be the first time he has given a man permission to marry his niece in order to insure the peaceful succession of a state."

"It is horrible," said Elizabeth.

"Why more horrible than cousin marrying cousin unto the third and fourth generation, which most of us scions of royal houses have to do until we become so inbred that we produce specimens like my brother Clarence's Warwick?" He crossed the room and lifted her chin with his fingers, the better to scan her lovely troubled face. "You and I are both intelligent people and of very suitable ages," he said.

"After all you have done to my mother's family how can you pretend to love me?" she flared indignantly; and could have bitten her tongue out afterwards, for Richard merely laughed at her.

"But I am not," he said cheerfully. "I have never pretended to love anybody but my fragile, uncomplicated Anne, God rest her sweet soul! And you of all people, Bess, should know that is true."

She did know—and knew, too, that some shameful part of her wanted him to make love to her because the cool, casual touch of his fingers stirred her more than the ardent kisses of Tom Stafford had ever done. That earlier madness had been but a prelude, the awakening of an inexperienced girl's senses; whereas now she was a woman emotionally awake, with all her father's capacity for ardour coursing through her veins, beginning to promise and torment.

"Of course I know you never wanted anyone but her," she answered awkwardly, jerking herself from his hold.

"Then we understand each other and can discuss this thing frankly," he said, wandering to the window. "It is an heir I want—born of your Plantagenet blood."

"You are brutal," she said, watching him warily as he stood there with his back to her.

"There are different kinds of brutality, as you may find out for yourself if you marry someone else," he said, shrugging that right shoulder of his which was almost imperceptibly higher than the left. "God defend me from being the kind of brute who leaps in and out of his wife's bed for the plain intent of getting himself a son and does not try to beautify the business for her by courting her mind!" He turned towards her as he stood in the window embrasure. There was that manliness about him which must, as he had said, have been bought in battle, and having come from some tournament at Smithfield he was wearing the straight tabard with the gorgeous quarterings of England and France which suited him best. "If you could bring yourself to trust me I do not think you would be unhappy," he said. "The life of a woman who was mine would never lack warmth and colour and kindness."

Because she knew this also to be true, Elizabeth made herself repel him the more frigidly. "You cannot force me to this. I am not your ward as my brothers were. My father left our marriages to my mother, and everyone in the country knows it."

"That is why I am asking you. I am not a humble man, but I am trying humbly to woo you. Or perhaps you consider the word *coerce* more fitting?"

Recognizing his ultimate power, Elizabeth shifted her ground. "And why do you want a son from me, whom you have publicly called bastard?" she demanded.

"Do you really need me to tell you?" he said, coming back to her. "You who are Edward's favourite daughter must know that both he and I would have done almost anything to keep the Lancastrians out."

"He himself once offered me to Henry of Lancaster."

"Only as a bait to get him into his hands. I was with him when he discussed it. He offered you to a number of men for political reasons, but I doubt if he was ever serious save for the King of France's son. Nothing less than a throne would have satisfied him for you." He stood there pushing the signet ring up and down on his finger. "To keep this throne strong I have let those priests and lawyers argue about your legitimacy; and for the same reason I will make sure that you do not marry Henry Tudor, with his Welsh blood and his Frenchified ways. He is sure to have heard of my unspeakable loss. As long as my son lived the Lancastrian's invasion would have been more of a gamble; but now, I suppose, to a good many of the people it looks a pretty good gamble. They don't want any more uncertainty about the succession. A few more years of civil war would so drain England that she might become a mere appendage of France. But with you as my wife there would be no more uncertainty about the succession, and no incentive for Henry Tudor."

He faced her with expressive hands and shining eyes, letting her see the whole purpose of his life. He looked almost fanatic—a man with one idea who had staked everything upon his hazardous convictions and who had hitherto been strong enough to sweep aside all opposition to his will.

"But, on the other hand, would not the people be repelled from you by the thought of incest, even with the Pope's permission?" she reminded him, momentarily half persuaded.

"To get a dispensation would take months, but *you* have their love—their complete trust," he said, speaking less fervently.

"Since you do not love me, are there not plenty of princesses in Europe whom you could ask?" she suggested.

"Say that I like you the better of two evils?" he countered, with a smile. "You are very beautiful."

"As you liked my brother Dickon the better of two evils?"

"As I like Dickon," he agreed, changing the tense.

Swift as a singing lark hope rose in her, just as it had when she chanced upon an entry among poor Anne's papers for the ordering of two silk doublets for "the Lord Bastard," and then realized that it really proved nothing, since Richard had a natural son of his own. "Then he is alive?" she cried, all question of marriages forgotten.

But Richard turned on her in anger, gripping her by the shoulder until it hurt. "Must you always come back to that?" he snarled. "Consider young Warwick. Since Anne's death you know very well—everyone knows—that I have had him sent to one of my castles up North at Sheriff Hutton. No one at Court sees him any more. Yet nobody supposes that I have had him destroyed. He has his apartments, his servants, his horse to ride every day—he could have a tutor, though much good it would do him! Ask Stanley—ask anybody—if that is not so!"

"Then if you will but let me *see* Ned and Dickon..." began Elizabeth, prepared to bargain.

Richard made a great effort to control his anger, but he either could not or would not answer her appeal. He walked away to the window, stood there as if engaged in some sharp mental struggle, and then swung round suddenly. "I swear to you on my wife's soul that I did not destroy your two brothers," he burst out. "Does that satisfy you? *Now* will you marry me and keep the things we both care for safe?"

For a moment Elizabeth stared at him in speechless joy; but she did not really believe him. He would say anything to persuade her to his purpose. Because he was King he could force her to marry him to-morrow, she supposed; but if it seemed that she was his unwilling victim he would have pushed the people too far. "Give me time! Give me time to decide!" she entreated desperately.

He let her go then, sending for Mattie to attend her. But once free from his presence, from the strange hold he had over her, she found there was no need to decide—only to pray for strength of purpose equal to his own.

"The King is superstitious. He would scarcely add blasphemous perjury to his crimes," argued Mattie, her only confidant.

"It might be that he has only sent them abroad and could not produce them," pondered Elizabeth. "Yet in my heart I feel sure that he lied. That if he considered it necessary, however much he hated the means, he would trick me."

"Whatever the Pope may say, and whatever they do in other countries, an incestuous marriage is sin," muttered old Mattie.

"And I would sooner die than marry my brothers' murderer," said Elizabeth; and going to her *prie-dieu* she fell upon her knees. "Forgive me for succumbing to his spell upon my senses," she prayed. "And somehow, dear God, show me a way to escape the widening web of his machinations!"

Elizabeth lay awake all night. And somehow, whether by prayer or by a process of elimination in her mind, the only possible source of help seemed to be shown her.

Chapter Fourteen

THERE WAS USUALLY SO much coming-and-going in the Lord
Steward's room, and so much urgent transaction of Court
business, that Elizabeth was fortunate in catching Lord
Stanley alone. She had waited while some foreign envoy concluded
his interview, and Heaven had helped her by sending the secretary
hurrying out after him with a bundle of forgotten papers. She could
see Stanley standing by the window, momentarily alone, and had
seized her opportunity to slip in through the half-open door. "As
you were my father's friend, milord," she begged in a low voice,
"take his place and help me now!"

He looked up in surprise from a map of the world he had been
searching for some foreign city and tried good-naturedly to hide
his annoyance. "Why, have they found you yet another objection-
able husband?" he teased, as lightly as though he were speaking to
young Cicely.

"Yes. This time it is the King," said Elizabeth.

The laughter left his round, jovial face immediately and he
strode to the door and kicked it shut in the face of an astonished
clerk and a couple of importunate place-seekers. "My dear Lady
Bess, you are distraught!" he said more formally, but with obvious
agitation. "You must go back to your apartments. This public rabbit
warren is no place in which to speak of such things!"

"Such a thing is not fit to be spoken of anywhere!" she said,
steadying herself against his table.

As if playing for both time and security, Stanley shot the door-bolt slowly. "It is probably only a rumour," he mumbled evasively, coming back to her.

"Yet I see that it does not really surprise you, milord."

"I understand that his Grace has discussed the—er—possible advantages of such a union with one or two of his councillors."

"But you were not one of them?"

"No," he admitted.

Elizabeth struck swiftly, taking him unaware with her daring. "Then you know that he does not trust you?" she said.

"Not trust me?" he bluffed, nodding significantly towards the pile of important-looking documents upon his table. But, in spite of the comfortable way in which he stuck both hands in his capacious belt, his laugh rang false.

"Queen Anne told me so before she died."

"Ah!"

The exclamation that escaped him was that of a man who suddenly finds confirmation of something he has long suspected, and Elizabeth was swift to pursue her advantage. She went down on her knees beside him and joined supplicating hands around the curve of his arm. "Listen, milord. In return for the vow you made my father to protect us I will make *you* one," she said. "But I warn you that I shall keep *mine*. I swear by his beloved soul that if you do not help me to avoid this horrible thing I will kill myself."

He saw that in spite of her obstinacy she was near to fainting, and, much as he deplored having to prolong the conversation, he was obliged in common humanity to raise her up and put her in his own chair. "But what can I *do?*" he asked grudgingly, his face the redder for the reminder of his vow.

"Send for Henry of Lancaster. Arrange for *him* to come and marry me, as Henry of Buckingham did."

"Buckingham was a fool," he blustered, stung by the comparison.

"He was a courageous friend."

"But what did you gain by it? The time was not ripe."

Hope began to shine in Elizabeth's eyes. "You mean that if it had been you might have helped us, as your wife did?" she suggested softly.

"The new King was still too popular," he added, too wary to answer her question.

Elizabeth stretched a pleading hand to him. "Then you think that now, when the people hold him responsible for my brothers and will be horrified at this rumour about his wanting to marry me, the time might indeed be ripe to let Henry Tudor know?" she insisted.

Thomas Stanley had regained his poise. He was again his successful, purposeful self. "There is no need to let Henry Tudor know," he said cautiously. "But I prefer not to discuss these matters with women. Forgive me for saying so, but there is always someone who tells a bosom friend. See what happened to Buckingham!"

He had named no one, but it was not difficult for Elizabeth to guess upon whom he cast the blame. She stood up and faced him. He was not a tall man and she looked directly into his eyes. "Although I have lived subservient to her, I am a very different woman from my mother. You, who have known me all my life, should know that," she said. "Just as you know that Margaret, your wife, saved you from trouble by her silence."

There was a new, steadfast dignity about Elizabeth which compelled him. And, even more than his ambitions, he loved his wife to whom she paid tribute. "Everything remains as it was before—save that we bide our time. Once he has been persuaded to put his hand to something, my stepson, Henry Tudor, is not the kind to let go," he began to say slowly, as if repeating some well-conned formula. "His uncle Jasper Tudor, who brought him up, is a tower of strength. The French King has promised ships. Bishop Morton's brains are of even more use to us now he is free overseas. Your half-brother Dorset keeps in touch. Margaret's man Lewis still comes and goes. There is no need to tell Henry Tudor anything."

Hope and excitement sprang in Elizabeth's heart. The colour came back into her cheeks. "So this time you will fight on our side!" she exclaimed.

But Stanley knew that it took subtlety to live through three such varied reigns. He had never been one to rely upon standard-raising and dramatics. "With four thousand armed retainers and a brother who has nearly as many it would probably be sufficient not to fight at all!" he said dryly.

"Then when Henry lands and Richard summons you to his aid—"

Stanley held up a plump, arresting hand. "Not so fast, dear lady! It is not as simple as all that. Do you suppose that the Lancastrian is such a fool as to risk putting himself into a noose without some written guarantee as to how many supporters are to be counted on, and in what places they will be? And, above all, a signed promise that you will marry him when he *does* come, and so lend his landing popularity and strengthen the weakness of his claim? Henry is capable, but cautious—a man after my own heart. Hearing through Lewis of your brothers' fate, he has even asked for assurance that if any accident should befall you—which Heaven forbid!—he may have Cicely."

Womanlike, Elizabeth saw the matter from a more personal angle. Such caution sounded too cold and calculating. Although she had never seen the man, she had begun to weave roseate dreams about him, thinking of him as her personal deliverer, so that now a cloud seemed to obscure her new happiness. "Then why do you not send him what he wants?" she asked almost coldly.

"Because I cannot write," said the great Lord Stanley, who commanded an army almost as big as the King's, besides half the strongholds in Lancashire.

To a daughter of Edward Plantagenet and Elizabeth Woodville his confession came almost as a shock; yet she knew that many of the powerful barons could write only such things as were necessary to the management of their estates. "But you have a whole army of scriveners," she said, smiling at him affectionately.

"And do you suppose that I would trust any of them?" he countered. "No matter how loyal he might be, the lives of all of us would be in that man's hands." He took a turn towards the door as if to assure himself that there was no one there, and then sat opposite to her, leaning across the table and taking her into his full confidence at last. "I tell you, Bess, the only hope of success in this momentous scheme is that the King shall learn nothing of my personal intentions until the last moment. His mind is alert, his espionage good. As you say, he has never really trusted me. Until after Henry's landing I must remain the necessary makeweight which both men need—the unknown quantity for which even an experienced soldier like Richard can make no certain calculations."

Elizabeth saw the deep, treacherous wisdom of his words. If she sickened at the treachery, she knew that it was only fair to remember that he had had to choose between unwillingly serving the new King or sharing Will Hastings' fate. The deep scar on his forehead bore testimony to the treatment he had already received for trying to withstand the usurper. "Let me write those letters," she offered, after a moment's thought. "Surely you will trust me, whom it most concerns?"

His fine brown eyes opened wide. He stared at her in surprised silence. Here was a solution he had never thought of—an offer too good to be turned down. He knew her to be clever and dependable—the one member of her family to whom all the rest turned when in trouble.

He decided that he could trust her discretion. "We could not risk doing such a thing here in the Palace," he said tentatively. "Anyone might come upon us at any time. You see, there are others besides ourselves who must be present. Men who have promised to raise troops and must subscribe their names before Henry will move."

"Where would you normally meet for such a purpose?" asked Elizabeth.

Now that there was something definite and dangerous to do he noticed how calm and practical she was. "I do not know. In some London tavern kept by one of my own people, probably."

"Then let me come with you to the tavern," she suggested, with as little fuss as though she were proposing to meet him in the rose garden.

Stanley regarded her with new admiration. Because she was young and gallant and his friend's daughter, the hazardous, long drawn-out enterprise suddenly took on a more hopeful and splendid guise and seemed more worth risking men's lives for. "But how?" he asked, almost as if it were she who was taking the lead.

"Dressed as one of your servants," she said promptly. "I tried it once before when I wanted to get out of sanctuary."

So she had not always been the meek, dutiful elder daughter he had supposed. "It should be possible," he said, considering the tall, slender lines of her figure. "I could perhaps find means to smuggle in to you the livery of one of my lads."

Elizabeth blew him a grateful kiss across the table and laughed with relief; and when she laughed she endeared herself to him by looking absurdly like her father. Or like luckless young Edward the Fifth for that matter—the family resemblance was so strong. "There is no need to do that," she said. "Somewhere in my clothes chest I have an old suit of Ned's which I expect I can still get into. Oh, nothing gorgeous or conspicuous, I assure you! So give me but the eagle badge of your livery and I will pin it on."

So once again she looped back her golden hair so that it fell straight to her shoulders and put on her elder brother's plain black suit; but this time she was neither alone nor frightened. In spite of what Stanley had said about women's tongues, she was obliged to take Mattie into her confidence because there must be someone to bolt the door after her and say that she was sick abed if anybody asked for her. And Humphrey Brereton, who was her devoted slave, had a horse waiting in the courtyard. And outside, where the roofs and towers of London made such a lovely silhouette against the pale evening sky, she knew that she had the strongest backing in the country—so strong a backing that the country itself must surely be overturned! After the heat of the day the breeze from the river was exhilarating, and they rode quickly without speaking through Charing village. As they passed through Lud Gate and the City houses began to close in upon them Brereton stopped at an inn, on the door of which someone had chalked an eagle's foot. He dared not help her to alight, but, calling to an ostler to take their horses, strode on before her up the stairs.

The room above was small and stifling with drawn curtains, and full of men who stood and spoke together in anxious undertones. They turned as she followed Brereton through the low doorway, and in that second she ceased to be a squire's page. Lord Stanley detached himself from the rest and went down on one knee and kissed her hand. Brereton leaned with drawn sword against the bolted door. Some of the men Elizabeth recognized as Lancastrian supporters, some of them she was more than surprised to see there. Sir Gilbert Talbot's presence showed her how uncertain were Richard's friendships. There were important personages like Hungerford, Bourchier, Sandford, Savage, Digby—all men with resolution written upon their faces, prepared to put their hand to what they had promised.

Candles and paper had been set upon the table; their plans were made and no man wished to loiter. Then and there Elizabeth sat in the midst of them in boyish doublet and hose and wrote to Henry of Lancaster all that they told her. As they named times and places the full momentousness of the plan unfolded itself before her. And she herself, by her promise to marry her Lancastrian rival, was the pivot upon which it all hinged. Never had she been more grateful to her parents for the careful education they had given her. When at last she had finished writing in her fine, clear hand about armies and supplies and landing ports she laid upon the table a sealed letter from herself—a love-letter telling Henry Tudor that she, as a woman, wanted him to come. And warm from her finger she drew a ring. "I pray you, Humphrey, give the Earl of Richmond these from me," she said to Brereton, who was to take the risk of being their messenger.

The ride back to Westminster was always in her mind a confused blur. This time they rode with Lord Stanley and the rest of his party. After that overcrowded room the fresh air outside was like wine. It was dark, and save for an occasional lighted window only the stars above the overhanging gables lighted their way through the narrow streets. Elizabeth was half frightened, half elated by what she had done. High-sounding words which had been said to her flitted through her mind. "The red and white roses will be united at last." "The country will know peace and prosperity." And closer and more personal her mother's tragic voice saying "Now my sons will be avenged!" And closer still Margaret of Richmond's lovely voice saying gently about her son, "He is studious and competent and gentle." Would he be gentle to her, his wife? Riding home under the stars, though she rode like a page at Stanley's stirrup, Elizabeth felt herself to be a Queen. A sovereignty which she was prepared to share. In her warm generosity all that she had she gave to Henry Tudor, who would come like a legendary knight to deliver her. "This night," she thought, glancing down from the immensity of the stars to her ringless finger on the reins, "I have perhaps changed the destiny of England."

Only as the dark mass of the Palace loomed before them did her spirits begin to fall. Elation passed and cold fear gripped at her because of the inevitableness of this thing she had done. Seeing a light still burning in the private apartments, she thought for the first time of Richard. Of Richard, not as the representative of a dynasty, but as a person. A person whom she had talked and laughed with—and betrayed. Betrayed to his death perhaps. Like herself, he was a Yorkist—not a stranger Lancastrian. Suppose, nagged her veering conscience, it should ever be proved that he was innocent of her brothers' death? Suppose young Ned still lived somewhere and she had deprived him, too, of all hope of his rightful inheritance. Might she not regret this night's impulsive work during all the rest of life? In spite of the cloak which Brereton had lent her, she shivered as they rode quietly into the Palace courtyard.

Seeing Lord Stanley, the guard saluted. Men stumbled from the guardroom, hastily fastening their belts. Grooms came for the horses and a sleepy servant brought a torch. Elizabeth, stiff from riding astride, slid down from the saddle as she had seen her brothers do. She let Humphrey Brereton's cloak fall where he would be sure to see it. "Here, boy, hold my hat and gloves a moment!" called Stanley, giving her an excuse to keep near him as they went through the gatehouse archway; and later gave her an unceremonious push towards the backstairs. "Up you go and get you to bed, or you'll be more of a dunderpate than ever in the morning!" he ordered, so that all should hear.

Elizabeth climbed the stairs with thankfulness, glad that the episode was over. Up to the present, excitement had kept her unaware of how much it had taken out of her. Now she trailed up yawning in the darkness, plucking the eagle badge from her shoulder as she went. Small need to tell her to go to bed, she thought, with a reminiscent smile. All she longed for was to get there. She would ask Mattie to stay and would snuggle down beside her.

At the top of the stairs Elizabeth paused to make sure that no one was about. Mercifully everyone else in the Palace seemed to be asleep. Through a closed door she could hear someone snoring. How good God had been to her!

In order to reach her unpretentious bedroom in the wardrobe wing she had yet to traverse some of the private apartments which were full of memories of Anne. She paused again to listen when she came to the Long Gallery at the end of them; but that, too, seemed to be deserted. A lamp was always kept burning beneath the arch at either end of it. The wind had risen and somewhere a casement banged, stirring the life-size figures embroidered on the wall-tapestries so that they moved a little in the shifting half-light as they so often did. Elizabeth stepped softly through the threshold, wishing she were well past them. And only then, when it was too late, did she see a figure at the far end detach itself from the more shadowy ones and move into the circle of lamplight beneath the archway.

Elizabeth's hand flew to her mouth, stifling an unborn scream.

It was the King himself standing there.

"He overlooked my part in the Buckingham affair. If he sees me now he will kill me," she thought in panic. The livery badge crumpled in her hand would be death warrant enough.

But his head was turned away from her. He was in his damasked bedgown and looking along the passage that branched off at right angles towards his bedroom. Moreover he was twisting the rings up and down his long fingers as he always did when ill at ease. Something in the nervous stealth of his movements suggested that he might be watching for someone or something.

Elizabeth was certain that he had not seen her.

She had only to step back as silently as she had come. To retreat into one of the other rooms and hide behind some piece of furniture. Or gain the backstairs, perhaps. And God would deliver her.

But before she could bring her petrified limbs to move Richard must have detected some sound. He swung round, his hand flying to his dagger. Quick as a man attacked from behind he had drawn it. Standing there motionless and mercilessly illumined, Elizabeth could imagine the sharp steel in her heart. She felt the blood drain from her face and was powerless to move. She just stood there looking at him across the length of the gallery with terrified and beseeching eyes.

She knew the strength of his wrists, the rare but terrible unleashing of his wrath. All the fine plans which had filled her mind for days were wiped out as if they had never been. Chance had delivered her up to him. "Now," she thought, "I shall join my brothers."

But the moments passed and Richard did not move. He only stared at her with a terror surpassing her own. Seeing his shrinking body and contorted face, coherent thought began to come back to her. For the first time it struck her as odd that beneath his damask bedgown he should be wearing a mail shirt and poignard belt. Instinctively she knew that he always wore it now, by day and night; and the inconsequent thought occurred to her that perhaps this had been the real reason why he would not sleep with Anne. He hadn't wanted Anne to know. In case she guessed at the fears which are bred by guilt...

Gradually the true explanation was seeping into Elizabeth's mind, quieting the beating of her heart but filling her with unspeakable horror. She remembered that she was wearing her brother Edward's suit, that her fair hair was arranged like his, and that she must seem spectrally illumined with the darkness all around her and the lamp above her head. She knew she must be deathly pale. And that Richard had not heard her come into the gallery, but had suddenly looked round and seen her standing there. As he stared at her in horror she was shaken to the soul by the knowledge that he believed her to be Edward's ghost.

His dagger clicked back into its sheath, useless against a murdered wraith. He covered his face with both hands as if he could bear no more, and fled down the passage back to his tormented bed. She supposed that no one else had even seen him shake with fear.

The moment Elizabeth heard his door bang she forced her trembling legs to move. Across that guilt-haunted gallery and the waving tapestries she ran, not daring to stop until Mattie let her into the familiar comfort of her own room.

Wildly she fell upon her knees, burying her face in the old woman's lap. Grief, horror, moral relief and gratitude for her deliverance were among the conflicting emotions that tore at her. "I know now. I know at last that he did it!" she cried incoherently. "Even my father could not blame me for betraying him. Whatever may come of the Lancastrians' plan, I regret nothing that I have done this night."

Chapter Fifteen

ALTHOUGH IT WAS ONLY August, the ling on the Yorkshire moors was burned to autumnal brown. The oaks looked clumped and heavy in the fullness of their foliage. The strong walls of Sheriff Hutton Castle were bathed in sunlight, and across the still water of the moat where the far end of the tiltyard merged into open country the ground shimmered in the noonday heat. It was almost too hot to move, and down in the outer bailey the Constable's hounds sprawled in the small patch of shade against the gatehouse tower.

Yet Elizabeth Plantagenet paced restlessly about the battlements, her mind too tensed to endure physical immobility.

It seemed hours since her young cousin Warwick had returned from his ride, docile between his two attendants, and looked up from the drawbridge to wave. And now it was nearly dinnertime and he had slipped away from them to sit near her, singing tunelessly as he thrummed upon the lute she had brought him from London. "At least it gives *him* pleasure that I am here!" she thought. For herself it was misery, because she was not allowed to go out of the castle at all. She was both a prisoner and a prize. Like the legendary princesses in their ivory towers, she was part of the guerdon for which two princes fought.

> "*Blanc sanglier* and Beaufort's son
> Are fighting for the crown—"

sang Warwick; and the silly jingle which he must have picked up from the guardroom went round and round in her aching head as giddily as the heat seemed to swim in the tiltyard. "Why must the poor lad choose to sing *that?*" she thought, pushing back the moist tendrils of her hair. "Of course it is only the means to the crown, not me, they are fighting for!"

"The white boar beats the Welshman back
And knocks his castles down,"

went on the boy's high-pitched falsetto.

"Heaven help me if he does!" prayed Elizabeth, sinking exhausted on to a low crenel in the wall. "The white boar being Richard, he will either kill me or force me to marry him. Neither of them loves me, but Henry Tudor does not kill people. He hates violence. His mother said so."

Elizabeth strained her eyes in an effort to see across the endless moors. If only she knew what was happening out there beyond them in the rest of England! If only someone would send her some news! Even bad news, she felt, would be more bearable than this suspense. All these important people who took one side or the other for politic motives did not realise how much more intimately it concerned her. The two descendants of prolific Edward the Third might be fighting even now for the crown, and because she had a better right to it than either of them she would be made to marry whichever of them won!

"This waiting will drive me as witless as poor Warwick!" she thought; and tried to steady her nerves by deliberately going over everything which had happened up to the day when she had left London. She suspected now that the King had heard of the Tudor's plans for invasion even when he was keeping that last splendid Christmas at Westminster; and as soon as he knew for certain that Henry's borrowed fleet had set sail he had sent her under strong escort into the heart of his own country, so that the invader should not get her. Some weeks before that he had had to give up for a time his own intention of marrying her. The temper of the people had grown too ugly. So ugly and menacing that he had even issued a public declaration to the effect that these rumours about his marrying his niece were all malicious gossip, and that he had never entertained any such idea. And because they went on muttering that Elizabeth had been living in the Palace since his wife's death, he had sent her for a time to live in Lord Stanley's town house. Considering his underlying mistrust of the man, that must have been the last thing Richard wanted to do, she supposed. But the indignation of the Londoners and the secret treachery among his barons had forced him to make many unwilling concessions of late.

It had been wonderful to be living freely in an ordinary friendly household, and the few days she had spent there had given her the longed-for opportunity to hear and discuss all the latest developments of those plans which had first been outlined to her so secretly in a tavern. And to her delight Stanley's intrepid Countess had risked a secret visit to them. Even now, sitting on the gatehouse battlements so many miles away, Elizabeth's strained face relaxed into a smile as she recalled those brief, happy hours during which she had listened with rapt intentness to Margaret of Richmond talking about her son. "If he is anything like you I shall be happy with him," she had prophesied, having already formed a deep attachment for the kind and spirited woman whom she hoped would soon be her mother-in-law.

"He should be happy, too, with anyone so lovely," Margaret had said. "Poor Henry, who has never known a father or had a home since he was a child!"

Elizabeth remembered how her pity had been stirred, contrasting such misfortune with her own happy girlhood.

"My first husband, the Earl of Richmond, died three months before Henry was born, and I was only fifteen," Margaret had explained. "Without my brother-in-law Jasper Tudor I don't know what we should have done."

"Only fifteen, Madam!" Elizabeth had exclaimed.

"The Tudors were ambitious and we Beauforts are descended from John of Gaunt, so Owen Tudor and Katherine of Valois got me for their elder son Edmund as soon as they could. But of course you know all that. Perhaps I loved Henry all the more because I was so young and he was all I had left," Margaret had added, as if apologizing for all she had since done for him.

Elizabeth remembered how she had sat entranced, listening to the romantic story of all that had happened to them. Margaret, the child-widow, had brought him up in Pembroke Castle until he was four, when the fortune of civil war had driven Lancastrian Jasper Tudor out, and then her own father, King Edward, had given the castle and the custody of both of them to Lord Herbert.

"Were they unkind to you?" Elizabeth had asked anxiously.

"Oh no, they were always kind," Margaret had assured her. "I loved Lady Herbert, and after Jasper was exiled and I was forced to marry again and leave Henry she was like a mother to him. The Herberts had a family of lively girls, so he was not too lonely. But when he was barely sixteen your father tried to get hold of him, and Jasper managed to get a ship and take him to Brittany."

Elizabeth's memory of all his hazardous adventures which followed was slightly muddled because she had been thinking about the lively girls who had been his companions. "Were they beautiful?" she had asked.

"Who?" Margaret had asked, breaking off in the middle of her thrilling story.

"Those Herbert girls."

"Really, I do not remember. There was one of them, Maude, whom he specially liked, I remember. But of course he was only a lad," she had added hastily, as if suddenly understanding the reason for Elizabeth's curiosity.

"Not much younger than you were when you fell in love with Edmund Tudor," she remembered saying, and blushed at the memory of such *gaucherie*.

But Margaret had only smiled and explained that Henry was not headstrong like herself, and that if, being half Celtic, his head had been stuffed with romantic dreams, that was probably as far as any of his amours had got.

Elizabeth was sensible enough to appreciate how much it would mean to the Countess to get her son home after so long a separation, and how she and people like Bishop Morton looked upon it as a Christian duty to try to put an end to these interminable wars of the red and white roses. But even while realising that she, Elizabeth, was but a necessary part of their plans, she could not restrain her thoughts from dwelling more and more upon Henry, the chivalrous knight, who was coming to rescue her from a marriage which must be dreaded in the sight of God and man.

She got up and leaned upon the battlements, trying to imagine how they would meet, her present anxiety almost forgotten. But it was difficult to picture him. He was only someone who had been described to her by other people, and since he had always been abroad she had never even seen a painting of him. Whereas Richard Plantagenet's face and figure and movements had been familiar to her all her life. They were sharp and clear-cut in her mind, insistently before her. In moments of irresolution she always made herself think of him as he had looked that night in the Long Gallery, hideously condemned by guilty fear; but since then she had seen him several times riding out to review his troops or talking to Sir Robert Brackenbury about the Tower defences, and almost always he had been wearing his blazoned surcoat and the burnished armour he had worn at the battle of Tewkesbury. A man who, like her father, became more vital at the threat of physical danger and went capably about his plans for meeting it.

During those last few days before she left the Palace he had seemed to stand out all the more spectacularly because he stood so much alone. He had issued a cleverly worded proclamation calling upon his people to defend their country, and consequently the Duke of Norfolk, Lord Lovell and many other faithful friends were away raising troops for him in their own counties; and just before the news of Henry's landing had reached him Lord Stanley had purposely asked leave to visit his estates. Because he had pleaded ill health the King could not very well deny him, particularly as he dared not offend a family who between them owned most of

Lancashire and Cheshire. But he would need someone else of high standing about the Palace to take his Lord Steward's place, he said. And unfortunately for Stanley his eldest son was present at the time. It was all being done as suavely as possible, but everybody knew that young Lord Strange was really kept at Court as a hostage for his father's fidelity.

"It is almost impossible to trick that man!" the Countess had said, commiserating with her husband's anxiety while superintending preparations for their journey into Lancashire.

But Henry Tudor, it seemed, had managed to do so a few days later. Hearing that his enemy intended to land at Milford, Richard thought only of the small port of that name near Southampton, and ordered his fleet to patrol all that part of the coast facing France; but the Tudor took a wide sweep round Land's End and landed at Milford Haven in Wales, disembarking only a few miles from Pembroke. Not only had he upset all Richard's military calculations but his move gave him all the advantage of a homecoming rather than an invasion. Jasper Tudor, Earl of Pembroke, was with him, of course; and the castle threw wide its gates in welcome. Seeing that popular warrior back again, all Wales rose in support of his nephew, marching beneath the fiery-red dragon banner of Cadwallader, the old British King from whom the Tudors claimed descent. Even now they were probably gathering more and more support as they swarmed across the border into England.

So much Elizabeth had heard; and she knew, too, that Richard was at Nottingham, his "castle of care," with twelve thousand men. Since then the Constable of Sheriff Hutton had heard nothing; but anyone looking out across the dried-up country could be sure that this time there would be no floods to help the Yorkist, and that the supporters of the Lancastrian heir were scarcely likely to be caught napping a second time with unprotected bridges over the Severn.

So somewhere between Pembroke and Nottingham Lancastrians and Yorkists must have met. Even now the fighting might be over. Thousands of people up and down the country might know the result of some stupendous battle and be discussing it in home and

street and tavern whilst she—to whom it mattered so supremely—
must wait in captive ignorance upon these accursed battlements.

Mercifully, Warwick had ceased his irritating singing. He had
climbed upon the low stonework beside her and was engaged in
flicking tiny bits of masonry down into the moat. "Look, horses!"
he said suddenly, clutching at her elbow. If his intellect were a bit
weak, there was certainly nothing amiss with his eyesight.

Elizabeth could see nothing but a cloud of dust. "Where?" she
asked eagerly.

"Beyond the tree they always let me ride to. Look, Cousin Bess,
there are a lot of them and they are level with it. Now they have
passed it. Surely you can see them, Cousin Bess?"

Yes, she could see them now. A party of horsemen making
straight for the castle. And the sentries must have seen them too,
for the Captain of the Guard was shouting orders; and soon the
portly Constable, badly winded from hurrying up the turret stairs,
was beside her. "Whoever comes here for your Grace is sure to be
from the winning side," he panted.

All her life Elizabeth would remember those moments of
suspense. The party was halfway across the tiltyard now and in a
matter of seconds the whole direction of her life would be known
to her, one way or the other. She scarcely dared to look. "Is there
anyone among them whom we know, Mattie?" she asked, as her
excited women came fluttering to the wall beside her.

But Mattie's eyes were old and dim and the horsemen, bunched
together, were but foreshortened figures who seemed to have
helmets but no faces. It was younger eyes and a simpler mind that
settled the matter. "No white boars!" lamented Warwick, for whom
the *blanc sanglier* stood for Westminster and the entourage of Aunt
Anne, the only person who had ever really made a home for him
since his parents died.

"It is true, what the young Duke says," corroborated the
Constable, to whom it meant the break-up of a lifetime's service.

"That looks *like* Sir Robert Willoughby riding in the middle of
them," ventured one of Elizabeth's women.

"And it certainly *is* Sir Humphrey Brereton raising his hand in greeting," said Elizabeth, closing her eyes in wordless gratitude. "How hot they must be, riding so fast beneath this fierce sun! Let us go down and welcome them."

Since whichever way the fighting had gone Elizabeth would be Queen of England, the Constable could do no less than obey. He barked an unwilling order, and as she led the way down the winding stairs they could hear the rattle of the drawbridge chains and the hollow thud of hooves above the moat; and by the time they all emerged into the sunlight at the bottom the courtyard was full of men of the garrison staring and dusty Lancastrians dismounting.

Sir Robert Willoughby was no sooner out of the saddle than he was kneeling to kiss Elizabeth's hand. "Lord Stanley sent me to give your Grace the glad news," he said. "At a place called Bosworth, outside Leicester, Henry Tudor was victorious."

So all her misfortunes and anxieties were over. Because she could find no adequate words, Elizabeth smiled at him through tears of relief. "The new King has sent me to escort you home to Westminster," he was saying.

"The new King?" she repeated.

"King Henry, may God preserve him!"

"You mean—they have already crowned him?"

"Milord Stanley crowned him upon the battlefield, and all men shouted 'Long live King Henry the Seventh,'" added Humphrey Brereton, coming, too, to kiss her hand.

But of course they could not have crowned him without her. Elizabeth stood upon the bottom stair looking at their exultant, upturned faces, and trying not to see the sullen faces of Yorkshiremen who stood in silent groups behind them. Most of them had fought at Tewkesbury, and for them she knew it was as if their God had gone. "But what could they crown him with?" she asked in bewilderment, her voice sounding singularly young and fresh as it echoed back between the ancient walls.

"A soldier found the crown of England in a thorn bush," Humphrey answered her eagerly.

For a moment Elizabeth did not see them at all, only a vivid picture of Richard Plantagenet on White Surrey with the golden circlet gleaming around his vizored helmet. While there was breath in his body, she knew, he would defend it. "Then Richard—?" she faltered.

"He is dead."

The crisp triumphant words came from Sir Robert, but Elizabeth heard a hard-bitten old archer sob. Even in the moment of their success the Lancastrian party must have been aware of the hatred and sorrow that surrounded them. At a word from their officers the garrisons would have murdered them. They looked towards the Constable, and the Constable, doughty warrior as he was, looked down at the ground. When there is nothing left to fight for, why give orders?

"The Plantagenet fought like a lion. Three separate charges he led, although bleeding from his wounds," stated Humphrey out of his young generosity. "But just as he had fought his way within grappling distance of the Tudor, we killed him."

The groan that came from a score of Yorkist throats was made more expressive than any words. "How many were with him when he fell?" their Captain asked tersely.

"Only Lord Lovell—and possibly his standard bearer," answered Sir Robert, and somehow, to his annoyance, for all the fine news he had brought, felt ashamed before them.

"He seems to have been fighting an army single-handed," said Elizabeth. Then, feeling that something quite different was expected of her, she added, with an effort at vindictiveness, "I wonder how *he* liked the feel of death?" and watched the hurt expressions of the men who had avenged her brothers change to appreciative grins.

"Let us go in and dine," suggested the Constable tactfully. "You must have ridden furiously, Sirs."

Washed and hospitably set at table their high spirits returned. "Where will King Henry meet me?" asked Elizabeth, picking at her pigeon pie and stumbling a little over the startlingly new title.

"He did not say, your Grace. Only that you were to take whatever time you needed for your comfort and that we are to escort you safely to your lady mother at Westminster."

Elizabeth pushed the pie aside with her new-fangled French

fork. "And he sent no letter—nor any ring?" she asked in a low voice, hoping that no one else at table would note her personal disappointment.

"Madam, he was but newly cleaned up from battle, in which he, too, had played an honourable part, and on his way to Leicester to give thanks."

"Of course," said Elizabeth, trying to stifle a feeling of flatness. It was scarcely the moment when a girl wants to go back to her mother. She was gay and beautiful and a promised bride. She wanted to share in all the excitement and ride in triumph through London with her future husband at her side. But of course what he had so arranged was considerate and proper. God must come first—God and the proprieties!

She had caught herself so often of late holding cynical conversations with herself like that. She must mention it as a fault to her confessor—she, who this very day had so much to be thankful for! In the meantime as soon as dinner was over she would give orders to her women about the packing of her gear. She must not keep Henry waiting.

"And my cousin of Warwick?" she asked, hoping the boy had not been forgotten.

"He is to come too," Sir Robert told her. So she leaned across the table to tell the boy. "We are going back to Westminster where there will be the acrobats and mummers that you like, and Katherine and Bridget to play with," she told him, vowing in her heart that she would try to be as kind to him as Anne had been.

"I will have my people pack everything to-night so that we may all set out in the cool of the morning," she promised Sir Robert and Humphrey. "And I shall forget about Richard," she added to herself, "when I get away from here and no longer see the faces of his men around me."

The next morning Elizabeth was happier than she had been for months. A light breeze had sprung up in the night, cooling the countryside. Puffy white clouds scudded across a blue August sky, the scent of honeysuckle was sweet in the hedgerows, and in the long fields red-gold barley ripened early to harvest. As they left Yorkshire behind people came out in all the villages to call down blessings upon her, and she knew the loving welcome which awaited her in London. "All my griefs and anxieties I am leaving behind," she thought, "and a new life lies ahead. New apartments are being prepared for my mother, who must be delighted at the outcome of it all. She will be one of the most important personages in the land again, and Margaret of Richmond, who cares less for these things, will have her son. Dorset and Tom Stafford and other attainted friends will be home again. There will be all the excitement of preparing for a wedding and a coronation and I must try to forget the past. And I shall have a good husband—and, blessed Mother of God, let me have children!" prayed Elizabeth. "And because God has delivered me from so much, though I be Queen of England," she vowed, "I will take the words 'Humble and Reverent' for my motto."

Chapter Sixteen

HALF THE NOBILITY IN the country seemed to flock in Elizabeth's wake to Westminster, and the Londoners' welcome was rapturous. The reinstated Queen Dowager met her with every show of tenderness, the return of her son Dorset seeming to have alleviated much of her bitterness; but although Elizabeth was officially in her mother's care she wisely insisted upon keeping some of their apartments to herself. They were the pleasantest in all Westminster Palace and Henry's courteous instructions for their comfort had been irreproachable; but although everybody had expected that he would want to strengthen his position by an immediate union with the Yorkist heiress, so far there had been no talk of marriage.

Elizabeth's first meeting with Henry Tudor had not been at all as she had pictured it in her romantic imaginings at Sheriff Hutton. After spending a long time consolidating his success in the various counties as he came southward, he had come to wait formally upon them. There had been nothing of Elizabeth's own impulsive gladness in his manner. She had found him a grave, reserved young man who looked considerably older than his age; and not quite so good-looking as his mother and the Stanleys had suggested. It was not that he was plain or lacked dignity, but his face was pale and a thought too long and narrow. But one could scarcely expect him to be gay or amusing after the hardships of his life, she supposed; and even if he spoke with a slight French accent, at least he appeared to have acquired no foreign mannerisms.

"Why does he so seldom come to see us?" she asked of Stanley, after the new King had finally taken up residence in the opposite wing of the Palace.

"Because there is so much for him to do," Stanley had said, excusing him either because he admired his stepson's industry or because he himself had just been rewarded with the earldom of Derby. "His Grace has already made himself popular with the London merchants, not by inviting them to lavish banquets as the late King did, but by knowledgeably suggesting fresh markets for them abroad. He is giving important offices to men of ability like Morton, too, with a view to curbing the barons' power and so preserving peace in the realm. And now he is calling his first Council so that preparations may go forward for a coronation."

"Perhaps he has said nothing about a wedding because he feels ill at ease taking precedence in my home," thought Elizabeth, very well aware of her superior rights. And on the occasion of one of Henry's rare visits, when for a moment or two they had been tactfully left alone, she had turned to him with all her habitual generosity. "I hope that you like living here," she had said shyly, thinking pitifully of his fatherless years. "You must know that everything I have and am is yours, Henry, in return for the risk you took to avenge my brothers. Lord Derby tells me how well the people have received you, and once my lineage is linked to yours…"

But to her hurt amazement he had seemed to want nothing from her, ignoring even his own slender Plantagenet claim through John of Gaunt. "My father's forebears were Kings of Wales, so I need no modern title," he had said cooly. "And apart from that I do assure you that there is no need for you to worry about me, Cousin Elizabeth, since I am King by right of conquest."

Feeling that her richest gift had been flung back in her face, Elizabeth's rare temper blazed out. "Even your conquest might not have been accomplished without my help," she told him, remembering her hazardous and secret visit to the tavern. "It was my promise to marry you, and Lord Stanley's strategy, that made it possible."

"And my Uncle Jasper's popularity in Wales," Henry had added, with maddening exactitude.

And so the weeks had run on into autumn and still no marriage had been arranged. But there had been a coronation. A coronation at which she and her mother and sisters had been honoured guests, but no more. For Henry the Seventh, having by his own quiet efficiency established himself strongly enough on the throne, seemed to resent the thought of taking his title through her.

"I do not see how you can be crowned until you are his wife," Margaret of Richmond had pointed out kindly, noting her outraged fury.

"It is not for *him* to give *me* the crown," Elizabeth had retorted haughtily, "since I already *am* the Queen."

"In reality—and in the people's hearts," Margaret had agreed gently. "Only give my son a little time to work for the reordering of this poor torn kingdom, my child, and your wedding will come later. And we shall see that it is very splendid. Apart from anything else, you must remember that, although you are only distant cousins, Henry has to wait for a dispensation from the Pope."

There was no gainsaying that. Henry was always so gallingly right. And so Elizabeth had waited in proud resentment, passing the time mostly in her own rooms, shamed once more because the man who was to marry her did not appear to want to. And whenever Tom Stafford and other young men who had been her friends came to pay their respects to her she was more delighted to see them than an affianced bride should have been.

There were three of them gathered together in her candlelit room one evening towards the end of October. Outside rain lashed at the window-panes, making their fireside companionship the more cosy. Humphrey Brereton read aloud the poem he had been writing about her, Tom Stafford thrummed his lute and sang her the latest love-songs, and George Strange, the only one of the trio who was not in love with her, regaled her with the latest gossip while her ladies handed round wine and sweetmeats. Elizabeth knew that she was looking radiantly beautiful in the soft candlelight, and altogether it had been one of those happy evenings which one stores in memory. "Now tell me about Bosworth," she invited suddenly, seating herself informally on a fireside stool. Remembering those tense moments on the battlements at Sheriff Hutton and the joy of her subsequent journey to London, she had the feeling that life had somehow stopped for her since then. "But surely you must have heard it all a dozen times, Madam!" the young men protested, joining her around the hearth.

"From my new Lancastrian entourage, yes," she admitted dryly. "But you must remember that I have been a Yorkist all my life. Could you not tell me everything just as it really happened—from both points of view? How Henry Tudor won and how Richard Plantagenet—was betrayed?"

"Although it is a long story, the actual battle lasted only two hours," began Brereton, suddenly sobered by the recollection.

"Yet it practically changed the face of England," said Stafford thoughtfully, laying aside his lute.

"And if ever a man were betrayed, it was Richard Plantagenet," corroborated George Strange, who should have known, being Stanley's son.

Their faces were grave now, yet eager, as they tried to relive it for their beloved Princess, and to be impartial. At an impatient wave of Elizabeth's hand the women had withdrawn to the other end of the room, and the only sounds about her were the homely crackling of the freshly thrown logs and the alternating depths and lightness of three manly voices.

"It was the sixteenth of August when Richard marched out of Nottingham with twelve thousand men, and he was in Leicester by sunset," began Stafford. "I remember the dates because I had managed to escape his restraint by then and join in this second attempt for the same cause for which my father lost his life. On the eighteenth Richard was about a mile from this place called Bosworth and our spies brought us word that he had had his men throw up breastworks and pitch tents."

"I marched eastward from South Wales with Henry Tudor," joined in Brereton eagerly. "He had only seven thousand men, so you can imagine we had been anxious all the way to know on which side Lord Stanley would fight! It was not until we reached Athelstone that your father and uncle met him secretly, George.

So secretly that Henry stole out to them quite alone, and almost lost himself getting back; and the rest of us hadn't an idea until the battle was almost over what your precious family meant to do."

"When the Lancastrians came up the two armies were in sight of each other, each upon a hill," George Strange explained. "But I noticed that my father placed his men slightly nearer to King Richard's so as to allay his suspicion until the last moment. You see, Lady Bess, I was a hostage with the Duke of Norfolk's forces and he had instructions to kill me at the first indication of my father's defection. Richard was never fool enough to trust any of us, once he'd gone back on his word about keeping your brothers safe."

"You must have spent some mightly uncomfortable hours, George!" said Stafford.

"I only wished they would get started. But Richard would not fight on the Sunday."

"He was such an odd mixture of ruthlessness and superstition!" murmured Elizabeth, sitting over the fire with chin cupped in hand.

"At least his suspense that Sunday must have been worse than mine!" grinned Strange. "For I think he had an inkling that my father and Henry Tudor had met. They say he scarcely slept till dawn and then waked in a sweat complaining that he had seen avenging ghosts."

"I hope my father's was one of them!" said Stafford, unobtrusively crossing himself.

"When he couldn't stand it any longer he called out for Lord Lovell and Catesby and went the rounds of the camp, leaving his tent so early that there was neither priest to shrive him before battle nor any breakfast," continued Strange. "Lovell told me afterwards that they caught a sentry sleeping and Richard stabbed him to the heart with that jewelled dagger he was always fingering. 'I found him asleep and have left him so,' he said."

"One can almost hear him saying it," laughed Brereton, half admiringly. "He was a fiend for discipline, and must have known there were traitors all around him."

"How would he have known?" asked Elizabeth, listening spellbound.

"It appears that Norfolk had already found some doggerel pinned to his tent flap," explained Strange. "A friend trying to warn him, probably. 'Jock of Norfolk be not too bold, for Dickon thy master is bought and sold,' it said."

"You may owe your life to that scrap of paper, George," observed Tom Stafford. "For John Howard of Norfolk must have known that if your father were on the winning side it would go ill with anyone who had harmed you!"

"Richard must have had good reason to kill that sleeping sentry too," added Brereton. "For we'd sent Sir Simon Digby to get through the Yorkist lines, and it was such laggards who made it possible. If spies could come and go like that the King must have realized that, splendid as his army looked, it was half full of traitors."

"It was then, wasn't it, that he sent an order for Lord Stanley to bring his forces close up against his own?" asked Stafford.

"'By Christ's passion, if they are not here by supper-time I will cut off his son's head!' he raved," confirmed Strange. He kicked at a fallen log as he spoke and the sudden blaze illuminated the reminiscent smile on his face. "And let all who dub my father a time-server remember that—dearly as he loves me—he dared to send back word that it was not yet convenient, and added a reminder that he had other sons. He did *that* for his civilized belief in a union which would end these everlasting wars."

"Poor Lord Stanley's heart must have been torn in two," said Elizabeth, "with his stepson the leader of one camp and his heir a hostage in the other!"

"Well, I imagine I should not have lived an hour after that had not good old Norfolk sent me with a small guard to wait until the fight was over," Strange told her. "I could not fight, but at least the Almighty allowed me to stand upon a hill from whence I could watch those who did. I would not have missed that battle at Bosworth for all the world!"

"However worried Richard may have been, it in no wise affected his military efficiency," commented Brereton. "He put his famous archers in front, under Norfolk and that brilliant young son of his, Surrey. Then he made a solid square of pikemen, bombards and arquebuses which he himself commanded. From the other side of this red-earthed field we could see him—conspicuous on his white horse—riding here, there and everywhere attending to each detail himself, quite regardless of our hopeful archers' aim."

"And what was Henry Tudor doing all this time?" asked the woman who was to marry him.

"He was doing all that befitted a man whose blood is half Plantagenet, Madam," said Stafford generously, knowing that the Tudor would take her from him. "First he made a stirring speech to his Welsh troops. You know the sort of thing, Bess—'Having come so far and put all to the hazard, this day must bring us either victory or death.' He understands the sort of thing to rouse them. Then he, too, put archers in the forefront and, with the help of Jasper of Pembroke's experience, commanded them himself."

It was Brereton, with his gift for narrative, who took up the tale of the actual battle. "At first the archers on either side bore the brunt," he said. "I am sure there cannot have been such a deadly flight of arrows since Agincourt. Then the trumpets sounded the charge and the whole field was a mêlée of single combat. Horse thundering against horse, and pikemen thrusting at each other. Hundreds of them were trampled underfoot, and even the archers, their quivers empty, snatched weapons from the dead. Knights who at home were neighbours and whose families were united by marriage, recognizing the familiar devices on each others' banners, yet fought each other to the death. In the middle of a charge I saw old Norfolk, his helmet riven in two, chivalrously spared by milord Oxford, only to be shot between the eyes with the arrow of some war-drunk Welshman. When young Surrey spurred forward furiously to avenge his father Clarendon and Sir William Conyers tried to rescue him, but were themselves cut down.

"Three separate charges Richard led, and would have won, he and young Surrey fought so brilliantly. But just as the battle was swinging in his favour the Percies of Northumberland withdrew their support; and—as you all know—at the crucial moment, Stanley ordered his troops to join his stepson's, not the King's.

"All of us knew that everything was over then. Only Richard, with a soldier's tenacious bid for the hundredth chance, refused to know it. Some misguided fool brought him a fresh horse and begged him to escape. 'Escape!' he scoffed. 'Bring me my battle-axe, and by Him that shaped both sea and land, I will die King of England!'

"There was only one chance left for him; and that was to kill the invader with his own hand. Stopping for a drink of water, he caught sight of Henry of Richmond with a few followers on a hill and pulling his vizor dawn, spurred White Surrey towards him. 'If no man will follow me I will try this last hazard alone!' he called out, leaving his dismayed and broken army behind him. And such was the inspiration of his valour that a few men *did* follow him—men like Viscount Lovell, Ferrars, Catesby and good old Sir Robert Brackenbury."

"And only Lovell is alive to tell of it," added Stafford.

In all the talk there had been about the battle no one had told Elizabeth this before. "You actually saw it?" she asked, scarcely above a whisper.

Surprisingly it was the deep voice of Stanley's son that answered her from out of the gathering gloom. "I saw it from that hill," he said. And although he spoke reluctantly, as became a confirmed Lancastrian, he seemed to be seeing it still. "The Plantagenet set his spear in rest and charged, leading that heroic little handful. His untiring sword seemed to cleave a passage for them. He looked like some inspired superman fighting his way through bare steel, with his horse slipping and stumbling over the dead and wounded he left behind. There was that burly giant, Sir John Cheney, I remember, standing guard before his Lancastrian master. But the King, slight of frame as he was, unhorsed him. With one stroke he slew Sir William Brandon, the Tudor standard-bearer, and, wrenching the silken banners from his dying hand, threw them contemptuously to the ground—then pressed on so that the proud Pendragon emblems were trampled into the blood-red earth by White Surrey's hoofs. There was no one between the two rivals then. Yorkist Richard had fought his way across the field and the

Lancastrian was almost within his grasp. I wouldn't have given a row of pins at that moment for Henry Tudor's life!"

"Riding back to help him, I could see his face, and it was livid," said Stafford. "Henry Tudor is no coward, but seeing that invincible surcoat of English leopards bearing down upon him he must have believed his last hour had come!"

"And then a miracle happened—"

"My uncle, William Stanley, moved for the first time. With his three thousand men he dashed in and surrounded Richard, cutting him off within striking distance of his prey—"

"Nothing could have been more neatly timed—"

"'Foul treason!' yelled Richard, turning in the saddle to strike in all directions," went on Brereton. "Catesby tried to get him out of it, but he just went on hacking and fighting his way through the growing number of Sir William's men. When his horse was killed under him he stabbed yet another man and stumbled forward, his hands outstretched as if to get at his enemy's throat. His head was bare, his gauntlets gone, and his green eyes were blinded with blood. He must have had a dozen wounds before they closed in and killed him…"

Elizabeth was thankful that the tall candles had burnt themselves out. "And then they set his crown upon Henry," she said in a proud calm voice, hoping that they would not notice that her face had been hidden in her hands.

"A soldier found it in a hawthorn bush and gave it to Sir Reginald Bray, and my father put it upon the Tudor's head and everyone shouted 'Long live King Henry,'" said Strange, repeating the words she had heard so often during the last few days. "The new King called all his supporters together and made a fine speech of thanks and then we all chanted the *Te Deum*. Towards evening, after we had eaten and cleaned ourselves, we rode with triumph into Leicester. No one dared to oppose us, so my father ordered all the trumpets to be sounded and my stepbrother was proclaimed Henry the Seventh of England."

They had told their story well, but somehow the recital of that splendid moment, which should have been the climax of it all, fell flat and stale. They talked a while of how well Henry had been received as they came southwards down to London, and of how modestly he had avoided all military display; but their minds kept going back to the battle.

"Where was Richard buried?" Elizabeth said, voicing the question she had long been wanting to ask.

"The Grey Friars in Leicester begged his body after it had been shown to the people at one of the city gates," one of them told her.

"That was kind," she said. "But how was he brought there? From Bosworth, I mean."

There was an uncomfortable silence during which Tom Stafford picked up his lute and Humphrey Brereton fiddled quite unnecessarily with a disarranged ribbon on his doublet. "George was the last to see him," he said evasively.

Tom Stafford moved behind her stool, swinging the gaily ribboned lute, and his free hand rested momentarily on her shoulder. "You do not want to hear that, Bess," he said gently. "After all, he was your uncle—and had been an anointed King."

"But I must hear," said Elizabeth, brushing aside his hand and still looking expectantly towards Stanley's son.

"His body was brought into Leicester across a horse," Strange said with slow reluctance. "Dusk was drawing on and after the long hot day it had begun to rain—that steady, hopeless rain that beats slantingly across open country."

It was quite dusk in the Princess's apartment and rain was beating hard against the window-panes. Elizabeth tried to picture those long, sodden, midland fields. "Not on poor White Surrey," she said, sighing.

"No. Some borrowed farm nag, I should think. But the sorry brute was so bespattered with his blood I could not really see."

Elizabeth could picture that too. It was her own blood—her father's… "If—he was so wounded—hadn't someone taken off his armour?" she managed to ask.

"They had taken off—everything," muttered Strange. "He was stark naked, with his head hanging down on one side and his feet dangling from the other."

"And his face?"

"I could not see it. His brown hair hung over it, all matted. And although they had pulled his body from beneath a pile of the slain, some sadistic fool had found it necessary to put a halter about his neck. I do assure you, Madam, this was no doing of my father's—"

Elizabeth had left the fireside with a swish of skirts and gone swiftly to the window. "Merciful Mother of God!" she moaned, leaning her forehead against the coolness of the painted glass.

"You should not have told her!" she heard Stafford hiss savagely. And then Strange's reasonable retort, "She asked me!"

"I did," she called back to him from the window. "Go on!"

The unfortunate young man had no choice. "The fellow who led the horse had hunched himself into his jerkin against the rain," he recalled, with a trained soldier's eye for detail. "It was quite dusk by the time I saw them, and they were crossing that narrow bridge that leads across the Soar into Leicester. And as the horse jogged over the hump of it so Richard's head bumped like a dangling wet mop against the wooden struts of the bridge."

"Don't!" cried Elizabeth sharply.

There was a long silence in the darkening room. The three elegantly dressed young men stood about discomfited until she rejoined them. It had been her own fault, and they all knew it. "He was the last Plantagenet King," she said apologetically, feeling like a murderess of her race. And then suddenly she clapped her hands impatiently. "Bring lights, some of you!" she called. "Are there no servants in the Palace that we must endure this abominable darkness?"

And when the servants came running and the lovely room sprang into soft golden light again she turned to her guests with eyes unnaturally bright—whether from excitement or from tears they knew not. "But what I have destroyed I will restore," she vowed. "From now on there will be Tudors. Born of my body." She seemed scarcely to be speaking to them, but rather to some unseen audience beyond the Palace walls, and with a gesture of magnificent certainty she passed her hands, palms spread, down her body from breasts to slender thighs. "With the agonies of childbirth I will pay for what I have done. Without warmongering or murder, I will give England and Wales a new dynasty. My children's children will bring this country peace and prosperity."

Then, dropping from her high prophetic mood, she began to laugh crazily and held out her hands invitingly to Stafford, drawing him into a gay measure. George Strange, relieved that their conversation was over, reached across the settle for his friend's lute and began to pick out an accompaniment to their steps. Humphrey Brereton's dark eyes lighted with half-envious laughter as he stood watching the two of them prance and turn about the room—watching Elizabeth dancing away the desolating picture of Richard Plantagenet's body being jogged ignominiously over Leicester Bridge.

E LIZABETH'S WEDDING HAD BEEN every whit as splendid as her mother-in-law had promised. There had been the beautiful ceremony in the Abbey and feasting in the Palace, and a procession through London with all the church bells ringing. And when, in their relief at the cessation of years of civil warfare, the people had lit bonfires and danced around them in the snow, Elizabeth knew that their singing had been a spontaneous expression of their love for her. All her sisters had begged to help dress her in her bridal finery, and Cicely and Ann, looking almost like stately grown women, had held her train. Remembering her mortification over her first wedding gown, Elizabeth had thanked God that this one betokened no lifelong exile in a foreign land. Instead of being covered with *fleur de lys* it had been lovingly embroidered with red and white roses; and when her kinsman, Cardinal Bourchier, placed her hand in Henry's, people had wept for joy because at that moment it had seemed that the familiar war-worn emblems had turned into a single bloom. A great Tudor rose, with red encircling white. And to her delight Henry had taken this as their mutual badge, and already it was woven on her bed-hangings and his chair of state and on the royal servants' liveries.

In the midst of her own triumph it had been good to see her mother's mended pride, and the happiness that shone in Margaret Beaufort's lovely, ageing face; but in her secret heart Elizabeth had been most grateful of all for Pope Innocent's considerate kindness when, in his dispensation, he had purposely alluded to her as "the undoubted heir of her illustrious father," thus killing for all time the ugly slur upon her name.

But even the magnificence of her wedding could not make her forget its tardiness. The battle of Bosworth had been fought and won in August, yet it was not until after Christmas that Henry had married her—and then only because Parliament, prodded by the angry mutterings of the people, had specially petitioned him to do so. And because Parliament had been astute enough to make the petition synchronize with their proposal to grant him poundage and tonnage for life, Elizabeth was never sure whether it was the remembrance of his promise or the considerable addition to his income which had persuaded him.

For her part, she had gone to her marriage with gladness. With all the natural sweetness of her nature she had striven against resentment, preserving her gaiety and trying to please him. Again and again she reminded herself that, except for hearsay, she and her husband were practically strangers, believing in her optimism that she would soon come to understand him.

"Have you seen what our loyal poet John de Gigli says about us?" she asked one morning, sitting up in their great state bed and laughing delightedly over an illuminated presentation scroll. "He calls me 'the fairest of King Edward's daughters.' Surely I am not more beautiful than my dainty sister Ann?"

She looked so much more beautiful, and her question was so provocative, that it was the moment for any new bridegroom to be passionately definite; but Henry Tudor had risen early and was putting on his furred bed-gown because he had a great many business plans for the day.

"Look, Henry, what the dear man says, too, about all the happiness we are going to bring our people!" persisted Elizabeth, waving the flattering verses beneath his nose.

Ninety-nine men out of a hundred would have let their business go hang and taken her fragrant body in their arms; but Henry only took the scroll. He did not care particularly about the personal happiness of a lot of Englishmen, but he skimmed through the lines politely. To his more critical, cosmopolitan mind they seemed more loving than polished, and overfull of pro-Yorkist enthusiasm. "I see the fellow has the impertinence to infer that your title has become mine," he remarked, laying the effusion down on the gorgeous coverlet.

Watching the frown gather on his forehead, Elizabeth remembered too late that this was just the impression he had been trying so hard to avoid. "But won't you read on?" she invited hastily. "He says all manner of admiring things about you later."

"I am afraid what Master de Gigli thinks of me is not highly important, and my secretary will be waiting," he excused himself, inserting his slender feet into his neatly placed slippers.

"Is your secretary so much more important than your wife?" pouted Elizabeth.

Henry smiled indulgently and bent to kiss her, explaining something about his plans for reducing the immense private armies of the barons which he was anxious to have prepared before Parliament reassembled; but Elizabeth scarcely listened because of the resentment rising hotly within her. "Does it mean nothing to you that other men consider me beautiful?" she demanded.

"It means a great deal," he assured her, straightening himself and passing a careful hand over his hair where she had ruffled it.

"Then why will you not sh-show it?" she persisted, her pansy-blue eyes filling with disappointed tears.

Instead of holding her close against his heart and showing her then and there beyond all possible doubt, Henry merely handed her his handkerchief. "Surely, my dear, I showed how proud I was of you in that so fine wedding procession which cost me more than my coronation," he pointed out gravely.

He was trying to please her, but the very temperance of his praise enraged her. And it did not help matters that his precise English sounded as if it had been conned out of a book, with occasional sentences arranging themselves like an exact translation from the French; although she supposed that in some people—people with more sense of humour, perhaps—it might have sounded charming. "In a public procession, where other men are judging what you got for your money—yes!" she cried, with a fine echo of her father's temper. "But what about when we are alone—in bed?"

She was talking straight out of her mind, just as her younger brothers were wont to do, without weighing her words. It was the way they all talked between themselves in her family. But, in spite of the adventurous life he had led, her husband was singularly full of inhibitions, and his obvious embarrassment made her feel crude. "Though, after all," she thought in exasperation, "bed is the only place in which he ever bothers to see me alone. And even that he probably looks upon as part of his state duties."

Seeing that she was really upset, he came and sat down beside her. "Marriages like ours are—only arranged," he reminded her patiently.

Obviously he could not comprehend the cause of her anger; but he looked thoughtful and considerate, and perhaps a trifle forlorn himself. "Of course you are right, and I have probably been foolish to expect—whatever I did expect," agreed Elizabeth, sniffing a little and absent-mindedly arranging his damp handkerchief in a square across her drawn-up knees. It was hard to admit that perhaps all that hopeful, rosy haze of romancing might have been on her side only. That while she was thinking of the all-important invasion in terms of rescuing knights and grateful meetings he had probably been thinking only about transport and supplies. Hard; but, after all, quite reasonable. And even after his arrival, while she had been eating her heart out impatiently and filling in time at Westminster, she knew that Henry had been busy establishing himself securely and making so many wise plans for the country that it had probably seemed to him no time at all.

"You are not imagining, are you, that I married you only because the Commons pressed me to it?" he said. "Had I wanted an excuse to delay our wedding still longer there was the sweating sickness in London; but, as you know, I disregarded it."

There was no gainsaying his argument, and the sweating sickness had been so bad that even her own mother had wanted the ceremony postponed because of the swift contagion. Elizabeth had found him to be one of the least pretentious of men, but was beginning to understand how extremely touchy he was about his own rights and capabilities. "I do not let other people move me," he went on explaining rather unnecessarily. "I do whatever I have planned neither sooner nor later than I have planned to do it."

"Like God Almighty!" thought Elizabeth irreverently; but, realizing once again that her spontaneous reactions were more worthy of her unregenerate young brother Dickon than of a Queen, she managed to answer with a suitable mixture of dignity and wifely submission. "I understand perfectly your reason for wanting to be crowned first, and I pray that our 'arranged' marriage, which was so necessary to your plans, has not proved too distasteful. We are neither of us children, and you have lived precariously abroad. Both of us have had ample time to meet and care for someone whom we might have *preferred* to marry." She was delighted to see how sharply and searchingly he looked up at her unexpected words, and forestalled him with any questioning there might be. "Has it been more difficult for you, Henry, because you were once in love with Maude Herbert?"

"How did you hear of that?" he asked, shaken out of his usual complacency.

"Your mother told me how kind Lord and Lady Herbert were to you when you were my father's prisoner in Pembroke Castle, and that you two were friends. But since you were little more than a lad when your uncle took you away to Brittany I hoped that you might have forgotten her."

An almost boyish smile curved Henry of Richmond's thin mouth. "You don't suppose that I submitted to exile as tamely as that, do you?" he said. "Your father and that war-mongering uncle of yours would probably have worried themselves into yet earlier graves had they known I was back home in Wales!"

"You were in Wales?" Elizabeth leaned forward, watching him. Watching the intrepid young Earl of Richmond he must have been. She was seeing him as a new person, and he had never interested her so much.

"More than once. Keeping my place warm against my return," he laughed shortly.

"And meeting Maude?" Somehow, because of his venturesomeness, she minded much more now about the Yorkist Governor of Pembroke's pretty daughter.

"Naturally, I went secretly to Pembroke. She and I had been used to ride and read together in the old days. Lady Herbert would have been glad for us to marry. But then your father saw fit to give her in marriage to Percy of Northumberland—" Henry, who was usually so precise, left his sentence unfinished and wandered away towards the window.

"Then you really loved her," said Elizabeth, regarding him with pity.

But he only shrugged and began collecting up some papers and hunting for a private notebook which he always seemed to carry somewhere about him, and Elizabeth began to fear that she would never really know.

"I suppose I did," he admitted, having found the precious notebook. "We lived in a fantasy of Celtic dreams. But as one knocks about the world one grows out of such things."

"Does one?" murmured Elizabeth softly, thinking of her Uncle Richard's lasting love for the Earl of Warwick's little daughter, who had befriended him in similar circumstances. "And more recently perhaps," she suggested, "you hoped to marry the Duke of Brittany's daughter, and that is why you regret—"

"My dear Elizabeth, I regret nothing," broke in Henry. He had already wasted much time and even *his* exemplary patience was wearing thin. "Why *should* I have wanted the woman? She is not half so beautiful as you. I meant to marry you, and I have." Merely by speaking so emphatically he kindled a glow of expectant happiness in his disappointed bride, only to damp it out again by adding as he turned away, "Besides, England is more important."

Elizabeth tried not to hate him for his calculating coldness. Probably when a man is cast out of his inheritance and forced to accept hospitality from foreign princes who would sell him at any moment that it suited them, she thought, the one thing he needs to acquire *is* calculating coldness. She tried to imagine Henry when he was very young, misfortunate and full of dreams. Before anxiety had etched lines prematurely upon his face or thinned his straight, brown hair. He could have been quite attractive then, she decided. And he was not much older now. Margaret Beaufort, she was sure, would not purposely have deceived her by overrating him. That was the way she, his mother, remembered him—as a fatherless, hardy and intelligent boy—and probably part of the way in which she thought of him now. For Henry always showed his mother a dutiful affection, freely acknowledging all that he owed to her; and one was so apt to think of people long beloved as a compound of their living selves and of all one's memories of the years that made them. She, his wife, must try to remember how considerate he had been to her and to all her family in material ways, and to hope that, once surrounded by security and love, all his carefully built barriers of coldness would gradually melt away. She must try to talk to him naturally, ignoring the difference of their ways.

"There is one thing I have been wanting to ask you, Henry," she felt emboldened to say before he left her.

"Yes?" he said, with a hand already on the bolt of the bedchamber door.

"It is about my uncle," began Elizabeth, not venturing to look at him. "They tell me the Grey Friars took up his—mangled body. He was your enemy, but he fought courageously—"

"And very nearly killed me," agreed Henry. He did not sound at all angry, so she need not have been afraid. Yet, without realizing that she did so, she began twisting his long-suffering handkerchief into tortured knots. "Will you not—could you not of your triumphant magnanimity—have him buried somewhere as befits—his blood?" she begged.

"His friends have leave to purchase a suitable tomb for him in Leicester," Richard's successor told her without any particular emotion. All her life, weathering the seas of adversity and joy, Elizabeth had been surrounded by warm family affection, and the complete detachment of his answer made her feel like a shipwrecked soul cast up upon some strange and inhospitable coast.

The industrious new King closed the door with relief upon her wifely probings and hurried away to his absorbing work. He thanked

God—and the admirable forbearance of Henry Tudor—that he had not lost his temper, or struck her or even rebuffed her for her feminine curiosity and her extraordinarily tactless demand. He had done none of these things, nor had he the least glimmering of an idea how much an honest display of feeling and a real, outspoken quarrel might have cleared the matrimonial air.

And as soon as the door closed against him, Elizabeth, his frustrated wife, buried her face against the grand Tudor rose embroidered on her pillow and wept hopelessly. "A man who is incapable of hate," she sobbed aloud, "may be incapable of love!"

Chapter Eighteen

EVERYONE SAID THAT IT was owing to the new King's clemency that Lord Lovell, the sole survivor of Richard Plantagenet's last charge, was back at Court. Still pale from his wounds and limping a little, he waylaid Cicely on her way to Mass. "Is it really true about the Queen?" he asked eagerly.

Having lost her adolescent plumpness, Cicely now bade fair to be the beauty of the family. She was soon to be the bride of Lord Welles and felt herself to be a grown woman of consequence. "Is what true, milord?" she enquired negligently, although perfectly well aware of the latest spate of Court gossip.

"That her Grace is with child—already?"

Cicely's own excitement over the prospect of becoming an aunt was so great, and Lovell's battle record so romantic, that her spurious hauteur soon vanished. "You should know by now, milord, that my brother-in-law the King is competent in all things," she told him, with mischievous blue eyes demurely downcast.

"I do—to my cost!" grinned Lovell, glancing ruefully at his bandaged sword arm. "And I know, too, that you are an enchanting hussy and Welles a fortunate man. But I thank God indeed for this news, Lady Cicely," he went on with a new seriousness which became him, "and so must every man who has the welfare of the country at heart. Without this future fusing of our interests in a living heir, all that we have fought for, on either side, might well have been in vain and all to do again, drenching the land in yet more bitter hatreds and bloodsheds, I pray you suit your gay steps to my wretched limp, sweet lady, and let us go into chapel and thank God together."

"And ask Him particularly to take care of my darling Bess," added Cicely softly, slipping a helpful hand beneath his uninjured arm. Like herself, he had been caught young in this maze of divided loyalties but, whichever side he had fought on, his affection for her family and the Yorkist cause was beyond dispute, so that she answered his questions about the Queen's health with a good heart. "She is often sick on wakening, which is but to be expected," she told him, assuming the matronly air of one soon to be married herself. "But, oh, Lord Lovell, there is a brightness in her eyes which has not been there since our brothers—died. She sits dreaming as she used to do, and then her lips begin to smile tenderly. Our Bess looks just like the Madonna in the Palace Chapel when she smiles that way!"

"Shall we see her there this morning?"

"No, they are in the private apartments discussing it—she and the King and the Countess of Richmond," Cicely told him, nodding her pretty head in the direction of one of the Queen's rooms in passing.

"What is there to discuss?" he asked.

"Lord, how dense you men are!" jibed Cicely. "Where she is to *have* the baby, of course, and what physicians are to be in attendance, and who shall be asked to be godparents, and all manner of things!"

But behind the closed doors of the new Queen's apartments it was Henry the Seventh and his mother who were doing most of the discussing. Elizabeth, the mother-to-be, sat in a high-backed chair by the window, smiling at her thoughts in the way that Cicely had described; and most of the discussion flowed over her unheard. Their serious voices arranging a fitting setting for so important a national event and planning for her material needs were just a benevolent murmur filling the sunlit room. "I was so afraid it would never happen—because my husband does not love me," she was confiding to the Mother of the Christ Child. "Yet now, before

Lent—why, it could not have begun sooner!" While the two Tudor voices rambled on, Elizabeth seemed to be wrapped apart in the haze of sunlight from the window. "I hope he will look like Dickon," she thought, certain in her happiness that her firstborn would be a boy. "Dear God, let him look just like a little Dickon—and I would not mind what I suffer or where they arrange for me to be. Almost, I could wish it to happen in a stable…Always, because of such consolation, I will strive to be humble and reverent…"

She became aware that her companions had risen from their chairs and that Henry was kindly motioning her to remain seated. "I shall leave the entire arrangements for the *accouchement* to you, Madam, since you must be more *au fait* with such feminine affairs than I," he was saying to his mother.

"And so the whole Court will move to Winchester," Margaret of Richmond answered on a note of triumphant finality.

"Why Winchester?" asked Elizabeth, coming out of her reverie.

Henry blinked at her in surprise—and disapproval. "Because my ancestor King Arthur is said to have been born there. And my Welsh heralds have just proved that my lineage goes back to the great British King Cadwallader. And by associating the birth of our son with Winchester I wish to impress these facts upon my people. Have you not been listening?"

Elizabeth's apologetic glance passed appealingly to her mother-in-law, who, as usual, understood. "I think our Bess is so over-come by her good fortune in bringing you an heir, Henry, that it is difficult for her to take in anything else," she explained, with an invaluable blend of her son's calm efficiency and her own saintly gentleness. "I shall stay with you, Elizabeth, so you do not need to worry your head about material details but can rest after all your vicissitudes and dream of this new comfort which is coming to your bereaved heart—and to our country. This is a consummation, my dear children, for which I have worked and prayed during most of my adult life."

And so by the time the Lent lilies had begun to rear their golden heads Westminster Palace was bustling with preparations for the journey down into Hampshire; and to her great delight

Elizabeth found that Henry had arranged for her mother and all the rest of her family to go with her. "All but poor Warwick," she remembered, when thanking him.

"A complete change of environment will be good for you. You have suffered too much in London," said Henry, although she knew that that was not the reason why he was sending her.

"And may not Warwick come too?" she asked, less because she wanted her poor witless cousin than because she hated the thought of his being lonely.

"I am afraid not," said Henry, intent upon a map he was unrolling.

"Why must you keep him in the Tower? What has he ever done?" she persisted, remembering how kind Anne Neville had been to the lad when she was Queen.

"It is not what he has done but who he is," answered Henry, leaning over the spread map to trace a route from town to town with a scholarly-looking forefinger. "Although your Uncle Clarence was so justly attainted of treason to your father, his son is still a potential source of trouble from my enemies."

"Yet Richard let him be about the Court," she said. But either Richard must have had less to fear from Warwick's better claim or else he loved his wife sufficiently to take a considerable risk in order to please her. And obviously Henry—for all his vaunted lineage—was taking no more risks than he could help for anybody.

"Does it concern you so much whether that good-looking nitwit comes or goes," he asked aggrievedly, "since *I* shall not be there?"

"*You* will not be there?" exclaimed Elizabeth, forgetting all about dead Clarence's son. "But I had taken it for granted—"

"Oh, I shall be back in Winchester before our son is born," Henry assured her, smiling at the happy thought. "But first I must go on a circuit up north. The security of the realm demands it."

Elizabeth moved closer to the table where he stood and for the first time looked down attentively at the place where his finger still rested. "Surely you do not mean that you will be going into— Yorkshire?" she said aghast.

"Among other counties, yes," he said, carefully placing a book and an inkhorn so as to prevent the parchment from rolling back.

Elizabeth looked up at his clever, preoccupied face. "But, Henry, you dare not!" she said, almost in a whisper.

"Dare not?" he repeated, straightening himself.

His voice was so calm that she felt she ought to warn him. "You are so lately come from abroad...I mean, perhaps you do not realize how particularly Yorkshire is the white-rose county. If you knew the passionate love they have for us—for Richard—and now for me..." she blundered, in genuine anxiety.

But Henry was so self-sufficient and always seemed to know all that was needful. "It is certainly unfortunate that you cannot come with me, since I make no doubt most of the people love you," he said politely. "But you will be doing me a far greater service by conserving your strength in Winchester."

He was not the kind of man whom women touched uninvited, but Elizabeth raised impulsive hands to his shoulders. Was he not her husband—the father of her unborn child—and courting very real danger? "Let me come, Henry!" she urged. "I am young and strong. I shall not mind the journey. And you do not know the temper of the Yorkists since you delayed so long to marry me and—and have not had me crowned. To them—crowned or uncrowned—I am Queen of England, and if I am there beside you, honoured as your wife, you will be safe."

Had Elizabeth not seen those white, scholarly hands of his clench in anger she would have been deceived by the evenness of his voice. "So you resent it that you have not been crowned?" he asked coldly.

She looked back fearlessly into his small, light eyes. "Whether I resent it or not, it cannot alter the fact that I am Edward the Fourth's eldest living child," she said steadily. "But I spoke only for your safety."

He had the grace to look shiftily aside. "It is quite impossible for you to come, Elizabeth; particularly as I already know that there will be trouble in certain towns. But do not disturb yourself. I shall go prepared." He spoke gently, appreciatively; but because he made no responsive movement her hands had slid foolishly, emptily, from the sober velvet of his doublet to her sides.

"What trouble?" she asked passively, quite certain by now that the troublemakers would come off worst.

As if moved by the quiet intimacy of the moment he answered her with unwonted candour. "As you so frequently suggest, my claim to the throne is not too immaculate," he admitted, with a shrug. "So I must expect trouble. Probably as long as Warwick or any other Plantagenet scion lives there will be plottings and pretenders."

Elizabeth searched his inscrutable face, and when she spoke her words were scarcely above a whisper. "But you would not—put him to death—like—like my brothers?"

Henry's thin lips smiled. "No," he said. "I am no murderer."

A sigh of relief escaped her. Had he not already proved himself magnanimous about Lord Lovell? In her gratitude for such new security Elizabeth would have liked to throw her arms about him and to infuse some warmth into their relationship; but he just stood there, with only civility preventing his attention from returning to his map. "I shall miss you—and pray for you," she said instead, schooling her warm heart to indifference and drawing a more suitably dignity about her.

"Yes, pray for me," he said, gratefully, apparently attaching more importance to her devotions than to her caresses.

Piqued, Elizabeth decided that, whatever the hazard of his enterprise, he could not depart soon enough; but when she saw the preparations for his departure she was secretly shocked. Plenty of money had been spent upon arms and stores and everything that was necessary—but little upon pageantry. "You forget that I have taken over a bankrupt kingdom," he said, in answer to her protests. "Buying impressive new trappings would not help me to refill my empty coffers or make me any the more popular in the war-savaged towns I shall be passing through. I would rather be able to remit some of their taxes."

Elizabeth acknowledged his wisdom but remembered how Richard—with full coffers or empty—had always ridden forth in a blaze of heraldry. So had her father, and her family had always considered such splendour necessary to the prestige of their blood. And, woman-like, she let her tender heart yearn a little over her impecunious but practical husband, so that it drove her out into Goldsmiths' Row to empty her own slender purse in exchange for some of the brightest jewels she could find, and then prompted her to sit up late at night with Mattie, stitching them into a shining diadem with which to adorn the serviceable plainness of Henry Tudor's helmet.

But Henry had lived too long alone to have the happy knack of making a glad occasion of a fond surprise. "It is a gift you can ill afford, seeing all that your dowerless sisters cost you," he reminded her, bending so that she might set the sparkling helmet upon his head upon the spring morning of his departure. "And, for that matter, neither can I; but I will reimburse you for these jewels and tell Sir Richard Empson to arrange for you to draw on my estates should you need any money during my absence."

It was the farewell of a thrifty husband rather than of an eager bridegroom. Before the assembled company Elizabeth thanked him dutifully and bade him take every care for his safety. Once more the warm impulses of her nature had been repulsed. She was a woman who loved to give and Henry seemed to need nothing from her. Because marriage was still a novelty she watched him ride away from Westminster with regret; and yet—to her shame—was conscious of relief, since his absence left her freedom to be more herself.

"Of course it was foolish of me to spend so lavishly," she confided to Stafford's sister Jane, whom she had chosen as one of her ladies. "I should have realised that after so many years of civil war we must be poor."

"He need not have mentioned it just then, Madam," said Jane Stafford bluntly.

"And the money was your own," muttered Mattie.

"But how right his Grace was in saying that my private inheritance from the Clare estates does not go very far between all of us!" sighed Elizabeth, who could not resist buying her sisters pretty things for their approaching marriages or her mother occasional presents for her special comfort. "From now on I am going to try to live 'out of my own,' as those unpleasant councillors, Empson and Dudley, are always saying. After all, my husband set me a fine example, spending less on the splendour of his coronation and more on pastimes for the people. He means to do such fine things for the country, and if I can help him over the first lean years it will be my share towards it. Only I wish someone had taught me how to economize!"

"You have never been really extravagant, Madam," expostulated old Mattie.

"Not to our way of thinking, dear Mattie. But then poverty is so relative. If I say that I will have my miniver cape turned instead of buying a new one for next winter, one must remember that most people do not possess any miniver at all."

"Perhaps they do not need it, being much less gazed upon!" laughed Jane Stafford.

"Well, anyhow, while I am waiting for my baby we will go over my wardrobe and see in what ways I can retrench," decided Elizabeth. "There is that crimson velvet of mine which has much wear in it, Mattie. I will have the tailor turn it. And I need not order so many caps. After all, I shall not be going out in public."

And so the busy days of preparation passed and Elizabeth was glad to find herself established in the sweetness of the country. The old palace of Winchester delighted her, and because it was summertime she scarcely noticed its draughts and inconveniences. She wrote frequently to her husband and thought the more of him because he had not excused himself from the danger of going north, and was amazed and not a little awed to hear how easily he had managed to quell all Yorkist hostility as he went and how he had finally been received without any outward show of resistance from the citizens of York. "We found every other inn had the sign of the white boar," he wrote pleasantly, "but they are all magically become blue boars now."

"When he comes back we shall have so much to talk about," Elizabeth thought, still hopefully envisaging that complete union of marriage which had so far eluded them.

But after Henry's triumphant return to London so many pressing affairs detained him that he did not reach Winchester until after the date upon which the strict etiquette upon which her mother-in-law was such an authority decreed that she should take to her room.

For days workmen had been stripping the worn old arras from the walls and replacing it with fresh tapestry embroidered only with flowers. There must be no scenes depicted upon it at all, lest the sight of lifelike human figures or animals in the chase should frighten her or make some bad impression upon her unborn child. Even the windows had been draped, except for one near the great fourposter bed from which she could look over the old cathedral town and the green Hampshire hills. And when all the preparations had been made according to the Countess of Richmond's instructions, the lords and officers of the Queen's household escorted Elizabeth to the door and there bade her farewell, passing over to her women their various duties so that, save for her physicians, she would see no man until the day of her deliverance in October.

Elizabeth, who loved the outdoor world, looked out upon the beech trees, wishing that they would begin to turn russet to their fall. Without her lively sisters the time might have dragged indeed; but, after all, it seemed to pass quickly, for towards the end of September, a month before such glad news was expected, the bells of Winchester Cathedral rang out and Elizabeth's son was born.

"The bells will soon be ringing all over England," she thought, "more gratefully perhaps than for any other prince!" And lying there, worn out and content, she knew that for so general a benison all her own personal griefs and strivings and disappointment had been worth while.

While her tired eyes were yet closed she could hear, more exciting even than the bells, the commotion of horses being brought out and messengers riding off to London with the news; and then someone was holding a cup of hot broth to her lips and Mattie was bending over her with a bundle in her arms, showing her her son.

"You have been wonderfully brave, my Bess," her mother was whispering, kissing her forehead with a new gentleness.

And from somewhere a little further off Margaret of Richmond's voice was saying, "Someone has gone to tell the King. He is out hunting. We did not expect this joy so soon, but he will be back soon."

And Elizabeth had lain there, thanking God. She was glad, of course, that at last she had been allowed to give Henry something; but she did not really mind how long he was coming. It was so much like Heaven lying there out of pain, and her mother had drawn the bed-curtain a little so that she could watch the tiny red-faced creature yelling lusty protest to the proddings of the doctors.

And when the door was flung wide and the King had come home from hunting, his eyes went straight to that same precious bundle, now lying contentedly in Mattie's lap before the fire, and in his eyes there had been the brightness of a man who sees the final seal set upon some hazardous task. "If I can ever hope to see Henry Tudor show emotion, I must look for it now," thought Elizabeth, watching him stand there, rubbing his hands together, with his mother beside him.

"Although so premature, the physicians say that he is a healthy child. We shall have to arrange for the christening in Westminster," Margaret was saying.

"Yes," agreed Henry. And then, tearing himself away from the new wonder of his heir, he had come briskly to Elizabeth's bedside. "And afterwards, in London, for my wife's coronation," he said, lifting her limp hand from the coverlet and kissing it.

"He is a just man who pays his debts, but very cautious," whispered some devil in Elizabeth's tired mind. "No heir—no coronation." And the ridiculous words kept repeating themselves in her bemused mind until, in the middle of whatever he was telling her, she forgot he was there and fell fast asleep.

Next morning, when she woke slowly and deliciously to a realization that she had a son and that her slender body was her own again, her sisters were gathered in her room. Elizabeth's glance went straight to the hearth, and there, sure enough, was small Katherine solemnly rocking the carved wooden cradle and dumpling little Bridget staring round-eyed at its sleeping occupant.

"Darling Bess!" cried Cicely, the moment Elizabeth stirred. "You have slept such a long time. Are you better?"

"Quite better," smiled Elizabeth. "Where is the Countess?"

"Resting," said Ann, perching herself on the other side of the great bed. "She has to rest some time."

Their glances met in understanding laughter. "My mother-in-law is kindness itself," murmured Elizabeth lazily. "But this is like being at home again. If only Ned and Dickon could be..."

"Is the King pleased?" asked Cicely quickly, seeing the tears gathering in her eyes.

"Enormously," said Elizabeth, blinking them away. "Tell someone to draw all the curtains and let in the lovely sunlight."

"There go the bells again," said Cicely, helping herself to some of the fine grapes the King had sent. "There's to be such a grand christening in the cathedral, and the Bishop and all the Chapter are scurrying about getting out their best vestments."

"I suppose the King's mother is arranging all that too," grimaced Ann. "Who is to be the precious poppet's godfather?"

"Milord Stanley says it will be the Earl of Oxford," said Cicely. "But he is so fat!"

"He may be quite kind," smiled Elizabeth.

"And the godmother?"

"Months ago, when I first knew that I was going to have a baby, I specially asked that our mother might be."

"Oh, I am so glad!" cried both girls in unison.

"She is ageing so, don't you think?" said Elizabeth. "And I was afraid she would feel hurt if Henry asked his own mother."

Katherine, gently removed by watchful Mattie from a self-appointed rocking task which was becoming too vigorous, came across the room to join them. "He is a lovely baby, Bess," she said. "But are you sure he is ours?"

"Of course. He is Bess's," they laughed. "Why not?"

"Then why," she asked earnestly, staring very hard at each of their heads in turn, "does he have brown hair?"

Elizabeth stretched out a hand and drew her small sister close until her inquisitive little snub of a nose was on a level with the grand rose-embroidered coverlet. She had noticed the same thing herself and felt that God had not, after all, bade her baby look much like Dickon. "His father, the King, has brown hair," she explained.

"Does he belong to the King too?" persisted Katherine.

"Of course, stupid!" said Ann.

"Then will he be called Henry?"

"No, my poppet, I do not think so," said Elizabeth, who had expected that too.

"Not Henry?" exclaimed the two older girls. "What *will* he be called, then?"

Elizabeth raised herself a little on her pillows. "I have just remembered what the King was saying—before I fell asleep. It was about our baby's name. He wants him to be called Arthur."

There was an amazed silence in the room. Even her busy bedchamber women stopped whatever they happened to be doing. "But we never *knew* an Arthur," objected Ann, voicing the thoughts of all of them.

"No," said the infant's disappointed mother.

"Then why… ?"

"Because of his ancestor—who lived here. Good King Arthur, who had a round table for his knights. Oh, you must *know*," went on Elizabeth, speaking a little impatiently because she was still weak and quite as amazed as they were. "There are all his fiery Pendragon banners and his Welsh ancestry—right back to the earliest Kings—"

"All right, poor sweet. Rest again and don't try to talk any more now. I don't suppose you like the name any more than we do," soothed Ann, bringing the rose-water to bathe Elizabeth's forehead.

But Cicely, snipping off another grape, suddenly began to giggle. "Well, at least Bess can count herself fortunate," she remarked disrespectfully, "that he didn't take it into his head to call the poor child Cadwallader!"

Chapter Nineteen

WHEN ELIZABETH TOOK UP residence at Sheen, that loveliest of places beside the gently flowing Thames, she
felt in her adaptable way that here at last was going to
be her married home. Henry had practically rebuilt the old palace
so that it was gay with walled gardens and turrets and large latticed
windows gleaming in the sun, and he and his mother loved it
better than any mansion they possessed. They renamed it with
their own family name of Richmond. "Here I will pass my days and
rear my children," thought Elizabeth, "after I have been to London
for my coronation."

But, for all his fine promise, Henry had done nothing about
her coronation. At first it had been impossible because she had
suffered from a distressing ague after her baby's birth—an ague
which had so undermined her health that she had been obliged to
linger a long time in the old town of Winchester, and had finally
had a chapel built in the cathedral there as a thank-offering for
her recovery. But by now it was high summer and she only a few
miles from London, and all her Yorkist friends began to mutter
angrily in secret corners about the Lancastrian King. Particularly
Dorset and Lovell and her cousin the gifted young Earl of Lincoln,
who—being son to one of Edward the Fourth's sisters—had been
considered heir presumptive until little Arthur Tudor was born.
And Elizabeth's mother grew dangerously indignant, lashing out
with her sharp tongue against Henry as she used to against Richard

and imprudently inveigling sympathizers to discuss his shortcomings in the pleasant apartments which he had provided for her.

"I pray that she will not begin her meddling again!" sighed Elizabeth anxiously, in the privacy of her own room.

"Do not worry about the sharp things she says, for she has no power now," soothed Cicely. "There is nothing she can *do*."

"Not personally," agreed Elizabeth. "But, all the same, I do not like the way Dorset and Cousin Lincoln keep bringing their friends to talk in her room whenever Henry is called away on state affairs to Westminster. And Henry has been away so much of late."

"It must be because of this young man in Ireland," said privileged Jane Stafford, who heard much outside news from her brother.

"What young man?" asked Elizabeth.

"The one all this pother is about," said Jane, inconsequently, supposing that the two Yorkist sisters knew all about it.

"What pother? And who *is* he, Jane?" persisted Cicely.

"That is what we should all like to know, Madam," began Jane blithely, preoccupied with setting out the Queen's embroidery silks. "At first it was believed that he was the young Duke Richard of York who—" Cicely's foot came down so heavily upon hers that she stopped short and blushed for her stupidity. "But now everyone says he is your Grace's cousin, the Earl of Warwick," she concluded hurriedly.

There was an awkward pause during which neither of them dared to look round at the Queen, upon whose face wild hopes and painful distress were gradually blotted out by bewilderment.

"But our cousin is in the Tower," said Cicely.

"He could have escaped," said the Stafford girl, mulish in her embarrassment.

"Escaped—from the Tower!" said Elizabeth, trying to laugh about it. "Come, come, Jane! Once the great Byward Gate or the moat portcullis had closed upon him even the wiliest of men could scarcely hope to do that. And surely nobody in their senses would believe that so simple a soul as Warwick, who is quite honourably treated here, could effect a journey to Ireland without the King's permission."

But it appeared that a great many people did. Perhaps only because they wanted to—or because the white rose was rooted so firmly in their hearts. All over the country there were chatalaines of manors who, symbolically, would not grow a red rose in their gardens. In spite of Henry's businesslike management of the country, they still wanted to have back the squandering charm of a Yorkist King. "Henry said there were bound to be pretenders," said his wife, moving with dignity to her embroidery frame. She longed to ask how much he knew of the matter, but, since he had not mentioned it to her, was far too proud to seek information from a chatterbox like Jane.

Instead she went to her mother, whose interest should run closest with her own. "There can be no truth, you think, in this rumour about Dickon being alive—" she began, having thought of nothing else since Jane's thoughtless words.

"None whatever," said the Queen Dowager, who never had believed for a moment in the ever-recurring rumours that one of her sons had been spared. "It is Warwick the young man pretends to be. And if his imposture does nothing else, it should at least make that secretive husband of yours show his hand. None of us has seen young Edward of Warwick for weeks. It is my belief that Henry is no better than your uncle and has probably had him murdered as your brothers were!"

"I am sure that he would not do such a thing," remonstrated Elizabeth in great distress. "Henry is too—civilized."

"Too cautious, possible," shrugged the Queen Dowager. "Does he suspect Dorset of being in this thing?"

Seeing the anxiety in her mother's shrewd, dark eyes, Elizabeth was more convinced than ever that they both were. "He has never mentioned the matter," she said coldly.

"Not mentioned the matter? To his own wife! Not even in the warmth of your own bed! And this play-acting upstart already crowned King in Dublin!" the Woodville woman railed disgustedly. "No wonder you cannot even get him to crown you!"

Angry and mortified herself, Elizabeth determined to force her husband's confidence. Hearing from Lord Stanley that Henry had been reviewing troops on Blackheath, she went down to the water-steps to meet him on his return. "Is it because Warwick has been crowned in Ireland that you are raising an army?" she surprised him by asking as soon as he had stepped ashore.

Henry cast her a quick look of surprise—almost of dislike. Dislike for intruding upon his reserve, perhaps. "My Deputy there, the Earl of Kildare, has seen fit to go through some kind of blasphemous ceremony with a *counterfeit* Warwick," he said, and turned almost immediately to call a brief order to his bargemaster.

But Elizabeth was not to be shaken off. "You could have told me instead of leaving me to hear of it like any stall-keeper's wife in Eastcheap," she said, falling into step with him as he took the garden path to the Palace.

"Why worry you when you have not been well?" he countered.

"An ague of which I am almost cured!" scoffed Elizabeth. "Do you suppose it was less harmful to my spirits to hear of it from my waiting-women?"

"It is a lot of moonshine, anyway."

Elizabeth looked him up and down with irritating calmness. "Is that why you are wearing your armour?"

"I am arming to deal with men like Lovell and your half-brother, who have eaten my salt and who are now supporting him in this country with a horde of foreign mercenaries," snapped Henry, without slackening his pace. "And afterwards," he added, with a slow kind of relish, "I will have my treasurer deal with the woman whose fertile brain invented all this spiteful idiocy."

Elizabeth knew that he spoke of her mother, and probably with good reason. So she saved her breath to keep peace with him. But once inside the garden door she caught at his arm and detained him. "Who *is* this pretender?" she asked, still thinking of her lost brother and the long months of uncertainty.

Almost to her relief, Henry seemed in no doubt at all. "A young lad of fifteen called Lambert Simnel. The son of some well-to-do tradesman in Oxford. A baker, I believe."

"A baker's son—posing as a Plantagenet!"

"Oh, it is not the young fool's fault. I am all in favour of more learning for the masses, but his parents must have given him an education above his station. His tutor, a cunning and ambitious rogue, was probably bribed. Your aunt, Margaret of Burgundy, may even have had something to do with it. She appears to have loved your father so extravagantly that she would lay her hand to anything that might annoy me."

"And people are really so credulous—"

"It is amazing what they *will* believe. Even the Londoners are beginning to be hoaxed by it, judging by the glum looks I met. It seems that this Simnel is upstanding and fair-haired like your family. Naturally, my enemies would have chosen such a lad!"

"The impertinence!" sympathized Elizabeth. "What will you do, Henry?"

"There is only one intelligent thing to do at the moment. Have the real Warwick brought here from the Tower, riding with an imposing retinue through the streets of London so that everyone may see him. And then, when the fraud is exposed, deal with his supporters who are crazy enough to try a landing in England."

Elizabeth looked at him with half-grudging admiration. Without ever trying to be spectacular, he was ever one to apply the simplest and most sensible remedies; and if for one moment she had disbelieved his assurances and suspected him of treating her cousin as King Richard had treated her brothers, she was ashamed.

As if almost guessing her thoughts, Henry turned back to her with a twisted kind of smile. "And I shall want you to meet him here and welcome him publicly. You, who have lived with him off and on since childhood," he said. "My subjects seem to find it difficult to believe that I do not murder people like my glamorous predecessor; but whatever *you* do or say they seem to believe in."

At Stoke, near Nottingham, Henry defeated his Yorkist enemies and crushed the Simnel plot. Using only the vanguard of his army, he outmanoeuvred them so that all their courage could not save them. The Earl of Lincoln, Lord Lovell, the Earl of Kildare and Martin Swart, who commanded their German mercenaries, all perished that day—only Dorset, who was preparing the way for them in London, persuaded the King of his innocence and escaped with a short imprisonment in the Tower. And Henry rode home more firmly established on the throne than ever; and almost casually, in his train, he brought Simon, the tutor-priest, and Lambert Simnel.

"What will you do with them?" asked Elizabeth, trying to divert attention from betrothed Cicely's uncontrollable tears for the twice-wasted gallantry of Francis Lovell.

Henry was a temperate eater, but after so much activity was enjoying his homecoming meal as much as any of them. "The priest will have to be imprisoned somewhere, of course," he said negligently, breaking a manchet of bread.

"Not hanged?" ejaculated Treasurer Empson, with disappointment.

"And Simnel himself?" asked Stanley.

Selecting a succulent chicken bone, Henry turned to smile at his wife. "You had better have him in your kitchens, my dear," he suggested. "Being a baker's son, he should be quite at home among the ovens."

There were men at the table who remembered his predecessor's summary way with traitors. They sat, knives suspended, and stared; and Cicely so far forgot herself as to burst into tears. "To think that men like Lincoln and Lovell should be k-killed," she stammered, "and this lout Simnel, who s-started it all, go free!"

Being in a good humour, Henry could afford to smile at another display of Plantagenet emotion. "Take heart, dear sister," he teased, his sharp eyes glancing down the long table to where she sat. "Lord Welles may not have so fine a leg, but his coffers are well filled, I assure you."

"I beg you to consider, Sir," expostulated Stanley, bringing him back to the matter in hand, "that Simnel had the effrontery to have himself proclaimed King."

"Then what good would it do, my dear Stanley, to make a martyr of him as well?" countered Henry pleasantly. "At the moment the Londoners must be feeling very foolish, and in that mood I am hoping they may lend me some more money."

"How right his Grace is!" laughed handsome Jasper Tudor, surveying his nephew with affectionate pride. "The sooner all this talk of pretenders is forgotten the better. There is something very apt about the turnspit idea, although we might all prefer to see Lambert Simnel hanged. And ridicule, I do assure you, is often a surer and swifter weapon than the sword." And because what the experienced, grey-haired Welsh chieftain said was usually worth listening to, no one discussed the matter at table any more.

But Elizabeth was more interested in the strange nature of her husband than in the fate of Simnel. "Do you really mean to make a turnspit of him?" she asked that night, when Henry came to her room.

"It should give the servants something to laugh at," he yawned, having none of the love for the common people that she had.

"And the real Warwick?"

"He can go back to the Tower to-morrow."

"And it really does not anger you that this baker's son dared to impersonate him?" she persisted, trying to understand him.

"As I told you before, it was not *his* idea," said Henry. "Probably he has no idea beyond food, and I have dealt with those who *had*— quite successfully. Really, Madam, I do not see why you should concern yourself with such carrion."

It exasperated her that he should call her Madam in the privacy of her own bedroom, and that he could neither love nor hate. Nor let anyone but his mother—and possibly that Morton man—look inside his thoughts. He would be called merciful over this rebellion business, she supposed; yet to be young and unprotected from ridicule was a cruel fate. Probably Henry would not show vengeance lest men guessed that he was afraid—that he knew the usurper's growing fear of anyone who had a better claim to the throne than himself, or who could make men believe they had. But whatever the cause, it was his uncaring mercy which was so much more terrible than rougher men's vengeance. Elizabeth knew herself to be no coward, and yet she was afraid of him. She had often stood up to Richard Plantagenet, with all his ruthlessness; but knew no way of defending herself against the impersonal civility of Henry Tudor.

Gradually, as the years passed, her resistance, her very personality, would be worn down. She, whose menfolk had had passion about them, wanted no man who yawned or called her Madam in her bed—and longed to have the right to tell him so. "I am his brood-mare, his chattel," she thought bitterly, submitting to his silent, businesslike embrace. "I who, by every Christian right, am Queen of England!"

In her chapel next morning Elizabeth confessed herself an undutiful wife and prayed anew for that humility which she had taken as her motto but which, alas, came so hardly to her. And later in the day she went to console her mother, who was wildly aggrieved because the King had cut down the allowance he made her. "The crown coffers were so emptied by war when he came," Elizabeth tried to explain loyally, "and the Commons would grant him only the half of what he asked—and then only as a loan."

"But it is so *unjust* when I did everything I could to help him against Richard!" complained her mother.

"And have of late been doing everything secretly to harm him!" flashed out Elizabeth, angered because her mother was still pretending innocence. "I do not think anyone can accuse Henry of being *unjust*," she added more gently, because the Queen Dowager had begun to cry. "It is probably *we* who have misjudged *him* by blaming him for delaying my coronation, when all the time he had this treacherous plot on his mind."

"That an ungrateful daughter of mine should speak to me so!" wailed the Woodville woman. "I wish this wretched Simnel were dead!"

"I daresay *he* does, too, by now!" said Elizabeth, returning to her apartments before her patience gave out.

And even there nobody seemed to be able to talk of anything else. "None of us has ever heard of a pretender being spared before," one of the Countess of Richmond's women was saying. "Anyone but our merciful Welsh King would have had him hanged, drawn and quartered by now!" And as Elizabeth passed close to two of her younger women, who had their heads too close together to notice her, she overheard one of them saying excitedly, "I peeped through one of the kitchen windows and saw him. They'd put a saucepan on his head and made him hold a poker for a sceptre. The poker was red hot, my dear…The head cook was letting people in from the street at a groat a time to look at him. You should have heard the other scullions hoot with laughter…"

Elizabeth passed on without even reproving their lapse from duty, but the painful picture stayed with her. It had sounded so like the guardroom torturing of the Christ. And this Simnel was of about the age her brothers would have been had they lived. It had even been supposed at first that he impersonated one of them, not Warwick. That thought and an uneasy sense of responsibility for what was happening among her own servants worried her all day. "I am going down to the kitchens," she announced towards evening, taking only two ladies with her. "And I will go in alone," she added, making them wait in the stone corridor outside.

In the main kitchen preparations were going on for supper, so that the cooks were all occupied, and at first the turnspits and scullions were too busy carrying crocks back and forth between the well and the great open fires to notice her. When the kitchen clerk came bowing and scraping from his little room she waved him aside. "Tell them to go on with their work," she said. "Which is the lad they call Lambert Simnel?"

A lonely figure bending before an open fire at the far end of the great vaulted room was pointed out to her. Clumsily and painstakingly, as though unaccustomed to the work, the unfortunate lad was turning a roasting pig before the blaze. His ostracism was patent and complete. "I will talk to him alone," said the Queen of England, lifting her skirts fastidiously to cross the brick floor.

Hearing someone approach, Simnel swung round defensively, lifting an arm to protect his head from the usual blow. His eyes were too reddened and bleared from the smoke to see her very clearly at first. Even his well-built body had been rendered ridiculous by giving him a kitchen smock which was far too small for him.

"Are you the tradesman's son who pretended to be an earl?" she asked.

"Yes, Madam," he answered, obviously wondering who she was.

"And now you are a turnspit?"

"By the King's grace," he said almost cheerfully.

"His Grace treated you better than you deserve."

"'Tis better than hanging. I did not want to die." The lad rubbed a hand across his aching eyes, leaving his face yet more smeared with soot. "I had no wish to harm him, Madam," he said, with uncowed independence. "I but did as my tutor bade me. I see now that it was wrong."

"It was very foolish," said Elizabeth, surveying his large hands and grease-smeared jerkin, and noticing for the first time the ugly bruise beneath his matted hair. In spite of the roaring fire, such rough clouts as he had hung damply to the strong muscles of his back, so she guessed that dishwater had recently been thrown over him.

"So you are content to work in the kitchens?" she said, with an effort to control her loathing of the way he stank.

"Grateful, my lady. Not content."

In spite of everything, there was a manliness about him, and apart from his broad country accent he spoke well.

"Are they—*very* unkind to you?" she asked gently.

It was then that he saw her for the first time as someone worship-fully beautiful. "I can fend for myself," he muttered awkwardly.

Because of the accessible humanity of her father, Elizabeth had had considerable contact with the cheerful courage of the people. Here, she thought, was the patient, unglamorous kind which had won fame for England at Crecy and Agincourt. And the thought passed through her mind, too, that probably Henry—who had passed this much-talked-of merciful sentence—would not even have recognized it. "What *would* content you?" she found herself asking, hating to waste a quality which she rated highly.

Warned by the smell of burning meat, Simnel gave the spit another turn. "I suppose they'd never let me go back home to Oxfordshire?" he said wistfully.

"I am afraid not," smiled Elizabeth.

He sighed and pushed back his grease-bespattered hair. For all her grand clothes, here was a lady one could tell things to, even if one hadn't much gift that way. "It's the open country—" he began diffidently. "Sometimes the other servants go out into the fields beyond the City walls—by the way these townsmen brag when they come back, it's mostly to tumble a wench, I reckon—saving your presence! But for me it'd be the space and the sky. And the clean smell of it. I hate this filth more than their fists." For the first time the tears welled in his eyes. "If I could only get outside these kitchens and hear the birds sing again—"

Elizabeth saw that his face beneath the dirt was fresh and ruddy, his mouth kind. "Do you love birds, then?" she asked.

"Yes, Madam. There's scarcely a call I can't imitate." His eagerness suddenly cooled to wonder. Perhaps he had become aware of the hushed servants staring from a respectful distance. "But why should the likes of you care? Who are you, Milady?"

"A woman who once had young brothers whom she loved," answered Elizabeth, her voice low and warm as it always was when she spoke of them. And as she spoke an idea was born. "Do you know anything about falcons, Simnel?"

"Well, not rightly," he admitted. "But back home I sometimes helped one of the Earl of Oxford's falconers clean their mews and in return he let me go along to watch them being trained. Once he let me carry his perch and unhood them. Quick to learn, he said I'd be. Their wings were so strong, and swift as lightning as they mounted!"

The lad's eagerness shone through his awkwardness and filth so that the Queen cared what became of him, and was angry with herself for caring. In her heart she knew that she had really come to this abominable place, as she would have gone down to hell, secretly hoping to see someone who faintly resembled Dickon. And this youth did not resemble him at all. Others might say easily, "He is upstanding and blue-eyed and fair"—but where was the slenderness, the grace? The gaiety and fine-bred intuition? She had ceased to listen to the turnspit's ramblings. "Do you know who this is?" she asked harshly, jerking from beneath the bosom of her gown an exquisitely painted miniature that hung about her neck upon a slender gold chain.

Startled by her seeming irrelevance, Simnel leaned forward to look at it. "I never saw the young gentleman before in my life," he affirmed.

"It is my brother, Richard Duke of York," she said, almost snatching it back from his gaze. "A pity, perhaps, that you did not see it before." Because this boy from Oxfordshire had convinced her that he was somebody with a decent personality she wanted to show him the enormity of the thing which he had done. "You are as much like a Plantagenet as that burnt pig there is like the sun!" she cried, raging at him out of the constant ache in her heart.

It was clear that he thought she had come to mock at him too, and by the stricken look on his face she saw that because of some worship that had grown in him the sudden disillusionment hurt more than all the cruelties he had endured. "But I will see what the King says about having you trained for falconry," she promised before she turned to leave him; and by the bemused way in which he stared and by the obsequiousness with which all the other servants made way for her she supposed that he must have guessed then who she was.

Whether it was the swaying of her emotions between pity and indignation or merely the smell of cooking, Elizabeth did not know; but back in her rooms she felt herself shaking with a return of the ague which she had supposed to be cured. Very sensibly she sat still for a while, quietly, in an anteroom by a favourite window which overlooked the peace of her herb garden, consciously trying to control the trembling of her hands as they lay idle in her lap. And as she sat there she wondered how she could have been so foolish as to have disturbed herself over a very ordinary young man caught in a clumsy fraud. He had nothing to do with the rich eventfulness of a life such as hers.

And all unexpectedly in the middle of such rare peace the great moment of her life was upon her.

The door of the anteroom was thrown wide for the King and he was standing there before her telling her that he had arranged Sunday, the twenty-fifth of November, for the date of her coronation.

The little room seemed suddenly to be full of important people with whom he had been arranging it, and judging by the pleased expressions of their faces Elizabeth suspected that they had used their utmost efforts to push him to this decision at last. Her good friend Stanley was positively beaming at her; Jasper Tudor, Earl of Pembroke, kissed both her hands; and even Bishop Morton's dark, secret face showed relief and satisfaction. "Henry and I have been two years married and I have given him a son, yet it takes a Yorkist conspiracy to convince him that it will be safer not to slight me any longer," thought Elizabeth involuntarily. She rose from her chair and made a deep obeisance to him and thanked him, trying to keep all signs of ague from her limbs and all trace of irony from her voice. Yet seeing the sheaves of notes in his secretary's hand and having to listen to the almost tediously careful arrangements which had been made, she came to the conclusion that Henry had intended to keep his promise, anyway.

"I have arranged for a procession through London, and my mother and I will watch your triumph from some window," he told her later, when at last they were alone. "You have waited with great patience, Elizabeth, and I want this to be your day."

Elizabeth looked up at him with a swift new hope of gladness in her heart. When he spoke appreciatively like that it was so easy to be beguiled into believing that he loved her; not merely that he was a just man, repaying her for producing an heir. "I shall love to ride through London, and be Queen," she said simply. "And I will try to make you proud of me."

"It should not be difficult, with your extraordinary beauty," he said, consulting his papers when most men would have been looking at her face. "And with the lavish sum of money I have set aside to spend on the pageantry."

It was unfortunate to mention money at such a moment, even though his early life may have taught him to count every florin. His wife's grateful radiance faded visibly, and as she stood watching him her thoughts strayed to her mother, that supreme opportunist who had always managed to advance some member of other of her grasping family upon each special occasion of her life—whether it were childbirth or crowning or merely her husband's latest infidelity. "Now is the moment to ask Henry for anything you want, Bess," she would almost certainly have whispered, had she been there.

But what was there to want, save what the irrevocability of Death had taken? Other women might ask for jewels; but jewels were cold comfort when all one longed for was the warm love of a man's heart.

"Is there anything that I can do for you?" asked Henry, as if reading the direction of her thoughts.

But really at that moment there was nothing that Elizabeth particularly wanted—which was, she supposed, the most subtle poverty of all. So, although it was to be her coronation gift, it was only a very small thing she asked for. Because she had always loved young people she suggested almost casually, "I would like that poor Simnel boy down in the kitchens to be transferred to the mews. He might, I imagine, be much happier with hawks than herded with pitiless humans."

If Henry felt surprise he did not make it manifest. The happiness of a baker's son was nothing to him. He did not even enquire whether she had ever seen Lambert Simnel, nor why she should make so strange and modest a request. "As you wish, my dear," he agreed. "I will have him apprenticed to my head falconer over at Charing."

Elizabeth saw him open one of his everlasting memorandum books and make a note of it, and was satisfied that he would keep his word. In her mind she saw also a pleasing vision of a clean and self-respecting young man standing beneath God's open sky again. And Henry—who had acquiesced so easily—saw, no doubt, another cheap opportunity of demonstrating Tudor clemency.

Chapter Twenty

For the long-looked-for coronation of the Queen all England seemed to be *en fête*. Elizabeth could have wished that it were summer-time; but mercifully the sun shone and, as Henry had promised, it was her day indeed. He had had her brought in the great state barge to London, with all her watermen wearing the new green livery with a great Tudor rose embroidered upon the breast of each. The whole width of the Thames had seemed alive with gaily decorated boats accompanying her. Young girls with flowing hair and white dresses leaned from a slender skiff to scatter red and white roses before the prow of her barge, and keeping pace with her a boatload of students from Lincoln's Inn made the air sweet with music; and for the delight of the spectators along the banks one barge was ingeniously converted into a dragon, copied from the proud Welsh emblem on the Tudor banners, which belched fire into the sparkling waters.

King Henry met her at the Tower. Even about that he had been considerate. Knowing her natural aversion to the place, he had satisfied convention by having her stop in the royal apartments there only long enough to rest and to refresh herself. "There will be so many people crowding about you and so much to do, taking a meal and changing for your procession through the streets, that you will scarcely have a moment to think of what may have happened here," he told her. And his words had proved true. Her thoughts had scarcely once strayed beyond the room in which they were dressing her. It was her day, and in a few minutes now she would be borne in a open litter beneath the gateway out into the City streets and in a glittering procession down the hill towards the Fleet Bridge, out through Lud Gate and along the Strand to Westminster.

"It seems incredible that after all that has happened to me I am still no more than twenty-two!" she said with awed excitement as her ladies set the final touches to her grandeur while Ditton, her youngest lady, knelt before her to hold her new glass mirror.

"A good thing you are reasonably tall to carry off the heaviness of this velvet!" laughed Ann Plantagenet, arranging the folds of ermine-trimmed crimson with clever fingers while Jane Stafford tied the heavy silken tasselled cords of it across the white damask of her gown.

"A good thing, too, that the King listened to the people's wishes and allowed your Grace to go to your coronation with your hair unbound, although you are no maid," said Mattie, who had brushed the gleaming mass of it until it outshone the golden circlet on her mistress's head and the caul of jewelled net with which they bound it.

Out in the November sunshine they seated her in a litter draped with a cloth of gold, and the bells of all the City churches rang out as her procession started. Before her rode her ladies on white palfreys, and stalwart knights of the Bath held a golden canopy above her. Immediately before her and heralding her approach, went Jasper Tudor on his charger—an ornament to any procession, as half the women said. The familiar streets were ablaze with colour, with richly woven tapestries hung from every house. And from every window—and even from roof-tops—smiling people waved, joining their cheers with those of the populace packed tightly in the cheering streets below. For Elizabeth their welcome was the best part of her day, for she sensed that it was neither curiosity nor subservience, such as both Richard and Henry had been given, which moved them, but a real loving welcome. They had known her since she was a child and were grateful for the assurance of peace which her marriage had brought them. However much she might have been called upon to pay for it in her private life, this union of red and white roses had at last enabled them to settle down to *their* lives, to their crafts and their sports and their love-making, in security. So Elizabeth, the first Tudor Queen, rode among them smiling, giving them that long dreamed-of blessing with all her heart.

As her glittering procession approached Westminster heralds sounded a fanfare which shrilled like silver against the deep-tongued clamour of the Abbey bells. In the stately beauty of Westminster Hall her ladies changed her crimson mantle for one of royal purple. Her mother-in-law followed behind her, and Cicely—pale and overawed for once—held up her train. In the sanctity of the Abbey itself mitred bishops and abbots, all in the rich colour of their vestments, awaited her. The Duke of Suffolk, her uncle by marriage—although still mourning the wasted death of his son Lincoln—was a resplendent figure bearing her sceptre; and handsome Jasper Tudor bore her crown. As Elizabeth went forward up the aisle the great west doors were closed behind her, shutting out the joyous abandon of the bells, and the swelling music of the organ took up their triumph in more solemn tones. All around was a galaxy of jewels and rich apparel, and a sea of expectant faces; and as she walked forward, head erect, Elizabeth was aware of Henry watching her from a curtained gallery which had been built beyond the pulpit. Enigmatic Henry, who, after two years' delay, was giving her a coronation so much grander than his own! Making a sign to Cicely to stop, Elizabeth pleased all beholders by sinking into a grateful and deferential curtsey before him, hoping that she had given him cause to be proud of her this day. Then, forgetting all earthly prides, she went straight on towards the waiting priests and the golden haze of tall wax candles and the blaze of gold plate upon the high altar; and all pomp and circumstance of the day was left behind her as she entered into the sacred hush of the sanctuary, to receive her crown from the hands of the beloved Bishop of Winchester and her dread responsibility from God.

After she came out from the Abbey there was a great feast at which all the highest in the land served her, and next morning

Henry joined her to hear Mass celebrated in St. Stephen's Chapel. For the first time she sat beneath a canopy of state as Queen of England; there were tournaments and masques, and in the evening the festivities came to an end with the splendid coronation ball to which her younger sisters had been looking forward for days. Never since her father's time had there been such gaiety in the Palace or such spontaneous joy outside in the streets, where the shopkeepers and their wives danced round the bonfires which their 'prentices had built. But the following day, to Elizabeth's delight, she and the King went quietly home to Greenwich and she was able to spend some hours with her year-old son.

Elizabeth was glowing with health and beauty. The excitement of the last three days was still upon her. She knew that she had been a success, and her sense of personal triumph made all things seem possible. And now for a while she and Henry would be at leisure and done with public ceremony. "To-night he will come to me and I will show him that I am grateful," she thought. "My foolish resentments will be gone and his bred-in-the-bone aversion towards us Yorkists will be wiped out. To-night our marriage will begin anew and be the satisfying thing of which I used to dream."

She had her women bathe her and comb out her wonderful hair and put on her new brocaded bed-gown of Tudor green which she had had made to please him; and then she sent them all away and went to her mirror. Studying her reflection by candlelight, she thanked God that she was desirable. And all that was warm and generous in her—all that aptitude for physical love which she had inherited from her father—was eager to find that completion which she desired and deserved in a marriage which had been so hazardous to come by. Somewhere in Henry must burn the poetic fires of his Celtic youth, and if only she could rouse them, she supposed with almost childlike simplicity, the happiness of both of them would be attained. And surely, surely, she thought, gazing at the reflected loveliness of her body, she could fail with no man this night!

But the evening wore on and Henry did not come. The tall candles began to gutter and burn down. And sitting in the gloaming staring at her untouched bed, Elizabeth—for no reason save that she was alone perhaps—began to think of his predecessor. Of how Richard's mocking touch had often stirred her pulses as her husband's never did. Of the strange attraction of his eyes, and of the effort it had needed not to yield to his advances. It was sin, of course. One of those shameful, half-committed sins which she had kept locked away in the back of her mind and never spoken of even to her confessor. And in the stillness of the shadowed room she could almost hear Richard's lazy, charming voice telling her that there were more subtle kinds of brutality which she might find out if she married someone else. The words had been meaningless then. But now, though Henry was no murderer, Elizabeth recognized their truth. There were brutalities of omission, committed week in, week out against a woman's happiness, which could be consistent with a man's self-righteousness and which called for no confession to any priest. It had been true, too, what Richard had said about the life of any woman who was his never lacking warmth or colour or kindness. There were some men, sensitive and imaginative, who saw to these things. But what would happen now—even if Henry came—save crude begetting, shorn of all thought for her? And, suddenly hungering unbearably for the precious trimmings of love, Elizabeth buried her hot cheeks in her hands, thankful that all the brave candles had at last burned themselves out.

Raging, she rose and paced her room, hands still pressed to cheeks; until, worn out with frustration—with all her warm urge to give thrust back upon itself—she threw herself across the bed-foot in the darkness, not even trying to stifle her sobs. It was so difficult to believe that there *was* no hope of married ecstasy—so humiliating to realize that with all her beauty it was beyond her womanly power to change this unsatisfactory mating. "If Henry comes a hundred times," she sobbed, "it will always be the same."

Next day Elizabeth was distrait and listless and her ladies attributed it to all the tiring ceremony of her coronation; but old Mattie, who had nursed her from childhood, knew that the newly crowned Queen had been weeping. "Shall I have the Prince brought?" she suggested, to cheer her.

But instead of nursing him Elizabeth only stood beside his cradle staring down at him while small Arthur, who was a solemn baby, stared unblinkingly back. "He is very like his father, do you not think Mattie?" she asked. "Do you suppose he will grow up like the King in nature?"

And Mattie, who had no book-learning, had looked into her mistress's face and read what was amiss. "His little Grace will be clever for his age," she said noncommittally. "But who can see into the future?"

"Perhaps that is God's supreme mercy," sighed Elizabeth, thinking of all the sorrows which had been hidden behind the door of her mother's marriage and deciding to risk Henry's displeasure and visit the Dowager Queen in her seclusion. Grief had once battered the Woodville woman into weeping on the floor in sanctuary, but it had never made her subservient.

And that night when Henry came to her room Elizabeth stood defensively outside the carved rail about their bed.

"I have been busy clearing up all the documents which have accumulated during your coronation, and last evening the French envoy stayed late," he stated briskly, as if excusing himself against her unexplained silence.

"And you still have the matter on your mind?" she said coolly.

"One does not want war with France."

Elizabeth watched him curiously. "Do you actually like fighting?" she asked.

"No," he laughed shortly. "And I cannot imagine how any civilized person can."

"My father and—my uncle—did."

He looked up at her uncertainly. "If you are comparing us to my disadvantage, I would remind you that I fight—and usually quite successfully—whenever I must," he reminded her coldly.

Elizabeth watched him lay aside the papers and the personal memorandum books which he seemed invariably to have with him, and the very way in which he arranged them infuriated her. "Do you ever do things—like the rest of us—just because you want to?" she asked, trying to keep the edge from her voice.

"For Kings it is not so easy as for—'the rest of us,'" he said, in those cultured sarcastic tones of his, and by the light of the bedside candle she could see his thin lips smiling complacently. "Perhaps it would be more correct to say that I often find pleasure in some of the things which I am called upon to do."

"Which things?" she asked, sincerely trying to understand him.

"Opening up new trade routes, for instance. Granting charters to merchants and helping to revive their shipbuilding industry as I have done at Bristol. And hearing all about strange, foreign countries."

"And seeing the things our seamen bring back."

"Yes. And talking to some of our City merchants at home. Some of them are remarkably shrewd men, and prosperous. Had I not been called upon to rule a country I think I could have quite enjoyed being a merchant and watching my affairs grow."

"And the money pouring into your coffers." For the life of her she could not help saying it.

Henry, in the act of taking off his bed-gown, looked sharply across the bed at her. But her face was expressionless, her eyes downcast. If he had suspected irony, he must have decided that he was mistaken. "Your room is chilly, Madam," he remarked, suddenly afflicted by that cold formality with which he invariably cloaked his embarrassment at those times when any woman would look for informality and warmth. "I pray you, let us get into bed."

Already he was standing within the rail of Elizabeth's curtained four-poster, taking off his slippers. Irrelevantly, resentfully she remembered how he always took time to place them neatly side by side. "I am a human being capable of passion and other men desire me to the point of distraction," she thought. "I will not be so coolly taken for granted—as a state duty or a habit!"

But first she must give him a chance—give both of them a chance. Plead with him and show him her heart. She came slowly to the other side of the bed, spreading out her upturned palms in a hopeless supplicating gesture above the turned-back sheet. "Henry, I would so willingly have given you everything. I am that kind of woman. Do you not realize it? Can you not understand?"

she pleaded, laying aside all her pride. "But there seems to be nothing you need. Nothing, that is to say, but what your mother and your clerks and a trollop could not supply you with. And it is hard to love someone who is so self-sufficient that he needs nothing at all."

Her lovely voice trailed away, defeated, because he just stood there with one elegant fur-lined slipper in his hand, staring at her. "Love—" he began; but Elizabeth never heard what he was going to say about that important subject, for the precise sound of the precious word on his lips struck her as so incongruous that she burst into idiotic little gales of laughter. "You don't even come to my bed because you want to, do you?" she challenged him across the place where he had lain with her in such complete silence. "You just make notes of when it will be convenient to come—in one of those h-horried little books of yours?" Trying ineffectually to stifle her merriment with one hand pressed against her mouth, she pointed shakily with the other towards his neatly piled documents. "When there is nothing more important to do or the F-french envoy has gone…"

Henry's slipper dropped smartly to the floor. "What more do you want of me?" he demanded, the angry colour mounting to his cheeks at last. "I have had you crowned, haven't I, and spent a mint of money on it?"

"Ye-yes, yes. It was w-wonderful," gasped Elizabeth, striving after her lost self-control.

"And I am not impotent, am I? I have given you a son, haven't I?"

"I had supposed—that it was I—" she countered, going off into another gale of laughter.

"Then what *is* it you complain of? And laugh about like— like that giggling young fool Cicely? Is it because I am neither a murderer nor a lecher, like the men in your own family?" If there was one thing the Tudor could not take it was ridicule. He thumped the great carved bed-post with his clenched fist. "What can you possibly have to complain of, Madam? Why, ever since the night of our marriage I have even been faithful to you!"

But Elizabeth was beyond reasoning. Born of an emotional race, she had suffered enough of that parsimony of demonstrative affection which starves a woman's body and warps her soul. Her husband might be the first Tudor King of England, but with all her inborn Plantagenet recklessness she gathered up his discarded bed-gown and bundled it back into his arms. "Then for God's sake go out and be unfaithful and come back human!" she cried out at him. "But not to-night!"

Chapter Twenty-One

NEXT DAY IT WAS not to her confessor but to Margaret of Richmond that Elizabeth went; for if anyone could judge of the provocation she had had or help her to understand Henry, surely it was his mother. "I sent him away. I denied my body to my own husband. Were I a mercer's wife and not a Queen I suppose he might have beaten me," she confessed bluntly, standing by the long oriel window in the beautiful austerity of Margaret's private room.

"But since you *are* a Queen—" submitted Margaret, bending over an exquisite altar cloth she was embroidering so as to hide a smile.

"It does not make my lack of wifely duty any the less."

"It is not so heinous, my dear. Even if Henry *were* a mercer I cannot imagine him being impatient about—whatever you did."

"That is just it," sighed Elizabeth, picking savagely at the silk cord of a crimson cushion lying on the window-seat. "Sometimes I wish he *would* beat me. Beat me or desire me. Or—or show *some* kind of emotion! I don't imagine he lacked ardour with that Herbert girl!"

"But this was a political marriage for the binding up of England's wounds—loving you both, I had hoped that it would turn out to be a love-match too." Margaret thrust her needle into the centre of a gold lily and let her lovely hands lie idly in her lap, giving the matter her full attention. "Henry does not show his feelings,

I know. Which is strange, considering the way his father loved me. And how his grandfather, Owen Tudor, must have swept King Henry the Fifth's little French widow Katherine off her feet—he being only her Master of Horse and she a Valois! So it would seem, perhaps because of the need of caution during his exile, that my son is scarcely a typical Tudor." After sitting for a while with a reminiscent smile illuminating the beauty of her face Margaret leaned forward and caught at her daughter-in-law's hand as she went pacing turbulently across the room. "But this I will tell you, child. Henry, of course, has said nothing of this matter to me; but I can see that he is hurt."

"I am truly sorry," said Elizabeth, looking down at her with deep affection. "If only because he is your son."

"You two are so different in nature that I think he finds you difficult to understand," sighed Margaret.

Elizabeth's blue eyes widened with surprise. "*I*, difficult! When even Cicely says I blurt out all I think?"

"And so embarrass him, perhaps. I wager, Bess, that he does not always understand how he offends."

"I will try to make amends," promised Elizabeth, without enthusiasm.

Margaret let go her hand to jerk forward a stool, and for a while they sat in silence, informally, each thinking in her different way about Henry. "Perhaps if you two were alone more often—if it were *he* who helped you to make all your decisions…" began the older woman thoughtfully. "If I were to go away for a while and stay in one of my manors or one of Stanley's, as I did before—"

But that was the last thing Elizabeth wanted. "Oh no!" she cried, laying a beseeching hand on Margaret's knee. "You have been so good to me. I know that I frequently see my own mother, but somehow she…" It was not easy to explain how the vagaries of Elizabeth Woodville could in time wear out the most patient of love, so her daughter did not finish the sentence. "I would not for worlds drive you away, Madam!"

"But you would not be driving me away," Margaret assured her pleasantly.

Elizabeth stared at her, remembering how Cicely and Ann always contended that she stole the place of their mother. "Do you mean—that you *want* to go?"

"It means a great deal to me seeing my son every day, after all those empty years."

"Of course. And your husband," prompted Elizabeth.

It was Margaret who now rose and wandered to the window. "Stanley is goodness itself to me, but it is a long time since we lived as husband and wife," she said, breaking a reserve which was as strong in her as in her son, although far less obvious. "You see—since you and I are exchanging confidences—I took a vow of chastity."

"You took a *vow*..." Elizabeth's gaze followed the gracious figure with the still youthful lines and prematurely greying hair. "Then no wonder you were not so shocked at me!"

"Oh, with my husband's consent, of course," explained Margaret lightly. "And not through any lack of dutiful feeling. It was at the time of the Buckingham rebellion. I felt it was not fair to endanger him because he let me help my son by a former marriage. And had it not been proven that we were no longer bedfellows King Richard might have found it difficult to believe milord Stanley ignorant of the plot."

"I don't think Richard ever trusted him, anyhow," said Elizabeth slowly. "But your absence may have saved his life." For a while the two women fell silent again until Elizabeth asked in bewilderment, "Do you really not like Court life, Madam? You, who so adorn it?"

"Were it not for Henry—"

"But all this is really more yours than his. You stood aside for him."

"England is not yet ready for a Queen regnant," said Margaret thoughtfully. "And I would sooner live quietly in a convent."

"You would make a lovely abbess! Looking like a stained-glass saint yet understanding the silliest peccadillo of your least-important novice!"

"That is the nicest tribute I have ever had," laughed Margaret Beaufort, turning to kiss her daughter-in-law. "But I have no vocation. Or perhaps I have been too much in love with life. I meant only that I often yearn for the peace and leisure to pursue those things which are of most value and which are so crowded out at Court. Such things as the fostering of learning and the contemplative life of the spirit."

"But you are so devout. And look how much you are doing in building colleges up at Oxford and Cambridge! And how you encourage Master Caxton with the printing of more and more books."

"I do not want the chance to learn to be locked only in our hands, but given freely to the people."

"Will it make them any easier to govern, do you suppose?" smiled the practical Queen.

"Perhaps not," agreed Margaret. "But they have a right to it. I am so proud that Henry is improving the conditions of the ordinary people."

"Only, I suspect, because it cuts down the power of the barons and makes him feel safer," smiled his wife. "Will he succeed as a ruler, do you suppose, Madam?"

"I am sure that he will," said the Countess. "You see, this Tudor dynasty of ours is starting with a new formula. Because Henry cannot rely upon having been born a King he is forced to make up for it by working harder than any of his subjects. Both Wales and England should benefit by this; and I, and many others who have striven to bring about this union of the Lancastrian and Yorkist branches, believe that it will give our country time to lick her wounds and live graciously. This was the dream for which poor Buckingham died. So I beseech you, dear Bess—even though you may derive no personal happiness from your marriage—to continue to see in it something more than the emotional satisfaction or dissatisfaction of two people. And, of your abounding generosity, I pray you pour into it all the patience and intelligence necessary to make at least a smooth outward symbol to the world."

When Elizabeth returned to her own apartments, full of good resolutions, she was greeted by gales of laughter and found to her relief that Henry had met her halfway in the matter of reconciliation. Although he may not have understood in the least how he had offended, he had sent her a peace-offering. A human peace-offering already surrounded approvingly by her laughing sisters. "In the pursuance of weightier matters I forgot that a Queen should have a jester," he had written in the letter which was handed to her. "And the bearer of this, although short of stature, has a large store of wit. Moreover, his Welsh heart is full of the music which you love."

Elizabeth accepted the gift, and the lack of rancour which it stood for, with alacrity. Already her rooms seemed full of laughter, and looking upon the small, misshapen fool she read a wealth of wisdom in his sad, simian eyes. "What shall we call you?" she asked, when he had sung to them of his native hills, plucking a wild sweetness from the strings of his beribboned lute.

"What but the Queen's fool, Madam?" he asked, squatting before her like a devoted dog.

"But he must have a real name!" insisted young Katherine, more delighted with his drollery than with his music. And the little man looked at his Queen with his big head on one side and said with all the liberty of inconsequent jesting, "Many's the lover sends a gift to his mistress to patch up a quarrel; and I, who wish you well, would be that patch."

"Then Patch you shall be," agreed Elizabeth, with a smile which sealed the beginning of a queer, enduring friendship.

And so Patch came into her household, teasing her ladies without malice and making absurd quips by day, and soothing her with his singing when she sat alone in the evenings waiting for her husband. And because a woman's senses may be starved and her body yet prove fertile, Elizabeth was soon able to promise Henry as *her* peace offering a second child.

"Let us hope it will be another boy," he said, kissing her gently.

"Yes, it would be greater charity to produce a son," she had agreed, "for at least they have the ruling of their lives." And he had looked at her uncertainly. She was always kind and dutiful these days, but often of late she had made odd, disconcerting remarks like that, and he had not known how to take them. But because, for all his studiousness, one of the few subjects he had not bothered to learn about was a woman's mind, Elizabeth was beginning to find that she could say them with impunity.

There was the same tedious etiquette of the lying-in chamber to be gone through, but this time Henry wanted her to stay at Westminster in order to appease the Londoners, who, it seemed, resented his heir having been born at Winchester. And whatever they wished for, this time the child was a girl. They called her Margaret after the King's mother, and upon this eldest daughter of his Henry came as near to lavishing affection as was in his nature.

These were the domestic years, with a growing nursery and a round of public royal duties.

There was the grand ceremony of the festival of the Order of the Garter to attend at Windsor, and all the excitement of her sisters' marriages, and—grandest of all perhaps—the marriage of her Aunt Katherine, Buckingham's widow, to the King's uncle Jasper. And it saddened Elizabeth a little when Henry proposed, for political reasons, to push Tom Stafford, who had loved her, into a union with the girl-heiress from Brittany. For everyone that summer seemed to be a season of marrying and giving in marriage. "Though for me," sighed Elizabeth, who so loved the sunshine and the countryside, "everything seems to happen in the winter! My marriage, my coronation—and even my babies."

But at last, in the midst of all the fullness of her life, there came a summer when her June baby was born at Greenwich. Born much more informally, in a room with windows open to the riverside gardens that she loved. He was lusty, good-tempered and a red-head, and from the moment old Mattie put him into her arms Elizabeth loved him with a delight which made all the disappointments of her marriage bearable.

"He might be one of us!" exclaimed Cicely, now a mother herself. "He does not look at all like the King."

"He is the adorable thing I have always wanted," said Elizabeth, holding him close. "You know, Cicely, I was ashamed to say so of so dear a son, but when they first showed me Arthur I was disappointed because he did not look at all like Ned or Dickon."

"This one may turn out a little like tall, handsome Ned," decided Cicely, reviewing the crumpled faced mite consideringly, "but he will be much bigger than either of them. Look at those limbs of his, Bess! Is it decided yet what they are going to christen him?"

"He is to be called after his father."

"How confusing!"

"It always is, but we can call him Harry," said his mother. "It is a jollier, more dashing sort of name, and somehow I think he looks like a Harry."

And because he was a second son Elizabeth was allowed to see more of him. While Arthur, the studious, was with his tutor, Bernard Andreas, at Croydon being taught all those grave things which were considered necessary for his future kingship, little Harry romped boisterously at Richmond or Greenwich and gurgled with laughter at the antics of Patch, who adored him—or, as he grew older, stood at his mother's knee listening attentively while she played upon her harp or her virginals. For even in the midst of his most exciting games the sound of music lured him, and as he grew older this formed a fresh bond between them. In the years to come Elizabeth was to remember with nostalgia all those care-free, homely hours. Looking back upon the days of Harry's childhood, it seemed to her, quite absurdly, that the sun must always have been shining then at Greenwich. And that, like most sunny days, they passed all too quickly.

For red-headed Harry was still only a toddler when Elizabeth first overheard someone talking about another mysterious young man in Ireland. Two clerks were loitering with their heads together outside the council-chamber as she passed, and when she enquired gaily of whom they were speaking so earnestly they bowed low and turned red about the ears and said they didn't know his name, but they believed he was someone the Earl of Kildare had befriended. He'd been mentioned, it seemed, in the despatches which had just arrived from Dublin.

And when Elizabeth mentioned the matter later among her women they all fell silent. But their very silence piqued her curiosity so that the same evening she questioned the King.

"Who is this young man in Ireland who was specially mentioned in the Deputy's despatches?" she asked, looking up from the score of a madrigal which she was striving to compose.

"Only another pretender," answered Henry carelessly, without raising his eyes from his book.

"And whom," asked Elizabeth, inking in a gay little semiquaver, "does he pretend to be this time?"

Henry looked up then, but it was a moment or two before he spoke, rather as if he were debating within himself whether to tell her or not. But the matter seemed so negligible, so patently absurd, that he told her the truth so far as he had been bothered to corroborate it. "People are always inventing fresh absurdities," he said, in that clear, rather expressionless voice of his. "They say this one is your young brother—Richard, Duke of York."

The half-finished score slipped from her lap and Elizabeth's heart seemed to miss a beat. "Dickon!" she breathed, almost inaudibly. And for a moment or two, instead of her solemn husband and the excellent furnishings of his room, she saw with the eyes of memory a slender young boy in black smiling back at her from the austere arch of the Abbot of Westminster's doorway.

"It is the sort of story these crazy Irish *would* think of!" said Henry irritably, turning over a page.

"Of course it is impossible," agreed Elizabeth, almost instantly, "when everybody knows that both my brothers were—murdered in the Tower."

Chapter Twenty-Two

TIN BUCKLES ON THE Queen of England's shoes! Oh no, Madam, I protest! Let me order silver ones," exclaimed Jane Stafford, holding out the worn footgear destined for repair.

"Four pence for hemming up the bottom of my old blue kirtle. Eight pence each for the bargemen's wages. Ten shillings to the carpenter for making that music chest," muttered Elizabeth, without looking up from the accounts before her. "But, my dear Jane, I cannot afford silver every day."

Tom Stafford's sister regarded the diligently bent head of her mistress with passionate devotion. "But the King can!" she ventured boldly.

Elizabeth laid down her quill and looked at her reprovingly.

"Will you not *ask* him, Madam?"

"Since you must know, Jane, I have just asked him for some more money. For my mother. And his Grace has increased her allowance almost to what it was before the Lambert Simnel affair. She is failing sadly and needs it."

Obediently, Jane laid the little shoes by ready for one of the pages to give to the shoemaker, which reminded her darting mind of some gossip she had heard outside a shop in Eastcheap. "They say the London merchants have made his Grace another loan," she said, taking advantage of the liberty which was often allowed to her loving, garrulous tongue.

"Because, to their amazement, he was punctilious about paying off the first one on the day it fell due." Elizabeth sat there smiling to herself and marvelling that some of the older men hadn't had apoplexy, considering their former less satisfactory dealings with a line of persuasive but impecunious, Plantagenets. "His Grace has even found better markets for their produce among the towns which he knows abroad. Our London merchants are beginning to find that it pays them very well to lend money to the King; and personally I suspect that he is a rather better business man than any of them."

"Everyone says he is growing rich," agreed Jane eagerly. "Which is all the more reason why—"

"It is no reason why he should keep all my relatives," snapped Elizabeth, hating the Woodville reputation for cupidity and determined to live it down.

Jane was on her knees in a moment, all repentance and concern. "Oh, Madam, we of your household know only too well where your money goes—always to your mother and sisters. Master Andreas, his little Grace's tutor, was saying only the other day that the love you bear your family is incredible. Fifty pounds each for the Princesses' private expenses," she ticked off on her fingers, "all manner of pretty gifts and an annuity to their husbands—"

"You run on about things you do not understand," reproved Elizabeth proudly, closing her account-book. "It is true that owing to the civil wars and my father's death my sisters have neither dowries nor suitable marriages with foreign princes. But they are still Plantagenets, and surely you do not expect us to be beholden to their husbands for the very food they eat?"

Jane bent her head very humbly to kiss the Queen's hand. "No, Madam," she murmured, "but it grieves me that your lovely generosity should leave you so poor." And because Elizabeth had a fellow feeling for any woman who had the courage to pursue her own argument, she lifted the girl's troubled face and kissed her. "God knows, I am not poor in love!" she said softly. Then, rising, she went to a side-table which, as usual, she had found strewn with an assortment of humble gifts. "Only look at the things my people have sent me this morning!" she cried gaily. "A fat chicken from some Surrey farmer, baskets of cherries brought in on their early-morning market carts—even vegetables from cottage gardens. And always the first of their crop, bless them! And posies," she added, picking up a tight little bunch of pansies and burying her face in their country fragrance. "Precious posies from the children!"

"Yes, we all know how they love you," laughed Jane, her brown eyes dancing again. "And then you must needs open your purse and send Ditton or Anne Percy or one of us out to them with twice as much as their gifts are worth!"

It was so true that Elizabeth had to laugh too. "Oh well, they are all so dear to me; and if I do have to go about with tin buckles on my shoes I am really a rich woman in my heart. Except, of course," she added to herself, "that I have no man to love me."

"Then you will not pore over such dull matters any more, will you, Madam?" said Jane, gathering up the account-book. "Surely it is enough that Decons, your clerk, is paid to do it."

"The King likes me to keep accounts, although I must admit that I find it very difficult," sighed the daughter of prodigal Edward. "And, Jane, when you or any of my other ladies hear people saying that his Grace is getting rich you should remind them of all the expenses he has. Preparations for war with France to help poor Brittany, which harboured him in his exile. And that lovely, lovely chapel he is building in the Abbey."

"I hate it!" exclaimed Jane, setting down the account-book with a bang.

The Queen swung round in her astonishment. "Jane! That heavenly beautiful building—"

"Oh yes, it may be beautiful," conceded Jane. "But Archbishop Morton says it is being built to enshrine the Tudor tombs. And I hate the thought that they will ever bury you—"

"You incredible goose! Take the account-book back to Decons now and—and try not to love me so extravagantly."

Left alone, Elizabeth, the Queen of England, stood for a while by her table touching each humble gift as if some specially precious benison had come with them, and wondering what her life would have been like had she married Tom Stafford and had this turbulent little beauty not as a lady of her bedchamber but as a sister-in-law. She might have found much quiet happiness, she supposed; but after all that she had now experienced she doubted if that would have satisfied her.

The pattern of her life had grown so much larger since the days when she had imagined herself in love with Tom. Although Henry made a confidant of no one, save sometimes his mother and Morton, a Queen lived at the hub of things. Those things which were never confided to her between the drawn curtains of her bed she inevitably heard discussed around the white napery of her board. Affairs of the country were talked about freely by knowledgeable men like Lord Stanley and his brother Sir William; Morton and the King's family bandied the names and news of European rulers who were personally known to them, while through the Palace flowed the widening influence of foreign ambassadors and envoys, the invigorating tang of spreading commerce and the culture of all the painters, writers, architects and printers whom Henry encouraged. Although Elizabeth never meddled, she learned. She took delight in hearing the management of her country discussed, and came to have a wholesome respect for her husband's mind.

"He cares so much less passionately than Richard, who loved the very earth of England, and yet in whatever he undertakes he seems to succeed," she thought. Conscientiously following his statecraft without the encouragement of his confidence, she came to understand it even better than some of his councillors. She knew, for instance, how hard he had tried to avoid war with France. The people, of course, clamoured for it. Through the centuries war with their nearest neighbour and traditional enemy had been the one thing for which they willingly voted supplies, the dangerous enterprise which they strained at the leash to join; and although it was their safety as well as his own that he was considering, they spoke disparagingly of Henry because he preferred to negotiate. Yet when Charles the Eighth threatened to occupy Brittany how efficiently the King of England moved! With no hatred of France inherent in his heart, he yet saw the danger it would mean to England if he allowed all the Breton ports across the Channel to fall into French hands. Although Spain and the Emperor of Rome, who seemed to be his allies, withheld their help, Henry sent forces to the defence of Brittany and, crossing to his own town of Calais, personally laid siege to Boulogne. While he was away Elizabeth made no bid for vicarious power, but wrote to him affectionately and often, telling him news of home and particularly of the progress of Arthur, who was already beginning to construe his Latin with Bernard Andreas.

The siege of Boulogne was short and resulted in no spectacular military victory. Charles, who had probably not bargained for such swift intervention, was glad to pay off his cool aggressor with good French gold and afterwards outwit him by persuading the orphaned heiress of Brittany to marry him, so that Henry sailed home in a sort of stalemate triumph which added nothing to his waning popularity. Military-minded men had sold their manors to win fame in France, the rank and file muttered bitterly because there had been precious little plunder and the hard-working populace at home wanted to know where their money had gone. But Henry returned unruffled. He had not been hankering for martial glory. Most of Charles's money had gone straight into his own pocket, England was once more at leisure to pursue her commercial prosperity, and—newcomer as he was—he had shown Spain and all the other European countries that he could manage his own affairs quite well without them.

It was some time before he found time to come to his wife's private apartments, but when he did he was rubbing his thin hands together with satisfaction. "Spain will be all the more anxious to carry on with our marriage proposals for Arthur," he congratulated himself, caring more in his long-sighted way for ultimate results than for the present feelings of his people.

"Then, although Ferdinand and Isabella left you to fight France alone, you still want him to marry their daughter?" marvelled Elizabeth, who had expected him to show strong resentment.

"Undoubtedly," said Henry. "I want Arthur to have the best

marriage we can arrange for him; and Spain, I am convinced, is the coming country."

"While you were away I was wondering whether you would want to cement your new peace treaty with a French alliance?" said Elizabeth, well versed in his ways.

"Later on, with one of the other children, perhaps."

"Margaret?" murmured Elizabeth, who, like a wise woman, had already begun to school herself for the pain of parting.

"No. I would sooner send her to Scotland," said Henry, so far forgetting himself as to take a born Yorkist into his confidence. "I have been pondering these many months upon the inestimable advantages of an alliance with Scotland. If in time the same King could reign over both countries, the way it already is with Wales—"

"And Ireland."

"If anyone could be said to reign there at all, with my own Deputy turning traitor!" laughed Henry shortly. "I have sent Sir John Egremont to arrest him."

"To arrest the Deputy of Ireland!" exclaimed Elizabeth. "Whatever has he done?"

"Made a complete fool of himself, I should imagine," said Henry, ferreting for his book to make a note of something he had forgotten to tell Egremont to do. "He sent for that ridiculous young man whom the Irish believe to be your brother and questioned him, as I ordered. But instead of publicly denouncing him he seems to have fallen under the spell of this—this extraordinary person himself. And it seems he actually allowed the Earl of Desmond to write to the Kings of France and Scotland telling them some cock-and-bull story about the real heir to the throne of England being alive. Just the sort of thing they would seize on at the moment to annoy me!"

"But of course they must know it isn't true," said Elizabeth, determined to keep a hold on commonsense and not let such things again stir up her past sorrow.

Henry took a turn or two about her room. In spite of the success of his campaign, he looked more perturbed than she had ever seen him. "The devil of it is," he said at last, coming to a standstill before her, "that this pretender was with the King of France in Paris when I was there. Charles treats him as if he *were* the Duke of York and has even given him a bodyguard captained by the Sieur de Concressault. Half the army knows this, and the fantastic rumour will be spread all over England in a week."

Elizabeth laid down the rings she had been drawing from her fingers. "Oh, Henry, not again! Immediately on your homecoming, and after all the trouble you had over that Simnel boy pretending to be Warwick!" she exclaimed, readily sympathizing with his annoyance. "But surely, now that you have won this campaign, you can insist that France shall not harbour him?"

"I have made that one of the clauses of the peace treaty. And unless Charles turns the impudent knave out bag and baggage he will get no daughter of mine for his Dauphin. I told you, did I not, that my succession was bound to produce a crop of pretenders? Oh, well, so long as they keep all their lunacy in France or Ireland…" laughed Henry ruefully. In spite of this fresh worry, Elizabeth was pleased that he was behaving so much more humanely, and even thought to commend her about something. "And, speaking of Simnel, that was not such a bad idea of yours, Elizabeth," he said, preparing to get into bed. "Though how you discovered that a baker's son had any feeling about birds is beyond me. They tell me at the mews that Simnel is one of the best men they have ever had for training a peregrine or a gyrfalcon. Knows just the moment to take a young wild bird from its nest, too. You'd better come hawking with me to-morrow and see him at work. My head falconer is getting past it and I could offer your late scullion a much lower wage for the same work."

It was the sort of small meanness which so often spoiled a pleasant concession, but next morning Elizabeth forgot it in the joy of hawking on the sun-swept heath at Hampstead. And her protégé proved himself well. He seemed quite unflurried by the King's scrutiny and more interested in the success of the birds he had trained than in a few envied words of royal praise. And as soon as the hawks were being chained again to their perches and the gay company preparing to return, Simnel himself came to lift the jessed merlin from the Queen's gloved wrist. Standing close beside her palfrey, he looked just as she imagined he would—upstanding and strong, with the wind in his hair.

That he must have worked hard she knew, and also that he was no longer a boy but a man. "You look happy, Simnel," she said kindly, looking down into his sun-tanned face.

"I am in love," he said simply. "She is a good country wench and will wed with me as soon as I can afford it. If one day I might bring her to the Palace to look just once upon your Grace's face—"

"I will ask one of my ladies to arrange it," promised Elizabeth, deeply touched. "And be patient with her goodness, for I think you may have a cottage of your own very soon."

"If ever there is anything I can do for you, Madam—" he said, inarticulate with gratitude. Elizabeth thought how dependable he looked, how typical of all that was best in rural England, and was glad when he laid his strong brown hand for a moment upon her rein. "I mean," he added, "anything at all."

Elizabeth called together her ladies and rode back to Westminster with a warm glow at her heart, for life had already taught her that, however exalted one may be, it is good to know of someone who will gladly serve one in any way at all.

Chapter Twenty-Three

IN ALL HIS DISPATCHES to the King of France Henry was careful
to speak of the mysterious pretender contemptuously as that
garçon, and Fox and Empson and his other councillors realized
that he was far more concerned about the coterie of discontented
Yorkists who were sneaking abroad to join him and forming quite
a pseudo-royal Court. Particularly when a man as influential as
Sir George Neville went. But Elizabeth noticed that her uncom-
municative husband was less prone to sarcastic sallies and cracked
his thin fingers less once the imposter was known to be over the
French border, homeless and presumably penniless, in Flanders.
Yet there was one danger which even Henry's astute mind had
overlooked, and that was the opportunity it gave to a woman who
hated him. Margaret Plantagenet of Burgundy, who had loved her
brother Edward this side of idolatry, lost no time in sending out an
invitation to the young man who claimed to be his son.

Nothing could have annoyed Henry more.

"Now that Charles the Bold of Burgundy is dead and she is
only a dowager duchess she has no political considerations to bind
her and can do anything she likes, I suppose," said Cicely, when
Henry's womenfolk were gathered together in the Queen's apartments to discuss it.

"But surely a Lambert Simnel sort of person would never dare to
accept," said newly married Ann. "Aunt Margaret would recognize
him for an imposter at once."

Cicely, more worldly wise, snorted over the purse she was embroidering for her husband. "Even if she did she would pretend not to!"

"She is my son's bane!" sighed the Countess of Richmond.

"He seems to believe she even started the Simnel business," said Cicely.

"But nobody *knows* that she did. After all, she never even saw him," protested Ann, who, in common with her brothers, had preferred this younger, livelier aunt from Burgundy to their staid Aunt Elizabeth of Suffolk or their shrewish Woodville aunt, Katherine.

"And even supposing this new pretender *were* the Duke of York, would she remember him? Well enough to be certain, I mean," queried the Countess of Richmond. "It is a long time since she saw him."

"His little Grace was eight years old when the Duchess came on that visit to King Edward," stated Mattie, with the liberty of long service. "Do you not remember, my lady Cicely, how he *would* take the deerhound he had for his birthday to show her and how the wild puppy creature bit a hole in her best gown?"

They laughed at the memory and by Mattie's loving precision the date was incontrovertibly fixed. "I do not think Aunt Margaret would accept anyone spurious as her nephew even to enrage the King," said Elizabeth, who had at yet contributed nothing to the conversation. "For in spite of the gown episode she delighted in Dickon."

Whether the Duchess would accept him or not was the Touchstone for which all Europe waited. Henry sent his spies abroad and all the Court waited for news. And soon the amazing truth was rippling through the Palace and men were marvelling about it in the streets. "The Duchess of Burgundy recognized him as her nephew." "'Like one given back to her from the dead,' she declares." "Not to be outdone by the King of France, she, too, has provided him with a retinue." "The young gallant goes everywhere with her."

"So that she may instruct him what to say about his supposed family and teach him manners," scoffed Henry.

"By what Sir Robert Clifford says he has no need to learn manners from anyone," said Sir William Stanley, who had recently been made the King's Chamberlain; but he waited to say it until the King had gone out of the room.

"Everyone we have questioned seems to agree that this person has a princely bearing and that his clothes become him," added Tom Stafford.

"But what language does he speak?" asked the King's mother.

"English, of course," said Lord Stanley, with husbandly terseness.

"With a strong foreign accent, no doubt!" laughed Elizabeth, remembering how even Henry had one when he first came.

"Why, no, quite perfectly, they say," said Sir William, evidently very much impressed. "And excellent French as well."

"Quite an accomplished tradesman's son the Duchess has found this time!" scoffed Margaret of Richmond elegantly. And younger Margaret, copying her, set them all laughing by declaring with true Tudor incisiveness, "We want no more baker's boys here!"

"Well, well, they will no doubt be crowning him in Antwerp or somewhere as Richard the Fourth!" said Elizabeth, with a hard note in her lovely voice, brought there by the bitterness of so much unnecessary suffering.

And to small Harry's delight Patch began parading up and down the Queen's gallery crowned with an upturned charcoal brazier and sweeping all and sundry aside with the skirts of a cloak improvised from the Queen's best Syrian rug.

Although she had joined in the jibing with the rest, Elizabeth slept but ill, and in the morning she took Jane Stafford and Ditton with her and rode out over the bridge to the convent at Bermondsey, which was in her Mortimer heritage. For there her mother, because of failing health and Henry's displeasure, had betaken herself to be nursed by the nuns.

"Her Grace is sleeping," said Mistress Grace, the Queen Dowager's companion, coming out to them and seeming to bar the bedroom door with her scrawny body.

"Then I will go in and sit with her until she wakes," said Elizabeth.

"It may be a long time," said Mistress Grace grudgingly.

"Then go and take a rest or gossip with my ladies out in the sunshine. You must be in need of change," ordered Elizabeth, wondering whether it was anything more than jealousy which made the woman unwilling for her to talk with her mother alone. But once within the quiet room, where conventual austerity blended pleasantly with the familiar furnishings of her family, and a great carved crucifix dominated all, Elizabeth forgot everything else and sat patiently listening to her mother's laboured breathing and looking pitifully at the high, white forehead and sharpened nostrils protruding so defencelessly above the neatly turned-back sheet.

"I do not think she will last long, Madam," said the Mother Superior, when she came in presently with a glass of cordial for her patient.

"That is partly why I came," said Elizabeth. "I am with child and near my time, so may not see her again. Also there is something I want to ask her before it is too late. And I would like to thank you and all your sisterhood for the tender care you have bestowed upon her."

The Mother Superior set down the glass. Before leaving she glanced from the crucifix to the face of her dying friend. "An earthly crown must be beset with thorns, too," she said. "Both she and your Grace have been called upon to suffer more than most women; but soon her soul will be at rest."

Upon first wakening Elizabeth Woodville seemed all bemused, fancying herself back in sanctuary; but a few sips of the cordial and the joy of finding that it was her eldest daughter who was ministering to her helped to clear the shadows from her mind. All difference of age passed from them. For a while they talked quietly together of past happenings. The Dowager Queen said how much she hoped that Bridget, her youngest, would make her vows and come to live in this peaceful place where she herself had received so much kindness, and Elizabeth was able to tell her how radiantly happy was young Ann now that she had been married to the Earl of Surrey as she had hoped.

"And your own husband has come back triumphant again, I hear," said the Dowager Queen, "although scarcely to a bed of roses, with this second pretender to plague him. But at least he cannot imagine that, sick as I am, I had any hand in the matter *this* time."

"Whatever he thinks, he has sent you some of his best grapes. I will have Ditton give them to Mistress Grace." Elizabeth moved to a window and drew the curtain a little so as to protect her mother's fading sight from the brightness of the morning sunlight. "Have you heard that Aunt Margaret has received the young man into her household?"

"Margaret of Burgundy?"

"She swears that he *is* Dickon," said Elizabeth, staring unseeingly out into the garden where her ladies and Mistress Grace were sitting together on a stone bench.

And after a moment she was surprised to hear the sick woman chuckling in the bed behind her. "I like your Aunt Margaret," she was saying, with a spark of her old malice. "I, too, would swear almost anything to annoy that solemn-faced husband of yours!"

Elizabeth turned to find those intelligent dark eyes still bright in the sunken face and felt that even with the breath nearly out of her body her mother was quicker in wordly wisdom than either of them. That here was someone to whom she herself could still turn for guidance as in the drawn-out days of her submissive dependence. "Tell me seriously," she said, coming back to the bedside. "Do you still believe that it cannot possibly be true—this constantly recurring rumour that one of them was spared?"

"You know that I do," was the uncompromising answer. "Your Uncle Richard was never the kind of devil to do things by halves."

Elizabeth hated to badger a sick woman, but pursue the matter she must. "Sir Robert Clifford, whom Henry sent to Flanders specially, saw this young man riding through Arras," she said. "And even he, who cannot possibly care one way or the other, says that he is the very spit of my father."

Edward the Fourth's widow chuckled again until it ended in a fit of coughing and the necessity for more cordial. "So he might, and it still not mean a thing," she said, when the paroxysm had passed. "If Margaret of Burgundy or any of our other Yorkist friends wanted to find a personable young man who looked sufficiently like your father to bolster up their tale, it should not be difficult. England is full of his bastards. And no doubt Flanders too, for that matter, since he spent some dull days of exile there."

So that was probably the simple solution, thought Elizabeth absently fingering the bowl of gillyflowers which the nuns had set upon a stool beside the great bed. "Jane Shore bore no children," she said inadequately, her mind going back only to the days of his most constant mistress.

"No. But there were plenty of others who did," said the Dowager Queen, with the growing irritability of weariness. "Grace here is the child of one of them."

Elizabeth had been used to seeing Grace and her young brother about the Palace at Westminster, and beyond a mild dislike had never particularly thought about them. "So that is why she has no other name?" she said, surprised at her own foolishness. "With those prominent predatory eyes she must take after her mother. Who was she?"

"I have long since forgotten," yawned the drowsy Woodville woman plaintively. "But now that no one cares about me any more Grace at least is kind and does what I tell her."

"I wonder what sort of things my poor mother does tell her to do? I wonder if, after all, they *did* have some hand in this?" pondered Elizabeth, trying to remember what the young brother had looked like; but she soon chased the thought away as ungenerous and undutiful. Her mother had fallen asleep with the suddenness of the very weak, and for a moment or two Elizabeth stood looking down upon her, remembering her vivacity and the dramatic skill with which she had always dominated any scene, and feeling sadly sure that it was the last time she would ever see her on this earth.

All that spring the whole country was seething with rumours about the so-called Duke of York across the water, and it appeared that an amazing number of people believed in him. To Henry it must have seemed that a weapon had been put into the Duchess of Burgundy's hand which could not only cause unrest but could also be used against him by any other foreign power with whom he was not friendly. He went about his affairs as usual, writing endless dispatches about the intended Spanish marriage between his heir and Ferdinand of Aragon's daughter, paving the way for a peace treaty with Scotland and granting charters to that intrepid mariner Jean Cabot to sail in the *Matthew* in search of treasure from the East, and tracing with his tapering fingers on the great map of the world the possible course of his return from Newfoundland. Elizabeth knew that in his own realm and abroad her husband was respected, and that for all his reasonable gentleness men feared him; but she often wished that some of them loved him. But then probably Henry did not want their love, she supposed, any more than he wanted hers. He went on making notes and amassing money and making sure that his elder son studied Greek and Latin and—above all—Spanish, at Croydon. He was becoming a little more near-sighted and a little meaner, and Elizabeth, knowing that she would never now have a real love affair, solaced herself more and more with the affection of her children and particularly with the amusing liveliness of Harry, whose health had never given her a moment's anxiety.

"We might be living in the Dark Ages instead of at a time when books are printed and fresh countries explored," complained Henry, accompanying her in the royal barge from all the unrest in London to the quiet of Greenwich. "The people are behaving like hysterical children."

"They were foolishly credulous about Simnel but you never seemed to care," said Elizabeth, sitting beside him beneath an awning resplendent with Tudor roses.

"That was a mere May revel compared with this. I had only to make the real Warwick ride through the streets to show them what fools they were. But now I have nothing to produce. Not even a murdered body." Without even noticing how her whole body winced, he turned to her almost in exasperation. "Elizabeth, has *none* of your family any idea where they were buried?"

"Would that we had! All we know is that it was in—there," said Elizabeth, trying not to look at the grimness of the Tower as their barge shot smoothly past. "The Tower priest must have known, I suppose. But he was old and ailing, and died before we came out of sanctuary. There was a squire of Richard's, called John Green, who took a message to Sir Robert Brackenbury. I tried to have speech with him, but Richard sent him away to the Isle of Wight. And poor Brackenbury, as you know, was killed at Bosworth."

"I will get to the bottom of this business if it takes me half a lifetime," swore Henry.

"Then may I never hope to forget it?" reproached Elizabeth. And because her time was nearly upon her he said no more.

It was a sad confinement, for her mother died at Bermondsey, and her baby, whom she called after her, did not live long. Her mother-in-law was not with her at the time, and when she came to visit her afterwards even *her* serenity seemed badly shaken. "There is something the King asked me to tell you, but which I am very loath to speak of," she began, when at last they were alone together. "Are you sure that you are quite strong again, Elizabeth? You have so little colour in your cheeks."

"Of course I am well," said Elizabeth, with a wan smile. "But naturally I have been grieving. And that wretched ague seems to have come back to plague me. It is often so in damp weather."

"Then I will tell you some other time," said Margaret, looking unaccountably relieved and preparing to go. But Elizabeth missed her mother-in-law's company. From the couch on which she was resting she reached out a restraining hand. "No, stay and tell me now," she begged, supposing it to be some finicky whim or new economy of her husband's. "Does Henry want to cut down my allowance again? Or must all my servants wear dragons as well as roses on their livery? Whatever it is, is it so terrible that you cannot stay?"

To her surprise there was no answering smile on Margaret's comely face. "It is more terrible than anything I ever heard," she said slowly. "And you, my dear daughter, will have to bear it."

Elizabeth sat up abruptly. "I? Then it concerns me—especially?" she stammered, with a great foreboding at her heart.

"You and your sisters. Henry has been making exhaustive enquiries about the disappearance of your brothers. He had to, Elizabeth—you must see that—to counter this growing belief that the younger one is alive."

"Yes, yes. I see that. And he has found out—?"

"That it is quite true that they were both murdered. With merciful swiftness, I assure you."

Elizabeth's hands flew to her blanched cheeks. Not until that moment had she realized how strong, how unquenchable, had been the hope that had flickered in her, nor how much she had allowed it to be kept alive by all these happenings. She felt it die in her now as if some part of herself died too, or a child in her womb. "God was very merciful to let my mother die when she did. But then, of course, she was so much cleverer than I. She never really believed…" Elizabeth's low voice trailed away into silence.

"It is no new grief, my poor sweet," consoled Margaret, without realizing how hope can outlive common sense. "Only the details. You are bound to hear of them sooner or later, and I could not bear that you should hear from some uncaring stranger."

"Tell me now," said Elizabeth, composing herself rigidly against her cushions and holding her hands very still. "I promise you I will not cry out or—faint."

"God give you courage!" prayed the Countess. "Henry went in person to the Tower and looked up the wages accounts. You know how methodical he is. There was a man paid to look after them called Slaughter."

"Black Slaughter. Yes, I remember. It was really through some woman of his that I heard," said Elizabeth, reliving those confused moments in the Abbot of Westminster's kitchen, when she had struck some lout for daring to say that Ned and Dickon were dead. "But I always supposed that he was kind to them."

"He may have been. Anyway, I don't think he had anything to do with it. But we could not trace him. He was probably killed in battle with his master. But it seems that while the Princes were in his care someone brought a message to Sir Robert Brackenbury."

"Richard's squire, John Green," supplemented Elizabeth, weary of the beginning part of the story.

"Yes. That was the name. Whatever Richard wanted Brackenbury to do, he refused. But he offered to give up the keys of the Tower for a night."

"It does not sound very likely."

"And then Richard sent Sir James Tyrrell."

"Tyrrell is still alive," said Elizabeth, leaning forward excitedly. "I always *wanted* Henry to question him."

"Well, he has questioned him now, offering reward and pardon. And the miserable man has confessed."

"That he did it?"

"He maintains that he did not see it done. That he stood at the bottom of the stairs and sent his man Dighton up, with some hired cut-throat called Forest."

Elizabeth waved the sordid details aside with shaking hands. After all these years the names of the murderers seemed to matter so little. "*How* was it done?" she demanded, in a voice which croaked huskily.

"*Must* you know?" asked Margaret, regarding her with anxious pity.

"Yes. Yes. If they suffered it I can bear to hear it."

"This John Dighton says that they—wrapped them around with the bedcovers and smothered them. That the little King was asleep but that the younger one called out to warn him."

"And are you sure that he did not escape?"

"How *could* he escape; with two strong men and another waiting below?"

Elizabeth's love for Dickon was such that even then hope died hard. "Or that he was not just left for dead and crawled away somewhere afterwards? Or that one of them did not take pity on him?"

"Those butchers carried down the bodies to show to Tyrrell."

"It is only this Dighton's word."

"And Tyrrell's."

"They were master and man. They would naturally tell the same story."

For a long time there was silence in the Queen's bedroom. Sad as the flickering out of the new life which had so recently been born into it, the gloom of such a deed seemed to put out the sunshine. "And those poor innocent bodies?" asked Elizabeth presently, her voice little more than a whisper.

"It seems that the two men were frightened and buried them hastily beneath the bottom stair as Tyrrell told them. But Tyrrell says that when King Richard heard of it he was uneasy. They were Yorkists, of his own brother's blood, he said. They must be buried in sacred ground and a solemn requiem said over them. Yet he had wanted them dead. Such inconsistency taxes my credulity."

"But Richard was like that. It was as if there were two Richards: one whom you hated and one whom you—came dangerously near to loving. I can imagine that he could deliberately kill and yet worry about the shriving of his victim's soul. And his family arrogance was prodigious."

"Then perhaps it is true. You knew him better than I," said Margaret, rising with a sigh. "At any rate Will Slaughter told somebody that the following night he saw a shuffling old priest and a man muffled to the eyes creep to the place and exhume them. And now, as you know, the priest is dead."

"And so all this renewal of agony has been to no purpose, Madam? Henry has not even their poor bones to show."

"But the public confessions of these two men have persuaded people that the Duke of York is dead."

Elizabeth lay back with closed eyes. "And I suppose that every tavern in London hums with it."

"Say rather every tavern in England!" said Margaret. "And everywhere the name of your Uncle Richard is execrated."

With the perfect timing of a man who has escaped an unpleasant half-hour with a woman, Henry came to join them. "I am sorry, Elizabeth, that you must go through all this again," he said. "But at least it will serve to kill this widespread belief that was becoming so dangerous to our dynasty."

"For the sake of our children's security I can bear it," Elizabeth assured him.

"I would not go so far as to say security," he said cautiously. "But how could I expect foreign powers to conclude marriages with them while pretenders kept digging at the foundations of my throne? Now we will invite the Spanish Ambassador to dine again."

"That must be a matter for much satisfaction," said Elizabeth expressionlessly. "But who, then, is the young man in Flanders?"

"Does it matter?" shrugged Henry.

"No, I suppose it does not," agreed Elizabeth. "And will Sir James Tyrrell be given a governorship or something on the Isle of Wight too?"

"Be patient, my child!" advised Margaret, touching her gently on the shoulder.

Henry eyed his wife with uncertainty, wishing she would not speak like that. "Let Tyrrell have his day," he said, gathering up some of his everlasting documents. "He has served my purpose. Later, you will see. I shall deal with him."

But for once Henry was over-optimistic. Belief that is based upon desire dies hard. There were many Englishmen who had cause to want back a son of Edward the Fourth. Archbishop Morton, as Chancellor of the Exchequer, had proved too clever an extortioner. Henry's trade reprisals against Flanders had hit the London merchants hard—so hard that they wrecked the rich Steelhouse wharf where foreigners from the Hanseatic towns reaped double harvest from the trade they might not enjoy. And practical as he was, the Tudor lacked the common touch which had made many a worse King better loved. So that, in spite of those hard-won and gruesome confessions, interest in the pretender grew.

It was like a cloud above the Tudors' lives. At first it had been just something which they joked about. But gradually, as the years went on and more and yet more people believed—or, for their own ends, pretended to believe—that a son of Edward's still lived, it began to darken their world—and perhaps even to cloud their own certainty. Because it affected them both it brought Henry and Elizabeth closer together. But it affected them differently. To Henry, with his poor claim to the throne, the whole affair stood for affront and fear; whereas to Elizabeth—although it brought fear for her family—it never really ceased to hold a shining element of hope. A hope which she wore herself out trying to extinguish, knowing it for the crazy thing it was.

Chapter Twenty-Four

ALTHOUGH THERE WAS LITTLE money forthcoming for the Queen to buy herself silver shoe-buckles, there always seemed to be plenty of money to pay the King's spies. Seeing that even murderers' confessions could not quench the rumour that one of the Princes had escaped, he drew carefully hoarded gold from his coffers and sent a whole posse of spies to comb the towns of Western Europe and to ferret around the household of the Dowager Duchess of Burgundy. They were a long time gone, and when they came back and began to piece their information together it was not very consistent. But they had at least found a name for the mysterious young man who was beginning to be known abroad as the Duke of York and sometimes—to Henry's exasperation—as Richard the Fourth of England.

It was the unromantic bourgeois name of Perkin Warbeck.

"Or was it Osbeck?" they debated.

They really did not seem very sure. But they were all agreed that he had lived in Picardy, in the prosperous town of Tournay.

"Then how is it," asked Elizabeth, who had been summoned to the King's room to hear them, "that he speaks such faultless English?"

"Jean de Warbeck, his father, being a free burgess of the town, sent him into commercial houses in Antwerp and Middlesburg, where he had much to do with English merchants," one of Henry's spies told her. "We have proof that one year he was there from Christmas until Easter."

"Not very long in which to learn a language," pointed out Sir William Stanley, sceptically.

"In order to perfect it, Sir, he was sent into Portugal in the household of Sir Edward Brampton, and remained there for months," he was told.

"But still in a foreign country," said Elizabeth, remembering for how long a time a faint French accent had clung to her husband's speech in spite of his being Welsh bred and born.

"It is possible that this young man may actually have been born in England, Madam, while his parents were on a commercial visit here," explained Archbishop Morton, who had been invaluable in assembling the varied and conflicting evidence. "Jean de Warbeck was, it seems, a converted Jew, and it has even been suggested that either for that reason or in order to encourage the Flemish trade your illustrious father himself may have stood godfather to the child."

"Are his parents dead?" asked Lord Stanley.

"His mother, Katherine de Faro, is thought to be still alive."

"And was this Katherine de Faro particularly beautiful?" enquired Jasper Tudor with a meaning smile, joining in the conversation from the chair to which illness now confined him.

"Of that we have no evidence, milord," the informers said solemnly, surprised by his seeming irrelevance. "But probably, since the young man himself is said to have the asset of good looks—"

"If you are suggesting, my good uncle, that this Warbeck child was something more than godson to my father," interrupted Elizabeth crisply, "then I think your ingenious idea is shattered by the unlikelihood of his Grace bestowing upon him the name of Peter, or any of its absurd diminutives."

"How did this Perkin turn up in Ireland in the first place?" asked Lord Stanley, returning more realistically to the matter in hand.

Archbishop Morton consulted a voluminous sheaf of papers. "For the sake of travel, or for some love of adventure which was in him, he appears to have gone there to assist a Breton merchant called Pregent Meno, who dealt in velvets and other expensive fabrics," he said.

"Then it was probably these fine fabrics bedecking his elegant person which so impressed the Irish and bedevilled them into believing that he must be some important personage!" suggested Stanley, with his rich indulgent laugh. "Well, write the whole matter down," ordered the King, who had been listening in attentive silence.

And as the Palace clerks made a great shuffling with their parchments and inkhorns milord Archbishop, who had been standing beside him, leaned closer. "It is an interesting story, Sir, and would look well in print," he suggested, his fine dark eyes glittering with lively intelligence.

"And probably more persuasive to the masses than in manuscript," agreed Henry, making a note to write yet again to his Holiness in Rome about a Cardinal's hat for so able a Primate. "Well, milords, that should lay this bogey for ever and set the Queen's mind at rest," he added more formally, in that precise, rather high-pitched voice of his, while drawing his gown about him and rising. "I would have you know that I have already written to the Archduke acquainting him with our findings and asking him to expel this gross impostor from Flanders. So now let us leave these good people to prepare their news for the printing press while we betake ourselves to the council-chamber. There are fresh dispatches arrived from their most Christian Majesties of Spain, and we would discuss the all-important matter of the marriage of our right well-beloved son the Prince of Wales with their daughter, Princess Katherine of Aragon."

Elizabeth, taking his courteously outstretched hand and allowing him to escort her from the room, was sensible of the new lightness of his step. "So you see it turns out to be, as I told you, just another foolish pother over another tradesman's son," he said smugly, at parting. But, while agreeing with the common sense of his words, Elizabeth shared nothing of his relieved lightness. As she passed along the gallery towards the garden with her ladies she experienced an extraordinary flatness, as if some hope held insanely in the back of her mind had once again been dispelled. So that coming upon Sir William Stanley and Sir Robert Clifford standing together beneath an archway, she felt impelled to ask, "And what do you two gentlemen make of it?"

Each of them held a document from which dangled the royal seal, and they had been so close in conversation and ceased speaking so abruptly at her approach that she was sure they had been still talking about Perkin Warbeck.

"In spite of all this reassuring evidence, the King has very sensibly issued orders to all of us to hold ourselves and our men in armed readiness in case of trouble," replied Sir William, covering his embarrassment with a statement of fact which was no answer at all.

"And what do *you* think, Sir Robert?" persisted Elizabeth, trying to make her voice as cold and casual as possible. "You who were at first so much impressed that you lived for several months in the pretender's entourage?"

Robert Clifford's position was a delicate one, and although he now enjoyed the King's favour the Queen's forthright way of speaking disconcerted him. "All the carefully amassed information we have just been listening to must, of course, be correct," he answered carefully. "But the backers in this business were singularly fortunate in finding a young man who so much resembles your Grace's family."

Although this was the very confirmation which Elizabeth's heart sought, her chin went up proudly and her hand went to the locket beneath her gown. "Surely your judgment must be at fault," she rebuked him, "if it ever saw anything in common between a mercer's son and my father's!"

Like a good Court Chamberlain, Sir William hastened to say the tactful word. "If either of us really believed for a moment that this Perkin Warbeck was your Grace's brother," he swore, tapping the summons he held in one hand with the back of the other, "your Grace must know that I would not lift my sword against him."

But Elizabeth left them feeling that the good man was both worried and uncertain. She wished above everything that she could see her Aunt Margaret of Burgundy and find out just how much that woman, whom she remembered with so much liking, had been activated by hatred of the Lancastrians and how much by belief in Perkin as a nephew. It must be more than ten years since Margaret Plantagenet had seen the real Dickon in England, when he was only a child of eight. After ten years, confronted by a grown man, could anyone be certain? Could she herself, who had seen him more recently? But of course her heart would cry out at sight of him and tell her. And it would all be confirmed because he would remember things—small foolish things which only the real Dickon would know. But why think about it? Why stand there with the tears in her eyes? Why keep recalling the loveableness of his personality, or the enchantment of his smile? Dickon was dead. Smothered, poor terrified precious, by Dighton's or Forest's rough, hell-hound hands. And had not she herself dreamed of Ned's crying out to her during that long night?

To hope to see Dickon again in this world was madness. Of course Margaret of Burgundy, whatever she believed, was acting merely as the adoring sister of a dead Yorkist King. Only the previous evening Elizabeth had heard her husband dictating his letter to the young Archduke Philip and complaining that her malice was both causeless and endless. Henry could not, it seemed, rid himself of the conviction that she had been responsible, too, for all that trouble when Lambert Simnel had impersonated Warwick. "Being a woman past childbearing, she now brings forth full-grown imposters," he had written. "Can she not instead be grateful for the joys which Almighty God serves up to her in beholding her niece Elizabeth in such honour, with children to inherit the throne of England?" As usual, Henry had set forth his arguments with reasonableness and restraint, preferring to conclude with a request rather than with the threats which he was undoubtedly in a position to make. "As Charles of France discarded this impostor," he had written, "so I entreat you to do the same."

And although the fifteen-year-old Archduke—advised, no doubt, by his father the Emperor—wrote back in due course, regretting that he had no power to expel the Dowager Duchess or her guests from his territory, Elizabeth felt that sooner or later Henry would find means to force him into doing so.

"And where will the poor *garçon* of Tournay go then?" she wondered, immediately chiding herself for the thought because it did not matter at all.

But all too soon she and Henry were to know.

"The pretender has landed in England," people shouted; and some, in their excitement, so far forgot themselves as to cry aloud with love in their voices, "Duke Richard has come home!"

All London was in an uproar. For an hour or two the Court seethed with excitement. And then fresh messengers clattered in over London Bridge, bringing more exact tidings, and the thing became a sorry jest, adding to Henry's prestige and somehow filling Elizabeth with secret, painful shame. The inglorious fact was that although Perkin's little borrowed fleet lay for several hours off Kent, with the money of his Continental backers behind him and the prayers of many a Yorkist wellwisher in England awaiting him, he himself had not set foot on English soil at all. He had sent a small advance party ashore to reconnoitre in some obscure fishing village, and the local Kentishmen, Tudor loyal, had lulled them with promises of food and adherence and then slaughtered them with whatever implements they could lay hands on, "trusting to God," as they put it, "that King Henry would come before the ships' companies landed and wreaked vengeance." But the foreign-looking ships had sent neither help nor vengeance, but sailed away, leaving their unfortunate comrades behind.

"Which proves that he is no Plantagenet!" declared Elizabeth disgustedly.

It had been such a pitiful attempt that the sudden shock of it was soon forgotten. De Puebla, the Spanish ambassador, even reported that his royal master—who had hitherto shown himself much concerned about the insecurity of Henry's claim—considered all such pretenders merely food for laughter. But Henry, more harassed than any of his subjects, had all the ports watched and his own Lord Chamberlain brought to trial. Nothing worse came to light concerning him than that he had sworn that if the would-be invader could be proved to be Edward's son he would not lift his sword against him, but this was sufficient to condemn him. Elizabeth, who had heard the words spoken in their innocuous context, supposed that Sir Robert Clifford must have reported them to the King out of spite or in order to wash out his own near-defection in the past, and she would have gone straightway to her husband about it; but Archbishop Morton assured her that it was known to both of them that Sir William had promised much of his wealth to this flickering Yorkist cause. And it occurred to her, as it might also have occurred to Henry, that the invader might indeed be Edward's son, and yet no Duke of York. The people were appalled that a man like the great Lord Stanley's brother should lose his life over so small an affair, all the more so in view of the King's habitual clemency; and yet they were impressed by the fact that neither family connections nor high places could protect a man from the results of suspected treachery.

And Elizabeth, covertly watching her husband, thought that he had become more secretive than ever and noticed how he had begun to age. She knew that, whatever private evidence he might have had of Sir William's guilt, he must have found it hard to sign the death warrant of a man whose intervention had saved the day for him at Bosworth. All his natural caution must have warned him of the risk of losing his own stepfather's loyalty; and more than anything else he must have hated to bring such bitter grief into the family circle of his mother.

Why had he done this thing, Elizabeth wondered, just when he could so ill afford unpopularity? Henry was not naturally cruel. Rather, he turned from violence. But fear, sometimes, could drive a naturally clement man to cruelty. Could it be possible that when it came to this question of the succession Henry was mortally afraid? That all his pride and self-sufficiency and vaunting dragon banners were but a cloak for the pitiful sense of inferiority felt by a man who had neither the clear right nor the personal attractiveness for the heritage he had usurped? A cloak which excluded the sympathy she would so willingly have given.

For the first time the wild idea occurred to Elizabeth that perhaps Henry might half believe in the thing which he had taken such pains to disprove. That he, too, was not quite sure that Perkin *was* an imposter.

But, whether he did or not, life went on much as usual. Elizabeth bore Henry another daughter, who, from the first moment of her gurgling baby laughter, brought her nothing but joy. They called her Mary, and young Harry, her brother, adored her. It was good for him, their mother thought, to curb his boisterous strength sometimes and play with her gently. Elizabeth was happily occupied with all her children. Arthur was mostly away at Ludlow with his tutor, and she was proud of his scholarly prowess, although sometimes of late she had worried over his health. She tried to prepare her elder daughter for the high matrimonial place which would undoubtedly be hers and at the same time to cure her haughtiness; and not to spoil young Harry, however much she was tempted to do so because of the turbulent affection he showed her.

Happy with her family at Richmond or Greenwich, Elizabeth saw little of Henry, who seemed to be perpetually going by barge to Westminster. He worked harder than most of his subjects, improving the courts of justice, controlling the dangerous power of the great barons by limiting their liveried retinues, and increasing the country's prosperity by creating markets abroad and by encouraging the discoveries of new countries by such splendid sailors as Cabot. He was full, too, of the prestige which would accrue to England from the proposed Spanish alliance, and spent hours closeted with de Puebla, the Ambassador, haggling about a handsome dowry and trying to arrange for a proxy marriage.

But the pretensions to a better Plantagenet claim which dogged Henry's reign were not to leave them in peace for long. There came a memorable evening when all their domestic activities were overshadowed by portentous news from Berwick. As they sat listening to the musicians after supper a messenger from that northern border town sought an immediate audience with the King, and hurried into the hall, dusty and exhausted, to report that Perkin Warbeck, forced at last from Flanders by the people's reactions to Henry's trade reprisals, had landed in Scotland. After two testimonies to the Tower murder and the printed pamphlets about his, Perkin's, parentage the sheer impertinence of it left the English Court breathless. True, Edinburgh was not much nearer in miles than Ireland or Flanders; but this time no protecting sea lay between.

"What are the Scots thinking of to allow it when your Grace has been to such pains to make a lasting treaty with them?" expostulated Sir Reginald Bray, who had done so much to strengthen the Tudor King financially.

But in the dispatches from the much fought-over town of Berwick it was clearly stated that Perkin Warbeck had landed by the King of Scots' invitation.

"You mean that James actually treats him as if he were royalty?" exclaimed Elizabeth.

"It would seem so," said Henry, still holding the letter between his hands. "As absurdly as Margaret of Burgundy did when I succeeded in prising him out of France."

"But James would not do so merely to annoy you?"

"One would scarcely suppose so after there has been talk of his marrying my elder daughter."

Elizabeth rose from her chair beside the fire and began to pace back and forth between the standing courtiers. "Oh no, not James!" she repeated, in sore perplexity. "In spite of all the border foraging that goes on, everyone holds James the Fourth of Scotland to be one of the most cultured men in Christendom. Bernard Andreas says he can turn a Latin phrase as fluently as he can talk French with Charles' envoys or discuss crofts and cattle with his Highlanders in their own Gaelic. His word is his bond. I have always thought he would be a son-in-law to be proud of." She stopped in front of her husband and spoke with urgent informality. "Henry, do you not see that if James acknowledges him it is because he really *believes* him to be my brother? This—torturing uncertainty—is coming very near home!"

All looked upon her with compassion. Even Henry could comprehend something of her distress and tried his best to reassure her. "There is no uncertainty at all after the conclusive evidence about your brothers' deaths and the facts we have now assembled about this impostor," he said. "And in any case James can never have seen the real Duke of York, so why should his opinion affect you?" Yet when the King turned to enquire of the messenger what forces Warbeck had brought with him the question sounded merely perfunctory. This wholesale deluding of sane people had gone on so long that it was becoming uncanny. It was not the material force of the young man that mattered but his personal magnetism. One could fight successfully against a stated number of ships or horsemen or archers, but where was the weapon with which to fight against charm? For, as the messenger admitted, the level-headed King of Scotland, who had but recently been discussing the advantages of a marriage with the Tudor King's daughter, had received Margaret of Burgundy's protege doubtfully, questioning him again and again with true Scottish caution; and yet he—like all the rest—had been persuaded.

"Why should my wife imagine James Stuart to be any better than the rest? He only *pretends* to believe in him," argued Henry, alone afterwards with Morton in the privacy of his own work-closet. "This brash young merchant is like a hostage held in all sovereigns' hands save mine, and they bandy him about between them. He is something they can throw into the scales against me, in order to undermine my security when they think I am becoming too powerful. And as a trouble-maker he is nearly as valuable to them spurious as real."

"It is only Clarence's son Warwick who is real," Morton reminded him. "And he is safely in the Tower."

And so they made themselves believe until James of Scotland gave his beautiful cousin, Katherine Gordon, to the so-called Duke of York in marriage.

Most people about the Court were reduced to horrified silence by this amazing move. Only the ageing Jasper Tudor had the hardihood to sum their thoughts in words. "One might give a man a bodyguard of gentlemen as a political gambit, as Charles of France did," he said, "but not a bride of one's own blood. That is inconceivable. Unless one genuinely believed in him."

The King himself came as near to rage as Elizabeth had ever

seen him, for Katherine Gordon was his cousin too. And it did not improve his temper that the suave de Puebla made some excuse to return to Spain, and that Ferdinand and Isabella let the matter of their daughter's marriage drop.

"*That* is what this poisonous imposter has cost me!" raged Henry, running his bony hands over his thinning hair. "For six years or more his antics have tormented me, and where will the end of it be?"

"And do you not see, Sir, that *any* pretender makes a cat's-paw for your enemies?" Elizabeth overheard Morton say. They are willing to take risks because if this little Flemish popinjay loses his life in some crazy venture Warwick will still be safe."

"And a thorn in my side!" said Henry thoughtfully, unaware that his wife stood within earshot. "Although he is weak-minded and his father was an attainted traitor, you think it is really Warwick whom Ferdinand and Isabella mind about most?"

The future Cardinal was easily the cleverest man in England and the only one in whom Henry ever confided. "I think," Elizabeth heard him say, "that there will be no Spanish marriage so long as Warwick lives."

Henry heaved the sigh of a very weary man. "Then it behoves me to catch the cat's-paw," he said, "and perhaps Heaven may show me how to use him myself."

THE WORDS THAT SHE had overheard meant little to Elizabeth at the time, and soon there were more urgent things to think about. In the autumn James and Perkin invaded England as everybody had expected they would; and although Henry's forces were so well prepared that the invasion extended not much farther than a border raid, its savagery was unprecedented. Perkin's foreign supporters had been added to James's troops, and the desolation of sacked villages which they left behind them was appalling. It was Perkin himself who appealed on behalf of the Northumbrians and persuaded James to turn back—partly, perhaps, through pity for people whom he claimed as his subjects, and partly because he had wit enough to realize that burning people's homes was a poor way to win their support. Such tactics might satisfy James's ambition by wresting from England the coveted town of Berwick, but they certainly would not help to smooth his own pathway to a crown.

For weeks the people of England lived in a state of tension. In northern towns there were constant outcries that the invaders were at their gates, and all over the country children were pulled into their homes at dusk with shrill cries of "The Scots will get you!" As usual Henry Tudor had set forth, if not to fight, at least to direct operations; and as usual he rode home to London triumphant. But he rode home a tired and irritated man. Besides the cruel loss of life, the invasion had cost so much money that he immediately summoned representatives from all the towns in his realm to a

Great Council at Westminster, where they willingly voted him a grant of one hundred and twenty thousand pounds for defence against Scotland and—much less willingly—the promise of loans to the amount of forty thousand pounds.

"Henry always makes his wars *pay!*" chuckled his Uncle Jasper admiringly; which must have been almost the last joke he enjoyed before he died. And the people who were left alive found it rather a poor one, anyway, because Archbishop Morton and Sir Reginald Bray not only set their underlings to collect the promised sums from every individual, house by house, and town by town, but were so extraordinarily thorough and extortionate in their demands that they were soon suspected of having enriched the King's coffers by a sum far in excess of the agreed amount. Morton, in particular, as Chancellor of the Exchequer, produced an ingenious device by means of which he delved into people's purses either by the argument that they paid too little or that they possessed too much. Men called it "Morton's fork" and many an honest man was ruined by it, writhing for years on one or other of its merciless prongs.

The popularity of Morton's royal master waned alarmingly. And when the time came for the tax-collectors to take up contributions in the West of England the men of Cornwall flatly refused to pay. Remote from the rest of England and completely indifferent to what happened there, they saw no reason why their hard-working lives should be still further impoverished in order to pay for something of which they had scarcely heard—"a little stir of the Scots, soon blown over." "Why should they, who laboured below ground in the tin-mines for a pittance, be expected to pay?" they asked. "Let the leisured people pay." A lawyer called Flammock inflamed them by assuring them that a levy was illegal, and a blacksmith of Bodmin called Michael Joseph sharpened their bills and sickles and led them through Devon into Somerset. From Wells Lord Audley, who had been extortionately taxed himself, led them through Salisbury and Winchester towards London, with their discontented numbers growing all the way. It was all very much like the Peasants' Revolt in Richard the Second's time, thought Elizabeth, who had recently been reading about it to Harry as part of his history lesson.

It became even more like the Peasants' Revolt when the stalwart Cornishmen encamped on Blackheath outside the very walls of London. Even Henry, whose whole attention had been centred on the army he was sending north to punish the Scots, was caught completely by surprise. But he acted promptly. He recalled the main army for the defence of London and put himself at the head of it, sending a smaller force merely for defence purposes to the Scottish border under Elizabeth's new brother-in-law, the Earl of Surrey. The Cornishmen fought valiantly; and although they had only obsolete weapons with which to oppose new Tudor cannon, they disconcerted their opponents by drawing a bow which sped an arrow long as a tailor's yard. It was a very shocking experience for the prosperous citizens of London to look down from their city walls and see an invading army gathered at their gates, and at first almost everyone believed that Perkin Warbeck was leading them. That this was the real invasion, or the return of England's King, who had promised to lighten their cruel taxes—whichever way one cared to look at it. And Elizabeth, who knew that it was only a horde of discontented West-countrymen, looked out over Blackheath too, and tried to imagine how she would have felt had it been her real brother Richard out there. Her despoiled brother battering at the walls of London and her own sons within. On whose side would she have stood? For the first time it came in full force to her understanding how the right of one must necessarily disinherit the other. And for the first time the secret hope that had always flickered in her heart became a fear. Much as she yearned after her young brother, she did not really *want* Perkin to be Dickon. And common sense had long ago persuaded her that he was not.

It was only afterwards that she knew how nearly the semblance of that very dilemma had come upon her. When Lord Audley had been executed on Tower Hill and Flammock and Michael Joseph hanged at Tyburn, Henry forgave the Cornishmen and sent them home, showing them none of the severity which had been used towards Perkin's followers when they landed in Kent. Indeed, as the Cornishmen themselves said, they had a sort of safety, because if the King were to hang everyone who objected to his taxations he would have no subjects left. But he could not forgo the opportunity to take some of their pitiful saving. Over and above what they owed, he fined them for their insubordination. So that as soon as they had returned to their far-off county and Perkin landed there they welcomed him as their saviour and clustered round him and bore him to Bodmin as their King. Three thousand strong they marched on Exeter, but Exeter—being a prosperous city which had benefited from Tudor encouragement to trade—would have none of them. Had Perkin landed a month or two earlier he might have been more fortunate; but now there was none of that first fine flood of enthusiasm which would have borne him along to the very gates of London. And Henry, hearing that the man who had caused him so many sleepless nights was in England and actually besieging one of his principal cities, left everything and hurried westwards with all the armed men he could raise.

Perkin, having fired the gates of Exeter and yet been repulsed, led his men on to Taunton, prepared to fight his way to London; but the Earl of Devonshire, to whom the Queen's sister Katherine was married, rose loyally for the Tudor. He called upon all the Devon Courteneys to surround Perkin's little army until the King's forces should arrive; so there was no more hope for the Yorkist pretender. With a small company of horsemen Perkin escaped in the night to the sanctuary of Beaulieu Abbey in Hampshire. Henry, delighted with the turn events had taken, presented his own sword to the gallant city of Exeter and promptly had Beaulieu surrounded. "Now, at last," he said to Thomas Stafford, who had ridden to Exeter with him, "the cat's-paw of Europe is in my hand!"

"Save that the ubiquitous pest is in sanctuary!" sighed the sore-tried Mayor of Exeter.

"For the peace of the realm the Pope would surely permit your Grace to drag him thence by force," pointed out Stafford.

"Your Grace could then put him to death and be rid of him for ever," the Earl of Devonshire backed him up eagerly.

"And have the truth about him go with him to the grave?" said Henry, with his tight-lipped smile. "No. Death is too easy. For six years he has cankered my life and set half Europe by the ears. He himself is nothing, yet lives and money have been poured out because of his impertinent pretensions. We do not want any more heroics about the Yorkists sung in Tudor England. I will make him confess again and again before all my loyal people and before all the poor fools whom he has deluded. By all we hear, he is a squeamish, sensitive fellow," he added more lightly, "and may as well pay for his pretty imaginings the price of ridicule. Did not my Uncle Jasper—God assoil him—once say that ridicule is the surest weapon of all?"

And so, in spite of all their urgings, Henry would not grant to Perkin Warbeck the importance of martyrdom, any more than he had to Lambert Simnel. "Give him a decent horse to ride and let him follow somewhere in the rear of our company to London. Neither served nor ill-treated," he ordered contemptuously. "Has any one of you heard news of my cousin, the lady Katherine Gordon?"

"They say that the first thing the impostor did upon landing, before ever the fighting began, was to have her placed for safety on that little rocky island off the toe of Cornwall which is called St. Michael's Mount," Stafford was able to inform him.

"If he did, it is the only decent thing I ever heard of him," said Henry. "Find out if she is with child, which God forbid, lest there be no end to this matter. And have her conveyed honourably by some other route to Greenwich, where she may be solaced by the Queen's kindness."

Henry saw to it that Elizabeth was at Greenwich when Perkin was brought into London. It was in order to spare her feelings, he said, since—being but a woman—she appeared at one time to have entertained doubts as to whether the rogue might really be her brother. So she was spared the sight of him riding defencelessly through London, with the mob throwing rotten vegetables and howling derisively at his heels. And of course there could be no doubt about his being counterfeit now, for, although the King's servants had never laid a hand upon him, he had been forced to read aloud a confession—not once or twice but many times. It was, in fact, that same biography which the King had had printed and circulated throughout the country, giving an itinerary of his short wandering life and details of his comparatively humble parentage.

Elizabeth was glad to be out of London, because merely hearing people joke about it afflicted her with the kind of vicarious shame which one feels about the exposure of theories or persons one once believed in. She was kind to Katherine Gordon and was glad to be able to assure her that once the hubbub of his arrival had died down Perkin would be allowed to live somewhere in the Palace of Westminster with no more restraint than a turned key to his apartments and a couple of guards. It was a triumph of Tudor clemency. But Elizabeth had to be very firm with Katherine about assuming that they were sisters-in-law. She found herself flinching every time the charming Scots girl referred to her husband as Richard, and—since nothing would shake her confidence in him—the Queen had to banish his name from their conversation.

Soon there was all their excitement of the Earl of Surrey's return from Scotland, and Ann's joy at welcoming him. Actually, he reported, there had been very little fighting. James challenged him to single combat with Berwick as the prize—which offer he had felt obliged to decline, since Berwick did not belong to him but to the King, his master. But with Perkin's claims puffed out like a candle James was clearly in a more conciliatory mood, and Henry, always tireless in the pursuit of peace and prosperity, took advantage of it to arrange a long peace treaty between the two countries and a marriage between the handsome, gifted James and his daughter Margaret. And with the arrival of the Earl of Bothwell and all the preparations for a proxy wedding and the making of much finery for their daughter, Henry could no longer keep the Queen away from Westminster.

"We Tudors will soon be the arbiters of the world!" she bragged merrily, peacocking before her sisters in her own new gown.

"We Tudors!" mocked Cicely, who had come back to London for the event. "Why, Bess Plantagenet, I believe you are really growing proud of this Welsh dynasty you have started! You look like a galleon in full sail, with your new purple velvet and your children grown up and marrying and going out into the world!"

"She looks lovely," asserted Ann, tweaking the pearled sides of her eldest sister's headdress to a yet more becoming angle.

"And you must admit that the Tudor himself will look most impressive in his state ermine as the bride's father!" laughed Elizabeth. "Henry must be at the peak of his power; and if hard endeavour goes for anything, he deserves it, and I am heartily glad for him after all the worry he has had. He is so pleased, Cicely, that our Margaret will be Queen of Scotland." Elizabeth walked to the window, her gorgeous train swishing after her, and raised her arms in a wide gesture of relief. "Think back upon those awful days of insecurity we endured during the Wars of the Roses, my dears, and imagine how fine it feels to have one daughter Queen of Scotland, my small, bright-hued Mary destined one day perhaps to be Queen of France, and Arthur married to the rich Aragon princess." Even if her children were growing up, Elizabeth herself was barely thirty-five, still slender and young enough to be foolish at times. She swung round and faced them, arms akimbo, as she used to do when encouraging or haranguing them when they were small. "As I say," she bragged again with an air, "we Tudors begin to bestride the world!"

They laughed at her, affectionately, glad of her high spirits. "And What about Harry, your favourite? What high honours is *he* destined for?" asked Ann, the perspicacious.

Elizabeth's face became all motherly concern immediately. "Oh, Ann, you must not say that! No mother should have favourites," she protested, yet at the same time realizing how precious it was to be still the centre of his world. "I am afraid the King has arranged no spectacular marriage for him yet. He is only a second son, of course, and recently since Henry has become so much more devout he has spoken about training him for the Church."

Irreverently, the girls burst out laughing. "Harry, a sober prelate!" they spluttered. And Patch, who had joined them unnoticed, placed a platter upside down upon his head, joined his fingertips together and raised his eyes to Heaven, treating them to a ridiculous mime of Prince Harry being solemn in a tonsure.

"Let us go and look at Margaret's gown for the proxy wedding.

That is what *really* matters," suggested Elizabeth, linking her arm in Cicely's. "The dressmakers are with her now." And as Ann had already seen it the two of them went along together. Margaret Tudor was standing in the middle of her room, a mere child in her bridal finery, with her women busy all about her. "She is too young to go to James yet," whispered Elizabeth, touched by the virgin freshness of her daughter.

"It does not seem so long since it was you standing like that trying on your wedding dress," murmured Cicely; and their smiling glances met, holding the memory.

"And to think how much I minded!" said Elizabeth.

"Minded?"

"About that odious Dauphin."

"All the same, that was your *real* bridal gown. For in a sense there has been no one since," said Cicely, with unusual understanding. "Or has there?"

Elizabeth shook her head sadly. "Only someone—I *could* have loved—"

"Tom Stafford?" said Cicely, still speaking in intimate undertones.

But Elizabeth had moved away and did not answer. To hide the colour burning her cheeks she bent down to examine the rose embroidery on her daughter's train. Life, for her, had never been as uncomplicated as that. And Margaret, having remarked their presence, was growing restive beneath all the measurements and pins. "Aunt Cicely, do you think I shall make a beautiful bride? Will the Earl of Bothwell like me?" she called across the heads of kneeling dressmakers. "I am so glad Lord Welles let you come to see me betrothed. But you ought to have come sooner, when all London was in an uproar about Perkin Warbeck! My father made him ride through the streets and read out loud all about who he really was. It was as good as a play, my laundress told me. She says they emptied their slops from upper windows all over that golden hair of his which he pretends is like ours, and even scooped up muck from the gutters and threw it in his face."

"Have you seen him, Bess?" asked Cicely.

"No. I am only now come from Greenwich."

"And I imagine none of us would want to!" said Ann, who had followed them, with a toss of her dainty head.

"But *I* have!" shouted Margaret triumphantly, emerging from the billows of satin which were being drawn over her rumpled head.

"You have seen him?" repeated the Queen in surprise. "Where?"

"From the window of that little anteroom beside the King's work-closet. It looks down on to a tiny walled garden where the monks used to walk. And Perkin Warbeck is allowed to walk there now. I saw him when I went to write my signature on some marriage documents. And the secretary told me that my father sometimes stands there and looks down too."

If Margaret had hoped to spring a surprise on her relatives, her sense of importance was satisfied. It was beneath a Queen's dignity to ask what so base an imposter looked like, but Elizabeth was glad when one of her sisters did.

"Oh, very ordinary," replied Margaret superciliously. "A fair, slight young man in plain worsted such as merchants wear. I could not see so much as a gash on him and he did not look even ashamed. After all the trouble he has caused, my father should have sent him whipped to Tyburn."

"Your father the King knows best," reproved Elizabeth sharply. "And it would become you to remember that your future husband was not so long ago this Perkin Warbeck's friend."

But the child's words had disturbed her.

"Why do you suppose Henry watches him like that?" she asked, returning with her sisters to her own apartments.

"Curiosity, I suppose," shrugged Cicely. "After all, whoever he is, this Perkin person has had rather an amazing run for his money."

"Like a cat watching a caught mouse," mused Elizabeth. "I sometimes wish he had put him to death. It might have been kinder. Henry did not even suggest making him a scullion. I wonder—what he is waiting for."

Cicely surveyed her anxiously. "Bess, you are not still fancying that he might really be Dickon? Not after what that awful Tyrrell man said—"

"No, no. Of course not. But, all the same, I should like to see him—just once."

After Cicely had rejoined her husband Elizabeth sat idly by her open window, watching summer thunder-clouds pile up above the sunset. The approaching storm made the evening still and airless. There was much to do for the entertainment of her Scottish guests, but her mind was not on her daughter's affairs. It had gone back to the things which Margaret had said with such young callousness. "Why is it that other people are allowed to see him and not I?" she wondered. "Why, half the people in London must have seen him. And I was always allowed to see Lambert Simnel. I went down into the kitchens that day. And I could see him now any day I liked, about the Palace or out hawking. And why was Henry so anxious to keep me away from Westminster?"

The storm spent its fury and passed, freshening the earth, and the morning of the proxy wedding dawned bright and cloudless. Yet, in spite of all the happy hospitable duties she had to perform, the thought nagged absurdly at the back of Elizabeth's mind. She could have asked Henry to let her see Perkin, of course. But even when their guests had retired, befriended and impressed, she could not bring herself to do so. He would probably laugh at her. Or refuse. And if he refused she would know that he himself, as she had once suspected, was not quite sure. That he was afraid that she, like her Aunt Margaret, might recognize him. The old quick fire of hope which she had supposed to be extinguished began to run through her again. In the evening, returning from vespers, she made occasion to walk with her ladies beside the old garden wall. Stopping for a moment or two and calling to one of them to adjust her shoe, she gave herself time to observe the strong iron gate. Seeing her, a couple of men-at-arms who had been sitting dicing on a log of wood beside it rose hurriedly and stood to attention. They were Perkin's guards, she supposed. A heavy old key hung from the belt of one of them.

When she went back into the Palace she found the King and the proxy bridegroom awaiting her. The Earl had come to make his adieux. He would be leaving in the morning. His master, he assured her, would count himself a very happy man.

"He will probably need to be a very firm one sometimes," laughed Elizabeth, with her usual candour. "But, happy as we are about this union, we shall be glad to have our daughter with us for a year or two longer."

"If Margaret is a little imperious sometimes, it is probably the effect of all this sudden ceremony and importance," said Henry, not liking to hear his favourite daughter even lightly criticized. "After so much excitement I think, Madam, it would be well if you took her to the quiet of our palace at Richmond to-morrow."

Elizabeth looked up quickly. "To-morrow?" she repeated involuntarily.

"I will tell them to prepare the barge."

But quite suddenly and definitely Elizabeth knew that she could not go to-morrow. There was something she must do first, even if it meant defying him. "If, by your Grace's leave, we might make it the following day—with all the clothes we brought—my own and the children's, it would be a little difficult to depart so soon. And I had hoped to spend a little time with Arthur before he returns to Ludlow—" she improvised. And because she was so seldom difficult—or because a guest was present—he could not well refuse to gratify so reasonable a request. "The day afterwards, then," he agreed pleasantly enough; but Elizabeth knew that it was a command.

"That gives me twenty-four hours," she thought, and wasted several of them lying awake. "He may change his mind and put this Perkin to death, and then I shall never see him," she thought. "But who is there to help me? Surely, among all the courtiers who daily pay me compliments, there is at least one who would arrange so small a thing?" Her mind roved over them, but not one, she decided, would risk the King's displeasure. She thought of Stafford, but he was married and a King's man now. Her mind moved down the social scale a little. Surely there was one of her own household—or one of the royal servants—who would find a way to serve her in this matter. And towards morning she remembered that there was someone who had said that he would do anything for her—anything at all.

Elizabeth rose early and, going to feed the parrot which Lord Stanley had given her, made loud lamentation that her new pet was ailing. And what more normal than to send for the King's head falconer?

"Why, of course, Madam," agreed her ladies. "He is so clever with birds."

Whatever important personages may have been going hawking that sunny morning, Simnel came immediately. He stood before her, feathered cap in hand and Tudor rose on jerkin, looking sturdy and dependable. And when, after asking him to examine the parrot, she managed to be alone with him for a few moments he made no elaborate protests of loyalty nor asked any inconvenient questions. He merely waited there, with the bird in his hands, ready to serve her.

"I want to get into that little old walled garden between the Palace and the Abbey," she told him as they stood beside the gilded cage. "But it is locked."

For a moment or two all his attention appeared to be concentrated upon the gaily hued wing outspread between his expert fingers. "How soon could your Grace be there?" he asked.

"In an hour from now?" The Queen's whisper sounded eager as a young girl's.

"It will be unlocked," was all he said.

The very simplicity of his loyalty disarmed her. "You will be taking a grave hazard, Simnel," she warned. "Even the Tudor does not forgive a man twice."

"Life is full of hazards, Madam," he said cheerfully, putting her parrot back carefully into its cage. "But with the ointment I shall send—a little on the wing daily—I think your Grace need have no further anxiety," he added in a louder voice as some of her ladies returned from the errand upon which she had sent them. He bowed then, feathered hat in hand again, and excused himself. "One of the King's favourite falcons has escaped, Madam," he explained. "So I must hurry."

"Oh, Simnel!" exclaimed the women sympathetically.

"I shall soon get her back, ladies," he assured them. "She may have flown into the yard of a private house or over some garden wall. But everyone will willingly let me in to search."

He was so goodnatured and such a general favourite that the Queen made no doubt they would. Even those two guards whom she had seen dicing away their tedium. "How long will it take you, Simnel?" she asked anxiously.

"No longer than to persuade people to lend me their keys in the King's name. And, of course," he added with an engaging grin as he bent near her to make sure the gilded cage was latched, "to see first that a falcon *really* escapes!"

Chapter Twenty-Six

I T WAS VERY QUIET in the little walled garden. Only the birds sang as they darted between the tangled bushes or strutted unafraid upon the daisy-strewn grass. The air was sweet with the scent of honeysuckle and the high walls shut out all sound of the everyday world.

Letting the heavy gate close behind her, Elizabeth felt as if she had stepped outside her normal life into a dream. Warmth and peace enfolded her and time seemed to stand still. Yet she found herself hurrying. As she followed one of the overgrown paths her feet began to run and her breath to come more quickly. Trailing brambles caught at the rich material of her skirts, and cobwebs, still dew-starred, brushed softly through her fingers; but she scarcely heeded them. She had waited so long for this encounter, yet knew not whom she would meet.

"It will be like the day I went to see Simnel in the kitchens," she assured herself, as she penetrated deeper into the garden. "This Perkin impostor will turn round and my heart will go blank as it did then. There will be the same sharp disappointment, like the cutting of a surgeon's knife, and then I shall be cured."

Suddenly, at a bend in the path, she came upon him. So suddenly that she stopped short with a hand on her racing heart. He was standing in the morning sunlight, a slim graceful figure outlined against a sunwashed wall. The light burnished his golden head as he bent over a book. This time there was to be no short, decisive cure. He might have been Dickon, grown to manhood, standing there.

"No wonder they all believed in him!" she thought.

Elizabeth supposed that she must have spoken the words aloud, for he turned then and saw her. Some grand lady in green and gold, staring at his solitude. Whatever surprise he may have felt, he had sufficient social poise to conceal it. He came forward a step or two, courteously, to greet her. "Madam, the morning was beautiful before your beauty adorned it," he said, with a delighted smile, "but now—"

Clearly, he had not recognized her. Elizabeth drew closer, looking into his face. Her eagerness may have betrayed her, or the rare jewels she wore. His mind worked like quicksilver. "But now it is home," he submitted smoothly, and stretched out both his shapely hands towards her.

It had never occurred to her that she might see him and still not be sure. But this was a man's face, with no boyish curves left. The fair skin was bronzed a little by the weather, the smooth flesh of cheek and chin tightened by shaving. There was about it a jauntiness, a wariness, and even an unfamiliar suggestion of hardness. Only the mouth was tender, as she had remembered Dickon's. Of course he, too, might feel uncertain and be taking a chance. But whoever he was he had the advantage over her, for he must often have seen her recent portrait in Margaret of Burgundy's house. Elizabeth withdrew her half-extended hands which had moved so spontaneously to meet his. "Are you the person they call Perkin Warbeck?" she asked.

By turning to lay his book aside upon the seat he gained a moment for reflection. But he must have decided to make no effort to gainsay her. "Or Osbeck," he shrugged, as if amused. "They never seem quite certain. And you, Madam," he said, bowing profoundly, "must be Elizabeth, the Queen."

"I came to see how you fared," she lied, "after all that they did to you."

"That was heavenly gracious of you. But their tormentings did not amount to much," he said, gathering up his cloak and spreading it for her across the stone bench. "Will your Grace deign to sit here?"

Elizabeth's limbs were trembling and she could not have refused him if she would. She sank down thankfully in the pleasant shade of an old mulberry tree. "Surely it was hard to bear, the hooting and the—things they threw?"

He winced, but she guessed that his fastidious pride was suffering less from the memory than because she had heard of it. He stood easily before her, expounding his philosophy of life. "One can always keep one's thoughts on something else," he said. "On a lark that is singing, on the thought of how badly the man in front rides, or upon the woman one loves."

"And that would help?" The Queen's voice was low and pitiful.

"Imagination can always rise above reality."

"You have certainly not been wanting in imagination! Imagination for which others have suffered," she said scornfully. He made an expressive gesture of regret and she relented. "But—when you read aloud your confession and they mocked you?"

"Ah, there I found it paid to employ other tactics," he told her, entering into the matter with absurd zest. "It was not *my* confession, of course. But, even so, one should join in the baiting, giving back shaft for shaft, steering their sense of the ridiculous, whenever possible, towards something else. Always with wit and good humour, *bien entendu*. For there is nothing your Londoner likes better than a good laugh. I assure you, Madam, I am becoming so experienced in these matters that I thought of employing my tedium here by writing a book for my fellow-unfortunates. 'Eloquence through rotten eggs,' perhaps, or 'Suitable sayings from the stocks.'"

"Don't!"

Grinning down at her, he looked more than ever like her memories of Dickon. "But why should you care?" he asked, teasing her with mock amazement.

"Because you remind me—"

"Ah!" He grew grave again, but did not pursue the advantage. The precious time was passing, and she had so much to ask him—so many traps to set. "Tell me about my aunt, the Dowager Duchess," she commanded.

"She is in good health and entrusted me with her love to you."

"Then she really supposed that you would get so far as to see me?"

"And so I have," he reminded her.

"But scarcely in the way that she intended."

"That will be a great disappointment to her," he admitted. "The Duchess was extraordinarily good to me."

"And you adored her." Illusion was so strong that it was on the tip of Elizabeth's tongue to add, "You always *did* adore her."

"Although I was grateful, I did not enjoy being beholden. Her Grace had too much the ordering of my life. And she could be vindictive. Particularly to the Tudors, of course."

"And it was she, I suppose, who really taught you English?"

"Heaven forbid!" he exclaimed, with a boyish burst of laughter. "She has acquired an execrable Lowland accent."

His own was pure native as the English hills.

"But she taught you all about us. Our names and habits, and how we looked and talked, so that you could speak of us familiarly. And about King Edward."

"There was no need. I remember my father perfectly."

"Jean de Warbeck, the merchant of Tournay?"

"If you say so, Madam."

Quite unreasonably, his good-tempered agreement angered her more than his pride. "Why do you so meekly say everything that is put into your mouth? Oh, I know that you had no choice—out there—when the King made you. But here—with me?"

His smile was both diffident and engaging. "Having failed, would it not be but poor kindness to persuade you?"

"You mean," she said, quick to pick up his thought, "that, so long as there was any question of your succeeding, it was my son or you?"

"And since my day is done let it be indubitably your son."

The insolence of his presuming to give her peace of mind infuriated her. "And probably not pressing his claim is just a clever way to avoid my questioning," she thought.

"How can anything that you do affect my son? Or anyone seriously suppose you to be a Plantagenet?" she demanded. "Men of my family do not persuade their allies to retreat. They fight like the third Richard fought at Bosworth, or ride out alone to face an angry mob like the second Richard did in the Peasants' Revolt."

The colour rose hotly in his cheeks. "Neither of them had to see their own country ravaged for the sake of destroying it, or Englishwomen raped by foreigners," he said.

He was too readily plausible, she decided. And then, just when she was sure of his guile, he was down on one knee beside her, neither parrying nor posing, but unfeignedly sincere. "I pray you give me news of my wife," he beseeched. "I hear that she is with you."

"She is well," said Elizabeth, looking down into his ardent face and thinking what a lover he would make. "I should like to be able to tell you that she is happy. But at least she is kindly treated."

"Everybody says you are the kindest Queen in Christendom!" he cried gratefully, bending to kiss the hands that lay in her lap.

In spite of herself, she was pleased with the compliment. She would have liked to touch his bent head. "Your Kate is easy to be kind to," she said smilingly.

"She gave up everything to follow me. She is sweet as the heather on the Scottish hills," he said. "Could you tell her that you have seen me? That I am shamefully well. And give her my undying love—"

Elizabeth released her hands from his eager hold and held up one to stay his importunity. "How can I tell anyone that I came here?" she reminded him. "Do you not suppose that I took some risk to do so?"

"Of course you must have done, ingrate that I am!" he agreed, rising to his feet.

But, seeing the disappointment upon his sensitive face, Elizabeth found the same difficulty in refusing him which had so often betrayed her into doing things for her young brothers. "She is coming to Richmond with me to-morrow, and one day I shall probably find means to reassure her," she half promised him.

"Bess—Madam—I will make a bargain with you," he began; and it was well done, she thought, that artfully dropped name even in the midst of his real sincerity. "If you will go on being kind to Kate I will go on playing Warbeck. I owe that much to her now—and to you."

"You have no choice," said Elizabeth, trying to speak coldly. "The King has made you confess yourself an impostor and may do so again."

"But if ever I came to the scaffold I could say anything. No one could prevent me in those last moments. And I look so inconveniently like you."

It was uncomfortably true. Sitting near him in the sunlight, Elizabeth could not deny it; and although she had almost persuaded herself that he was not Dickon, the idea of anyone so like her brother standing on the scaffold was unbearable. "What do you remember about your father?" she asked abruptly, as if to allay the thought.

Instantly his wariness seemed to change to pleasure and there was a reminiscent smile upon his lips. He seemed to be upon sure ground and there was no talk now of the Tournay merchant. "Chiefly how tall he was, and how good to look upon. And how pleasantly his clothes smelt of musk or amber. There was a locket, he wore, I remember, and straight bands of pearled beading across his breast."

"Most of which you could have gathered from his portraits," said Elizabeth.

"Of course," he agreed without offence. "But no painting could show how the room came alive with his vitality when he came into it, or how even the most ordinary things suddenly became interesting. How he was always laughing and telling Will Hastings to do all the dull things. And how, when he had time, he made one love his books and yet seemed always to be either coming in hungry from the chase or in a tearing hurry to go to it!"

"Aunt Margaret could have told you all that."

"But she couldn't make you feel it, could she? Not the laughter and the *security*. When I was small and he lifted me on to his knee and let me build castles on his table. Or the bursting pride in my breast when he swung me up high above his head and called out in his great voice: 'By Christ's breath, Will, this youngling of mine is the most diverting companion of them all!' It is one's *feelings* one remembers."

Elizabeth was leaning forward, spellbound. "What did you build your castles *of* upon his table?" she asked.

He stopped in full spate and frowned uncertainly. "I do not really remember. It is so long ago. Little blocks of wood of some sort, I suppose."

"Pieces of type?" she suggested eagerly—and saw her mistake too late. How useless to ask leading questions and then be beguiled into supplying the right answers.

She was watching him so intently that she caught the momentary gleam of satisfaction on his face; yet his voice sounded indifferent enough. "Yes, it could have been something like that," he said, and began negligently exploring the contents of the purse at his belt.

"Do you remember watching his funeral from a window?" she persisted, and immediately he described it. But he was clever enough to talk mostly about the wooden effigy clad in the King's state clothes which would naturally have made most impression upon a small boy.

His passing reference to the hole made in the Palace wall when they went into sanctuary sounded convincing and the sort of thing a child would remember, but of course he could have been told that too. She must think of something which he could not possibly have been told. "And do you remember what I said to you when—when I last saw you? As you went out of the Abbot of Westminster's door?"

He stared at her for a moment, seemed about to say something and then changed his mind. Playing for safety, no doubt, she thought. Finally, he shook his head. "It is so long ago," he murmured. But Dickon, who loved her, would have remembered.

It was queer. She could swear that he remembered some things—up to a point. But not those more recent things which were most vivid to her. Probably her mother's explanation was right. "But of course you remember Mistress Grace?" she asked carelessly.

"Grace? Grace?" he repeated; and she supposed that he must be picking his words very warily now. "I seem to remember the name."

"She was always about the Court."

If he knew who she was he kept a noncommittal silence.

"She is said to have been a love-child of my father's and was devoted to my mother, who, of her charity, brought her up."

In her intense desire to make him betray himself Elizabeth leaned towards him eagerly; but he only shook his head. "My life has been so wandering, and spent in different countries. I have met so many people since then," he explained. Which was, of course, reasonable enough.

"Like me, this Mistress Grace had a younger brother," added Elizabeth meaningly.

"And you think that I am he?"

"I think that so many people have told you so many lies about yourself for their own ends that—"

"By now it is difficult for me myself—"

"To know which to believe."

He was uncannily quick at picking up her ideas, but was smiling broadly as he recapitulated them. "Then you will go so far as to permit yourself to think that I am one of the King's bastards? And that this Grace woman, to please the late Queen in her last illness, sent me to the Duchess. That is very ingenious."

"It is at least as likely a story as any."

They were talking now in quick, half-finished sentences as only those can whose minds are intimate. Not since the older Richard rode to Bosworth had Elizabeth talked like that with a man who seemed to be of her own blood. And she found it a mental release to talk so again, with someone who picked up her half-spoken thoughts, who did not kill conversation by taking light expressions literally—someone whom she could argue with and yet like, disbelieve in and yet trust. And it made her realize sadly how stilted had been all her conversations with Henry Tudor—and how impossible it was for even a lifetime of such barren utterances to lead them to see into each other's minds.

"I do not deny that you may be half Plantagenet," she conceded.

And because the scent of the lime tree was so languorous and life had been so hard—because she took such pleasure in his looks and the time she dare stay with him was so short—Elizabeth let the peace of the moment steal over her. With an almost drowsy gesture she patted the bench beside her invitingly and when he sat down she leaned against him. "I am glad you have this garden and not some horrible cell," she murmured.

"The King's kindness has been—incomprehensible," he said. "I hope he is kind to you?"

"Kind?" Thoughtfully Elizabeth stirred the little pebbles of the path with the point of her shoe. "Yes. If you call it kind never to be rough—nor inconsiderate about my comfort. He never forgets to buy me anything he promises—nor what he paid for it. He makes notes of everything I am to do in his little day-book."

"How horrible!"

"It probably helps to make up for all the years when he wasn't important enough to arrange even his own life."

"What a way to talk about your husband!" laughed her companion.

"How should I talk about him?" asked Elizabeth, rousing herself to look up at him.

"One does not analyse a person one loves. One just loves them as they are."

"But I did not say I loved him," said Elizabeth, and her head went back comfortably against his shoulder.

"Have you no other lover?" he asked after a moment or two. "Surely anyone as beautiful as you—"

It was not the first time the idea had occurred to her. She wiggled the point of her shoe and looked down at it consideringly. "Would a woman dare to, who was married to Henry?"

"I suppose not. His mercy is so much more terrible than Uncle Richard's ruthlessness. But for a woman who is made for love as you are—"

"I try to fill my life," Elizabeth said. "I have my children. And there are so many pleasant and amusing things—"

"Which would be so much more than pleasant or amusing shared."

"Ah!" The shadow of the great Abbey was creeping over the

grass, passing as inexorably as one's most precious hours. In a few minutes the bells would be ringing for Matins, and she had promised to go then. She felt her companion's arm slide warm and comforting behind her along the back of the seat, and suddenly, inexplicably, she found herself telling him things of which she had never spoken even to her sisters or to her confessor. "There is nothing that we really share, except our formal strutting through a reign of history—towards that grand tomb which Henry is preparing in Westminster. Have you seen it?"

He shook his head.

"Even our coming together physically is—routine. Though we had to marry—to graft the Tudor roses—it should not be, should it?"

"It should be a losing of oneself to find ecstasy. A fire, a completion, a fusing of flesh and spirit. Human comfort—yet the moon and the stars."

"As it is with you and your Kate?"

"Yes."

"And even though you are separated—though she may lose you for all time—she has had that ecstasy. She is richer than I," sighed Elizabeth.

"My poor Bess!"

She thought that his lips touched her hair. Even though she did not really believe in him—even though young Dickon was dead—it was sweet to hear him say her name much as Dickon might have said it. Unutterably sweet to let herself *pretend* to believe—for the space of these few minutes which were left. "It is so hard to know that life is passing. That I am thirty-five. That I have beauty and the capacity for passion. And that neither in marriage nor illicitly have I lived through one single night in the arms of a lover. There are women who accept my kind of marriage meekly, I suppose; and men who think we have no desires. Or never think of us at all. Oh, I know that I should strive after patience and righteousness. And if I strive hard enough I may even attain a small heavenly crown," she finished, with a little shaky laugh. "But never in this life shall I have known—the moon and the stars!"

"I suppose that women in convents who take vows—" he began,

seeking for some way in which to comfort her. But her interruption was sharp with bitterness.

"They are not nightly reminded of what might have been—and then frustrated," she said.

He withdrew his arm from the bench and leaned forward, grinding fist in palm as though, in his almost feminine sensitivity, he endured some part of her raging against the way life had cheated her. "Odd that such men are so often respected—that there are such different kinds of brutality!" he muttered incoherently.

Elizabeth sat up very straight and stared at him. "Why do you say that? Whom have you heard say it before?" she demanded.

His surprise was patent, and the question brought them both back to the commonplace. "No one, so far as I know. But it is true, is it not?"

"Yes, yes," she agreed, with hurried self-consciousness. "But I do not know what made me speak of such things. And above all to you."

He was smiling again, his charming, casual smile. "Because you are not likely to see me again," he suggested. "And so it will not matter."

"Yet I came to question you—not to talk about myself."

"It may ease you to have found someone to whom you *could* speak of it—just once."

"Because we speak the same language."

"Then why do you find it so difficult to believe me to be Dickon?" he asked.

"It is not difficult. It might be desperately easy if one had no common sense. And if the King had not disproved it." Elizabeth was quick to forestall any protest with a question of her own. "Why do you sometimes talk as if you might soon die?"

He shrugged and turned away. "I do not want to. I love life. But I am a restless sort of person," he said lightly. And even as he spoke the great Abbey bell began to ring.

Elizabeth, a creature of kept promises, stood up immediately; but it was difficult to go. "I have always worn this," she said challengingly, drawing the miniature of her brother from the bosom of her dress. "Surely if you claim to be the Duke you must have something which belonged to our father?"

"When a terrified child with his brother's screams still in his ears is carried from the scene of murder and put into a swaying boat he does not stop to collect his childhood treasures," he told her grimly.

"No, of course not. It was foolish of me to ask. And I really knew that James of Scotland had tried to prove you with the same question, and that you could produce nothing."

The young man's hand went again to his wallet. "Only these," he said, holding out a few pieces of a printer's type. "And they scarcely seemed worth showing to a realistic King like James."

With a little cry Elizabeth was bending over his open palm, turning them about. "Dickon!" she cried. "They are Master Caxton's. See, they have the impress."

"They must have been in the pocket of the old coat they bundled me into that night. I suppose I kept them—sentimentally—or as a kind of mascot."

"Of course. You were building a castle with them on the King's table. Don't you remember that day when—" Elizabeth stopped abruptly. This time she had the sense not to give him a clue.

For her it would always be the day when the Dauphin jilted her. But Dickon had been too young to realize. Breathlessly, alternating between hope and fear, she waited for him to say eagerly, "Of course! That day when we younger ones played weddings in the garden. And I brought in the big book and found you sitting crying in the King's chair. And I asked you why, if it were not particularly comfortable, so many people wanted to sit in it."

But he just stood there looking at her. Either he could not or would not supply the all-important words. And why had he not produced the little blocks of wood before? She had looked up quickly—quickly enough, she fancied, to catch the triumphant quirk of an eyebrow. And then she remembered. "How clever of you!" she said, in a voice low with anger. "But, of course, Caxton was with Margaret of Burgundy before ever he came to us. You might have picked them up anywhere—as a novelty. And a while back, when I was fool enough to mention them, you felt in your wallet to make sure they were there."

She walked swiftly away from him, her head held high. She was not even aware that he followed her. When she reached the garden gate she detached the heavy old key from the chatelaine swinging against her skirts and let herself out. The ordinary world looked desirable enough in the June sunshine. She could hear excited voices from somewhere in the direction of the Palace and guessed that the escaped falcon had been found. Simnel had probably beguiled the impostor's guards into joining in the chase. Neither of them was in sight. Elizabeth put the key back in the outside of the lock, paused for as long as it takes to make a sudden, crazy decision, and then went on her way. "Madam, you have forgotten to lock the gate!" a gay voice called after her. He must be standing at the little grille, watching her go up the Palace path. Was he mocking her because he knew that she could not find it in her heart to go back and lock it? How dared he stake such an undreamed-of chance of liberty upon the assurance of his charm? Most men would have profited in silence by a woman's whim of kindness, not given her a chance to change her mind. Or was he actually warning her, at his own expense? Giving her a chance to undo such dangerous foolishness? In any case she was sorry she had taunted him with cowardice. For he had proved himself to be sensitive and kind. And in a world where there were so many different kinds of brutality, might there not be different kinds of courage?

Chapter Twenty-Seven

Perkin Warbeck's escape was a nine days' wonder. Why should he have wanted to escape at all, people asked, when he had little further hope of raising a following and was at least reasonably safe? Everybody about the Palace precincts had been concerned all morning about the King's lost falcon, and it was not until they took Perkin his midday meal that his negligent warders found that a much more important prey had escaped.

The Queen's ladies rushed to tell her the news, and in their excitement about the doings of a man whose strange adventures had for so long intrigued everybody they chattered so much that they scarcely noticed how little the Queen herself said. And it was not surprising, of course, that deaf old Mattie, who knew all her secrets, should make no remark at all. And soon the arrival of Katherine Gordon made them start discussing it all over again.

"What will they *do*?" Perkin's wife asked distractedly.

"The King has closed all the ports," they told her.

"And even if he had not, do not raise your hopes that your husband will get any more following abroad," Elizabeth warned her.

"He might get back to Scotland?" the girl suggested hopefully.

Elizabeth put down the book of devotions she was pretending to read. She was sane now, freed from the spell. Cured, she supposed. "Scotland, Flanders, France—what difference does it make?" she asked wearily. "As soon as he left each of them the King, in his wisdom, made friendly alliances with each country so that they could never invite him back. Do you suppose that your Cousin James would risk for an adventurer's sake his own marriage with our daughter?" But Elizabeth's own hopes were still divided. She wished that Perkin would get clean away and never trouble them again. Yet so long as he lived and was at liberty Henry's anxiety would be as it was before. Anxiety which had prematurely aged him. Elizabeth had acted upon the spur of the moment, and now that she had time for reflection she was afraid of the enormity of the thing she had done; afraid both for herself and for the King's head falconer. Yet, strangely enough, not even the guards were called to account; and when she next saw Henry he looked neither angry nor unduly worried. He even went hawking in Richmond Park the very next day—perhaps in order to show his subjects of how small consequence the matter was. But during the weeks which followed Elizabeth often caught him watching her with that thin-lipped, mirthless smile which gave him what old Mattie so disrespectfully called his cat-and-mouse expression. And recalling what her daughter had said about his looking down from his anteroom window, Elizabeth began to wonder if he could possibly have seen her leaving the garden that day.

Torn by a variety of emotions, she was glad of the distraction afforded by their removal to Richmond. It had given her something fresh to think about and less time to see the strained anxiety in Katherine Gordon's eyes. "If he can get abroad and make some sort of life for himself, however humble, I would live with him," the poor girl kept saying. "Do you suppose, Madam, that the King would let me?"

"No," said Elizabeth uncompromisingly. "Is it not enough that his Grace is kind to you and makes you an allowance? You should thank the blessed saints that you were not with child by this impostor or he might have been forced to act differently."

"But, after all, I am his cousin, and I think he likes me," mused Katherine.

"Yes. I am sure that he likes you," replied Elizabeth, pausing before her mirror and deciding that it was not only Henry who was ageing. The strain of all that she had been through was beginning to tell on her, and for the first time she discerned faint lines which might in time mar the serenity of her beauty. She had brought to her husband the benefit of her popularity and given him a fine family to unite the red and white roses, which was probably all that he had ever wanted of her. So perhaps the reason why he did not often come to her bed now was that he liked this pretty Scottish cousin of his too much. The thought annoyed but did not hurt her. "And I am afraid I grow more and more apt to misjudge him," she thought.

During the days that followed Elizabeth strove hard to keep her thoughts from Katherine Gordon's attractive husband and all that had happened in the monk's old garden. And the simplest way was to make up her mind once and for all. She was convinced that she could never have felt that kinship with him and opened her heart to him had he not had Plantagenet blood. For the sake of her own peace of mind she accepted her mother's solution of the matter. He was some bastard brother who looked extraordinarily like Dickon. How else could he have had that fineness of feature and that charm of manner? And her mother, she guessed, had secretly contrived the affair with her all too willing sister-in-law, Margaret of Burgundy. Ill as the Dowager Queen was at the time, Mistress Grace, who was so devoted to her, could have sent her own younger brother as the tool that Margaret sought. A tool so likely that he must have appeared to her as a gift from Heaven with his looks, his knowledge of Court life and his inherited charm. A counterfeit so plausible that for more than six years he could put fear into even the self-sufficient Tudor. But whoever the young man was Elizabeth did not like to think of him, hunted and hungry, hurrying from one watched port to another, pitting his nimble wits against her husband's.

Her imaginings were groundless, for in the end the King's men caught him within a stone's throw of Richmond Palace. Even then he dodged like a hare and escaped them and managed to enter the sanctuary of Sheen Priory.

"You see," said Katherine Gordon triumphantly to all who would listen to her, "were he not really your Richard of York how could he have known that sanctuary was at hand?"

"He had time to look round," snapped Jane Stafford, knowing how this constant use of the name affected her mistress. "A noble priory with acres of land could scarcely be mistaken for a farmstead."

But for once the Queen overlooked the use of the forbidden name and drew their guest gently aside. "I am sure that it was the Palace, not the Priory, he was originally making for," she consoled her. "He must have loved you very dearly to risk his life to see you, Kate."

In spite of her anxiety, the girl's fair face flushed with happiness. "But how could he possibly have known that we were coming here?" she asked, after a moment's consideration.

But that the Queen had no intention of telling her.

"Well, at least he is safe," they both sighed.

But he was not, for there was an end even to Henry's patience. This time the King disregarded the laws of Holy Church. Perkin Warbeck was a disturber of the public peace, he contended firmly, and demanded that the Prior should deliver him up. It was well known that Henry never offended the Church if he could help it, and more and more frequently he had made valuable religious foundations and bequests; but the common sense of his request roused so much sound backing throughout the country that the Prior agreed to hand over the pretender on condition that his life should be spared. And judging from the spirited way in which he bargained with the King, it seemed probable that during the few short hours of his unwanted guest's sojourn the wise old Prior, too, must have succumbed to some inherited Plantagenet charm!

The whole nation marvelled when Henry acquiesced, merely having the impudent impostor set in the stocks for the whole of a forenoon before Westminster Hall and then again at Cheapside, and then imprisoning him for life. "Put him in one of those cells beneath the Earl of Warwick's room," she heard Henry tell the Lieutenant of the Tower. And there, presumably, he would eat his young heart out, forgetting the warmth and sunshine and the song of the birds, not being even allowed to walk on the battlements as her poor Cousin Warwick did.

The year limped away and Elizabeth resolutely turned her mind from that grim place. More and more she spent time and money on the sick and the distressed so that she came to be known as Elizabeth the Good. She tried not to criticize anything that her husband did and to keep her mind dutifully upon the concerns of her own household and family. Now that her mother-in-law had withdrawn from Court, Elizabeth relied more and more upon her own judgement; and although she never sought any of the spectacular power so beloved by the Woodville side of her family, she was pleased to find that within her own sphere she had much quiet influence. Her children adored her and she counted herself fortunate in the frequent companionship of her sisters. Although Katherine Plantagenet was now one of the Devon Courteneys and absorbed in their affairs, and young Bridget was already a novice, Ann—who had married the brilliant Earl of Surrey—was often in attendance upon the Queen. And when Cicely's rich old husband died it was Elizabeth to whom she came for advice. For life was blossoming anew for Cicely because she need no longer make a secret of her love for Sir Robert Kim, a gentleman of Lincolnshire. "But of course the King would never hear of my marrying him," she would sigh.

"What he does not hear of he cannot prevent," pointed out Elizabeth.

Cicely stared at her favourite sister in surprise. "You mean that you, who took "Humble and Reverent" for your motto, seriously advise us to marry without his permission, Bess?"

"Only if you are prepared to live away from all the gaiety of Court. In some quiet country manor perhaps. Think well, my sweet. You need to be very sure, you who have always been so lively and so feted."

"Oh, Bess, for Robert I would live *anywhere!*"

"Then that is the answer," said Elizabeth, with a new firm assurance.

"And you would do what you could for us if the King is angry?"

"I would do what little I could."

"I suppose I should not ask this of you, but you do not know how awful it is to be married while one is still young to a man whose touch is like salted fish on Good Friday!" explained Lord Welles' new young widow.

Elizabeth took her sister's piquant face between both her hands and kissed her very tenderly. "Darling Cicely, I understand better than you suppose," she said quietly. "*I* was heir to a throne and had no personal choice. But for one whose happiness I desire above all things I would say 'Take a man who will be your mate.'"

That her elder children could not marry for that reason Elizabeth knew and accepted. But James of Scotland was manly and generous, and the Spanish girl by all accounts had been well brought up. So she did what she could to prepare the characters of Arthur and Margaret and their knowledge of foreign languages, and their wardrobes for their approaching marriages, in spite of the fact that the Spanish sovereigns seemed still to hesitate. "But Henry is sure to find some way to persuade them," she told her anxious friends, being more confident than ever of his power and wisdom.

And then one day all London was suddenly agog with the news that Perkin Warbeck, whom people had baited in the stocks, had tried to escape again.

"But surely, nobody ever escapes from the Tower!" exclaimed Elizabeth, when her brother-in-law, the Earl of Surrey, came to tell her. She was sitting talking with Thomas Stafford and his sister, and her old friend Lord Stanley, and in her sudden agitation she rose from her chair, scattering her embroidery silks upon the floor.

"Nobody ever will, Madam," Surrey assured her. "But few people have ever succeeded so nearly as he. They were by the Byward Tower—almost on to the drawbridge—when they were taken."

"They?"

"Your Grace's cousin, the Earl of Warwick, was with him."

"Warwick!" exclaimed Jane Stafford, down on her knees gathering up the silks.

"It appears they had concocted some sort of plot—" explained Thomas Stafford, who had heard of it before but been warned by his sister not to speak of it before the Queen.

"My cousin of Warwick concocted a plot!" protested Elizabeth. "I ask you, my dear Tom, would he not be hard put to it to arrange the simplest hawking party?"

"Then it must have been this Perkin who concocted it," surmised Lord Stanley, whose mind had been slipping from Court affairs since his brother was executed. "No doubt Warwick, tired of years of constraint, lent a willing enough ear. We all know that obliging way he has. He probably did everything Perkin Warbeck bade him."

"What puzzles me, milords," said Jane, squatting back on her heels with the silks in her lap, "is how, if Perkin were locked in one of those terrible cells, the two of them could meet?"

"The cell was found unbolted," said Surrey. "True to type, he must have managed to make friends with his guards."

"But they were all four specially chosen. Strangeways, Blewet, Astwood and the man they call Long Roger. I heard the King appoint them," said Elizabeth, unaware that she was providing his stepfather, who had cause to know Henry so well, with a possible clue. "Each of them had already proved himself zealous in serving the King."

"Perhaps they *were* serving him," suggested Stanley blandly.

Elizabeth swung round on him in understanding surprise. "You mean that this time the clever pretender was fooled? That he was the bait?" she demanded angrily.

"Well, anyhow," summed up Surrey, trying, as usual, to smooth matters over, "they are both taken now and held for trial. And we all know what the end of them will be."

"Oh no!" cried Elizabeth. "The King would not do *that*! Everyone knows how merciful he is, and he must realize as well as we do that whatever happened Warwick could not really have been responsible."

"But no doubt—saving your Grace's presence—it would clear the path to the Spanish marriage miraculously were the trial to go against him," remarked Stanley.

And this time Elizabeth said nothing. She was recalling those words of Archbishop Morton's which she had accidentally overheard. "So long as Warwick lives there will be no Spanish marriage." And she shivered as if someone walked over her grave. Was her son's marriage to be paid for in Plantagenet blood? Just as Henry made his wars pay, had he used the cat's-paw of Europe for his own ends at last?

When the day came for Edward, Earl of Warwick, to be executed on Tower Hill, Elizabeth the Queen, as was most fitting, went alone into her oratory to pray for the passing of his gentle soul. There were tears in her eyes for his untimely death and for the pitifully useless days of his life. But the thoughts of her heart were really at Tyburn, where another young man who had wished him no harm, and who probably deserved to be hanged, waited beneath the common gallows. Even in the midst of her prayers Elizabeth pictured him standing on the scaffold in the morning sunlight, gay and dramatic, above the gaping English crowd, confessing to the last, with an engaging smile, that he was the son of a merchant of Tournay. And it was almost as if she could hear his voice saying again, in the warm, walled garden, "Since my day is done, let it be indubitably your son."

Chapter Twenty-Eight

ELIZABETH STOOD ON THE dais in Westminster Hall with all the wealth of Tudor pageantry around her. It was her elder son's wedding day and the culmination of the hard-won union of two great powers. Spanish splendour, in which the elegance of black played so effective a part, vied with the more richly hued familiar devices of the English. All the previous week there had been magnificent comings-and-goings to meet the Princess of Aragon, and a scurrying of servants to prepare for the impressive reception of her numerous entourage. And on this happy day itself the bells of all the churches had rocked their steeples, and the people, packing the street, had thrown their caps in the air and shouted a spontaneous welcome to the youthful Prince of Wales and his auburn-haired bride. The water conduits ran with wine, altars and sideboards gleamed with gold plate, and all the best horse trappings and heraldic banners in the country had been brought out. Never, since the Tudor mounted the throne, had there been such lavish expenditure.

"A wildly successful procession through London, a wedding in St. Paul's, a tournament in front of Westminster Hall, every kind of masque and mummery, and now a state banquet—truly so much celebration is exhausting!" laughed Elizabeth. "By your leave, Henry, I will go and rest a little while before the final spectacle."

"I would that I might join you!" smiled the King, in rare good humour. "As you say, a week of playing hosts upon such a scale is apt to bring it home to us that we are not so young!"

"But it is so wonderful, Madam!" protested their younger son Harry, escorting her to a secluded gallery and setting a chair for her. "I beg you not to stay away long."

"Do you never tire, child?" she asked, marvelling at his enthusiastic energy as she brushed his flushed cheek with loving fingers.

"How should I when there is so much to see and hear and do? I wish Arthur were married every day. And how I wish I could have tilted out there with Uncle Courteney and Thomas Stafford and all the rest!"

"Perhaps one day you may do better than any of them," she foretold, regarding his tall muscular body with pride.

"Then it will be *your* favour and no silly chit's that I shall wear in my helm," he vowed, setting a stool for her feet and then bestriding it as if it were a horse. "Tell me, dear one, did I carry it off well, escorting my new sister-in-law through London to St. Paul's?"

"It was nice of the King to let you," Elizabeth reminded him. Looking down upon the procession, she had in fact been eaten with pride in him, but she always tried not to feed his exuberant vanity.

"Katherine is quite human really, once one can get behind all that rigid etiquette with which those priests and duennas surround her," he ran on, not really noticing whether his mother had answered him or not. "And she has such exciting clothes. That wide-brimmed Spanish hat she wore when she was riding her Andalusian mule beside me, and the long lace thing they call a mantilla she had on in church. But oh, Madam, did you notice her ladies in the procession? Each of them accompanied by one of our Court beauties. A charming thought. Only our fool of a Chamberlain had forgotten that in Spain side-saddles are girthed from the opposite side, so that the poor things had to ride back to back as if they had just quarrelled violently!"

"Harry, you must not speak so disrespectfully of milord Chamberlain!" she reproved him. But the boy could see that she, too, was smiling.

"Even the Aragon girl had to laugh," he chuckled, rising restlessly as some fresh frolic was started in the hall. "They will be beginning the dancing soon. Did you hear that Arthur is so afraid of making some mistake in those slow stately dances the Spaniards do that he has decided to play for safety and partner Lady Guildford in an English one? You know, Madam, whatever sort of a buffoon I made of myself I would dance with my bride, not with my sister's middle-aged governess!"

"But then Arthur is more prudent than you. He looks ahead like his father and so avoids mistakes."

The Tudor's second son indulged in a ribald grimace which he had learned from one of his grooms. "A good thing it is he who will be King and not I," he remarked without rancour. He was tall and ruddy and vital. He had none of the fineness of feature or sensitivity which her beloved Dickon had had as a boy, nor was he unduly concerned for her weariness as her small brother would have been. But Harry was her son. As yet there were no other loves in his life, and she was still the centre of his world. He needed the sweetness of her approval as a budding rose needs dew. "I am going to dance with Margaret after Katherine and Arthur and their partners have finished," he told her. "You will come back before then and watch me, will you not, Madam?"

"I shall come and watch Margaret. She dances very well," said Elizabeth, because she thought the snub was good for him; but there was a smile in her voice as she said it. Not for worlds would she have missed the dancing of any of her children; but just now she must rest for a minute or two.

"Shall I tell the servants to bring you some wine?" he asked, craning his neck to see what was going on below.

"Please, Harry," she answered. "And do you go back to your revelling. It is a shame that you should miss any more of it for me."

After he was gone Elizabeth leaned back against the cushion he had brought her and closed her eyes. She seemed to have spent hours listening to exalted personages speaking through interpreters. And then she had had to make suitable replies and try not to muddle up their foreign titles or offend against their complicated Court etiquette. And all the time part of her mind had been worrying a little as to what her exquisitely mannered little daughter-in-law would think of the outspoken utterances of her own more freely brought up family.

Elizabeth sipped the wine which had been brought her and tried to relax. From where she sat she could see the glittering company of her guests passing to and fro about the central hearth, from whence leaping flames lit up the great hammer-beam roof of this loveliest of halls. The whole Palace seemed to be full of lights and laughter, music and movement; yet here, in her curtained recess, it was comparatively quiet and cool. She chided herself for needing to rest; but since last year she had not been so strong. Not since the shock of those two young men's executions, she supposed, for some spring of vitality seemed to have snapped in her then. And it had been a hot, airless summer, with the plague rife in London again, and she had been grateful when Henry had taken her across the sea to their town of Calais. Knowing that he was not the kind of man to run away from the plague on his own account, she had thought it very considerate of him. But it had turned out that, like most of his kindnesses, it fitted in with plans of his own, for Calais, it seemed, was a very suitable place from which to throw out feelers for a good European marriage for their small daughter Mary. Of course Elizabeth knew that Henry had been acting like a wise father; but to her Mary was still an adorable bundle of childish curves and amusing laughter, and she did wish that her husband would not be so secretive. Why could he not have taken her into his confidence before leaving England and discussed so personal a matter with her instead of talking of it cautiously behind closed doors with Archbishop Morton? But Elizabeth was glad now that she had accepted the situation meekly enough. The King's plans always turned out for the best; and she had more reason than she could ever explain to be grateful to him for so complete a change of scene and thought.

And as soon as they had returned to London she had been caught up in all the bustle of preparation for her daughter-in-law's arrival. "Poor little Katherine of Aragon, having to part from such doting parents!" she had thought. "And coming from the warmth and colour of Granada, by way of a vile Channel crossing, to travel from Plymouth over our appalling roads in the cold grey of November rain!" Mercifully Henry himself had gone to meet her, and Elizabeth was sure that his satisfaction and his graciousness must have done much to mitigate the poor child's misery.

She was still thinking how well success became him when she found him at her side. "You, too, are tired?" she said sympathetically, pouring his wine with her own hand. "I do not wonder, for you undertook that terrible journey to Plymouth, which I was spared!"

"Sometimes I think I am always tired," he sighed. "But it has been worth it."

Although he took the wine from her hand he did not look at her, but stood gazing over the body of the hall. Whatever his private weariness, there was an air of triumph about him. "I just heard de Puebla telling the French Ambassador that England has not stood so secure for five hundred years," he said.

Elizabeth rose and stood beside him. "That will be an even more lasting memorial to you than your beautiful chapel," she said softly; and in the expansiveness of the moment his hand pressed hers. Among so many other things God had given him, He had even turned a Yorkist woman into an understanding wife. "There have been times I have thought that this would never happen," Henry admitted, indicating with a nod of his neatly shaped head the distinguished company of their guests. "But now there are no more pretenders. Ferdinand and Isabella and everyone else knows that there is no better Plantagenet blood than mine left. We stand secure, unchallenged—we Tudors."

Elizabeth shared his sense of security, but she made no answer; for even in the midst of her thankfulness she was thinking of the price. "I like our new daughter-in-law," she said presently, watching the girl play her part with a touching young dignity. "I like the way she looks one straightly in the eyes. She is not particularly beautiful, perhaps; but she has been well trained for queenhood, and I think that she will prove kind."

"Let us hope that she will prove fruitful!" said Henry shortly.

"They are very young to be married," demurred Elizabeth dubiously.

Henry surveyed them dispassionately across his lifted glass. "My mother bore me when she was not much more than fifteen," he reminded her.

"People did in those days," said Elizabeth. "And then, of course, she was desperately in love with your father. I do not think that Katherine cares very much for Arthur."

"Does it make much difference?"

"A great deal, I should imagine. Not that I think Arthur would realize. Sometimes I think his head is full of Latin verbs and dreams about the future. You know, Henry, I have been very worried about him of late. He looks so pale."

"It has been a long and trying day for a lad of fifteen."

"But Katherine bears it well. Although she is but a year older she is much more mature. Foreign girls are, I think. But see, Henry, how Arthur keeps passing his hand across his brow."

"A trick he has caught from me."

"And then that cough he has. He tells me he got wet through waiting out on the plains while those fussy duennas of hers decided whether or not he might meet her before they were married. Just as if we lived in harems like the Saracen women!"

"You worry too much about his health, Elizabeth. You always have worried about him more than the others because he was born prematurely," said Henry, setting down his glass. "Well, I must go and say a few words to those Spanish priests. And after the dancing I suppose it will be time for the final procession to bed the bride and bridegroom."

Elizabeth caught at his arm. "But they are so young!" she repeated. "You will not let them—"

"Come, come! I must have heirs," he laughed. "A grandson to consolidate our union."

"Arthur is shooting up so. The doctors tell me he may have overgrown his strength. Would it not be better for them to wait a year?"

"Well, I will talk to the doctors about it," agreed Henry, half sharing her anxiety but finding it difficult to believe that anything so nebulous as an adolescent's health could interfere with his plans.

"But formally they must be bedded to-night. To omit that part of the ceremony would be to offend Spain."

"Spain! Spain!" thought Elizabeth, watching him return to the dais to receive a group of important-looking prelates. "Must the lives of all of us revolve around Spain! He is so far-seeing, so wise. Is this merely an obsession with him, or will that country one day wax so great that it will take some other Tudor's utmost wit and strength to curb her?"

But for the moment Henry looked more contented than she had ever seen him. He was always at his best in public—dignified, urbane and cultured. And now, it seemed, he was at the peak of his power. The respect shown him by all foreign ambassadors and envoys indicated how much his name stood for abroad. And as he sat there, a reserved but gracious host, he had something indeed to be satisfied about, for few Kings had ever accomplished so completely all that they had set out to do. The power of the barons was broken so that they could no longer make a battle-ground of England, the people were contented and prosperous, the empty coffers refilled, and—above everything—the royal succession assured. And better than anyone Elizabeth appreciated what it must mean to Henry Tudor that his elder son was no longer Prince of Wales only in name but, after being educated in that beloved country, was going there with his wealthy young bride to rule it. To set up his own Court where the great Pendragon and his other remote ancestors had once held sway.

For all the Plantagenets' splendour, Elizabeth had to admit that they had seldom had such material benefits to boast about. And she was shamed at the remembrance of how often she and her sisters had secretly made fun of the way Henry rubbed his hands together in satisfaction like a successful shopkeeper. She realized now how much that element of a businessman in him had helped to bring about their country's present prosperity.

Hearing the musicians strike up a galliard, she clapped her hands for her ladies and went back to watch the dancing. Arthur appeared to have abandoned the idea of partnering Lady Guildford and won rounds of applause performing a minuet with Cicely, and his bride chose to dance a stately measure with no man at all, but with two other ladies. But the success of the evening was when Margaret and young Harry took the floor, prancing with youthful high spirits in a typically lively English country dance. In fact, so high did Harry volt and caper and so warm was the hall that his fair skin was soon glistening with perspiration; whereat, nothing deterred, he broke up the formality and delighted the company by throwing off his fine new velvet top-coat and dancing the whole thing over again with enormous energy and enjoyment. Elizabeth laughed with the rest and Henry beamed at the pair with paternal pride.

After a splendid pageant, during which live doves were loosened as a special compliment to the bride, she and Arthur were bedded in the Bishop of London's house, and then the young Spanish bride was given back to the care of her ladies pending her people's return to Spain and her own departure with her husband for Wales. So Elizabeth hoped that her anxious counsel to her husband had carried weight.

And if she was a little lonely at Richmond after their departure, she was consoled by unusual demonstrations of affection from her elder daughter, Margaret, who seemed to cling to her mother more now her own time for parting was so near at hand. For as soon as it was summer and the roads became drier Margaret Tudor was to set out north with an imposing retinue to become James Stuart's bride and Queen of Scotland.

Chapter Twenty-Nine

AFTER ALL, IT WAS not her elder daughter whom Elizabeth was called upon to part with that summer. For by the time the roads were dry and the hedges green there was no marrying, only mourning. Elizabeth was still abed on the shining morning when the news came from Wales.

"It is Prince Arthur," her women said, white-faced and stammering.

Elizabeth, who had been dreaming, as she so often did, that she was back in the monks' deserted little garden at Westminster, sat bolt upright. "Is he ill?" she asked, as if it were news which she had been expecting. But after a moment or two she knew by their frightened silence that he was dead.

That Arthur—the son whose throne had been made so secure—was dead. But as yet she knew it only as a fact accepted by the mind, not as a desolation to which one must learn to attune the heart. "How? What happened?" she asked.

"We do not know," they answered, tying the last fastenings of their hurriedly donned clothes. "It is said that there were some cases of plague—"

"Or there might have been some accident—"

"No," said Elizabeth, with a mother's certainty, "it is just that his Grace has never been really strong."

Jane Stafford came and put loving arms about her. "We all wanted so much to let you sleep in peace a little longer," she said. "But the King is asking for you."

"He needs you," said Ann Howard, her sister, hurrying in to join them. For Ann knew well that the best help she could give was to tell her beloved Bess that someone needed her.

Elizabeth looked at her bleakly. "I have been married to him for sixteen years and he has never really needed me," she said, too stunned to realize that she spoke her thoughts aloud.

"They say he is distraught," said Ditton, tenderly holding a cup of hot milk to her mistress's lips.

Elizabeth pushed the milk away untasted. Swinging her long slender legs over the side of the bed, she slipped her feet into the slippers they held for her. Then, tremblingly, thrust her arms into the gown they brought. She had been too suddenly roused from sleep and her mind was so stunned that she moved as obediently as a puppet. If her husband needed her she must hurry.

Outside in the anteroom she saw Patch, hunched against her door like a dog that keeps watch. His big brown eyes, the one thing of beauty which he had, gazed up at her in an agony of compassion. For once his glib tongue was stilled, and she knew that the soul within his ugly body rendered her much of the worship which should have been his Maker's. He was only her fool, but at such times devotion takes on a higher value than degree. Elizabeth stopped in front of him. "What am I to do, dear friend?" she asked simply.

The squat shoulders shrugged beneath their gay silk motley. "A market-woman with broken eggs in her basket, if she be wise, counts those she has left," he muttered.

The Queen bent down the better to hear him. "But, Patch, how can I comfort *him?*"

Patch's gaze was sure and steady. "Only you," he said, "can refill his basket."

Like everyone else in her immediate entourage, he probably knew that it was a long time since the King had come to her bed, and that she was content to have it so.

She went on her way. It was odd, perhaps, to ask advice from a fool, but she saw that he was right. And when she came to the King's apartments she did just as Patch had told her.

She found Henry sitting at the foot of his great four-poster, where, on happier mornings, they had so often sat together, resplendent in their furred bedgowns, to receive the birthday gifts of courtiers; only now Henry's face looked grey and the embroidered leopards of England sprawling across the bed-head behind him seemed to be snarling maliciously. The gentlemen-of-the-bedchamber withdrew at sight of her, and Elizabeth went to him and laid her arms about his bowed shoulders. "As your Grace's wisdom is renowned all over Christendom, you must now show proof of it," she urged.

"But *Arthur*—" he said incoherently, his hands clinging to her encircling arms. "Arthur for whom we had such dreams and who had so much promise…Arthur who was to have been King…"

Elizabeth smoothed her husband's thin, disordered hair. "I know, dear heart," she comforted; and in that moment they ceased to be a politically married couple who had little in common and were but two unhappy people who had begotten and lost a beloved son. "But consider, Henry, how your mother in all these marriages had no child at all save you, and how God has preserved and prospered you. Whereas we have still another son and two fair daughters."

Henry sat silent, his hands still clutching her like a startled child's. All his plans lay broken about him, far bigger and more important than a child's toys. Even now he must inevitably be thinking not only of his grief but of his fine new dynasty. "If anything should happen to that reckless young hot-head Harry—" he whispered.

Elizabeth kissed him and stood smiling down at him. Even her own grief was forgotten in her desire to assuage another's sufferings. Past affronts and frustrations were forgotten. She remembered only Patch's words. "God is still where He was, and we are both young enough," she said, humbly offering her husband the privilege he had lately spurned.

He rose from the bed then and kissed her with real gratitude. Some virtue seemed to have passed from her to him. His weakness had passed. He was the King again. "How can you appear so serene?" he asked, the more amazed because he was intelligent enough not to minimize her grief. "You Yorkist Plantagenets have courage!"

It was an accolade. The only compliment he had ever paid her. And Elizabeth knew it to be sincere. But his thoughts did not linger upon her. "This unspeakable loss is something quite outside my calculations," he said, beginning to walk back and forth in thought. "What about Katherine of Aragon now?"

"I do not know," said Elizabeth. "Except that we must send for her at once and be very kind to her—until such time as she goes back to Spain."

"Back to Spain?" The words escaped the King's thin lips sharply. "But there is her dowry. Twenty thousand scudos."

It shocked Elizabeth inexpressibly that he should think of it at such a time; but undoubtedly it was a contingency which he would have to deal with almost immediately.

Henry's pace quickened. He walked briskly to the door dividing his bedroom from the anteroom and closed it against the curiosity of the courtiers who waited there. "And we arranged that Arthur should make over to her a third of his estate, you remember? But now that she is widowed—we should have guarded against this—" A new excitement informed him. It had nothing to do with the lad Arthur who lay dead. Elizabeth watched him go to the table beside his bed, take a key from his wallet and unlock a drawer. She hated the eager fumbling of his fingers, the hungry light in his eyes, the sharp look upon his face. He might have been some money-lender making certain of a payment. She was sure that for the moment he had forgotten her. "I cannot remember how it was worded. Morton and de Puebla were there…" he was muttering. He had drawn forth the precious notebook, which was always kept under lock and key or about his person. But his bony hands were trembling and, incongruous as it seemed, his eyes were still blurred with tears. He turned over the pages, holding them close to his well-shaped nose. But in his haste he waxed impatient. "Here, look for me, Elizabeth," he ordered, pushing the book into her hands. "My sight grows worse every day. It is all those accounts. Why, only yesterday I began a letter to my mother and could not finish it. The entry should be headed 'Spanish marriage' and made some time at the end of fourteen ninety-nine or the beginning of fifteen hundred. Somewhere about here, look you."

Obediently, disinterestedly, Elizabeth did as she was bid. It should be easy enough to find. His small, neat writing was as clear as his high-pitched voice.

"January, December, November," she read aloud, flicking the closely filled pages over backwards. "It must be on this page. You began to reopen negotiations for the Spanish marriage immediately after—after—"

Remembering, he reached out a sudden hand. "No matter! No matter! I can see it for myself now you have found the approximate date," he said. And, noticing that she now seemed loath to relinquish the book, he almost clawed it from her.

But not before Elizabeth's quick glance had lighted upon something which interested her very much. Although certainly it was not headed "Spanish marriage." It was just a small, enigmatic note made a little further up the page. Against a date in the previous November her husband had written: "Tell D. to leave both doors unbolted."

Both doors? What doors? Even through her personal misery the significance of the entry penetrated her mind. That was the very week when Perkin Warbeck and her cousin Warwick had escaped, when Sir John Digby was Lieutenant of the Tower. Even before Henry had found the information he sought Elizabeth knew, in dazed horror, that in his circuitous way he was as much a murderer as her uncle.

She left him with his notebook in his hands. The necessity of settling an immediate problem would take his mind off his grief. He would have to call a Council and discuss what was to be done about Katherine of Aragon—and her dowry. For herself there was no such merciful necessity. She would not have to plan for the future, and all her thoughts would be with the precious past.

She went back to her room and sat by her window. The scent of summer flowers came up to her and the voices of her younger children at play. And for the first time she really realized that Arthur, her firstborn, was dead. Not just as something which someone had said to her in a second or two, but as a bitter loss which she must live with all her life. Delivered from the duty of comforting her husband—and bankrupt of any further desire to do so—she sat there and wept and wept.

As the day wore on Ann became worried for her health. She knew the strain under which her sister had lived, how the long-drawn-out uncertainty about Perkin Warbeck had played upon her emotions, and that since then Elizabeth had not seemed so strong. And in her anxiety Ann, Countess of Surrey, sent to tell the King, begging that his physicians might come. Instead, Henry came himself and was extraordinarily kind. It was *his* turn to comfort now, he said. But because he had disappointed her dreams Elizabeth loved her children far more than she had ever loved him. A few hours ago it had seemed that the shared sorrow of Arthur's death might be bringing them closer together, but now she knew for certain that he had ordered those prison bolts to be drawn, luring two young men to their deaths. The full meaning of what she had accidentally read now came to her with shattering clarity. And although Henry was her husband she felt that she hated him. She wished that she had not been so ready to comfort him with the promise of more sons, for he would certainly see that she kept her word. And in this hour of misery she, who so loved children, did not want to bear him any more. She was feeling utterly exhausted, and she told herself that if they two should come together again she would die of it.

It was only a passing hysteria, of course. Being Elizabeth of York, she mastered it. She thanked the King for coming and gradually regained her habitual expression of outward serenity and went on being a dutiful wife. And as soon as the first violence of her grief had subsided her first thought was for her dead son's widow.

"We must find out if she is pregnant," said Henry portentously.

"Everything turns upon that," agreed Morton.

"Your Grace's physicians could examine her, or the lady might be asked to attend a select committee," suggested Sir Reginald Bray.

"Has not the poor child suffered enough?" asked Elizabeth, marvelling at the complicated processes of their masculine minds. "Would it not be very much simpler if I just—asked her?"

So she had a specially comfortable horse litter prepared for her daughter-in-law's journey and paid for the black-velvet curtains out of her own purse. For Henry, she found, was not nearly so ready to spend lavishly on his daughter-in-law now; and Elizabeth knew that, pregnant or not, the poor girl would want privacy from the morbidly gaping crowds.

She made a point of greeting her personally, treating her in public as the chief mourner in the tragedy, although everyone must have known how much deeper her own sorrow went. In spite of trailing weeds, the Aragon girl did not look at all tragic. Somehow her black only succeeded in accentuating her young fairness, and there was about her an air almost of levity and relief. "Madam, it is for you that I grieve," she said, with a disarming generosity.

"I will try to be as good to her as Margaret Beaufort has always been to me," vowed Elizabeth. And she realized that even if the girl had not loved Arthur she must be feeling very lonely after such sad happenings in a strange land, and very unsure of the future, finding herself no longer married to the King's heir. Although, of course, everything would be much the same were she to be the mother of Arthur's child.

"Are you with child?" asked Elizabeth, scarcely able to frame the words for thinking of her own son Harry, who might be disinherited. But to her relief Katherine shook her head.

"Then the marriage was never really consummated? You see how important this is. You must be quite sure about it."

The Spanish girl's eyes met her with candour equalling her own. "No, Madam. Arthur talked big—how do you say?—boasted—a good deal before the pages after our wedding night. But it was only—boasting. And after that, as you know, I went back to my women. And then he seemed ill—"

"Then you are still virgin. And I am sure it will not be long before your parents find you another husband," said Elizabeth gently.

"Then shall I be allowed to go home?" Clearly these were the pathetic words of longing which Katherine must have been saying to herself over and over again during that long, jolting journey in the closed litter; but before her mother-in-law's kindness she managed to keep their eagerness within the bounds of courtesy.

Elizabeth, who liked her, was touched. She bent to kiss the ingenuous young face. "My poor Katherine, I really do not know. Certainly not until we have heard from Spain. The King and de Puebla and all of them are in the council-chamber discussing it now. But we have been so completely stunned with grief that nothing has been arranged. So you must stay here for the present, and it has occurred to me that one of my ladies, another Katherine, who is widowed and lonely, may help to console you. But I have heard the King and Archbishop Morton speak about a house for you at Croydon where you can have your Spanish priests and set up your own household."

"The King has been very kind," murmured Katherine, who did not in the least want to go away to some quiet place called Croydon. "He sent me a message that he will let me have back my personal jointure which my father had put in his Grace's keeping."

Elizabeth was surprised. Evidently Henry wanted to keep the girl's favour. "But I doubt if you will ever see the rest of your dowry again, if he can find means to keep you in England!" she thought. In the meantime Elizabeth was at a loss how to entertain her guest, seeing that the Court was in deep mourning. "How the sun shines!" she said, going to the window. "After being in that cramped litter for so many hours each day perhaps you would like to go out in the gardens? We cannot devise any entertainment in public, of course, but if there is anything you would like to do—"

Katherine joined her at the window. The lovely gardens of Greenwich were spread before them and down in the courtyard the horses were being brought round. In spite of the sad quiet that reigned within the Palace, there was bustle and laughter down there. For Prince Harry was going riding in the park with Charles Brandon and a few other lads of his own age. Although they were all dressed in sober black, one could not expect young people to be decorous all the time or quite broken-hearted. And to the Spanish princess who had spent several miserable months constrained by the failing health of a sick husband they must have looked very gay. Perhaps she remembered how her brother-in-law had made her laugh during the bridal procession. "If it please your Grace," she said, brightening, "I, too, should like to go riding in your so beautiful park—with Harry."

After Spanish Katherine had gone to don her becoming velvet riding-habit with the wide-brimmed hat which Harry so much admired, Elizabeth stood for a while watching him mount his horse. Whatever her husband had hoped, she was more thankful than she could say that the Spanish girl was not pregnant. Harry was a very important personage now. And what a King he would make, with those long, strong limbs, that unaffected, infectious laugh...Elizabeth turned as some one came into the room behind her. "Send the Lady Katherine Gordon to me, Ditton," she said, and went on watching from the window until Arthur's lively widow had joined the informal cavalcade and ridden out towards the park with young Harry Tudor obviously teasing her about her strange foreign saddle. "A pity," thought Elizabeth, looking into the future, "that there is so much difference in their ages!"

A soft footstep and the rustle of a skirt behind her recalled her to the commonsense present.

"Your Grace!"

Kate Gordon, sweeping an obeisance to a Queen she adored, was a thing of slender, lovable beauty. If she had thought to be Queen herself, it was a thing which was never spoken of between them; for both of them knew that it was love and not ambition which had induced her to follow the fortune of the man she still believed to be the rightful King of England.

"Ah, come and sit here," said Elizabeth, inviting her to the window-seat. "I sent for you because I want you to comfort that other poor Katherine—"

"Comfort?" The word came scornfully.

"Ah, no, dear child, I know her grief is not of the heart like—ours. But just bewilderment. But you are so sweet and gentle and more of her age than I. Will you try to befriend her?"

"Anything that your Grace wishes I will do," promised the Scots girl, thereby unconsciously accepting from a discerning mistress some measure of healing for her own deep hurt.

"My new daughter-in-law wants to go back to Spain," said Elizabeth.

"It may bring her happiness, though for myself I have no desire to go back to Scotland. For no matter where one goes one's heart travels with one. Madam, have I leave to ask you something?"

"Yes, dear Kate."

"Just now you said 'her grief is not of the heart like—ours.' Do you, too, believe—"

Elizabeth rose restlessly. "Oh no, no, of course not! Did I say that? I do not feel too well to-day. This morning on rising I thought perhaps—" Before her companion could ask an eager question the Queen broke off suddenly and turned to ask *her* one. "All the same, I do often think of your husband and his ridiculous claims because it concerns—I mean it might have concerned—my son. But, Kate, I am Queen of England. I cannot go around to this person and that asking about such things. Or even voice my thoughts, lest they give rise to misconception. But surely they told *you*. Surely you must know?"

Kate Gorden stared at her in bewilderment. She had never seen the serene Queen so agitated before. "Know what, Madam?"

Elizabeth glanced towards the open doorway through which she could see Jane and Ditton sewing, and lowered her voice. "How two young men, one of them feeble in mind and weak physically perhaps from long confinement, could possibly come within a hair's breadth of escaping from the Tower. Even supposing"—Elizabeth's voice stumbled a little and the colour rose in her pale cheeks— "even supposing communication between them had purposely been made possible—it could never have been intended that they should so nearly *really* escape. My brother-in-law, Surrey, said they very nearly did, and must have given the Governor of the Tower a horrible fright. It is known that they got as far as the Byward Tower. That means that there was only the drawbridge between them and freedom—out in Thames Street. I never shall understand it. There must have been scores of men-at-arms about, and those two may not have had so much as a dagger between them. It sounds fantastic, Kate!"

The Scots girl was standing before her, her head held high. "Neither of them was much over twenty, and for ten minutes they held the entire Tower garrison at bay!" she confirmed proudly, her eyes shining as if she could see them doing it.

"My cousin was no coward," said Elizabeth, watching her. "But whatever they did must have been contrived in your husband's fertile brain. But what?"

Katherine Gordon came out of her trance of pride. "Why, Madam, do you really not know," she said wonderingly. "But *I* know. Once they had won their way nearly to the gates, with half the garrison at their heels, Richard ran to the place where you English keep the King's wild beasts. I cannot imagine how he knew where to find the bolts. But he let the lions loose and kept their pursuers at bay."

Elizabeth, the Queen, should have reprimanded her severely. The great Scottish Earl of Huntley's daughter had been forbidden to call her husband anything but Perkin. But the girl was so passionately excited, and somehow the Queen's words of reprimand would not come. Elizabeth really *did* feel ill. The faintly freckled face of her companion, the wide latticed windows and the sunshine seemed to be slowly fading away, and in their place Elizabeth seemed to see an arched doorway in the Abbot of Westminster's parlour and a slender boy in black walking away from her towards it. She could hear her own voice calling gauchely, "Dickon, remember the lions!" He was going through the doorway, farther and farther away like the walls and everything else. And it was growing cold. But once, before he disappeared, he turned and smiled—that far-off, gay, enchanting smile…

Elizabeth, who even in the direst moments of her varied life had never before fainted, sank down unconscious upon the cushions of the window-seat. And Kate Gordon, who had no clue with which to link her words to such sudden collapse, shouted in frightened amazement to Jane and Ditton to come quickly and send for a doctor.

Chapter Thirty

N O ONE THOUGHT THERE was anything strange about the
Queen's indisposition. Her Grace had complained of
not feeling well that morning; and, later, while talking
to milady Katherine Gordon, she had fainted. And the royal
physicians had confirmed the fact which all had suspected. Her
Grace was pregnant again. "Please God the baby will prove to be a
son," prayed her friends, recognizing a dutiful effort to console her
husband's grief. And in spite of young Harry's robust strength the
King must have hoped this more fervently than any of them.

But the Queen herself received the doctor's assurance listlessly.
There was none of her usual joyousness at the thought of another
child. She would sit silent for hours as if turning something over
in her mind; and her thoughts were certainly not upon her coming
confinement, for when one of her ladies would try to rouse her with
some question about the tiny garments they were embroidering
Elizabeth would start and answer absently. Her sisters noticed that
this time no tender, Madonna-like smile curved her lips. Instead
of looking forward to the future it seemed rather as if she were
brooding upon the past and saying farewell to someone whom she
had loved. And naturally all of them supposed her sad thoughts to
be wholly of Arthur, who was so like his successful father and who
would have made such a wise and prudent King.

"I hope I shall be allowed to have this new baby here in
Greenwich, without any fuss," she said one day to Jane Stafford.

"My mother-in-law is no longer at Court to insist upon so much ceremonial, and one has less heart for it now that our beloved Mattie is dead."

"This place is home to you now, is it not, Madam?" said Jane.

"Yes. I like to sit here by the window and hear the younger children playing in the garden. I must be getting old, Jane."

"Old, at thirty-seven!" laughed Jane, appealing to Ditton, who was coming in at the door. "I wonder, my dear sweet, if you have any idea how beautiful you look at this very moment with the sunlight on your hair?"

"Whatever beauty I had must be fading fast!" smiled Elizabeth. "Unlike most women, I seem to have had no love affairs to keep it warm."

"It is only deepening and maturing," said Jane. "And you are still so enviably slender."

"If you have a few lines round your eyes it is because you have suffered so much, Madam," added Ditton, setting down a bowl of the Queen's favourite pansies which she was carrying. "Lately you have seemed as if you liked to be alone, sorting out your mind perhaps. Or just—remembering. But we have all missed your Grace's laughter."

"My poor dears, what dull company I must have been!" Elizabeth reproached herself. "But I promise you I will mend my ways. I have been resolutely locking away the past, and now I must turn my thoughts to the future. So now you may hope to hear me laugh again—though not quite so boisterously as that young roisterer Harry, I hope!"

But the laughter seemed to be struck from her lips almost as soon as the promise was said. For before the morning was out the King's secretary waited upon her with a formidable-looking list of instructions. "It is his Grace's arrangements, Madam, for the coming happy event," he explained.

"Is the King so busy that he cannot come himself to talk them over?" enquired Elizabeth.

The secretary bowed so obsequiously that he missed the spirited reproach in her eyes. "The King is always busy," he said.

"Yes, amassing money and making notes until his pale eyes go blind!" said some new demon of unforgiving hatred in his wife's mind. But she knew that this was not true, and that Henry also worked conscientiously for the order and improvement of his realm.

"Then he will probably have need of you, Master Secretary," she said aloud. And, being dismissed, the man seemed uncommonly glad to go.

Elizabeth carried her husband's letter to the window and the more favoured of her ladies waited, grouped about her. "Well, Bess, where is it to be this time?" asked Ann, her sister, whose turn it was to be in attendance.

It was several moments before Elizabeth answered, and she had already read and refolded the letter. Her eyes looked out hungrily upon her beloved gardens, now all aglow with flowers. "The Tower," she said at last, quite tonelessly.

"The Tower!" they all gasped.

"Yes. The Tower, of all places! For a Welshman Henry has singularly little imagination. He might have spared me that!" It was the first time that she had ever criticised the King aloud before her gentlewomen, but the words were torn out of her.

"But why?" asked Jane, aghast.

"I do not know," said Elizabeth wearily, sitting down upon the window-seat.

Ann came and sat beside her, putting a comforting arm about her waist. "It may not be so bad, dear Bess," she said. "The royal apartments are right away from the—dungeons. And the King is sure to have them done up."

"If he can spare the money!" muttered Ditton daringly.

"And there is a little garden," said Jane, making her small contribution to their meagre sum of consolation. It was the dear, intuitive sort of thing a Stafford *would* say.

"But the rooms are so damp and her Grace suffers so with ague. And it will be winter again then," Ditton reminded them.

"Yes, it will be winter again then, Ditton," agreed Elizabeth. "But let us not think about it now."

It was easy enough to say. But how could one *not* think? They hung about for a few minutes in unhappy silence. Of course the Tower was a royal residence like any other and children had been born there before, yet they all felt as if the morning's brave sunshine had passed behind a cloud. And presently they drifted away, leaving the two Plantagenet sisters together.

"Would it be any good asking Henry—" began Ann, as soon as they were alone.

But they both knew that it would not be. Elizabeth did not trouble to reply. She just sat there with her back to the window and the crumpled letter in her hand. When the Tudor ordered something one obeyed. "He must have some very particular purpose, Ann," she said slowly after a time. "Henry never does anything without a purpose."

"No, I daresay not," agreed Ann anxiously. "But the damp and the depression will kill you!"

"Perhaps," said Elizabeth, looking straight before her, "that *is* the reason."

"Bess, you must be mad!"

They were quite alone in the quiet room. Only to one of her sisters could Elizabeth have said such a thing and hope to be understood. And this new thought that had come to her was so utterly terrible that—even though she might be wrong—she must voice it just once.

Ann, the quick-witted, was down on her knees in a moment with protective arms about her. "You mean—because of this Aragon girl?"

"Because of her dowry. And the alliance. Henry, God help him, has not enough heat in his blood to put his worst enemy away for the getting of a girl. But this love of money grows on him. And this obsession about Spain."

They were close together and they spoke in frightened, jerky whispers. "And if you were to die—naturally, in childbirth—he would be free," said Ann, reading the thoughts from her sister's eyes and repeating them as if she were learning some incredible lesson.

"And he could probably get a dispensation from the Pope, because Kate says the marriage with Arthur was never consummated.

Then he could marry her himself. And keep the alliance—and all that money…"

"Twenty thousand scudos!" remembered Ann.

But suddenly Elizabeth pulled herself together, getting briskly to her feet. "But of course it is impossible!" she decided. "He could not be so wicked. It is I who am wicked ever to have harboured such a thought. It is just because I have been unwell and depressed." She bent down and took her sister's anxious face between her own two cold hands. "Dear Ann," she implored, "forget that I ever said it!"

At the sound of approaching voices Ann rose from the cushion upon which she had been kneeling and began hurriedly rearranging the pansies. "You are not the kind of person to have harboured it without some cause," she said judiciously. "But you must try to put the suspicion from your mind, dear Bess. You know that I have always disliked Henry; but whatever his shortcomings as a husband, he is no murderer."

"N-no," agreed Elizabeth, with so much uncertainty that Ann gave her a swift, surprised glance. Elizabeth had been thinking of the undrawn bolts in the Tower; but because there were people about she said no more. Everything was stir and movement again. Curly-haired Mary had escaped from her nurse and was running to Elizabeth with an eager request to hear the pet parrot talk, and Margaret was wanting to tell her about the pet parrot talk, and Margaret was wanting to tell her about the finished splendour of her wedding-dress. Margaret would wait now until the Court was out of mourning and until her mother's baby was born, and then she would go to Scotland and really be married to handsome James.

There were so many things to see to and Elizabeth was naturally so cheerful that life began to interest her again. The wide, spacious life of the Tudors. She felt better and she began to laugh again. And to be ashamed of her feelings towards her husband. And one day the King came to her with an important-looking letter in his hand impressed with the great seal of Spain. He looked, she thought, immensely pleased. A great and confident King, whose policies were in all ways to be relied on. "Read this, Elizabeth. It concerns you," he said almost genially. "It is from our good friends Ferdinand and Isabella. They are agreeable to their daughter staying on in England. Staying in our care and learning our language and our ways—until Harry shall be old enough for marriage. I sent for him last evening and talked to him about it and tried to instill a little of Arthur's seriousness into him." Elizabeth held the letter in her hands but scarcely took in the sense of it. Her husband's words had been enough. Enormous relief uplifted her, swiftly followed by self-reproaching shame.

"And you really think that his Holiness—"

"Mercifully the marriage was never consummated. It is more a matter of the difference in their ages."

"Then you have been trying to persuade her parents?"

"I had thought of it, but made sure they would object because Katherine is so much older than he. But now Queen Isabella herself makes this suggestion about Harry. It seems they have heard such fine reports of his growth and prowess."

Henry was rubbing his hands together with satisfaction, and Elizabeth looked up at him searchingly, leaving the letter lying unread in her lap. She would much rather have read his mind. Quite obviously he was enormously relieved. But had their most Christian majesties raised the objections which he had expected would he not have found some other means of keeping Katherine? He, who never allowed anything less compelling than death to stand in the way of his plans? Her suspicion of his motives might have been but sickly imagination. Yet why had he arranged for her baby to be born in the Tower? She would never know. Never understand the enigma that was her husband.

"I could ask him now whether, after all, I need go there now," she thought, "and if he says I need not I can be certain of his original reason." But perhaps, since she must live with him amicably, it would be easier to bear the courtesy of half-truth. "And heaven knows," she thought, "I should be accustomed to the nagging cruelty of half-truths by now!" And in any case he would be sure to say in his precise way, "Why change now when our plans are already made?" And she would be none the wiser.

For Henry Tudor was not the man to spoil his policy for want of an alternative scheme or to alter arrangements of state to suit a woman's whim.

So all that Elizabeth said was, "I have always wanted Katherine of Aragon for our Harry. She will make him a good wife."

"I was sure you would be pleased," said Henry pleasantly, taking back his letter. And Elizabeth did him the justice to be sure that he was too. He would keep the alliance and the money without having to exchange an intelligent and fruitful wife who was used to his ways for an imperious young chit who might expect him to be romantic. It would all suit him so much better. "And to the end," thought Elizabeth, "he will have the sanctimonious satisfaction of showing himself to the world—and to history—as the pattern of a faithful husband."

She would make the best of her confinement and keep about as long as possible doing all the pleasant and interesting things which, thanks to her marriage, made up her life. Whatever Henry had cheated her of, he had more than kept his promise of material security. This lovely summer morning the sun was shining, and the Tower was a long way off. She could hear young people's carefree voices out in the garden and Patch was coming to persuade her to join them.

"The new heir of England has just stopped a tennis ball on his nose," the fool reported jubilantly.

"Oh, Patch!" she exclaimed, jumping up immediately. "Does it hurt him?"

"If it does he will not stop his sport to have it attended to, Madam. Not satisfied with an hour's bashing on the tennis court, he is now determined to get his revenge for the beating young Charles Brandon gave him yesterday at the butts."

It was Patch's way of getting her out into the sunshine. "Then let us go down and watch," she agreed. And followed by a few of her ladies and preceded by the capering fool she went down the Queen's staircase into the sundrenched garden. It was high noon and midsummer, with the sparkling Thames at full tide. And as she made her way towards the archery butts her velvet skirt, swaying over the close-clipped lawn, was no greener than the grass. Surely nowhere in the world could there be such refreshing loveliness as these riverside lawns, nowhere such profusion of roses! To live in the present was all one asked for on a June morning.

She found her son with his boon companion young Brandon, whose father had been Henry Tudor's standard-bearer at Bosworth, standing among a group of young friends, sports enthusiasts and pages. Even some of the servants, taking time off from their duties, must needs stop to watch the contest. As usual he had thrown off his coat, and even at a distance it was easy to pick him out as the tall red-head in shirt and doublet. Harry might speak fluent French with his tutor or love music with the passion of a Welshman, but out here at sport he was sturdily English. Coming quietly closer, Elizabeth considered him objectively, less as her son than as a future King. He lacked the fine-drawn features of some of his ancestors and much of their Norman culture, but he had an air of command, and there was a directness about him, a forthright manner of speech, which made easy contact with those about him. Even with the watching servants and the unimportant pages who raced to retrieve his arrows he had the right jest, the common touch. That thing which his father, for all his wisdom, lacked. Yet standing there with legs braced and a man's-size bow drawn between his hands he seemed to dominate them all. And suddenly Elizabeth felt very proud.

"Humble and Reverent" she had taken as her motto, and, although born of a fiery race, she had striven to live up to it. She, a Yorkist, had submitted herself to a Lancastrian. In years to come people might not remember much about her. But here was the gift she had made to her country. The fusion of the red and white roses into one strong Tudor rose. And looking at Harry she felt assured that all she had been through of uncertainty and suffering was worth the outcome; for surely it was no small thing to mother a dynasty which was close to the heart of England?

She watched her son play out the contest. Red-headed Harry— strong, gifted, handsome—the future Henry the Eighth of England, with all his father's hoarded wealth to spend and all the security of his mother's unquestioned blood, a splendid marriage and all his shining path of youth stretching before him. "What will he make of it?" she wondered, wishing with all her heart that she could see into the future.

He had seen her now and aimed his best. Whether it were tennis, wrestling or archery, he always liked to have her there, watching his sport. That he played up to an admiring audience there was no denying, but his backers knew that whether he won or lost he would accept the issue just as cheerfully. "Right on the inside rim of the red! That brings the score even, Charles. Heaven send I get a gold!" he shouted, applauding his opponent's marksmanship. "Never mind all this solemn talk of marriage, this is what I call a fine morning's sport!"

"And what will you call your fine Spanish son?" jibed Patch, from the pathway. But Harry Tudor's mind was on the score, his eye upon the target. At fourteen the thought of marriage does not mean much. "I have no idea," he said, turning his head smartly towards the mark and drawing the mighty bow.

There was a moment's tense silence. All eyes were upon him. The string was drawn back almost to the golden down upon his cheek. He sighted the tip. And then the arrow flew, whistling through the air to strike the golden centre of the target hard and true. The glad laughing shout of sportsmen went up for joy of it, and young Harry's laugh rang out loudest of all as he thumped Charles Brandon on the back. But no sooner had the watching crowd relaxed than he ceased to be a sportsman, and became just a spontaneous boy. He pushed his bow into a page's hand and without waiting to shed either leather bracer or tab, ran to his mother, throwing his arms about her with such thoughtless vehemence that Jane and Ditton, careful of her condition, cried out to restrain him. But even though he hurt her Elizabeth did not mind. She looked radiantly happy.

Still hugging her tight, the future King grimaced over his shoulder at the grinning fool. "But, I tell you what, Patch," he said, finding himself at leisure to continue their half-finished conversation. "If ever I have a *daughter* I know what I shall call *her*!"

"What will you call her?" asked Elizabeth, knowing as well as he.

"Why, that is easy!" he laughed, releasing her. "How else, Madam, but after you—the loveliest mother a man ever had? She shall be Elizabeth."

Reading Group Guide

1. The book opens with Elizabeth's rejection by the French prince. Right away, Elizabeth becomes "a woman aware of the ambitious cruelties of men." How is this moment the trajectory for all that follows in the story? What other men have cruel ambitions that affect her?

2. The dowager queen is certain from the outset that Richard is intent on obtaining the throne for himself. Yet Thomas Stafford tells Elizabeth, in chapter four, that Richard's initial intentions had been to see Edward crowned, but that the council persuaded him to take it for himself. If Tom's words are to be believed, how might the suspicions and actions of the dowager queen also have played a part in Richard's change of heart?

3. What characteristics does Elizabeth exhibit while she and her family are in sanctuary that prepare her for her future role as queen? How does she later utilize these skills and innate characteristics to be a "humble and reverent" queen?

4. In chapter nine, Buckingham thinks the following of King Richard: "There were men, [Buckingham] knew, who seemed to have two personalities." What other characters show two sides? Elizabeth Woodville? Henry Tudor? Others?

5. Ms. Barnes does an excellent job of painting Richard III as a duplicitous character, a man of immeasurable charm and yet one

who is not to be trusted. She makes it difficult for the reader to reach a definite judgment of him. Buckingham says of him, "Every line of him…was a baffling contradiction. How could one assess him, or be sure?" What were some moments when you were unsure how to judge him as good or bad? What was your final assessment of him?

6. In chapter four, Elizabeth calls Henry Tudor her "archenemy." Then in chapter 14 she thinks of him as her "personal deliverer." Which of these does he turn out to be? In what ways is he both?

7. Elizabeth often reflects on Henry's inability "to neither love nor hate." Instead, there is a certain level sensibility about him. She, however, comes from a long line of fiery, passionate kings. But which has history shown to make for a better king, or political ruler in general?

8. Elizabeth often laments that Henry neither wants nor needs her love. Do you agree with this? What are some ways in which Henry does need Elizabeth? Are there any moments when he shows that he does in fact need and love her?

9. "We Tudors begin to bestride the world," Elizabeth claims in chapter 24. Historically, how is this true?

10. What is the motivation behind Elizabeth's "sudden crazy decision" to leave the garden gate unlocked in chapter 25? What is she really trying to prove with this test? Who is she testing? Perkin? Or Henry?

11. Early on, Henry promises Elizabeth that he is no murderer, and yet she suspects it of him more than once, even suspecting him of wanting her to die in childbirth. What is your verdict of Henry—is he a man capable of murder? Is he indeed a murderer?

12. Margaret Campbell Barnes's writing career first took off in the years following World War II. She published ten books of historical fiction between 1944 and 1962. She was a volunteer in the ambulance service during the war and lost her eldest son in the battles in Normandy, "a bitter loss which she must live with all her life." All of this—the climate of the times, her own personal loss—came to bear very strongly on her writing. Where is this influence apparent in *The Tudor Rose*?

Reading Group Guide written by Elizabeth R. Blaufox, great-granddaughter of Margaret Campbell Barnes

About the Author

MARGARET CAMPBELL BARNES LIVED from 1891 to 1962. She was the youngest of ten children born into a happy, loving family in Victorian England. She grew up in the Sussex countryside and was educated at small private schools in London and Paris.

Margaret was already a published writer when she married Peter, a furniture salesman, in 1917. Over the next twenty years, a steady stream of short stories and verse appeared under her name (and several noms de plume) in leading English periodicals of the time, including *Windsor, London, Quiver,* and others. Later, Margaret's agents, Curtis Brown Ltd., encouraged her to try her hand at historical novels. Between 1944 and 1962, Margaret wrote ten historical novels. Many of these were bestsellers, book club selections, and translated into foreign editions.

Between World Wars I and II, Margaret and Peter brought up two sons, Michael and John. In August 1944, Michael, a lieutenant in the Royal Armoured Corps, was killed in his tank in the Allied advance from Caen to Falaise in Normandy. Margaret and Peter grieved terribly the rest of their lives. Glimpses of Michael shine through in each of Margaret's later novels.

In 1945 Margaret bought a small thatched cottage on the Isle of Wight, off England's south coast. It had at one time been a smuggler's cottage, but to Margaret it was a special place in which to recover the spirit and carry on writing. And write she did. All together, over two million copies of Margaret Campbell Barnes's historical novels have been sold worldwide.